MAMA DEAR

Few things are more valuable or dear to us than our mother's love. And there is no better time to celebrate that special love than Mother's Day. Join Arabesque authors Cheryl Faye, Monique Gilmore, and Angela Winters in three delightful stories that tell of the love that only mothers can give.

SENSUAL AND HEARTWARMING
ARABESQUE ROMANCES FEATURE
AFRICAN-AMERICAN CHARACTERS!

BEGUILED   (0046, $4.99)
by Eboni Snoe
After Raquel agrees to impersonate a missing heiress for just one night,
a daring abduction makes her the captive of seductive Nate Bowman.
Across the exotic Caribbean seas to the perilous wilds of Central America . . . and into the savage heart of desire, Nate and Raquel play a
dangerous game. But soon the masquerade will be over. And will they
then lose the one thing that matters most . . . their love?

WHISPERS OF LOVE   (0055, $4.99)
by Shirley Hailstock
Robyn Richards had to fake her own death, change her identity, and
forever forsake her husband, Grant, after testifying against a crime syndicate. But, five years later, the daughter born after her disappearance
is in need of help only Grant can give. Can Robyn maintain her disguise
from the ever present threat of the syndicate—and can she keep herself
from falling in love all over again?

HAPPILY EVER AFTER   (0064, $4.99)
by Rochelle Alers
In a week's time, Lauren Taylor fell madly in love with famed author
Cal Samuels and impulsively agreed to be his wife. But when she
abruptly left him, it was for reasons she dared not express. Five years
later, Cal is back, and the flames of desire are as hot as ever, but, can
they start over again and make it work this time?

*Available wherever paperbacks are sold, or order direct from the
Publisher. Send cover price plus 50¢ per copy for mailing and
handling to Penguin USA, P.O. Box 999, c/o Dept. 17109, Ber-
genfield, NJ 07621. Residents of New York and Tennessee must
include sales tax. DO NOT SEND CASH.*

MAMA DEAR

Cheryl Faye
Monique Gilmore
Angela Winters

Pinnacle Books
Kensington Publishing Corp.
http://www.pinnaclebooks.com

PINNACLE BOOKS are published by

Kensington Publishing Corp.
850 Third Avenue
New York, NY 10022

First Printing: May, 1997
10 9 8 7 6 5 4 3 2 1

Printed in the United States of America

CONTENTS

SECOND CHANCE AT LOVE

Cheryl Faye

Dedications
For my mother, Barbara R. Smith.
I love you, Mommy.
Thank you for *always* being there for us;
and
Euvetta Tiburcio.
Thank you for your kindness throughout,
I love you, too;
and
for Mothers everywhere!

ACKNOWLEDGMENTS

Thanks first to my Lord and Savior, Jesus Christ. Nothing is impossible with you in my life.

Michele Kimbrow (Shelly K), thank you for being such a good friend and for your continued support *and for the names* (smile).

Monica Harris, my editor. Thank you for being so good at what you do.

Thank you to everyone that purchased my debut novel, *At First Sight*.

To all who wrote to me, *an extra special thank you* for your good wishes. All of this is for YOU!!

Chapter 1

It was a cold night in the beginning of February, and Rachel Waters was exhausted. She had just finished working a double shift at the hospital because one of her nurses was out with the flu. Being the head nurse of the pediatric ward, and because she could not get anyone else to do it, she had been forced to work the extra hours so there would be enough bodies on duty.

As she wheeled her Volvo 740GL onto her block, she prayed that one of the kids had cooked something for supper. The last thing she wanted to do was stand in front of a hot stove for the next hour fixing something to eat. Her feet were killing her.

She steered the car into her driveway and activated the automatic garage door opener in one smooth move. Hell, if they didn't cook, she decided, they'd eat pot luck. *They aren't babies,* she said to herself. She turned off the car engine and sighed. She did not immediately exit the vehicle. She was dog tired and quite comfortable in the plush leather driver's seat of her car.

After five minutes, she reached into the passenger seat and grabbed her pocketbook. She engaged the car door handle and pushed the door open with her foot. Once she had stepped out of the car and closed the door, she raised her hands over her head, stretching her back and neck slowly. With much effort, she lumbered to the door that separated the garage from her kitchen.

"Hi, Mommy!" her teenage daughter greeted her cheerfully. She was at the kitchen table doing her homework.

"Hi, baby," she groaned. "Did you cook?"

"No, but I'm not hungry. I made myself a sandwich."

"Jenny, that meat is supposed to be for your lunch," Rachel said as she laid her pocketbook on the table next to her daughter's schoolbooks and picked up the mail from the adjacent counter.

"There's still plenty there," Jennifer said.

"Where's your brother?"

"He didn't get home from practice yet."

"Doesn't any mail come for me that's not a bill?" Rachel asked, mostly to herself.

"You look tired, Mommy. Are you hungry? Do you want me to fix you anything?"

"No, I ate at the hospital. I'm just gonna go upstairs and run myself a bath and soak for a while."

Rachel picked up her pocketbook and replaced it with the mail she'd just opened. As she started out of the kitchen, Jennifer called to her, "Mommy, can I go to Cynthia Patterson's party this Saturday?"

Rachel didn't stop or turn back but she asked, "Who's Cynthia Patterson?"

"A girl at school," Jenny called behind her. "She's having a sweet sixteen party this weekend. Everybody's gonna be there. Can I go?"

"I'll see."

Just as she reached the staircase leading to the second floor, the front door flew open and in ran her son.

"Hi, Mom!" he said in a huff as he dropped his schoolbag and basketball in the foyer and ran past her and up the stairs two at a time.

"Where are you rushing off to?" she yelled at his back.

"I've gotta go to the bathroom. *Bad!*"

She heard the door slam on the bathroom before she was even halfway up the stairs. As she walked past the closed door, she called, "Don't forget to get your mess up from in front of the door, Malcolm. You know how you have a habit of forgetting things."

By the time she reached her bedroom, he was exiting the bathroom. "I'll get it, Mom. How you doin'?" he asked as he followed her to her bedroom, stopping at the door.

"I'm tired. I hope you ate, cause your sister didn't fix anything, and I'm not about to."

"That's all right. I'll get something to eat. Maybe I'll run down to the pizza shop and get a couple of slices. You really look tired," he added.

"I am," she sighed as she sat down on her bed. "How'd practice go?"

"Good. We've got a new coach, though," Malcolm said.

"What happened to the old one? What was his name?"

"Coach Jeffreys. I heard they fired him. Somebody said he was messing with one of the girls in school."

"And all they did was fire him? They should have arrested him."

"I don't know how true it is, but anyway, our new coach seems pretty cool. I think he knows more about coaching basketball than Coach Jeffreys did anyway. We have our first game with him in two weeks. Are you gonna come?" he asked.

"I'll try. I have to check the schedule at work first," Rachel said as she kicked off her white nurse's shoes.

"Well, it's gonna be on a Thursday night at six. The eighteenth. So maybe you can get that day off or something," Malcolm suggested.

"I'll see, Mal. I can't promise you, though."

"Okay. Well, let me go get my stuff," Malcolm said as he turned away from the door. Before he walked away, he turned back and asked, "Do you want me to get you anything from the pizza shop, Mom?"

"No, baby. I'm okay."

"Okay. I'ma leave in about fifteen minutes."

She just nodded her head and waved her hand.

"Close the door, Malcolm," she called to her son after a
few seconds.

Rachel stepped into her private bathroom as she pulled down
the zipper on her uniform. She stepped over to the tub and
turned on the faucets. She moaned as she bent over and reached
under the faucet, catching some water and rinsing the tub
quickly. She stood and reached into the cabinet over the toilet
and removed her lavender bubble bath. She then leaned over
and engaged the drain stop on the tub and poured a few capfuls
of the sweet-smelling liquid into the tub under the running
water. She adjusted the water temperature, favoring the hot
water.

As the tub filled, Rachel took a deep breath, inhaling the
lavender scent. As she turned to leave the bathroom, she caught
a glimpse of her reflection in the medicine cabinet mirror.

She did look tired, just like her kids said. "I need a vacation,"
she mumbled.

She went back into her bedroom and pulled her uniform over
her head and tossed it carelessly onto the bed. She removed
her slip, then pushed her pantyhose and panties off in one move.
She reached back and unfastened her bra and added it to the
pile of discarded clothes on her bed.

As she pulled the pins from her hair and removed the colorful
band that held her ponytail in place, she gazed at the picture
of her husband that sat atop her dresser. "Hi, baby," she said
with a sad smile. "I wish you were here right now. I sure could
use one of your back rubs."

Rachel's husband, Malcolm Waters Sr., had died eighteen
months ago of a heart attack. He had been just forty years old
at the time. His death left her feeling as though the biggest part
of her heart had crumbled.

She and Malcolm had been childhood sweethearts. They met
when Rachel was in the ninth grade. Her parents would not
allow her to date him until she was seventeen because he was
four years her senior, but they knew that they were meant for
each other long before then. He had respected the wishes of
her parents, and had never even made the slightest advance on
her, but they spent hours on end talking and learning all there

was to know about each other. During the time before they were allowed to date one another, they both saw other people. Rachel, of course, because of her tender age, was much less exposed to the dating scene than Malcolm was. They, however, shared the experiences of most of the dates they went on.

Rachel even went so far as to ask Malcolm's advice on attracting certain boys that she was interested in. Oddly Malcolm schooled her, giving her pointers on how not to behave in order to win the attention of a male contender. He later told her that it never bothered him that she asked his advice about boys. He said he had always been confident that she would be his girl one day, regardless.

Though Rachel had not been Malcolm's first lover, Malcolm had been hers. They dated for a year before she gave herself to him on her eighteenth birthday. She had been frightened, despite the fact that her body had cried for his closeness on many occasions. Her birthday was the day after Christmas, and Malcolm had been home from school for the holidays. He had brought her flowers and took her to dinner before asking her to spend the night with him at a motel across the river in New Jersey, as they both lived in New York City at the time. She agreed without pause. He was, after all, the love of her life.

When they arrived at the motel, Malcolm gave her the first of two birthday presents he had purchased for her. It was a sheer black negligee. He asked her to wear it for him, and though she was shy, she gladly did as he asked.

She went to the bathroom to change, and once she had donned the see-through garment, she returned to the bedroom to find him wearing only a pair of silk boxer shorts. All of the lights in the room were out, and three scented candles were lit, illuminating the small room in a soft light. He had poured champagne into two plastic goblets for both of them, and he handed one to her as she came near him.

It had been impossible for her to miss the effect the negligee was having on him, for his body was clearly outlined in the soft fabric of his undergarment. The sight was quite arousing to her, and her stomach knotted in anticipation of being with him.

Though he had told her on many occasions before this that he loved her, when he whispered the words to her that night, it was different. Rachel knew there would never be another man for her. He was her sun, her moon, and her stars. He was her life.

"I have something for you," he'd breathed close to her ear then.

She simply gazed up into his soft brown eyes, unable to speak, so caught up in his aura she was. He reached over to the dresser and picked up a small box that until that time she had not even noticed.

He opened it and removed the contents as he gazed lovingly into her eyes.

"I love you, Rachel, with all my heart," he'd said. "Will you do me the honor of being my wife?"

It was only then that she realized he was holding a diamond ring between his fingers. She looked down at the ring, then back up into his eyes and smiled as tears formed in her eyes.

"Yes, Malcolm. Oh, yes," she'd answered. "I love you with all my heart, too."

As Rachel lowered herself into the steaming tub of bubbles on this night nineteen years later, she recalled that scene as if she had lived it yesterday. Her eyes watered at the memory, but she smiled. Despite the very real ache she still felt in her heart at his physical absence, she was overjoyed at the wonderful memories she had of him and their life together.

Chapter 2

The telephone was ringing when Justin Phillips entered his apartment that same night. He had just left Frederick Douglass High School in Hackensack, New Jersey, his new place of employment. This evening he had coached his first practice session with the Rockets' basketball team. He was quite impressed with the skill of some of his players.

He had lucked into this position, really. Justin was formerly a pediatric surgeon at County General Hospital in Los Angeles, California. He had worked at the hospital for fifteen years. He had also taught at the University of California, Los Angeles Medical School, for six years. As much as he had once loved the medical profession, the job had really burned him out.

In the last year, he would become quite depressed every time a small child was brought to him for some form of surgery. He would gaze into their sad, sick eyes and find himself close to tears. When he realized that he could no longer be objective in treating his patients, he knew it was time to get out.

Aside from his hospital and teaching duties, however, Justin's real passion had been the time he spent at the inner city youth center, where he volunteered three nights a week. He had been the athletic director and basketball coach. He loved every minute he spent at the center. Working with the kids, coaching them in sports and in life, had been one of the most fulfilling experiences of his life.

One of the reasons he left Los Angeles was because his mother was up in her years and sickly. She had done everything but beg him to come back home. He could not deny her.

His longtime friend and college roommate, Marcus Vinton, was the principal at Frederick Douglass, and when Justin told him he was moving back East and changing careers, he immediately offered Justin the position of biology teacher/basketball coach.

The drastic cut in pay that he was forced to take on returning to his hometown of Hackensack was never a concern of Justin's. Due to some very wise investment choices, and a substantial sum of money left to him by his mentor, Dr. Tyler Austin-James, upon his death, Justin was pretty much set for life.

Neither did he have any family on the West Coast. A couple of years ago, he would have hesitated to leave. At that time, he had been engaged to be married to a woman he thought was the best thing that ever happened to him. What a rude awakening he received when she ran off with his best man on their wedding day.

He dropped his duffel bag and took three giant steps into his living room. "Hello!" he answered in a rush to catch the call before his answering machine switched on.

"Hi, baby."

"Hi, Mom," Justin said as a warm smile spread across his handsome pumpernickel-brown face. "How's my favorite lady feeling today?"

"Oh, I'm fine, sweetheart. How's my favorite son?" Mrs. Phillips asked.

Though Justin had two older brothers that he knew his mother loved as much as him, they always greeted each other this way. He was the baby of the family and growing up had suffered terribly with asthma. For a number of years, his condition was such that it prohibited him from doing a lot of things other children his age were able to do. As a favorable consequence of his sickness, however, Justin's parents, along with his older brothers, had spoiled him.

"I'm fine, Mom. I met the kids on my basketball team today, and I must say, I've got a heck of a team."

Justin never swore in the presence of his mother; not even so much as "hell."

"That's good, baby. I spoke to Jared today. He and Emma are coming up this weekend and bringing the children. I hope you'll come by, too. He's so looking forward to seeing you."

Jared was the elder of his two brothers. He was ten years older than Justin. He and his family lived in Washington, D.C. Jared was the senior partner at a law firm that he and a fellow colleague had formed twenty years ago.

"Sure, Mom. I'll be there. When are they coming, Saturday or Sunday?"

"They're coming for the weekend. I'll be so happy to see those children. They've grown so much since Christmas . . ."

Justin pulled off his overcoat and made himself comfortable on his sofa. He could tell his mother was in a talkative mood. He didn't mind, though. There was nothing he wouldn't do for his mother.

Chapter 3

Malcolm Waters Jr. was the star of Frederick Douglass' basketball team, the Rockets. He averaged twenty points per game and was an outstanding defensive player as well. Basketball had, at one time, been his first love. It currently took a close second only to girls, but that was normal for a healthy seventeen-year-old boy.

His love of basketball was inherited from his father. Before the senior Malcolm's death, he and his son spent numerous hours either watching—at home and at Madison Square Garden —or playing the sport. Though they rooted for opposing teams many times, and had many boisterous debates, they also shared a very strong bond that had nothing to do with the game. Malcolm Sr. had been his son's best friend. Malcolm Jr. had always had a very open and honest relationship with his father. They talked about everything. Though Malcolm had taken his father's death very hard initially, he was able to put his grief aside after a few weeks because he felt he had a responsibility to his mother and younger sister. He was now the man of the house, and like his father before him, he intended to be a rock for his family.

Malcolm was a very good-looking young man. He was actually just a younger version of his father. Though he was two inches taller than his father had been, he had his father's pecan-toned face. Pictures of Malcolm Sr. as a teen were very often mistaken as shots of his son. Both had thick, dark eyebrows and long lashes that complemented bright, cheerful brown eyes. Their noses were somewhat flat and wide but not unbecoming. Their mouths were the only feature they did not share. Malcolm Jr. had his mother's full sensuous lips.

The second half of the Rockets's basketball season had begun two weeks ago. It was now the beginning of March, and the team's record under their new coach was four wins and no losses, so far. When Malcolm came in that evening after their fourth win, he was feeling jubilant. He had played an excellent game, having made ten of the eleven shots he attempted.

"Hey, Mom," he said cheerfully when he entered the house from the yard entrance. He stepped right over to where she stood at the stove and kissed her cheek. "How you doin'?"

"Fine, baby," Rachel answered. "How are you?"

"Great! Wow, that smells good. What are you making?"

"Curried chicken and rice and peas."

"Uhm, I can't wait. I'm starving."

"How was the game?"

"Excellent. We won again. Of course," he added with a smirk.

"Of course." Rachel smiled as she glanced affectionately at her son.

"Hey, Mom, what are you doing on March seventeenth?" Malcolm asked as he opened the refrigerator, looking for a quick snack.

"Hey, wash your hands."

"Oh, sorry," he said as he moved to the sink. "So what are you doing that night?"

"Nothing, why?"

"Well, you know we're trying to raise money for our senior trip. We're going to Disneyworld, Memorial Day weekend. If we can raise a good portion of the money, we won't have to hit up our parents for the majority of it." Immediately after drying his hands, Malcolm returned to the refrigerator and removed a biscuit left over from breakfast and the jar of grape jelly as well. As he prepared to lather the biscuit with the jelly, he continued, "One of the ways we're going to raise some of the money is by having a Spring dance. It's on the seventeenth. We need chaperones. Would you be willing to be one?"

Rachel snickered. "Chaperone a teen dance? Where's it going to be?"

"At the school. In the gym."

"I don't know, Mal."

"Come on, Mom. It'll be fun," Malcolm insisted.

"For who?" she responded with a chuckle.

He chuckled, too. He took a large bite of the jellied biscuit and with his mouth full said, "You'll have fun, Mom. There'll be other parents chaperoning, too. I think Mrs. Washington is going to be there that night."

Rachel moved from the stove to the kitchen table and began to set the table with the plates stacked there. "What time does this dance start?" she asked.

"It starts at seven and ends at twelve."

She moved to the counter next to the sink and opened the drawer that held her silverware. "What will I have to do?"

"Nothing really. Just be there."

"I'm sure there'll be more to it than that," she said as she gave him a sidewise glance.

"Well, you can call Miss Jennings at the school. She's coordinating the whole thing along with the senior class G.O."

She sighed.

"Come on, Mom. You haven't been going out or doing anything really fun since Daddy died. I think this would be a good way for you to start getting out again."

"Yeah, right, by hanging out with a bunch of kids at a kids' party?"

"There'll be other adults there." Malcolm moved across the kitchen to where his mother stood and wrapped his arms around her. "Please, Mom. I already told them you would do it."

"Oh, you did, did you? Well, that's a lot of nerve," she said with a frown.

"I know," he said softly. "I'm sorry. I just thought you

wouldn't mind doing this for us. We're really trying to do everything we can to save you and the other parents the expense of sending us away.''

Malcolm lowered his head like a little boy ashamed of having done something to incur the wrath of his mother. This was a maneuver he learned when he was a young boy, and it was one that usually softened Rachel's heart.

At that very moment, Rachel, knowing that Malcolm was trying his prize-winning little-boy ploy, could not ignore the resemblance he had to her deceased husband. She remembered that Malcolm Sr. used to use a very similar ploy when he knew she was not pleased with him.

As usual she could not stay angry with her son. She looked up into his brown eyes and seeing his father, the love of her life, she smiled and shook her head.

She did not respond, but Malcolm knew he had won her over. "So you'll do it?" he asked cautiously.

"I guess so."

"Thanks, Mom," he said happily, hugging her once again. "I'll tell Miss Jennings to put your name on the list. Do you want her to call you?"

"If there's anything special I need to know, yeah."

"Okay, I'll tell her. I really appreciate this, Mom. It'll be fun," he said, nodding his head confidently.

"Yeah, we'll see. Go get your sister. Tell her dinner's ready."

Chapter 4

"Hi, Coach Phillips."

"Hello, Jennifer," he answered with a smile as he passed her and a number of her grinning and giggling female classmates in the hall between classes.

Jennifer Waters, like a great number of the young ladies in the eleventh and twelfth grades, thought the new basketball coach was gorgeous. Though most of the juniors and seniors were staunch supporters of all of the school's varsity teams, basketball had always had the largest following. Since Justin Phillips' arrival a month ago, however, the crowd now consisted of a greater number of female onlookers.

Jennifer was also on the cheerleading squad and as a result was relatively popular and knew all of the players and the coaches. It didn't hurt, either, that her older brother was the star player of the basketball team. Girls at school very often tried to befriend her in the hopes of getting an introduction to her brother, Malcolm.

Jenny took it all in stride, though. Despite the many opportunities she had to take advantage of her "connections," she rarely did. She was a genuinely nice girl, and plenty of her fellow classmates liked her on her own merits.

However, due to Malcolm's position on the basketball team, she was happy to let her fellow female classmates know that Coach Phillips knew her by name. Many of them were envious of this, especially since he was not her biology teacher. A good number of the young girls that Jennifer associated with had innocent crushes on Justin Phillips.

Understandably so—he always had a ready smile for everyone, teachers and students alike. Those that had him for biology thought he was very fair-minded and almost always even tempered. The students simply liked him.

Though Jennifer had never really spoken to him at any length, she found it almost impossible not to notice what a nice person he seemed to be. Aside from being the best-looking teacher in the school—she and her fellow cheerleaders had taken an official vote on this matter—the students at Frederick Douglass High School embraced him warmly on his arrival at the school because of his pleasant demeanor.

"Hey, Jenny," someone called from behind her as she headed toward her next class.

She turned and saw the young man that she was secretly infatuated with, Marvin Elliot. All thoughts of Coach Phillips flew out of her head. She stopped in her tracks and smiled shyly. "Hi, Marvin."

When he caught up to her, he asked, "How you doin'?"

"I'm fine."

Marvin smiled appreciatively. He concurred with her answer. "You going to the dance?"

"Uh-huh." Jennifer held her books against her chest, hugging them close in the hopes that he would not notice how her heart was pounding at being so close to him.

"Did you get your ticket yet?"

"No. I was going to get it from Mal."

Marvin was a senior like her brother. He was also one of Malcolm's teammates.

"Listen, how about . . ." Marvin hesitated.

Jennifer looked up into his eyes and saw the doubt there. She felt she had to say something so that he would be encouraged to continue. Of course she had no idea what he had been about to say, but she was hoping . . .

"I was wondering if you would mind going to the dance with me?" Marvin said before Jennifer could open her mouth.

She thought she was hearing things. *Did he really ask me to go with him to the dance?* Were those fireworks she was seeing in the hallway at school? *He asked me to go to the dance with him!* The realization hit her like a Mack truck. She tried to contain her elation.

Involuntarily her face broke into a wide smile and she answered, "I would love to, Marvin."

"Great. Don't worry about your ticket. I'll pay for it."

"All right." She was deliriously happy and stifling the urge to scream out her joy was very difficult, but she maintained her composure as best she could.

"Would it be all right if I picked you up that night?" Marvin continued. "I mean, would your mother mind?"

"Oh, no, she wouldn't mind. I'm allowed to date, even though I'm not dating anybody right now." Jennifer felt she should make that perfectly clear, in case he was wondering.

"Oh, good. I'm not dating anyone, either."

Despite his dashing good looks, Marvin was very shy.

It was unanimous among the female population of the school that he was in the top ten as far as looks were concerned. His toffee-complected skin was flawless, and he wore a thin mustache atop the most kissable lips Jennifer had ever seen. He was the product of an interracial marriage: his father was African-American and his mother was Philippine. His black hair was short and naturally curly, and his eyes slightly slanted. He was tall, six feet three inches, though he was only seventeen years old. He towered over Jennifer, as she stood a mere five feet four inches in the two-inch heels she was wearing at the time.

He walked her to her next class, which was just two doors away, and they made plans to talk more at lunchtime.

When Jennifer took her seat in her history class, her face was covered with a smile that remained there for the duration of the forty-five-minute lesson.

Chapter 5

On the evening of Frederick Douglass's Spring dance, Rachel tried on five different dresses and wasn't happy with any of them. It had been so long since she had been out anywhere that required her to dress up that she didn't feel comfortable in anything.

She stood over her bed with her hands on her hips and looked at the five dresses she'd tossed there. She shook her head in disgust.

"Why did I let Malcolm talk me into this?" she asked herself aloud.

"Mommy." Jennifer entered the room with her face all aglow. "Do you think Marvin will like this dress?"

She had on a navy blue tuxedo-styled coat dress that stopped just above her knees. It was doubled-breasted with navy satin-covered buttons and white satin lapels and cuffs.

Rachel smiled and replied, "If he doesn't, he has no taste. That looks great, baby. How're you going to wear your hair?"

"I figured I'd just put it up in a bun and have a couple of curls falling down in front," she said with a shrug.

"That should look cute."

"What are you wearing?" she asked, noticing the dresses decorating Rachel's bed.

Rachel sighed. "I don't know. Everything looks so . . . Oh, I don't know." She plopped down on her bed in defeat.

"Mommy, what's wrong?" Jennifer asked as she sat down next to Rachel. She put a comforting arm around her shoulder.

Rachel shook her head before she looked into her beautiful daughter's eyes. "I wish I hadn't said I would do this."

"Why?"

"I'm just . . ." She sighed heavily. "It's been so long since I've been out anywhere, I don't know what to wear. I don't have anything to wear."

"You have plenty of stuff, Mom," Jennifer said as she quickly rose from the bed and moved to Rachel's walk-in closet. She immediately grabbed a dress off the line. "What about this?"

She was holding up a red silk fitted sheath that belted at the waist. The neckline dipped gently, and the sleeves were long and tapered at the wrist.

Rachel choked back a sob. "Your father gave me that dress a couple of Christmases ago."

"I know. Why don't you wear it?"

Tears came to her eyes involuntarily. "I miss him so much, Jenny."

Jennifer rushed to her side and embraced her. She could not help but cry, too. "I know, Mommy. I miss him, too, but I don't think he would want you to stop living just cause he's not here anymore."

Rachel hugged Jennifer tightly. "I'm just so scared. I've never loved anyone else. I don't know how to live without him," Rachel cried.

"Mommy, it'll be okay." Jennifer didn't really know how to comfort her mother. She had begun to notice in the past few months, whenever Rachel would talk about her and Mal's father, she would cry.

Jennifer missed not having her father around, too. He had been her hero, and she had been his angel. She had always dreamed of one day marrying a man just like him. She knew her parents had been very happy together; that they loved each other deeply. She felt the love they had for each other extend to her and Mal.

She knew their father wouldn't want Rachel to close herself off from the world. Jennifer wished she would go out sometimes and maybe meet someone that could keep her company and make her happy again. Whenever her aunt Janice, their father's younger sister, tried to get Rachel to go out with her, she always made up an excuse.

Jennifer was glad that Malcolm had talked her into chaperoning the Spring dance. Even if it was just a kids' party, at least this way she could meet some other grown-ups and maybe make a few friends that she could go out with on other occasions.

Rachel had begun to regain her composure. "Jenny, I'm sorry."

"That's okay, Mommy. I bet you're gonna have a good time tonight."

"I don't know if I want to go."

"You have to. They need you," Jennifer said as she rose from the bed and began to hang the other dresses back in her mother's closet. "And besides, you need to get out more. This is the perfect opportunity. There won't be any pressure or anything. It'll be fun," Jennifer assured her.

Rachel looked into her daughter's eyes and smiled. "You're not going to let me get out of this, are you, Jenny?"

"Nope. I need a chaperone," she said with a bright smile.

Rachel reached for the red dress Jennifer had laid next to her on the bed. She picked it up and held it in front of her on the hanger. "So you think I should wear this?"

"Yeah. You look great in that dress."

"Come here," Rachel said softly as she held out her hand.

Jennifer took her hand and sat next to her on the bed. Rachel put her arms around her and hugged her. "I love you, baby."

"I love you, too, Mommy."

She kissed her softly on her cheek and said, "Okay, let me start getting myself together."

"Yeah—me, too. Marvin's gonna be here at seven."

"How are you guys getting there?" Rachel asked.

"I don't know," Jennifer said with a shrug. "I didn't ask him."

"Well, I can give you a lift if you don't think he'd mind riding with your mother."

"He won't mind. And if he does, too bad," Jennifer said as she turned and left the room.

By seven o'clock, Malcolm had already left for the dance. His three buddies that picked him up were all dressed in suits and ties. Malcolm wore a tuxedo that had belonged to his father with a cummerbund and bow tie made of authentic kente cloth. Rachel had had it altered to accommodate the two-inch difference in their heights. When she finished helping Malcolm tie his bow tie, she was amazed once again at how much he resembled her late husband.

"You look very handsome, baby," she told him with tears brimming in her eyes.

Malcolm saw the emotion filling his mother, and he gently embraced her. "Thank you, Mom. You look really pretty yourself. I'm sure you're going to be a big hit tonight."

"Yeah, right. With who? Your friends?" she said with a smile.

Malcolm had always had a way of making her laugh when she became overcome with emotion. She was grateful for his gift at that moment.

"You boys all look so very nice. I'm not used to seeing you this way," she told his friends.

When Malcolm and his friends were leaving, she called after them as they walked out, "Make sure you fellas go straight to the party. Don't go getting into anything on the way there."

They all laughed.

Jennifer's date arrived promptly at seven o'clock. He, too, was smartly dressed. He wore a navy pinstriped suit, white shirt, and a blue and gray print tie.

He brought a beautiful corsage made of gardenias for Jennifer. When Rachel walked into the living room to meet him, Jennifer was struggling to pin the corsage on her lapel.

"Hello. You must be Marvin." Rachel offered her hand.

Marvin took two steps toward her and said, "Hello, Mrs. Waters. It's nice to meet you." He shook her hand gently as he asked, "How are you?"

"I'm fine, thank you. How are you?"

"Fine, thank you."

"What a beautiful corsage."

"Thank you," Marvin and Jennifer responded simultaneously.

"Here, let me see," Rachel said as she stepped in front of Jennifer and expertly pinned the corsage to the lapel of her dress. As she did, she leaned in closer to Jennifer and whispered, "He's cute." Rachel then took a couple of steps back and studied her daughter with a loving smile. "You look beautiful, baby."

"Thank you, Mommy. So do you," Jennifer said lovingly.

Chapter 6

Justin arrived at the Spring dance almost an hour after it began. That morning his mother had asked him to take her to visit an ailing friend, and though he didn't stay with her during her visit, when he returned to pick her up at four o'clock that afternoon, she had not been quite ready to leave. He ended up having to spend an hour there, during which time his mother and her friend prayed together and said their goodbyes.

By the time he got his mother back to her apartment in the senior citizen complex she lived in, it was close to six o'clock. When he got back to his apartment, he immediately headed for the shower. He had been playing basketball while his mother was with her friend, and he felt quite uncomfortable. He washed himself quickly but thoroughly.

When he stepped out of the shower, he turned on the nineteen-inch television in his bedroom to catch the start of the Chicago Bulls–New York Knicks game as he got dressed. Though he was fully dressed thirty minutes later, he waited until halftime before he left.

When Justin walked into the gymnasium where the dance was being held, he was glad to see such a big turnout. The kids looked great, he thought. Most were very nicely dressed: the boys in suits and ties and the girls in fancy party dresses.

He had started to wear one of the many designer suits in his wardrobe but at the last minute decided on something a little more comfortable. He was wearing a pair of black wool slacks and a black silk knit mock turtleneck sweater under a deep red collarless wool blazer.

A number of years ago, Justin's hairline had begun to recede and his hair started to thin on top, so about six months ago he shaved his head, opting for a hairless scalp as opposed to a thinning one. He wore a pencil-thin mustache and a closely cut goatee.

Almost immediately, he was greeted by one of his colleagues.

"Hello, Justin. I was wondering if you were going to make it."

He turned to his left and looked down at the very attractive woman standing next to him. "Hello, Barbara," he said with a warm smile. "I got a little tied up."

"Ooh, are you into that?" she asked with a wicked grin.

Justin chuckled and shook his head in amazement.

Barbara Jennings was one of the school's English teachers. She had been quite forthright in her flirtations with him since the week he arrived at Frederick Douglass. Though she had hinted on a number of occasions that they get together outside of their work environment, Justin had purposely played dumb each time.

She was a bit too forward for his taste. He didn't have a problem with a woman coming on to him—actually he was quite flattered, for she was a very beautiful woman, but he did like to feel that he would at least have to "try" before he got to first base.

As they stood there, Barbara went into a litany about all the work she had done to bring this party off. Justin half listened to what she was saying. He learned early on, as a number of the other faculty members had warned him, Barbara Jennings liked the sound of her own voice.

After a few minutes, however, he began to feel like she was

suffocating him, so he excused himself. Before he got away, though, she made him promise to save her a dance.

Justin moved along the edge of the gym and greeted a number of his colleagues, though he never stopped his forward movement. Some of the kids greeted him, and at one point, as he passed by a group of girls huddling close and talking in whispers, he was greeted with a chorus of "Hi, Coach Phillips."

He finally stopped on the far side of the gymnasium and slowly surveyed the hall. Everyone seemed to be having a good time, and though for the moment he was content with staying to himself, he was caught up in the positive vibes that filled the place.

Rachel was asked to attend to the punch bowl and keep the small plastic cups filled. She was happy to oblige. This was an easy task, and she was not required to really socialize.

Though it was obvious that the kids were all having a great time, she really couldn't wait for the night to be over. She was one of only three parents that "volunteered" as chaperones for this event. The other adults present were all members of the faculty, and though everyone was polite, no one went out of their way to be very friendly.

She could see that Jenny was having the time of her life with Marvin. They stayed on the dance floor for almost every song played. When they weren't dancing, they either sat or huddled close together, talking and grinning in each other's faces. Rachel was relieved, at least, that Marvin appeared to be a gentleman. Or maybe he knew she was watching him closely, albeit covertly.

She noticed, too, that Malcolm seemed to be all over the place, flirting with this girl and that one, never staying with anyone for too long a period of time. *Oh Lord,* she thought, *I hope I don't have a young Casanova on my hands.*

As she waited for the partygoers to retrieve the cups of punch from her table to make room for more, Rachel's gazed traveled across the hall. They came to rest on a face she had never seen before. The man stood on the other side of the gym by himself, one hand shoved into the pocket of his trousers.

He had a subtle smile on his face, as if he were either watching or remembering something that tickled him. She wondered if he was one of the three parents that had volunteered since she still hadn't met the other two.

She noticed that he smiled and nodded when a couple of the kids greeted him. *What a handsome man,* she thought as she continued to stare at him.

His face seemed very warm and friendly, and she could see that his eyes sparkled, even from the distance they were apart. He began to walk slowly in her direction, though he kept his eyes on the kids as if he were a cop on the beat.

The man stopped suddenly and smiled broadly at a couple of kids that were showboating on the dance floor. A crowd had begun to form around the couple as they did what seemed to be a choreographed routine.

As Rachel continued to watch him, he suddenly turned and looked directly at her.

Their eyes locked for a moment, and Rachel noticed that the smile he was wearing slowly fell from his handsome brown face. When she realized that she was staring directly into his sparkling eyes, she lowered her head and felt her face heat up from embarrassment.

Almost frantically, Rachel began to fill cups with the punch and line them up on the table so she wouldn't have to look into his eyes again.

Justin was getting a kick out of the young couple that seemed to be performing for their classmates. The dance routine they were doing had to have been rehearsed, he reasoned. They moved together in tight synchronization.

When a young lady he recognized as a senior at the school squeezed in front of him to get a better look, Justin turned his head toward the front corner of the gym. He looked right into the eyes of a breathtakingly beautiful woman standing behind the drinks table.

He immediately forgot about the exhibition that was taking place in front of him. She was looking right at him, and for a moment he was held spellbound by her gaze. Suddenly she lowered her eyes and quickly picked up the ladle lying on the table and began filling cups with punch.

Who was she, he wondered. He stood where he was for a while longer and studied her as best he could from his vantage point. He tried not to be too obvious. He could see how uncomfortable she became when she realized that he was staring back at her.

The woman's face was framed by long black curls that fell past her shoulders. She looked young, maybe early thirties, he guessed, and appeared to be somewhat shy. He thought she was very sexy though. The red dress she wore fitted her nicely, loosely conforming to the curves of her body. She wore a single strand of pearls around her slim neck and pearl earrings in her ears that seemed to give her a somewhat pristine appearance.

He started in her direction slowly. He wanted to meet this beauty. Despite his efforts to appear cool, calm, and collected, his heart raced. He couldn't understand it. No woman had ever had such an effect on him without a word passing between them.

As he continued toward her, two of his ball players stopped at the drinks table and greeted her. She smiled at the boys, and they stayed and chatted with her while they each emptied two cups of the red liquid. Her smile was warm and sincere, and she appeared to know them. *She must be one of the chaperones,* he thought. Since he had arrived at the party so late, he hadn't had an opportunity to meet any of them.

"Hi, Coach Phillips," someone called to him.

He turned in the direction of the voice and greeted the three students he had just passed.

"Hey, kids. Are you having fun yet?" he asked with a smile.

"Yeah, it's the bomb!" one of them responded animatedly.

He laughed. When he turned back to the beauty at the drinks table, she was once again standing alone. When he was just a few feet away from the table, she looked up at him briefly. She was even more beautiful close up. She lowered her eyes as he approached.

"Good evening," Justin said easily.

She looked up at him, and he felt as if he would drown in the dark pools that were her eyes.

"Good evening," she said softly.

"I've never seen you at the school before. Are you one of the brave individuals that volunteered as a chaperone for this evening?" he asked with a mischievous smile.

Rachel chuckled and raised her eyebrows as she said, "You mean gullible, right?"

Justin laughed affably. He offered his hand. "I'm Justin Phillips, biology teacher and basketball coach."

"Oh, hello. I'm Rachel Waters. Nice to meet you." *So this is Mal's coach,* she thought as she shook his hand. Malcolm had told her that the girls at the school were all crazy about Coach Phillips. Rachel could see why.

"Likewise, I'm sure." Justin tipped his head to the side inquisitively and said, "Waters. Are you by any chance related to Malcolm Waters?"

Rachel's smile brightened. "Yes, he's my son."

"Oh! Mrs. Waters, I'm so glad to finally meet you. You have quite a young man in Malcolm. He's a hell of an athlete," Justin said sincerely.

"Thank you—I've been told. I'm ashamed to say I haven't seen him play at all this year. I'm a nurse, and I work some really crazy hours sometimes. I've heard a lot about you, though."

"Well, I hope some of what you've heard was good."

"It was all good. Malcolm thinks very highly of you."

"Well, that's nice to know. The feeling is mutual. He's a great kid," Justin said warmly.

"He has his moments. He actually suckered me into this gig," Rachel said with a smirk.

"Did he?"

"Yes, he told me I would have a blast."

Justin laughed again. "You mean, you're not?" Rachel had to laugh also.

At that moment, Malcolm walked up on them. "Hey, Mom—I see you've met my coach."

"Yes."

Malcolm put an arm around Justin's shoulder and said, "This is the man, Mom. He's the man."

Justin smiled, but Rachel could tell that he was slightly embarrassed. "No, Malcolm, you're the man." Justin turned back to Rachel. "Has Malcolm told you that he's the star of our team?"

"Not in so many words," Rachel commented.

"You've gotta come to one of our games, Mom," Malcolm insisted.

"I will, Mal, as soon as my schedule changes."

At that moment, one of Malcolm's female classmates passed nearby. "Hello, Coach Phillips. Hi, Malcolm," she said demurely as she smiled sweetly at him.

Malcolm's arm fell from Justin's shoulder, and his head turned in the direction of the girl. "Hey, Juanita. You sure look good."

It seemed as though he had completely forgotten that his mother was standing only a couple of feet away.

"Thank you," she said coyly.

Justin and Rachel witnessed Malcolm's obvious distraction with apparent humor. They eyed each other and shook their heads as Malcolm said to them, without turning away from his friend, "Uh, excuse me." He started to follow Juanita, then paused and turned back. "Mom, you're not going to stay behind that table all night, I hope."

"Go tend to your business, Malcolm," Rachel countered.

"I'm coming back for a dance," Malcolm called as he hurried off behind his young friend.

Justin chuckled as he watched Malcolm moving away from them. "God, was I ever so blatantly eager to get next to one of my classmates?" he wondered aloud.

Rachel laughed and said, "I'm sure you were, just like most of us old-timers."

He turned back to her and nodded his head in agreement. "So you're not going to stay back there all night, are you?"

"What?"

"You're not going to stay back there all night, are you?" he repeated.

"Oh, well . . ." she sputtered.

He reached out a hand to her and said, "I need a dance partner."

"I haven't been dancing in so long—I'd probably embarrass you and me," Rachel said, not immediately taking the hand he offered.

"I doubt that."

"I don't know the latest dances," she said as a means of avoiding the inevitable.

"I stopped keeping track of the latest dances a long time ago."

He continued to hold out his hand to her. He could see she was searching for another excuse to give him for not dancing. "Have you ever seen *Lady Sings the Blues?*"

"What? Yes!"

"You gonna let my arm fall off?" Justin said in his best Billy Dee Williams imitation.

Rachel was confused for a moment until she realized what he was doing. She lowered her head but could not conceal her laughter. She took the hand he offered and allowed him to guide her around the table.

"That was one of my favorite scenes," she admitted.

"Mine, too," he said as he led her onto the dance floor.

Chapter 7

Jennifer was having a great time with Marvin. He either kept her in stitches with his sharp wit or giggling from the many compliments he paid her. She was pleasantly surprised to find that he had such a wonderful sense of humor. She had always thought that he was unusually quiet, considering the group of boys he usually ran with. She could see now that it wasn't until he was comfortable that he seemed to come out of his shell.

She was delighted that he was so interested in her. She had never imagined that he would ask her on a date, much less to the school dance. Earlier in the evening, he asked her if she would mind being his girlfriend. *Would she mind,* she thought to herself. Shucks, if it was up to her, she would have it printed in the school paper!

She and Marvin were dancing to a love ballad when Jennifer noticed that her mother and Coach Phillips had met. She was glad. Jennifer noticed that her mother seemed to be enjoying Coach Phillips's conversation. She hadn't seen her mother appear so comfortable in the presence of a man since her dad died. She sincerely missed her father as much as her mother did, but she also wanted her mother to get on with her life.

She wanted Rachel to start dating so she wouldn't be alone

when she and Malcolm went off to college. Malcolm would be going away in September, and she would be following him next year. She didn't want to leave knowing her mother was unhappy. She knew there would never be anyone in her mother's life to replace their father. He was, after all, perfect as far as Jennifer was concerned, but she hoped her mom would meet a special man that she could share her time with.

Jennifer thought someone like Coach Phillips was perfect for her. He was handsome, kind, and seemed like a trustworthy sort of person.

The music had changed, and as she and Marvin now danced to one of Naughty By Nature's big hits, Jennifer watched as her brother joined them briefly before running behind one of his "girlfriends." She noticed that Coach Phillips was holding his hand out to her mother, probably asking her for a dance, Jennifer figured. When she didn't take it immediately, Jennifer silently prayed that she wouldn't turn him down. Her mother looked to her to be making excuses, but Jennifer noticed that Coach Phillips did not give up easily. After a moment, she took note of her mother laughing at something he said before she took his hand and allowed him to lead her onto the dance floor. Jennifer smiled so brightly that Marvin asked what she was thinking. She looked up into his eyes and answered, "I'm thinking about what a wonderful time I'm having here tonight."

When the two songs they danced to had ended, Coach Phillips escorted her mother off the floor. They stood for a moment talking before her mother turned and headed back to her station behind the drinks table. Jennifer did not miss the look on Coach Phillips's face as he watched her mother walk away. She smiled with satisfaction at the idea that he might be attracted to her.

"I'll be right back, Marvin." Jennifer headed off the floor and over to the drinks table.

Rachel saw her approaching and smiled. "Hi, baby—having a good time?"

"I'm having a great time! Are you?" Jennifer asked as she stepped behind the table and linked her arm with her mother's.

"Yeah, it's okay."

"I saw you dancing with Coach Phillips."

Rachel observed that Jennifer's smile seemed to be rooted in some form of mischief. "Yeah, so?"

"Isn't he cute?" Jennifer asked.

"He's all right," Rachel said nonchalantly but avoided Jenny's stare. She definitely thought he was "cute."

"Mommy, you know he's more than just 'all right.' "

"What's that supposed to mean?"

"What did he say to you?"

"What do you mean, what did he say? He asked me to dance."

"Yeah, but I saw you. You weren't going to dance with him at first. What did he say to make you change your mind?" Jennifer wanted to know.

"Have you been watching me all night?" Rachel asked, ignoring Jennifer's inquisition.

"I just want you to have a good time, Mommy. I'm glad you met him. He's really nice. I think he likes you."

"How can you say that? We talked for all of ten minutes, and you were nowhere around."

"But I was watching you," Jennifer said as she hugged Rachel briefly.

"Get away from me, Jenny," Rachel said good-naturedly. "Marvin's looking for you."

Chapter 8

After her dance with Justin Phillips, Rachel's attitude about being at the Spring dance had changed. She was no longer upset that she had allowed Malcolm to "sucker" her into being a chaperone.

Though initially she had been nervous as she watched him approach her, once he had introduced himself, she began to relax.

Since he first started at the school, Malcolm had nothing but praise for his new coach. He told her how Coach Phillips had won the team over by not being as serious minded as Coach Jeffreys had been.

Coach Phillips told them that it was more important to him that they have fun while they played than it was for them to win. Whereas their former coach had played only the guys he favored on the team, Coach Phillips made sure that at every game, each boy had an opportunity to participate. If one of the players was not particularly skilled in the game, Coach Phillips made sure that his supporting teammates were able to take up the slack. He encouraged everyone to do the best he could. That was all he ever expected of any of them. Being that he was so fair-minded, all of his players gave him their all during competitions, and his popularity grew rapidly among the students.

Rachel got the impression that he was a very easygoing person. He seemed very comfortable with himself and his soft-spoken manner led her to believe that he was very adept at making people comfortable around him.

She smiled as she recalled his Billy Dee Williams impersonation. She had been reluctant to dance with him, since she hadn't been out dancing for months before Malcolm Sr.'s death. She had been sure that she would trip over her own feet or step on his. When he recited the line from the movie, however, there was no way Rachel could refuse him.

They chatted amiably as they danced. He insisted that she was quite the dance aficionado. She could not deny how much she enjoyed dancing with him, either. He made her feel safe— as though he would gladly accept her exactly as she was, with any and all flaws. She didn't feel as though she had to try too hard to impress him.

When they left the floor, he thanked her graciously and asked if she would do him the honor of dancing with him again later in the evening. She gladly said she would.

She thought it was funny that Jennifer had seemed to zero in on them. Rachel didn't know whether Jenny was right when she said that Justin Phillips liked her, but she knew that he was the first man since Malcolm that had even piqued her interest in the slightest.

Justin wanted to talk to Rachel Waters some more, but he knew he had to restrain himself. She was a married woman. The gold band on her left ring finger evidenced that. Besides, her son played on his basketball team. How would it look for him to be coming on to her, even subtly?

He was undeniably attracted to her though. He had watched her closely as they danced together. She kept her eyes straight ahead for the most part as they danced, and because he was so much taller than she, her view was basically of his chest.

He was overwhelmed by her beauty, but he thought he

noticed a bit of sadness in her eyes. He did not miss, however, how they shone with pride when Malcolm came over to them. He would have bet his life savings that she was a very loving and caring mother.

The few times she had looked into his eyes while they danced, he thought he recognized a timidness about her. She had even blushed when he complimented her on her dancing.

Why are you letting yourself get so worked up about this woman? he asked himself as he stood near the gymnasium door and eyed her surreptitiously. He knew there was no chance of them becoming better acquainted, but he could not put aside the longing in his heart. He wanted to get to know her. He wanted to be her friend. He wanted to do whatever he could to remove the sadness in her eyes.

Halfway through the dance, Rachel was relieved of her "punch duty." She took this opportunity to stroll around the gym and talk with some of the faculty members on hand. They were all very pleased with the turnout at the dance. The kids were all enjoying themselves, and the school had raised a good bit of money to help allay some of the costs of the scheduled trip to Disneyworld.

As promised, Malcolm grabbed her during one of her conversations and pulled her onto the dance floor. As they were dancing, Jennifer came over and joined them, and the three of them enjoyed a moment of familial joviality. None of them noticed how they were being watched from across the room by Justin Phillips.

After a while, Rachel returned to the sidelines, and as she stood there watching the kids dancing and enjoying themselves, she realized that she was having a wonderful time. She had to make sure she gave Malcolm and Jennifer big hugs when they got home that night. She was glad they had been so insistent about her getting out.

Barbara Jennings joined her after a moment, and they talked about what a success the dance had turned out to be. Miss Jennings was one of Malcolm's teachers, and he did very well in her class. She took this opportunity to let Rachel know just how well he had done on a recent exam she had given.

As Rachel listened to Miss Jennings going on about some of the other students she taught, she noticed that her attention was never fully directed at her. She seemed to be looking for someone in the gym.

Rachel thought she was an attractive woman and actually looked not much older than the students she taught. She was wearing a very provocative black spandex dress that was cut low, exposing an abundant cleavage. Her face was heavily though expertly made-up, and her hair was severely combed away from her face in a bun that sat atop her head. There was not a loose strand of hair anywhere. Though she was very pretty, she appeared almost mannequin-like.

While they conversed, a number of the young men at the dance acknowledged Miss Jennings, giving her what Rachel thought to be highly improper glances.

Quite suddenly Miss Jennings caught her off guard. "Now that's one man I'd like to see in the buff," she said.

Rachel was taken aback by her comment for a second before she looked to see whom Miss Jennings was referring to. She followed her gaze and realized that she was talking about Mr. Phillips.

She felt herself blushing and though she didn't respond, Rachel had to agree that she was pretty sure she would enjoy that sight herself.

"Isn't he just the most delicious-looking man you've ever seen?" Miss Jennings continued.

Rachel didn't know how to respond. She was actually surprised that this woman was being so uninhibited around her. After all, she didn't know Rachel. For all she knew, Rachel could have been offended by her words, or she could have been one of those parents that was quick to run and tell the principal about her licentious ways.

As Miss Jennings continued to ramble on about what she would like to do to Mr. Phillips or have done to her by Mr. Phillips, he started toward them. Rachel was embarrassed because she felt as if he could tell that they were talking about him.

He seemed to be looking directly at her, whether he was or not. He also seemed to have a very appreciative smile on his handsome face. He was probably admiring Miss Jennings's shapely body in her tight-fitting garment.

"I was wondering when I was going to get that dance, Justin. I thought you forgot about me," Miss Jennings called before he had even reached them.

The music was slow, and the floor was jammed with young couples dancing closely. Rachel took a step away from Miss Jennings, certain that he was indeed coming to dance with her.

"Sorry, Barbara," he said with a shake of his head. "I promised this dance to Mrs. Waters." He held out his hand to her and said, "Shall we?"

Rachel was stunned. She looked up at him wide-eyed for only a second before she took his hand and allowed him to lead her onto the floor. She turned back to Miss Jennings briefly and could see that she was quite annoyed at being so quickly brushed aside.

When Justin put his arm around her waist and pulled her close to him, Rachel's heart rate doubled.

"Thank you for not making me look like a complete liar, but I've been trying to avoid getting trapped by Miss Jennings all evening," Justin said close to her ear.

Rachel looked up at him and smiled. "She seems to be quite smitten with you."

"Lucky me," he said sarcastically.

She lowered her head and laughed softly. She was tickled that he was so uninterested in Miss Jennings after hearing the way she felt about him. She was also a bit flattered that he had chosen her over the young temptress.

"So Mrs. Waters, are you enjoying yourself?"

She looked up at him with a smile. "Actually I am. I really didn't think it would be so much fun."

"I see your husband didn't allow Malcolm's silver-tongue to convince him to attend our little shindig."

Justin felt her body tense immediately with his words. Her

eyes seemed to cloud over, and the smile she had been wearing fell from her lips.

"My husband passed away, Mr. Phillips," Rachel said just above a whisper.

Justin wanted to kick himself. "Oh, I'm sorry," he said immediately. "That was a really dumb thing to say."

He had a frown on his face, and Rachel could see that he was beating himself up for no reason. "That's okay—you didn't know," she said as she looked into his eyes.

She had the saddest eyes he had ever seen. She was right, of course—he hadn't known that she was a widow, but he still felt terrible about what he'd said. Now he could understand her sadness.

He wondered how long it had been.

They continued the dance without exchanging any words between them for the next minute or so. He was trying to think of something to say to her, but he was afraid he would put his foot in his mouth once again.

"This is the first time I've been out dancing since he died," Rachel suddenly said. "Malcolm and Jenny have been trying to get me out of the house for the longest time now."

He could tell she was trying hard to be cheerful, but he could feel her pain as sure as if it was his own. "How long has it been?" he asked gently.

She sighed. "Almost two years now."

Justin was pleased that she felt comfortable enough with him that she hadn't pulled away. Almost unconsciously, he tightened his hold on her as he felt an overwhelming need to comfort her.

"I thought it would get easier as time passed, but it hasn't. I still miss him so much."

Rachel was becoming very emotional. Though she felt comforted by Justin's strong arms, she couldn't help wishing that she was being held by her beloved Malcolm. Against her will, she began to cry.

She missed Malcolm desperately. Missed the times when he would hold her as Justin was now; missed hearing his laughter and seeing his smile; missed his tender loving.

When Justin realized that she was crying, he asked anxiously, "Mrs. Waters, are you all right?"

With her head lowered, she shook it, indicating that she wasn't.

She moved away from him. Her face was wet with tears. "I'm sorry. Excuse me," she cried softly as she turned and hurried toward the exit.

"Mrs. Waters," he called after her.

Justin stood there dazed and confused and feeling totally responsible for this beautiful woman's discomfort.

"What did you say to her?"

He turned and looked into the angry eyes of Malcolm Waters Jr. "I . . ." Justin stammered. He didn't know what he'd said to make her so upset.

Malcolm turned away from him and went after his mother.

Rachel rushed out of the gymnasium and past a group of kids that were mingling just outside the door. She found a bench at the far end of the corridor and sat there trying to collect herself. She was so embarrassed. The last thing she had wanted to do was cause a scene, but that was exactly what she had done.

He must think I'm crazy, she thought of Mr. Phillips. She had really tried to keep her emotions in check, but standing in his arms and talking about her husband had just been more than she could bear.

"Mom! Are you okay?" Malcolm asked as he hurried to her side. He sat next to her and immediately embraced her. "What did he say to you, Mom? What did he say?"

She shook her head and tried to compose herself. "He didn't say anything, Malcolm. It's not his fault. We were talking about your dad, and you know how I get. I'm sorry," she cried.

Malcolm held her tighter and tried to comfort her. "Mom, it's okay. It's okay. You don't have to be sorry."

His eyes began to water. He hated to see his mother cry. He wished there was something he could do to make her pain go away. "Mom, it's gonna be all right. I promise you."

"Mommy?" Jennifer was there. "Mommy, what's wrong?" she asked worriedly.

Rachel felt terrible that she had upset her children this way. She held both of them, each on one side of her. "I'm sorry, babies. I'm okay. It's nothing. I just got a little emotional when we started talking about your father. I didn't mean to ruin this for you."

"You didn't, Mom," they said together.

Rachel took a deep breath and looked toward the ceiling, trying to get herself together. "I'm sorry. I'll be okay now," she said, looking from one to the other. "I'm so embarrassed. I can't believe I did that."

"It's all right, Mom," Malcolm assured her.

Her children sat with her for the next few minutes as they all comforted one another. When Rachel felt she had her emotions in check, she asked them to go back to the party. She told them she needed a moment alone before she went back inside. They were both reluctant to leave her, but she assured them that she was all right.

Justin's insides were knotted anxiously, wondering if Rachel was all right. He'd wanted to follow her when she ran from the gym but thought better of it when he saw the way Malcolm looked at him. *Why did I have to say anything about her husband,* he asked himself. *She had been laughing and was having a good time until I had to go and spoil it for her.*

He knew everyone was wondering what he'd done to upset her. He could see the way they were all looking at him.

After agonizing over it for nearly ten minutes, he decided he had to make sure that she was all right. When he left the gym, Malcolm and Jennifer were coming toward him. Their faces were filled with sadness, and his heart ached because of it.

"Malcolm, is she okay?" he asked with genuine concern. "I didn't mean to upset her."

"You didn't, Coach," he said solemnly.

"Where is she?" he wanted to know.

"She's down there," Malcolm said, pointing toward the end of the corridor.

"Is she all right?" he asked, looking down the hall in her direction.

"Yes," Jenny answered.

They continued past him and reentered the gym, though neither of them was in a party mood any longer.

Justin walked toward Rachel tentatively, not sure she would be willing to see him. She sat with her hands in her lap, looking so sad it broke his heart.

"Mrs. Waters?" he said softly.

She looked up at him immediately when she heard his voice. "I'm sorry that I—"

"No," he stopped her as he sat beside her and took her hand. "I'm sorry I upset you."

"It wasn't your fault. I try to . . . It's just hard to talk about it even after all this time."

"I understand."

"I'm sorry if I made you uncomfortable," Rachel said as she looked into his eyes. She could see that his concern was genuine.

"No, don't apologize. It was a stupid thing for me to say."

She shook her head and said, "You couldn't have known."

They sat in silence for the next few seconds.

"Are you okay?" he asked finally.

She nodded and tried to smile. "We were childhood sweethearts. He was the only man I ever loved, and it's hard to get used to him not being around anymore."

"I understand."

Rachel took a deep breath and sighed. "Malcolm and Jenny worry about me so much. I feel so bad that I lost it in there."

"Mrs. Waters, there's no reason for you to feel that way."

"Please call me Rachel."

He smiled. "I'm sure they understand how hard it is for you, Rachel."

"I don't know what I'd do without them." Rachel sat up straight and leaned against the back of the bench. "I'm sorry if I ruined your evening."

"Oh, how could you think that?" he said as he looked at her in astonishment.

"Well, I'm sure you weren't expecting to have some strange woman crying on your shoulder tonight."

"I don't think you're so strange," he said with a warm smile.

Rachel couldn't help but smile, too.

"I'll make you a promise, though," Justin began. "The next time I see my foot heading toward my mouth, I'll be sure to duck."

Rachel laughed. She looked over at him and saw that he was smiling at her, too. Still feeling a bit embarrassed by her uncontrollable show of emotion only minutes earlier, Rachel was comforted by his sense of humor and appreciated his compassion.

"You know, Mr. Phillips . . ."

"Justin."

"Justin. Malcolm has a way of making me laugh when I'm feeling really down or if he sees I'm about to lose it. Thank you for being so gracious."

"It's not necessary," he said softly. "You know, I kind of know what you're going through. I lost someone that I cared for very deeply, too. She didn't die on me, though I'd be lying if I said I haven't wished it since."

Rachel looked at him strangely after that remark.

"See, a little over a year ago, I was engaged to be married, and my fiancée left me at the altar."

"Oh, no."

"Yeah. She ran off with my best man. It was very hard to deal with. It took a long time to get over that. At least, I think I'm over it," he added as an afterthought. "So just like it's hard for you to get on with your life, it's been very hard for me to trust anyone, so I can identify with what you're going through."

"That's a terrible thing to do to someone that you know loves you," she said, feeling genuinely sorry that it had happened to him.

"Yeah, it is."

They sat together again in silence for the next few minutes, though they were very comfortable with one another.

"We're a couple of sad sacks, aren't we?" Rachel said with a sad smile after a while.

Justin chuckled. "Yeah, how 'bout that."

"Oh," Rachel sighed. "I'm going home."

"Are you really?"

"Yeah, I think this is enough for my first time out."

"Well, if it's any consolation, Rachel, I think you did just great."

She smiled graciously. "Thank you, Justin."

"I hope you had a good time," he said as he gazed into her beautiful eyes.

"I did." She nodded. "I really did."

"Good."

"Would you do me a favor? I really don't want to go back inside. Would you mind telling Malcolm I'm going home."

"Do you need a ride?" he asked.

"No, I'm driving, thank you."

"Are you going to be okay?"

"I'll be fine. Thanks for being so understanding," she said sincerely.

"Anytime," he said fondly. He took her hand and added, "It was a pleasure meeting you, Rachel. I hope to see you at one of our games soon."

"I'm going to come to a game, I promise. It was nice meeting you, too, Justin," she said with a smile.

He rose from the bench but before he walked away, he said, "Good night, Rachel. Drive safely."

"Good night."

Rachel watched him as he walked slowly back to the gym. There was a jumble of emotions flowing through her that night. She loved her husband and missed him tremendously, but she realized, with some trepidation, that she had met a man tonight that awakened something in her that had been asleep since Malcolm died.

Chapter 9

Sunday morning Rachel rose and went to the nine o'clock service at Calgary Baptist Church, where she had been a member for over ten years. Though she was usually enthralled by Reverend Williams's unfailingly moving and enlightening sermons, on this day she sat in the pew thinking of Justin Phillips.

His handsome face was a fixture in her mind's eye, and his gentle manner left her feeling comforted. *Was she wrong to feel this way?* she wondered. Did this mean that her feelings for Malcolm were changing? She didn't want them to. The nineteen years they had together were the greatest years of her life. She didn't ever want to lose the memory of that time with him.

Would Malcolm understand her feelings for this man she had met only yesterday? Was she getting in over her head? How did she know he was even interested? Maybe the only reason he had been so nice was because she was Malcolm Jr.'s mother. But something in her gut told her that her instincts were right. Justin Phillips was interested in her. After all, he had approached her. Both times they danced together, he had come from across the gym to get her.

Before meeting Justin, she had never even considered becoming friendly with a man again, but she could not deny that she did want to be friends with him. She felt as though he was someone she could trust with her feelings.

When the service was over, and she had exited the church, her sister-in-law, Janice Waters, leaned into her and asked, "So where was your mind this morning?"

Rachel was caught off guard. "What?"

"You heard me. You can't tell me you were listening to Reverend Williams's sermon. You looked like you were in your own little world."

They were walking over to Rachel's car in the church parking lot. Janice was coming back to the house with her for lunch.

"I don't know what you're talking about, Jan," Rachel remarked with a wave of her hand.

"Uh-huh," Janice said with a smirk.

When they were seated in Rachel's car, and she had started the ignition, Janice asked, "How was the dance last night? Did the kids have fun?"

"Yeah, they had a ball. I made a fool of myself, though," Rachel answered matter-of-factly.

"What do you mean?"

"I was dancing with Mal's basketball coach, and he asked me why my husband didn't come to the dance. So I told him. Then we started talking about Malcolm, and I started crying and embarrassed myself and the kids and probably Justin, too."

"Who's Justin?"

"Mal's coach."

"You're on a first-name basis with Mal's coach?" Janice noticed.

"Well, after crying on his shoulder, don't you think I should be?"

"What happened?"

"Oh, I don't know. It was strange. One minute we were dancing and laughing and the next, I just lost it. I ran from the gym, and he came to see if I was okay. We sat outside talking for a while until I got myself back together, and then I went home."

"What does he look like?"

"Who? Justin?"

"Yeah."

"He's handsome. And he's really a sweet man. The kids at school are all crazy about him, from what Mal and Jenny say. He's new. He's been there only since last month."

"You said he's handsome and he's really sweet. So you think you'd want to see him again?"

"Janice, I'm not thinking about that. I'm not ready to date anyone," Rachel insisted.

"Why not? Malcolm's been dead for almost two years, honey, and I know you love him—but you need to get on with your life. You know he'd want you to."

"Justin was just being nice."

"I don't think you believe that. You were thinking about him today in church, weren't you?"

Rachel looked straight ahead. When she didn't answer, Janice continued, "Honey, I think it's great if you've met someone that you're interested in. Don't feel bad about it." She reached over and squeezed Rachel's shoulder gently.

Rachel looked over at her sister-in-law and could not keep her eyes from filling up. "I feel guilty for liking him, Janice. I just met him. I don't really know anything about him."

"Well, maybe you should get to know him. You owe yourself that chance, Rachel. You deserve to be happy. You look so sad all the time. And besides, maybe he has a nice friend for me."

Rachel looked over at Janice and smiled. "You've got a one-track mind, you know that."

"I know."

Chapter 10

For the next few days, Justin went about his life, business as usual, with one major difference. The memory of Rachel Waters had taken up permanent residence in his mind.

When Rachel left the dance Saturday night, Justin's desire to remain there left with her. Being a member of Frederick Douglass's faculty, however, he could not shirk his duty, so he stayed, but it seemed that the remaining hour and a half of their allotted time there was the longest of his life.

He visited his mother on Sunday, as he usually did, and before he realized what he was doing, he was telling her about this incredible woman he met the night before.

He was standing at the door of her kitchen when he said, "You know, Mom, before I found out that she was a widow, I was wondering why such a beautiful woman would look so sad. She had these sad eyes that kind of drew me in, and I felt this overwhelming desire to hug her."

"It's sometimes very hard to get over the death of a spouse, Justin," his mother said. "Your father's been dead for over seven years, and though I've accepted his death, I still feel as if I've lost a piece of my heart. I'm just glad I've got my children. Knowing that I can see him each time I look at one of you does my old heart a lot of good."

"She depends on her kids a lot, too, I think, for that same kind of comfort. Her son is one of my players, and her daughter is on the cheerleading squad. She told me that they're always trying to get her out of the house. She said last night was the first time she'd been out dancing since he died."

Justin's mother gazed at him from across the room for a long moment. "You sound like you've got a thing for this young woman, honey."

Justin blushed. "I . . ." He sauntered over to the kitchen table where his mother was seated. He sat across from her and in a soft tone, said, "Yeah, I guess I do."

"Be careful, baby. She may not be ready for you."

"I know, Mom, and I'll be cool but she's just . . . She's touched something in me. I feel like . . . I want to get to know her. I'd like to be her friend."

"But if she's not ready for that, you have to let her be."

He sighed. "I know, but I think she felt comfortable with me. I'll go slow, though. The last thing I want to do is scare her off."

On Tuesday afternoon, the Rockets had a game against their biggest rival, Hackensack High School's Cougars. It had been a tense and very exciting game from the opening buzzer.

The boys on the team were all eager to beat the Cougars, because everyone had them slated as being the underdogs in this match. The game was played on the Cougars' home court, and Justin's players came with their games faces on.

Marvin was the team's starting center, and Malcolm was the team captain and lead guard. The two of them had a rhythm on the court that came naturally and was nearly unstoppable. By the end of the second half, Malcolm and Marvin had led the team to a seven-point advantage over the home team.

Justin was happy that the guys had pulled off such a major upset. He was very proud of his boys. The way they played tonight showed exactly how much they had grown as a team since he first started coaching them. Aside from Malcolm, Marvin and a couple of the other team members that were exceptional players, the other boys all worked hard to improve their skills. They supported each other in true team fashion. He liked to think that he had something to do with their sportsman-like attitudes.

When the game was over, and the guys had changed back to their street clothes, Justin offered a few of them a ride home. Marvin, Malcolm, and two other boys, Gary Lennett and Felton Stevenson, all gladly accepted his offer.

Justin drove a Mercedes Benz 560D, and when the boys saw it, they became very excited about the prospect of being driven home in a such a classy automobile. During the ride, they all rehashed major plays of the game, talking and laughing loudly as they were all in a very jubilant mood.

Malcolm was riding shotgun with Justin, so he was the last to be dropped off. Actually that had been the plan all along. Justin wanted to talk to Malcolm alone. He wanted to inquire about his mother.

"You guys played a great game tonight, Malcolm," Justin said.

"Thanks, Coach. It seemed like everybody was on their game."

"Well, you all have a great rhythm between you. You connect well."

"Yeah. Before you came, we weren't playing this well. Coach Jeffreys didn't let everybody play. I think the guys appreciate that you give them all a chance."

"Well, that's why they signed up to play, so they could get some play."

"That's true. I wish Mom could've seen this game," Malcolm said.

Justin had his opening. "How is your mother, Malcolm?"

"She's fine."

"I was really worried about her the other night."

"I know, but she's okay. She gets real teary when she talks about my father."

"That's understandable."

''If my dad was still alive, he wouldn't have missed any of my games. He was like the quintessential basketball fan.''

''Yeah?'' Justin looked over at Malcolm with a smile.

''Yeah. He used to get season tickets for the Knicks. We went to all the games.''

''You and your dad were really close, huh?''

''Yeah, but we all had good relationships with him. He and Mom were best friends, you know. Even me and Jenny could see it.''

Justin listened raptly as Malcolm spoke about his father and mother's relationship. Rachel had already told him they had been childhood sweethearts, but from what Malcolm told him, they had always been a very close-knit family. Aside from yearly vacations with the whole family, Malcolm Waters Sr. took his wife on a ''second honeymoon'' every year as well.

He began to admire this man that he would never have the opportunity to meet and could understand why even after nearly two years, Rachel would still miss him as if he had just died yesterday. He also began to admire Rachel even more. Despite her husband's death, she still had to go on. She still had to make sure her children did not lack anything in the way of parental guidance, now that she was a single parent—and from what he could see, though he didn't know Jennifer that well, she was doing a great job. He knew for a fact that Malcolm was a parent's dream. He was well mannered, considerate, loyal, and very supportive of his family.

Having worked with teenaged boys when he was in Los Angeles, he had met several that had no fathers in their home, but also many that had lost their fathers during their formative years. Raising a teenaged boy without a positive male role model on the scene could be a very difficult task. From what he could see, Rachel and her husband had raised their children to be strong, independent, but supportive individuals—positive additions to the human race.

When they pulled up in front of the Waters's house, Malcolm thanked Justin for the ride and offered his hand before he got out of the car.

Justin liked this kid tremendously. As he shook Malcolm's hand, he said, "Tell your mother I said hello, okay?"

"Why don't you come inside and tell her yourself?"

"No, Malcolm, I don't want to impose," Justin said, though he truly wanted to gaze at her lovely face if only for a minute.

"You won't be imposing. I'm sure she'll be glad to see you," Malcolm assured him.

Would she really? Justin wondered. *Did Malcolm know this for a fact, or was he just guessing?*

"Come on, Coach," Malcolm urged as he leaned down and spoke through the glass on the passenger side of the car.

Justin turned off the car and opened the driver's side door. He followed Malcolm up the walk to the front door, and with each step his heart beat faster. He tried not to give away that he was extremely excited about the prospect of seeing Rachel again.

Malcolm unlocked the door and stepped inside. He held the door for Justin as he stepped over the threshold and into the house.

"I'll be right back," Malcolm said as he headed toward the kitchen. "Mom, I'm home."

Rachel was just setting the table for dinner. Malcolm stepped over to her and kissed her cheek. "Hi, baby. You're just in time for dinner," she said with a smile.

"Perfect timing."

"How was the game?"

"It was great. You missed a doozy. There's someone here to see you, by the way."

"Who?"

At the same moment, Jennifer came downstairs from her room. She was surprised to see Justin standing just inside the door.

"Hi, Coach Phillips."

"Hello, Jennifer. How are you?" he said with a pleasant smile.

"I'm fine. How are you?"

"Good."

"How was the game?"

"It was great. It's too bad we didn't have our head cheer-leader there," he said and playfully tapped her on her shoulder. "We really creamed them."

Jennifer had a doctor's appointment that afternoon so she hadn't been able to attend the game. "Well, that's good. Sounds like you didn't really need me."

"We always need *all* of our cheerleaders," Justin said with a warm smile.

Rachel heard his voice before she saw him, and her heart fell into her stomach. *Be cool, girl,* she told herself.

"Hello, Justin."

He turned from Jennifer at her voice, and his face broke into a radiant smile, one that Jennifer did not miss. "Hello, Rachel. How are you?"

"I'm fine. How are you?"

Jennifer noticed the smile that had suddenly dominated her mother's face as well. She could not help but grin at these two. She discreetly left them and went into the kitchen with her brother.

"I'm fine, thank you. I just dropped Malcolm off, and I thought I'd come in and say hello. I hope you don't mind."

"Of course, I don't mind. I'm glad you did. How was the game?" *God, he looks so good,* she thought as she gazed up into his brown eyes.

"It was great. We won. The guys played their butts off today." *Damn, it's good to see her,* Justin thought as he stood there admiring her beauty.

"That's good. So you're still undefeated, huh?"

"Yeah. A perfect record." *She's so beautiful,* he was think-ing. What he wouldn't do to pull her into his arms at this moment.

"That's great. When's your next game?"

"Thursday. At the school."

"I'll be there," she told him.

His smile seemed to brighten at this bit of news. "That's great! We need more cheerleaders."

Rachel laughed and said, "I'll bring my pom-poms."

Justin laughed with her.

They stood there for a moment in awkward silence, as both of them had run out of witty conversation and were just so overwhelmed at seeing each other that they had suddenly become tongue-tied. Rachel broke the silence.

"We were just sitting down to dinner, Justin. Would you like to join us?" she asked softly.

He wanted to say yes more than anything in the world, but he wanted their first dinner together to be a little different. He wanted to take her out; to romance her; to wine and dine her. Besides, he didn't want to impose on his first visit with her.

"Thank you, Rachel, but I wouldn't want to impose," he said graciously.

"You wouldn't be imposing. There's plenty, and you're more than welcome to join us."

"Well, I really can't tonight, but I appreciate the offer."

She was disappointed, though she tried to hide it. "Well, maybe another time."

"I'll definitely take you up on that, though," he said, smiling exultantly.

"Good." She was delighted.

"Well, I'd better be going. I don't want to hold up your dinner. I just wanted to come in and say hi, see how you were."

"I'm glad you did. It's great to see you again." She looked up at him with dovelike eyes.

"It's great to see you, too, Rachel, and I look forward to seeing you on Thursday," Justin said ardently.

"Likewise."

He turned to the door and opened it to leave. "Good night, Rachel."

"Good night, Justin. Drive safely."

As Justin walked back to his car, a feeling of warmth spread throughout his body despite the cold temperature that night. When he reached his car, he turned and looked back at the house and was pleased to see Rachel still standing there. She waved at him one final time before closing the door.

As he slowly wheeled his car away from her house and

toward his own, he felt as though his life was finally about to come together. He could be wrong, but he felt certain that he had just gazed into the eyes of the woman he wanted to spend the rest of his life with.

Chapter 11

When Rachel walked into Frederick Douglass High School's gymnasium on Thursday evening, it was packed. The game was already under way. She had decided at the last minute to go home and change from her nurse's uniform to a pair of jeans, a white turtleneck sweater, her black leather riding boots, and a black leather bomber jacket. She was fortunate that Jennifer's cheerleading squad was sitting near the entrance she had used, because when Jennifer spotted her, she asked one of her friends in the first row to make room for her on the bench.

Just as she was sitting down, Malcolm drove the lane and slammed home a basket which immediately brought the crowd to its feet. Rachel was swept up in the excitement aside from being a proud mother. She cried out, "That's my baby!"

Despite the high level of noise in the gym that began with Malcolm's basket, and continued when one of his teammates stole the ball and scored again, somehow Justin heard Rachel's voice over the din. He turned in the direction he thought it had come from but did not see her. After searching the crowd for a few minutes and still not spotting her, he turned his attention back to the game. *Damn, now I'm hearing her voice,* he thought.

The first half of the game continued, and the level of play

was high throughout. The Rockets were leading at halftime by nine points. Jennifer's squad took the floor at the half and performed an exciting combination of acrobatics and step-dancing.

The air was filled with a jubilance the likes of which Rachel had not been a party to for years. She was a bit ashamed of herself when she realized that she hadn't been to any of Malcolm's games since her husband died. So many things had changed with his death. She had literally put her life on pause. Simple, enjoyable things such as attending her own son's games had become one of the many activities she had avoided because of the memories they evoked. She realized that she had been cheating her children as well as herself.

"Rachel!"

She looked around when she heard his voice. He was off to her left, near the Rockets's bench. The team was on the floor, warming up for the second half. He was wearing a blue and white running suit, a white T-shirt, and white running shoes. She smiled and waved as he started over to her.

"How are you?" he called as he approached.

"I'm fine, Justin. How are you?" They were practically yelling over the noise of the young crowd and the music that filled the air from the public address system.

"Great—I'm glad you made it." She was standing in front of the bench, and he came right up to her. "I was looking for you at the start of the game."

"I didn't get here until just before the half ended."

"Did you catch that run Malcolm started?" he asked with a big smile.

"I sure did. Didn't you hear me yelling?" she asked with a laugh.

"You know, I thought I heard your voice—but when I looked around and didn't see you, I figured it was my imagination." Justin laughed. "Did you bring your pom-poms?"

"They're in my bag," Rachel joked, tapping her shoulder bag.

The horn sounded then, signaling the start of the second half.

"I'd better get back over there," Justin said, tilting his head in the direction of his team's bench.

"Okay. I'll be cheering."

"See you when it's over."

Rachel watched Justin walk back over to the bench and smiled. She genuinely liked him and hoped that the feeling was mutual.

He grabbed Malcolm and let him know that she was there. Malcolm ran over and gave her a big hug and kiss before taking the floor.

From the opening tap, the second half was just as exciting as the few minutes she had caught of the first. The Rockets won the game once again, bringing their record under Justin's coaching to nine and oh.

Malcolm came over to her at the end of the game. Rachel grabbed him immediately and hugged him. "Oh, baby, you were great. You were so good."

"Thanks, Mom," he said, overjoyed that she was there. "I'm glad you came."

"I am, too. I'm so sorry I haven't been coming to your games, baby. I promise I'm gonna do better."

"It's all right, Mom. You're here now."

Jennifer joined them. She gave Malcolm a big hug and kissed his cheek, too. "You were awesome, Mal."

"Thanks, sis."

Marvin then joined them. "Hi, Mrs. Waters."

"Hi, Marvin. Great game."

"Thanks." He slipped an arm around Jennifer's waist, and she tiptoed and kissed him on the mouth. They moved away from Rachel and Malcolm as Justin stepped over to them.

"Great game, Malcolm," Justin said as he slapped him five.

"Thanks, Coach. I'm gonna go shower and change. Mom, I'm going to stop with the guys at the pizza shop so don't worry about dinner." He turned to Jennifer and Marvin. "Hey, sis, y'all coming to the pizza shop?"

"Yeah," Marvin answered.

"Do you guys have homework?" Rachel asked Malcolm and Jennifer.

"I don't," Jenny answered.

"Me, either."

"Okay, you two. Don't be too late. Remember, tomorrow's a school day."

After a few minutes, Malcolm, Jennifer, and Marvin walked away leaving Rachel alone with Justin. She looked up at him and smiled. "At least I don't have to cook."

"Are you hungry?" he asked.

"I'm starving. I'm going to pick something up on my way home."

Though he wanted their first dinner together to be more of a wine-and-dine event, he figured it might be a little awkward for her if he asked her on a date right here in the middle of the gym, with her kids only a few yards away. Since she really had no idea how attracted he was to her, he decided that something a little more informal might be more appropriate.

"You know, Rachel, there's a great little soul-food place about a block from here. I was going to go by there and get something myself. Why don't you come with me?"

"Is it any good?"

"It's very good. I mean the place is no big deal. It's actually a little hole in the wall, but the food is so good I don't think the customers pay the decor any mind."

Rachel agreed to go to the diner with him. Though it was only a block away, they both drove their cars there so they wouldn't have to go back to the school when they were finished. Rachel was tickled when one of the two countergirls greeted Justin by name.

"You come here a lot, huh?" she asked.

He blushed. "Yeah, I guess."

The menu was a two-sided sheet of paper laminated to keep stains off. The tables were close; actually there were six tables and a counter that seated ten. All of the tables seated four, but it really didn't look as though they could accommodate twenty-four people at once.

Rachel and Justin took a table near a window which looked out onto the parking lot. She studied the menu, having a hard

ime deciding what she would have—everything sounded so
good.

"What are you having?" she asked him.

"The smothered chicken."

"I was looking at that. Is it good?"

"The only time I've tasted better is at my mother's house."

"Really?"

He nodded.

"Are the pork chops any good?"

"Yup. Everything I've ever tried here is good, and I've had
almost everything they serve at least once. Except the chitlins.
I don't mess with that."

"Me, either."

As Rachel continued to study the menu, Justin studied her.
She was wearing her hair in a ponytail with a few strands softly
curled and falling down along the right side of her face. She
wore no makeup, and he noticed that her skin looked flawless
and soft as silk. He wanted to caress her face; to feel her skin
against his fingertips. An appreciative smile played on his lips
as he dreamt of holding her in his arms and kissing her full
sensuous lips. She was so beautiful to him.

Rachel looked up from the menu to ask him a question about
the barbecue ribs and noticed him staring. "What?"

Though he was sitting right across the table from her, he did
not hear her immediately.

"Justin!"

"Huh?"

"Why are you staring at me like that?"

"Was I staring?"

"Yes."

He appeared flustered for a moment, which Rachel thought
made him look adorable.

"I, uh . . . I was just thinking that you don't look old enough
to have two teenaged children."

"I started early."

The waitress appeared at their table. "Are you folks ready
to order?"

Rachel started to order the barbecue ribs but changed her

mind and decided on the smothered pork chops with mashed potatoes, collard greens, and corn bread. Justin ordered the same sides with his chicken. After taking their orders, the waitress gathered their menus and left, promising to return quickly with their food.

"Malcolm told me you're new to the school. Where were you teaching before?" Rachel asked Justin as she folded her arms in front of her and rested her chin in her hand.

"Well, I was in L.A. I just moved back here in January. I was teaching out there but at a different level."

"Really?"

"Yeah, I was at UCLA Medical School. I used to be a pediatric surgeon."

Rachel was stunned, and it showed on her face.

"I know. It's a big change."

"That has to be the understatement of the decade. Why'd you give that up?"

He explained how he had come to the difficult decision to give up the medical profession. She listened intently as he explained how he had become overwhelmed by the job he had at one time loved. He told her that he had too much compassion to be a surgeon. He felt that in order to be a really brilliant surgeon, one had to be able to separate the fact that the little people he operated on were nothing more than bodies on a table that needed fixing. He couldn't do that. He had spent as much time with the children he treated as possible, which made it all the more difficult for him when an operation was not successful.

He also added that when his fiancée left him, he pretty much lost his focus. He told her that being in L.A. reminded him mostly of what she'd done to him.

Rachel could see the pain and anger in his eyes when he spoke of her. They had been engaged for two years, and his best man had been a doctor that he worked with every day. Though when they ran off together they left the area, Justin found that after a year, he had come to hate L.A. and never wanted to return there.

She felt bad for him. She could see that he still had a hard time coming to terms with the betrayal of this woman and his friend. She wanted to hold him, to comfort him. "I'm sorry they hurt you that way, Justin," she said as she reached across the table and gently covered his hand with her own. "I think that's worse than having a loved one die. I mean, you give a person your heart, and you trust them to handle it with tender loving care, and to do something like that . . ." She shook her head.

"How'd your husband die, Rachel?"

"Heart attack. He was a pediatrician, too."

"Really?" Justin smiled.

"Uh-huh. I work in the pediatric ward at the hospital myself."

"I guess we've got a thing for kids, huh?"

"Yeah. I love 'em," Rachel said with a smile. "Don't you ever miss it?"

Justin leaned back in the seat and thought for a moment before he answered. "I miss the kids, but I love what I'm doing, too."

He told her about the youth center in L.A., and Rachel noticed that his eyes shone as he spoke of the young boys he used to coach. Rachel could see why the kids at school had all taken to him in the short time he'd been there. He seemed very passionate when it came to children, young and old.

Their meals came quickly and like Justin said, Rachel found the food to be delicious. They laughed when she admitted that the reason she changed her order from the ribs to the pork chops was because she would be a bit inhibited in picking them up with her fingers in public.

During the course of their meal, Justin talked about his mother and the relationship he had with her, and Rachel talked about Malcolm Sr. She told him about their relationship from the time she was a teenager. She talked about the relationship she had with her children and told him how proud she was of both of them.

"You should be proud. You have two great kids."

As they waited for the check, Rachel said, "That was great, Justin. I really enjoyed that."

"I'm glad. I enjoyed your company, Rachel."

She blushed. "Likewise."

"Do you think we can do this again sometime? I mean, I'd really like us to be friends, if that's all right with you."

"I'd like us to be friends, too, Justin," Rachel said demurely.

"Besides that, I'd like to take you to dinner," he continued in a hushed tone, "at a real restaurant."

She laughed.

When they stepped from the diner into the parking lot, Justin walked Rachel to her car which was parked four spaces from his. "Thank you for dinner, Justin."

"You're welcome."

"Don't forget, you still have to come by my house for dinner one night."

"Oh, I won't forget. I never turn down a home-cooked meal twice," he said with a grin.

She smiled back at him. She pulled her keys from her pocketbook and proceeded to open her car door.

"Rachel?"

"Yes?"

"Would it be okay if I called you sometime? You know, just to talk."

"Of course," she said with a warm smile. "I'll give you my number."

"Oh, I have it. I have the phone numbers for all the kids on the team," he explained when Rachel looked at him questioningly.

"Oh, yeah. That would make sense."

They stood outside her car for the next few seconds in an awkward silence.

"Listen, I'm, uh . . . I'm going to follow you, to make sure you get home okay."

She looked up into his eyes and realized for the first time really that she'd had such a good time with him that she didn't want to leave him. "All right."

He wanted to kiss her. His heart was pounding in his chest from the excitement he felt at being so close to her. He could tell that she liked him as well but figured she might be taken aback if he went with his feelings. He knew she hadn't been with anyone since her husband died, and the last thing he wanted to do was scare her off. He reached for her hand and brought it to his lips. "Thank you, beautiful lady, for your company. Next time we'll go somewhere more befitting a lady of your caliber."

A chill ran down her spine when he pressed his lips to her skin, and she blushed involuntarily. *What a man,* she thought. When he released her hand, she whispered, "Good night, Justin."

"Good night, Rachel."

For practically the entire fifteen minutes that it took Rachel to drive from the diner to her house, her face was lit with a smile. She found Justin to be warm, sincere, funny, and charming. He talked about his mother with pride and love, and she got the impression when he told her about his fiancée's betrayal, that he was a man not ashamed of showing his true feelings. She couldn't ignore the similarities he had to her dear lost Malcolm. She glanced repeatedly in her rearview mirror at his car behind her. She really couldn't wait to see him again.

When they reached her house, Rachel turned into her driveway and rolled down her window as he pulled up alongside the curb. His passenger window slid down, and he leaned across the front seat and called to her, "I'll call you tomorrow."

"Okay. Good night," she said as she waved to him.

He tapped his horn gently as he pulled off. Rachel watched until his taillights disappeared before she pulled into her garage.

When she entered the house, Jennifer was at the kitchen table, and Malcolm was at the refrigerator.

"Hey, Mom, where you been?" Malcolm asked.

"Oh, I stopped to get something to eat," she answered, embarrassed. She started through the room with no intention of stopping for their third degree.

"All this time by yourself?" Jennifer inquired.

"No, I was with Justin. Mr. Phillips," she quickly corrected. She left the kitchen quickly, not waiting for her children's response.

Like she guessed, they were surprised by her answer and were slow in recovering. When they did, she was on her way upstairs to her room. Jennifer looked across the kitchen at her brother, and a big smile broke on her face.

Friday evening Justin called Rachel. Jennifer picked up the telephone when it rang and was surprised when she heard, "Hello, Jennifer. This is Justin Phillips. How are you?"

"Hi, Coach Phillips. I'm fine." She was in the kitchen with Rachel, and she gave her mother a wicked grin. "Hold on, she's right here."

Rachel took the phone from her daughter, trying hard to ignore the look she was giving her. "Hello," she said coolly into the receiver. "I'm fine, Justin. How are you?"

Jennifer took a seat at the table and rested her chin in her hand, literally looking down Rachel's throat as she spoke.

"Hold on a minute, Justin," Rachel said suddenly. She put her hand over the mouthpiece and said, "Get out of here, Jenny."

Jennifer couldn't help but giggle, though she immediately rose from the table and left the room. Rachel's look indicated that she was not joking. Once she was gone, Rachel resumed her conversation. She and Justin were on the phone for forty-five minutes. They made plans to have dinner together the next evening.

After the call, she left the kitchen and headed upstairs to her bedroom. She was there for all of two minutes when Jennifer entered.

"Hi, Mom," she said with a cheesy grin.

"Hi."

She sat on the bed as Rachel went about the task of preparing for her nightly bath. "So how's Coach Phillips."

"Fine."

"So-o-o . . ."

"So what, Jenny?"

"Come on, Mom. What's the story with you and Coach Phillips?"

"There's no story."

"You had dinner with him last night, and now he's calling you. You guys were on the phone for almost an hour."

"Oh, were you timing us?"

"Yeah!"

Rachel had to laugh. She thought it very funny that Jenny was so inquisitive about them.

"Are you guys gonna start dating?"

"Jenny, we're just friends, that's all, so don't go getting your hopes up."

"But Mommy, he's so cute. And he's nice, too."

"I know he's nice. I'm not ready to start dating anyone though."

Jennifer looked heartbroken. "So you're not going to go out with him again?"

"I haven't gone out with him yet. Last night wasn't a date. I was hungry, and he told me about that soul-food place near the school. That's it."

"But you're not going to see him? I think he would be perfect for you, Mom."

"How do you know that? What do you know about him?"

"I know he's a nice man, and I know he likes you."

"How do you know he likes me?"

"I can tell," Jennifer said knowingly, as though she had some secret power.

Rachel didn't say anything else. She continued to remove her clothes. When she stepped into her bathroom, Jenny called behind her, "Mom, can we go to the mall tomorrow after my dance class?"

Well, now I guess I have to tell her, Rachel thought. "I can't tomorrow, Jen," she called from the bathroom.

"How come?"

Rachel stepped back into the room but stopped near her dresser and gazed at her daughter. After a few seconds, she moved over to the bed and sat next to her. "Jenny, you know I'll always love your father."

"I know, Mom."

Rachel sighed. "I don't want you to get the wrong idea, but

. . . Justin's taking me to dinner tomorrow night. He's picking me up at six.''

Jennifer's face broke into a bright smile. ''That's great, Mommy! That's great!''

''It's just dinner.''

''Yeah, but you've gotta start somewhere.'' Jennifer reached over and hugged her. ''I'm so happy, Mommy. I'm glad you're giving yourself a chance to be happy again.''

Chapter 12

Dinner Saturday was wonderful.

Justin took Rachel to Morton's Steakhouse in New York City. Afterward they went dancing at S.O.B.'s. Rachel had the time of her life. Justin was the perfect gentleman all night, tending to her every need, catering to her every whim and desire.

Justin was simply ecstatic about being with Rachel. He went out of his way to make her comfortable at every turn. He marveled at how different she seemed from their initial meeting. She laughed easily and told him some of the funniest stories about her late husband and the kids. He could see that she still had very strong feelings for Malcolm Waters Sr., but she spoke of him without the sadness he saw the night they met. Justin felt from what Rachel told him that he would have liked him had he the opportunity to have met him.

When they left the restaurant, Rachel told him what a nice time she had at the school dance, admitting that she hadn't realized how much she missed dancing until that night. That was when he suggested they go to S.O.B.'s. The music played that night had a largely Latin and Caribbean flavor. There was live music as well as a deejay. When the band played a merengue, Justin took Rachel's hand and started for the floor.

She resisted. "I don't know how to merengue."

"I'll teach you. It's easy."

"I'll probably look ridiculous."

He took a step closer to her and softly said, "You are too beautiful to ever look ridiculous."

Rachel blushed and joked, "My, what a sweet-talker you are."

He laughed lightly and she gave in. He started slowly showing her the steps, and in no time they were dancing across the floor like two veterans. "I thought you couldn't do this," he said close to her ear.

"I couldn't."

"Well then, you're an awfully quick study."

She gazed up into his eyes. "You're an awfully good teacher."

They were at the club until 2 A.M. On their drive home, they didn't talk much. Rachel sat next to Justin with her eyes closed but with an unmistakable look of joy on her face. She was smiling. He looked over at her at one point as they waited at a traffic light.

"Penny for your thoughts."

She opened her eyes and said, "Just a penny? Haven't you ever heard of inflation?"

He laughed. "Okay. Fifty cents."

Rachel laughed then. When she recovered, she looked over at him and said, "I was just thinking of what a wonderful time I had tonight. Thank you, Justin."

He smiled at her words. "You're welcome. I'm glad you enjoyed yourself."

"I really did. I can't remember the last time I felt so good."

He was pleased to hear this.

"Malcolm . . ." Suddenly she fell mute.

"What?"

"Never mind."

"Talk to me. What were you going to say?"

She sighed. "I was going to say that Malcolm used to take

me dancing all the time, but I'm sure you're tired of hearing about my husband.''

He did not answer right away. He wasn't sure if he was tired of hearing about him or not. He was learning a lot about the person she was from the stories she told him of their relationship.

"Rachel, I want you to be comfortable with me. I don't want you to feel as though you have to watch what you say around me. We're friends, and I don't mind being your sounding board. Anything you want to tell me, I'm here and I'll listen."

She looked over at him for a moment without saying anything. She felt a lump in her throat. "Thanks, Justin."

The remainder of the ride was made in relative silence. When Justin pulled up in front of her house, Rachel started to thank him, but he stopped her. "I'll walk you to your door."

"Oh, you don't have to do that."

"Yes, I do. If I don't and my mother finds out, it'll be my hide. I picked you up at your door, and I'll leave you at your door."

She shook her head and smiled. Rachel waited for him to come around and open her door. He reached in and helped her out of the car. He held her hand as they slowly walked to her door.

Rachel turned to him. "Thank you again, Justin, for a wonderful evening."

He reached for her other hand as well. "You're welcome. I'm really glad you had a good time. I had a great time, too. You're a great dancer, and we've definitely got to do this again."

They stared into each other's eyes for only seconds, though it seemed like an eternity. He wanted to pull her into his arms and kiss her, but he knew he had to go slow. He knew he had to take his time; he couldn't rush her. He didn't want to do anything to mess this up. He was sure that she cared for him, but he could see an iota of doubt in her eyes, so he simply leaned over and kissed her softly on the side of her mouth. "Good night, Rachel."

"Good night, Justin."

He turned then and started back to his car. She turned and went into her house. A smile was on her face as she remembered their night together.

She was surprised to hear the television in the den. She walked to the doorway, and Malcolm was sitting there.

"Hi, Mom."

"You waited up for me, didn't you?"

"No, I was just watching T.V."

She gave him a look that indicated that she didn't completely believe him.

"Did you have a good time?" he asked softly.

She smiled at him and answered, "Yes, Mal, I had a very good time."

"Good. That's all that matters then."

Her heart swelled with love for this young man that she had brought into this world. She felt that she was the luckiest woman in the world to have two wonderful children that cared so much about her happiness.

"Is Jenny in bed?"

"Yeah."

She walked over to where he was sitting and bent over to kiss him. "Good night, baby."

"Good night, Mom."

"Don't stay up too late."

Chapter 13

Over the next few days, Justin called Rachel every day. Each time they talked, there was an abundance of laughter that filled the Waters's household. Malcolm and Jennifer noticed the change in their mother and were happy about it. They both felt that Justin Phillips was good for her.

On Tuesday of the following week, Rachel attended Malcolm's game at the school. The Rockets suffered their first loss under Coach Phillips. Malcolm, however, was not too upset. He chalked it up to life. "Nobody wins all the time."

Justin took Rachel, Malcolm, and Jennifer to dinner that night after the game. He enjoyed being around her children almost as much as he enjoyed being with her.

The following evening, Rachel invited him for dinner. She made a pan of lasagna, a tossed salad, and garlic bread. Justin arrived at six o'clock, and while Rachel and Jennifer put the finishing touches on dinner, Malcolm entertained Justin in the den. When their father was alive, Malcolm had always gone to him for advice about girls and such, and now that Justin was around, he felt he once again had a man that he could confide in.

"Dinner's ready," Rachel called from the kitchen.

Justin and Malcolm went to wash their hands before they headed for the kitchen.

"Wow, it smells great in here," Justin said as he entered.

"Well, I hope you like lasagna," Rachel said cautiously.

"I love it," he said as he gazed at her amorously.

Jennifer giggled softly as she was simply thrilled that her mother was dating this hunk of a man.

When they were all seated at the table, Justin said grace. Rachel bowed her head initially, but before he was through, she looked up at him across the table. She hadn't felt this kind of nervousness in her stomach since she first started dating Malcolm. She lowered her head again before he was finished, and in unison they all said, "Amen."

"Mom, you haven't made lasagna in a long time," Malcolm said as he immediately reached for the serving spoon lying next to the lasagna pan.

"Malcolm, Justin is our guest. Let him help himself first," Rachel insisted.

"Oh, no, no, no—I don't want any special treatment. Malcolm, you go right ahead. I'll help myself to the salad."

Malcolm looked at Rachel briefly, then back at Justin, then back at Rachel and smiled before he continued on his same course. She just shook her head. Jennifer took in the whole scene in silence.

"This is delicious," Justin said after taking his first bite of the meal. "This is really good. Do you have some Italian in your blood?"

Malcolm and Jennifer laughed. Rachel blushed. "I'm glad you like it."

Malcolm dominated the conversation over dinner, talking mostly about the team and some of his and Jennifer's classmates. Jennifer commented occasionally on things that her brother said, but when she led the conversation it was, for the most part, about Marvin. Justin listened intently to everything the kids said. He was in his element. He felt like a member of their family. A few times he looked across the table at Rachel, and she would blush under his scrutiny, but he could tell that she was just as happy as he was in this setting.

After dinner Justin and Malcolm retreated to the den once again to watch the playoff game that was on. The Knicks were playing and Justin was a diehard Knicks fan.

Jennifer helped Rachel clear the table and wash the dishes because she wanted to talk about Coach Phillips.

"You really like him, don't you, Mommy?"

Rachel was washing the dishes, and Jennifer was drying. She handed her a wet plate as she softly answered, "Yes."

"I saw the way he kept looking at you across the table. I think he's in love with you."

"How can you say that? What do you know about love, Jenny? You're just a child."

"I'm not a child, Mom, I'm a young woman, and I know what it's like to be in love. Besides, I read all the romance novels that tell how a man looks when he's looking at the woman of his dreams. It's like he's here, but he's really not here. He's thinking about being alone with you on a deserted beach under the stars, making love to you—"

"Jenny!"

"Well, Mommy, I'm not stupid. I know where babies come from. Besides, I've heard you and Daddy."

Rachel was mortified. She couldn't believe her teenaged daughter was talking to her this way. She had always been very open with Jennifer about boys and sex but never about her own sex life.

"Mommy, don't be embarrassed. I know how much you and Daddy loved each other. I thought that was beautiful. When I look back at it now, I can understand why you miss him so much. He was the man of your dreams."

She looked over at her daughter, marveling at how mature she really was. "Yes, he was."

"But you know, I think Daddy would've liked Coach Phillips. He kind of reminds me of him in some ways, you know. The way he takes the time to listen to me and Malcolm and the way he looks at you. Daddy used to look at you like that, Mommy—that's why I said he's in love with you."

"No! How can you say that?" Malcolm's voice carried from the den into the kitchen. He and Justin were in a debate about what team was better, the New York Knicks or the Orlando Magic. They had been having this loud discussion for some time now, though Rachel and Jennifer had ignored them up until this moment.

"God, they're loud," Jennifer said.

"Yeah, aren't they?"

"It sounds like Daddy's in there," Jennifer said without thinking. She immediately regretted her words when she saw the pained look in her mother's eyes. "I'm sorry, Mommy, I didn't mean to say that."

Rachel turned off the faucet and moved to the table to wipe it down. "That's okay, baby." She chuckled lightly. "It does kinda sound like him. Remember, he and Mal couldn't watch a game together unless they were fighting over the players."

Jennifer didn't respond. Rachel turned to her with tears brimming in her eyes. "I like Justin, but I still miss your dad so much." She sighed heavily.

Jennifer moved over to her and put her arms around her. Rachel was comforted by her daughter's embrace. After a couple of minutes, she collected herself and said, "Come on, let's go in the den."

When they appeared at the door to the den, Justin was about to respond to Malcolm's last statement about Patrick Ewing. He realized suddenly that they had been making an inordinate amount of noise, and he quickly apologized.

Rachel raised her hand to stop him. "It's all right, Justin. To be perfectly honest with you, it's been far too quiet in here during the playoffs. I'm used to a lot more cheering coming out of this room when a game's on than there has been lately."

Malcolm explained. "Me and my dad used to always argue about the Knicks. He was a diehard fan, just like you."

"He was obviously a very wise man," Justin commented.

They all laughed.

Justin left that evening at about ten thirty, when the game was over. He said good night to Malcolm and Jennifer before Rachel walked him to the door.

"Dinner was excellent, Rachel. Thank you," he said as he reached for her hand.

"You're welcome, Justin. I'm glad you enjoyed it."

"I did. And I enjoyed spending this evening with you and the kids. I'm glad they don't mind me coming around."

She smiled and told him, "They like you almost as much as I do."

Justin was greatly moved by her words. "That's nice to know, Rachel." He looked deep into her eyes. "Are you going to be busy this Saturday?" he asked.

"No."

He stepped closer to her. "Can I see you?"

"Yes."

"We'll go to the movies or something. Whatever you want to do."

"All right."

He kissed her suddenly. His lips were soft against hers, and though he didn't devour her the way he wanted to, he held his lips to hers long enough to let her know how much he wanted her.

"I'll call you tomorrow," he sighed.

"Yes." She was totally lost in the moment.

"Good night, Rachel. Sweet dreams," he said as he gently caressed her face.

He turned to the door and opened it. As he stepped through, she found her voice. "Good night, Justin. Drive safely."

He turned back briefly and smiled before he blew her a kiss.

Chapter 14

Justin's mother called him Saturday morning and asked if he would take her to the mall to do a bit of shopping. Though this was the one thing he had little patience for, he gladly obliged her.

It was just after one o'clock in the afternoon, and the mall was packed with people doing their last-minute shopping for Easter. Due to his mother's age, they were forced to stroll through the mall at a leisurely pace. Mrs. Phillips had always been one of those women that loves to comparison shop. She never bought anything the first place she saw it. She always had to shop around to see if she could get a better price. As such, she and Justin were in and out of stores for the last three hours and had made only one purchase.

They were just stepping out of a Lane Bryant shop when Justin spotted Rachel a few feet ahead of them in the corridor. He didn't want to yell, but he didn't want to let her get away without speaking to her, either.

"Mom, I'll be right back," he said in a rush.

"Justin, what's wrong, baby?" she asked with a frown.

"Nothing, Mom. I'll be right back."

He left his mother where she stood and hurried to catch up

with Rachel. He caught sight of her as she followed Jennifer inside The Limited. "Rachel!" he called when he reached the entrance.

She turned from the clothing rack she was standing near. "Hi!" she said brightly. She walked back to the entrance to see him. "How you doin'?"

He reached for her and kissed her gently on the mouth. "I'm fine, hon. How you doin'?"

"Good."

"Hey, Jenny," Justin said, waving to her.

Jennifer put the slacks she was holding back on the rack and joined them. "Hi, Coach."

"Doing a little shopping, huh?" Rachel said.

"No, I'm here with my mother. She's the shopper. I really don't have the patience for malls," Justin admitted.

"Justin?"

He turned at the sound of his mother's voice. Mrs. Phillips stood just outside the store with an anxious look on her face.

"Oh, Mom," he said as he stepped closer to her and placed his hand gently around her waist. "This is Rachel Waters and her daughter, Jennifer. Honey, this is my mother."

Rachel noticed the resemblance he had to his mother immediately. "Hello, Mrs. Phillips," she said as she offered her hand. "It's so nice to meet you."

Mrs. Phillips's face changed from one of anxious anticipation to the gentle, friendly, and caring face of a loving parent. "Hello, dear. It's good to meet you, too. I've heard so much about you, sweetheart, I feel as if I already know you." She grabbed Rachel's hand firmly in both of hers. "How are you?"

"I'm fine, thank you. How are you?" Rachel asked, returning her warm smile.

"Oh, I'm just fine, sweetheart. Hello, dear," she then said, addressing Jennifer.

"Hello," she answered with a shy smile.

"You have a beautiful daughter, Rachel," Mrs. Phillips said as she smiled at Jennifer.

"Thank you," Jennifer and Rachel said in unison.

"When Justin ran off, I thought something was wrong. He didn't tell me he had seen you."

"I'm sorry, Mom."

"That's all right, baby," she said, looking up at him fondly. "I can understand your motivation. Are you ladies shopping for your Easter outfits?" Mrs. Phillips asked, turning back to Rachel.

"Oh, no, ma'am. I got that out of the way a couple of weeks ago. This is sort of an every other weekend bonding thing that Jenny and I do. She tries to find ways to spend my money, and I try to find ways to keep it."

They all laughed.

"Well, I know my boy here is about tired of following me around in here. He's humoring me, I know." Mrs. Phillips leaned in closer to Rachel and whispered conspiratorially. "He hates these shopping malls. Always did. Isn't that right, Justin?"

"Mom, you know I'd do anything for you," he responded as he hugged her playfully.

"He's the baby of the family, and he's spoiled rotten but he's a good son."

Rachel and Jennifer chuckled when they noticed Justin blushing.

"Is your son here, Rachel?"

"No, he refuses to go shopping with us."

"Smart guy," Justin said under his breath, but Rachel heard him.

"Well, Justin, you have to bring Rachel and her children by my house one weekend for dinner. I would love to meet your young man. Justin speaks very fondly of both of your children, and it'll also give us a chance to get better acquainted," Mrs. Phillips offered.

"I'd like that, Mrs. Phillips. Thank you," Rachel answered.

"Good. Well, I won't hold you up any longer. I know my baby wants to get out of here, so I'm gonna have mercy and cut this little excursion short. It was such a pleasure meeting you, Rachel and Jenny."

"It was a pleasure meeting you, too, Mrs. Phillips." Rachel leaned closer and kissed her cheek.

"I hope to see you again soon."

"Likewise."

She released Rachel's hand and turned to walk away. Justin stepped in closer to Rachel and brushed her lips with a kiss. "I'll see you tonight. Bye, Jenny."

"Bye."

Justin and Rachel had dinner at an East Indian restaurant that night. Rachel loved East Indian food, and though Justin had never tried it, he was game to try anything once. Rachel was delighted when he told her how much he enjoyed his meal. Afterward they took in a movie.

Rachel didn't want to stay out too late as she and the kids were planning to attend the eight o'clock Easter service at church the next morning. Justin pulled up in front of her house at eleven fifteen.

"Thanks for turning me on to that restaurant, Rachel. I know so many people that don't like East Indian cuisine, I just figured I wouldn't care for it, either."

"I'm glad you liked it, Justin, 'cause like you said, I don't know many people that like it, either. At least now I have a friend with that in common."

He leaned over in the seat of his car and responded seductively, "I'd love to find out what else we have in common."

Rachel blushed and lowered her eyes. A wave of heat coursed through her body at the deep tone his voice suddenly took on.

Not missing her sudden discomfort, Justin reached over and took her chin gently in his hand, tilting her head up and around so he could look into her eyes. "You know, I care for you very much, Rachel."

"I care about you, too," she said nervously.

She would not look into his eyes. Her stomach was in knots, anticipating what he planned to do next. She was sure he was going to try to kiss her, and she had fantasized about this moment—but now that it was a reality, she wasn't sure if she could handle it.

"Look at me," he murmured.

She did as he asked. The look of desire in his eyes was unmistakable. Her heart began to beat even faster.

Slowly he leaned in still closer. He still held her chin gently in his hand. She was afraid to move. Her lips parted involuntarily as his face came slowly closer and a sigh escaped her.

His mouth was soft against hers, but she already knew it would be. Wednesday night when he left her house, he had kissed her lips for the first time and she fell under his spell. He released her chin and pulled her closer with his free hand as he pushed his tongue between her teeth. He was so gentle and he moved inside her slowly, teasing her tongue and tasting the inside of her mouth. She closed her eyes and relaxed a bit and moved her tongue in chorus with his, enjoying the feel and taste of him. When Justin felt her relax, he went for broke. He pulled her as close as he could, considering the console between them, and placed a hand behind her head in an attempt to totally consume her.

Rachel luxuriated in his kiss, loving the way he was making her feel. Her hand moved to caress his face, and she savored the smoothness of his skin. It felt as though he had shaved only moments before.

Suddenly the face of her late husband flashed in her mind's eye, destroying her pleasure as if it were a sparkling pane of glass crashing to the floor. She pulled away from him as if she had been burned.

"Rachel, what's wrong?" he asked in alarm when he noticed the intense look of distress on her face.

She sat bolt straight in her seat. "I'm sorry. I'm not ready for this, Justin." Her eyes filled with tears, and her chest began to rise and fall quickly as she tried to fight the urge to cry. She lost the battle. "I thought I was, but I can't do this."

"Rachel," he said in a caress. "It's okay. It's okay, darling. I won't rush you." He reached over and stroked her face tenderly. He gently brushed her tears away with his thumbs as he took her head in his hands.

She looked into his eyes with her tearful ones. "I'm sorry."

"Shh. There's no reason for you to be sorry, sweetheart. I know this isn't easy for you, but I want you to know that my feelings for you are real. I care so much about you and Malcolm and Jenny, and I want to be a part of your lives. But I won't rush you. I'm here and I'm not going anywhere. Okay?"

She tried to smile, but she still felt so bad that she wasn't comfortable enough to speak. She nodded her head in response.

He released her and opened his door and got out of the car. He walked around the front of the car to her door and opened it. He helped her out of her seat, and when she was standing in front of him, he placed his arms around her and held her tenderly. "I love you, Rachel," he said in a whisper.

His words, though meant to reassure her, frightened her instead. Despite the fact that she genuinely cared for him, she was afraid of hurting him. *Am I being unfair to him, knowing now how deep his feelings are and knowing that I can't offer him the same comfort by reciprocating those feelings?* she asked herself. *I don't want to lose his friendship.*

She held him tighter and rested her head against his shoulder. When she felt her composure returning, she looked up into his eyes.

He could see that she was apprehensive about his confession, but he wanted her to know that he would be there for her and that she was safe with him. He didn't say anything—instead he placed a tender kiss on her lips.

After a while, they turned and started up her walk. When they reached her door, she turned to him and with her head lowered said, "I'm sorry if I ruined your evening."

He smiled and said, "You didn't. Please don't think that."

She looked up at him. His smile was warm and sincere. "I really care about you, Justin."

"I know."

She stepped in closer and kissed him gently on his lips. "Thank you for being so understanding."

"Rachel, when you're ready, I'll be right here. With you is where I want to be."

She smiled up at him gratefully. "It's good to know I have a friend like you."

He wrapped his arms around her and held her for a moment before he brushed her temple with a kiss. "Good night, Rachel," he said as he released her.

"Good night, Justin, and thank you."

When Rachel entered the house, she stopped and talked briefly with Jennifer and Malcolm before heading up to her room. Once there, she sat on her bed and stared at the picture of Malcolm Sr. on her dresser. She began to cry.

She reached for his picture and held it in her lap as her emotions overflowed. "Why'd you leave me? Why'd you have to leave me?"

She held his picture to her bosom as her tears flowed seemingly without end. She began to question herself. *Will I ever be able to love again? Will I ever be able to live again? Will I ever be able to let you go?*

The next morning, Rachel, Malcolm, and Jennifer met Janice at church for the Easter service. The church was serving breakfast for the congregation afterward, but Rachel did not care to stay. She was still feeling a bit depressed about the night before. Though she wouldn't tell anyone what was bothering her, they all knew it was something so they didn't push. They went straight home instead.

Once there, Rachel went about preparing something to eat for all of them while the kids went upstairs to change their clothes. Janice took this opportunity to try to find out what was bothering her sister-in-law.

Janice took an apron from the hook on the inside of the pantry door and tied it around her waist. "Honey, what's wrong?" she asked with sympathetic concern.

Rachel just shook her head. She was laying strips of bacon in a large skillet and at Janice's question, stopped suddenly.

She lowered her head and closed her eyes against the tears she felt welling up inside her.

Janice stepped up behind her and placed her hands on her shoulders. "Is it Justin?"

"Oh, Janice," she cried as she turned to her and let her feelings flow.

Janice embraced her gently as Rachel told her about last night. "I can't let him go," she sobbed. "I can't let him go."

"Oh, honey, I'm sorry. I'm so sorry." Janice continued to hold her until Rachel had cried herself out.

"What am I going to do?" Rachel asked as she stepped out of Janice's embrace.

Janice thought for a moment before she answered. She knew how close her brother and sister-in-law had always been. She and Rachel had been friends since childhood, too, as they were the same age. "Rachel, Justin sounds like a good man, and I know Malcolm would want you to be happy. I know how much you love him, and I know how much he loved you. I know you care about Justin, but you can't be afraid to let yourself go. Trust your heart. Malcolm would understand if you fell in love with someone else. He can't take care of you anymore. You have to let him go."

"Why do I feel so guilty?"

"Well, Malcolm's the only man you've ever known. He's been a part of your life for most of your life. But remember, before you guys got together, he was never selfish when it came to you. Even when he couldn't see you or date you, he always talked to you about your other male friends because he loved you so much that your happiness was the most important thing to him. That hasn't changed, Rachel. I know he's up there watching over you and the kids, and I know that he would want you to be happy." Janice's eyes filled with tears at the memory of her older brother. "That's just how he always was. The people he loved . . . he always wanted to see them happy."

"I know." Malcolm Waters Sr. had been the most selfless person Rachel had ever known. His family had always been his first priority. Their comfort and happiness had always been

most important, and he did everything in his power to ensure
it.

"Justin said he would be there for you when you're ready.
Trust him and trust yourself. You're not doing anything
wrong."

Chapter 15

Over the next three weeks, Rachel and Justin saw each other practically every other day. He came by the house most evenings, and he either had dinner with her and the kids or he took them all out to eat. Two Saturdays in a row, he took them all to the movies, and the second Sunday, they all went to his mother's house for dinner.

Mrs. Phillips loved having them over. None of her grandchildren lived nearby, so she took the opportunity to dote on Malcolm and Jennifer as if they were her grandkids. Malcolm hadn't been looking forward to the visit. He told Rachel that there were plenty of things he could do with his Sunday afternoon than spend it in the home of an "old lady" he didn't know, but she insisted he go. Needless to say, when they were ready to leave, Malcolm volunteered to come by the following day after school to help Mrs. Phillips do her food shopping.

Mrs. Phillips was an exceptional cook. She roasted a turkey and made her own stuffing. She also made macaroni and cheese, candied yams, string beans, and the softest, fluffiest dinner rolls Rachel had ever tasted. Malcolm had always had an enormous appetite, and when they ate out, he was never satisfied. When Mrs. Phillips saw how much Malcolm was enjoying his food, she insisted he have seconds. He had been afraid to ask for more, knowing that Rachel would probably be embarrassed, but when she offered, he dug right in. Mrs. Phillips was delighted as she watched him eat. She loved cooking for people that loved to eat, and nothing did her heart better than a young man with a healthy appetite. Of course when dinner was finished, she served dessert: pineapple upside-down cake. Ironically that was Malcolm's favorite dessert.

When she learned that pineapple upside-down cake was Malcolm's favorite, Mrs. Phillips promised to bake one especially for him.

After dinner they sat around and played a game of Monopoly. Justin and Rachel sat the game out but got a kick out of watching Mrs. Phillips, Malcolm, and Jennifer. Justin was delighted to see his mother so happy. The last time he'd seen her so excited was when his niece and nephew were visiting. She loved children, which is probably where he inherited his love of children.

By the time they left her apartment at nine thirty that evening, Malcolm and Jennifer were calling her Miss Lou. She thanked Rachel for bringing the children by and praised her and her late husband for having raised such respectable, loving children. She made Rachel promise to come back the following weekend after church and to bring the children with her. Seeing as how her parents were no longer alive, and Malcolm's parents lived in Florida, Rachel was more than happy to do it. Like her children, she, too, had taken to Justin's mother.

When Justin took them home that evening, after saying good night to Malcolm and Jennifer, he sat in the den with Rachel for the next half hour.

"You know, you made my mother very happy by bringing the kids over today," he told her.

"Oh, Justin, your mother is a wonderful woman. I loved being there with her, and I think the kids did, too. You know, Malcolm didn't want to go," she admitted.

Justin laughed as he said, "Yeah, and he didn't want to leave, either."

"They don't have their grandparents nearby."

"Mom's grandkids aren't either. She was right, you know,

about what she said. You and Malcolm did an excellent job of
bringing them up. I'm sure if he could see them now, his chest
would be out to here," Justin said as he extended his hands
outward from his body.

She looked into his eyes and realized that she could love
him. He was such a sensitive man. Knowing that he would do
anything for his mother, and seeing how he was always there
for her and how patient he was with her, she knew she could
love him.

They were sitting together on the sofa, and she was resting
her head on his shoulder. She surprised him when she turned
her head toward his and placed a soft kiss on his lips. This was
the first time she had ever initiated any intimacy with him. He
pulled her into his arms then and seized her mouth with his.
Rachel wrapped her arms around him, pulling him even closer
as she was swept away by his tenderness. She wanted to give
herself up to the passion that raged in her belly but was still
afraid to let go completely.

Justin's hands moved slowly across her back. He was revel-
ing in the feel of this tender creature in his arms. He took her
kiss as a signal, letting him know that she was ready for him.
He wanted to love her, to feel her body next to his, to become
one with her like never before. His love for her was all consum-
ing. There was nothing else that mattered to him. Being with
Rachel was what he aspired to. It was what he lived for now.

"I love you, Rachel," he moaned in her ear.

She pulled back ever so slightly to look into his eyes. "I
don't want to lose you, Justin."

"You won't, sweetheart. I'm here for the duration," he said
as he smiled at her tenderly.

"You are so wonderful," she said joyously as she caressed
his face with love and appreciation. "How could I be so lucky
to have you in my life? I don't think there are many men that
would be willing to wait for me the way you have."

"There aren't many men that could love you the way I do."

She didn't respond to him with words but instead touched
her forehead to his. She loved being in his arms, being close
to him this way. She tried not to think of Malcolm, but his

memory pushed itself to the front of her mind. She closed her eyes for fear that Justin would read her thoughts. Malcolm had loved her that way. He had waited for her, too.

"Next Saturday I want you to come to my place for dinner. I'm going to cook for you, and we'll spend a quiet evening together. I want to show you how special you are to me, Rachel. I want to show you how much I love you," he murmured.

Rachel had known the day would come when he would want more, but she wanted to be with him, too. She could not deny the physical desire that coursed through her body each time he touched her. Her only hope was that she didn't disappoint him.

"I had no idea you were such an excellent cook," Rachel indicated when they were finished eating, as she helped him clean up.

"Well, you have to admit, I had a great teacher," he said as he handed her a towel to dry her hands.

Justin had prepared a dinner of chicken cacciatore over spaghetti with broccoli and cauliflower.

"Did you make those rolls yourself?" Rachel asked as they moved from the dining room to the living room.

"No. I confess. Mom prepared the dough. I just stuck them in the oven."

She laughed.

"I might as well tell you, too, that was my best dish," he admitted.

"Well, I'm flattered that you pulled out all the stops for me."

I would do anything for you, he thought, but he said, "Would you like another glass of wine?"

"Yes, I would. Thank you."

He poured for both of them before he joined her on the sofa. "You missed a great game on Thursday," he said when he was seated.

She'd had to work late that night and didn't get home until after ten. "I know. Malcolm told me. He said it was close throughout."

"Yeah, it was. This was the best game of the season, I think. Those guys made us work for that win."

"It was nice that you took them all out to eat afterward."

"Well, they deserved it. They played so well that night. I just wish I could have done more."

"I'm sure they appreciated it. From what I understand, you're a big hit with the kids at school."

"Well, it's nice to be appreciated."

Rachel looked over at him, thinking that she was glad to have him as a friend. "I hope you know that I appreciate you, too, Justin," Rachel said softly.

He set his glass on the table and took hers from her hand as well. He closed the distance between them on the couch, though it was only a matter of inches. He slipped his arm around behind her and pulled her even closer.

"I hope you know that I love you," he said with his mouth only millimeters from hers.

He pressed his lips against hers gently, almost teasingly. His tongue emerged from between his lips, and he swept it across her lips seductively. She opened her mouth to receive him, but he pulled back slightly, teasing her with soft pecks and little licks on her mouth.

His body was hard for her. He wanted to ride the waves of ecstasy and carry her to a level of excitement she had never experienced. He wanted to invade her sweet nest of heavenly soft womanhood and be captured by her body as her walls contracted on him.

Rachel arched her back up toward him in an attempt to get closer. She was on fire for him. Feelings that she hadn't experienced in years coursed through her body with each kiss he planted on her skin. Each time his tongue touched her, she felt her skin sizzle.

She gave herself up to him, allowing him to do with her as he pleased. Her body fell limp in his arms and she closed her eyes and savored his tender affections.

Justin gently eased her back on the sofa until she was lying flat. He stretched his body out across the length of her, sighing as the curves of her body fit with those of his like pieces of a puzzle.

Rachel raised her hips, grinding seductively against the evidence of his desire.

"Oh, lovely sweet Rachel," he growled.

He moved slowly down her length, nibbling on her neck, gently biting the lobes of her ears as he bathed each with his tongue. His hands found her breasts and he massaged her mounds with an urgency he could not hide. Her blouse buttoned in front, and in truth, he wanted to rip it from her torso, but he restrained himself. He prolonged his torture by undoing each of her buttons with his teeth.

Rachel sighed in pure bliss as he kissed and fondled her. She felt his mouth on her left breast as his thumb and index finger teased the nipple of her right mound. He took the bud between his teeth, biting gently enough not to hurt but with enough pressure to push her to the brink.

"Oh, yes!" she sighed with pleasure.

Her mind traveled back to the many times he had pleasured her this way, taking his time and making her suffer in a manner that she loved. The thought of feeling the fullness of him inside her again, coupled with the reality of his hands and mouth burning against her skin pushed her to the limit. Her hands found his backside, and she pressed his maleness to her forcefully as the explosion that started between her legs traveled to her brain.

She ground her body against his, thrashing wildly, not able to control herself. "Oh, God! Oh, yes! Yes! Malcolm, yes!"

Justin's body froze. She clung to him still as the climax had not yet subsided. His heart shattered as his body went limp. He pushed himself off of her and rose to his feet.

Rachel opened her eyes, and the instant she saw his face, she knew what she had done. She opened her mouth to apologize, but before she could get the words out, he barked, "My name is Justin! Justin! Not Malcolm!"

She sat up immediately. "Oh, God, I'm so sorry," she cried as she covered her face, horrified by what she had done.

Justin strode from the room. He went to his bedroom, slamming the door behind him and began to pace the length of one wall as he tried to contain the anger that welled up inside of him. He closed his eyes and tried to close his mind as well to the sobs he heard coming from the other room. *How could she do this? Why did I let her do this to me?* The anger won over the pain that burned in his shattered heart.

Rachel heard a loud bang come from the other room as Justin pounded his fist into the door of his bedroom before he emerged. He stormed back into the living room.

"I can't do this, Rachel. I've tried, but I can't compete with your husband's ghost! I know you love him, and that's fine— but he's not here. I am!" he stated, poking a finger in his own chest. "He can't take care of you anymore. He can't love you anymore. I love you, but if you want to die with him, I can't be there for you. I can't. I don't want to take his place, Rachel. I *won't* take his place!"

"Justin, I'm sorry," she wailed.

He looked down at her, and as much as she had hurt him, he could not be mean to her. "So am I," he muttered.

She sat where she was, crying uncontrollably. He stood over her, wanting to comfort her, but he couldn't. If she was not willing to give him a chance to love her, there was nothing more he could do. He had tried to be patient with her. *No,* he thought, *I have been patient!* He would have waited as long as she wanted, but he would not allow her to use his love as a replacement for another man. That was where he drew the line.

He reached for her pocketbook, which she had thrown on his recliner. He handed it to her. "Come on, I'll take you home."

He was angry, but he felt sorry for her more than anything else. She was a beautiful woman, full of life and love, but she was too afraid to live her life independent of a husband that could no longer return the love she so fiercely held on to.

She fastened her blouse with difficulty before she rose from the couch and took her bag from his hand. She looked up into his eyes through her unending tears. Rachel was distraught. She wanted to say something to him, but all she could think of was *I'm sorry.* How could she explain to him that Malcolm was the only man she had ever known? She knew she had pushed him past the point of reasonable patience. She couldn't expect him to understand anymore.

She could see the hurt in his eyes that she had caused, and she felt so ashamed that she lowered her head and slowly lumbered to the door.

Not a single word passed between them during the ride to Rachel's house. The tension between them was so thick it made the short fifteen-minute drive seem like an hour. Tears continually streamed down Rachel's cheeks, though her sobs had ceased for the time being.

Justin, too, was distraught but he kept the depth of his pain hidden. He thought he had found in Rachel the woman he was destined to spend his life with. Though he had been engaged before, and had loved his fiancée dearly, what he felt for Rachel went so much deeper. He had been positive that he would share a life full of unparalleled happiness and love with her and her children and hopefully, one day, children of their own. He had been made to feel welcomed in her home and her life from the beginning. He wanted to be a part of their lives and have them as a part of his. Now, instead of the joy and happiness he felt only hours before, he was filled with an emptiness the likes of which he had never experienced before.

When Justin pulled up in front of Rachel's house, he still did not utter a word. He simply sat and waited for her to get out.

She sat beside him, and though she did not speak immediately, he could feel her eyes on him. "I never meant to hurt you, Justin," she said as her voice broke from the sobs she tried to contain. "I've never been with anyone else. I'm sorry."

Her crying ripped what was left of his heart to pieces, but he could not console her. His own pain was too great. She had to make the decision on her own as to whether she wanted to continue to live in the shadow of her husband's memory or stand on her own and make the most of what was left of her life.

When Justin did not respond, Rachel knew she had lost him. He stared straight ahead, his face like that of a man of stone.

She reached for the door handle and pushed it open slowly. It was an effort for her to stand because she didn't want to believe that it was over between them. She knew once she was completely out of the car, she was out of his life as well. When she was on the curb, she turned back to close the door and apologize once more, but as soon as the door closed, he engaged the lock and drove away.

Rachel stood where she was, devastated, as she watched his taillights disappear in the distance. She turned and ran toward her house. She fumbled for her keys in her pocketbook, having a hard time seeing because her eyes were filled with tears. When she was finally able to negotiate the lock, she ran into the house and up the stairs, not bothering to acknowledge either of her children.

"Mom?" Malcolm called from the den.

She ran straight to her room and fell down on the bed and cried in great racking sobs.

"Mom? Mommy, what's wrong?"

Jennifer and Malcolm rushed to her side. "Mommy, what happened?" Malcolm asked worriedly.

"Nothing. Just leave me alone, please," Rachel cried.

"Mommy, please tell us what happened," Jennifer begged.

"I don't want to talk about it. Just leave me alone."

"Mom—" Malcolm started.

"I said, leave me alone!" she yelled through her tears. She rose from the bed and moved to the door. "Go!"

Malcolm and Jennifer were hurt that she would not confide in them or allow them to comfort her. They rose from the bed slowly, and both eyed Rachel questioningly as they were extremely worried and curious as to the reason their mother was so upset. When they had passed through the door, they turned to look back at her only to have the door slammed in their faces.

Chapter 16

Rachel slept until ten thirty Sunday morning. She didn't get out of bed until an hour later. Her sister-in-law Janice had called her that morning when church services ended, wondering why Rachel had not attended. She pretended to be asleep when Jennifer called her to the phone. Unbeknownst to Rachel, Jennifer told her aunt Janice that she thought something bad had happened between her and Justin. She asked that she come and see about Rachel.

When Rachel came downstairs that morning, she pretended that nothing was wrong. She went about preparing her breakfast like any other morning. She didn't realize that her children were very in tune to her feelings, and also, despite her attempts to appear unfazed by whatever had happened last night, her face was a picture of melancholy. They did not question her, however. The memory of how distraught she had been last night was something they did not want to rehash.

Over the next two weeks, Rachel went about the business of her life like she had in the months following her husband's death. She divided all of her time between her job, her home, and her children. There was no joy in her heart, though she tried to put up a brave front.

Malcolm and Jennifer did not miss, nor could they ignore, the undeniable sadness that had suddenly engulfed their mother. Still she would not confide in them.

They noticed, too, that Justin had stopped calling. They figured that the night she had come home crying, they must have had a serious argument, but neither of them wanted to believe that their friendship had ended so abruptly.

After a week of not hearing from him, Malcolm decided to pay Justin a visit at his office at school. Maybe he could find out what had happened from the coach.

"Come in," Justin responded to the tapping on his door.

He was not really surprised to see Malcolm. In truth, he was surprised that he hadn't come by sooner.

"Hey, Coach."

"Hi, Malcolm. What's up?"

"Can I talk to you for a minute?" Malcolm asked before he stepped all the way into the room.

"Sure. Come in and sit down," Justin offered.

Malcolm closed the door behind him and took a seat in the chair directly in front of Justin's desk.

"What's on your mind?" Justin asked, though he was sure he could guess.

"I know you'll probably tell me that it's none of my business, but . . . how come you stopped calling my mom?"

Justin stared into Malcolm's eyes for a moment before he answered. *He's such a nice kid,* Justin thought. He honestly felt as though he had let him and Jennifer down by not coming around or calling anymore, but what could he do?

"You're right, Malcolm, it's not your business and I won't discuss it with you," he said sympathetically.

Malcolm had come to look forward to Justin being around. Not only was he pleased that he had been looking out for his mother, but he had begun to look up to Justin, as well. He knew his mother missed him, but he missed him, too.

Malcolm lowered his head for a moment before he spoke

again. Justin was surprised by the look of anguish on Malcolm's face when he asked, "Don't you even care about her anymore?"

What was he supposed to say? Of course, he cared about her. He loved her. Still. In fact, more than ever.

When Justin didn't answer, Malcolm rose from the chair. His face was now awash with anger. Justin didn't want to leave it this way, so he tried to make him understand. "Malcolm, this is between your mother and I."

"Yeah, right," Malcolm sneered as he moved toward the door. "I don't know why I ever thought she would be happy with you."

Malcolm's hand was on the doorknob when Justin said, "I do care about her, Malcolm, but this is something we have to work out between ourselves."

Malcolm did not respond. He simply yanked the door open and stepped into the corridor.

The next day, when school was over, as Justin left the building, he ran into Jennifer as she was leaving school.

"Hi, Coach Phillips," she said with a cautious smile.

"Hi, Jenny. How are you?"

"I'm fine, thank you," she answered as she fell in step beside him.

They walked a few feet in silence before Jennifer asked, "Coach, are you still going to help us on Mother's Day?"

Malcolm and Jennifer were planning to cook a big dinner for Rachel on Mother's Day which was just five days away. They had recruited their aunt Janice and Justin to help with their plans. Janice was going to help them prepare the meal, and Justin was responsible for getting and keeping Rachel out of the house long enough for them to do it.

He looked down at her sadly and murmured, "I can't, Jenny. I'm sorry."

She stopped in her tracks and looked up at him pleadingly. Her eyes began to water, so she turned away from him and quickly started in the opposite direction.

Justin stood where he was and watched her walk away. He felt terrible, but he could not bend. Rachel had to come to *him*.

Chapter 17

Rachel had not attended the last two games Malcolm's team played because the prospect of seeing Justin was too painful for her. She traded shifts with one of the nurses she worked with at the hospital—thus she was able to use the excuse of having to work on those days so she would not have to lie to her son.

The Thursday before Mother's Day, however, was the start of the citywide varsity playoffs. The Rockets had the best record of all the schools in the league, so naturally they were in the running for the championship. Malcolm practically begged her to come to this first game as it was one of the most important games of the year. Rachel could not refuse him.

She arrived at the school gym that afternoon before either of the teams had emerged from the locker rooms. Though Jennifer's squad was on the floor doing warm-up exercises, and she had reserved a seat for her in the first row of the bleachers, Rachel opted for a seat higher up in the stands. She did not want to make herself too obvious, on the slight chance that Justin was looking for her. Besides that, she wanted to have the opportunity of watching him, without it being completely obvious that she was doing so.

She was grateful that Jennifer and Malcolm had stopped asking her about their relationship. There was really nothing she could tell them, anyway. She would never tell them what had happened between her and Justin, and she hoped they didn't believe he had done her wrong. How disappointed they would probably be to learn that she had been wholly responsible for their breakup.

When the Rockets emerged from the locker room, they appeared to be more than ready to start this playoff game. They took the floor and immediately set themselves up for their shooting and passing practice exercises. Rachel stood immediately when she noticed that Malcolm was looking in the stands for her. His face broke into a smile that warmed her heart when he spotted her. He blew her a kiss.

She tried as hard as she could to concentrate on Malcolm and his teammates, but she could not keep her eyes off of Justin Phillips. He stood near the team bench, talking with the officials at the scorer's table. His face was set in a frown of concentration. It was obvious that his mind was on the impending game and nothing else. She thought he looked more handsome on this day than ever before.

He was dressed in a black double-breasted suit. His white shirt looked crisp at the collar, and his red and black tie was knotted expertly at his neck. His feet were ensconced in a pair of black leather slip-on oxfords that finished off his attire handsomely.

He called Malcolm to his side, and as he stood there listening to Justin's directive, Malcolm looked up at her. She noticed that when Justin was finished speaking, Malcolm said a few words to him. As Malcolm ran back to the floor, Justin turned immediately and looked up at her in the stands. Though his lips did not move, he nodded his head slightly in acknowledgment of her. Her eyes immediately began to water.

Just before the game started, Rachel watched painfully as Barbara Jennings sauntered over to Justin and grabbed his arm, pulling him closer so that she could whisper in his ear. She smiled at him seductively when he straightened up to his full height, and Rachel burned with curiosity because she was not able to see the expression on his face. She immediately remembered the things Miss Jennings had said to her on the night of the Spring dance, indicating how much she would love to get next to him. She wondered if Justin would pursue her now that they were no longer seeing each other. She was an easy enough conquest. He wouldn't have to do any work in that regard. He had been in an extremely amorous mood the night of their breakup; she wondered if he had or would satisfy his hunger with Miss Jennings.

An inferno of jealousy raged in Rachel's heart at the mere thought of them together. Seconds later, however, she was berating herself. *You blew it, remember? You had him in the palm of your hand and you let him slip away.* Why shouldn't he go after Miss Jennings, she reasoned. She was young and beautiful and obviously hot to trot. Even if he didn't consider her seriously, Rachel would not be surprised if he turned to her for physical comfort.

She sat in the stands for most of the game, not really concentrating on the players but more so on the many things she should have done or could have done to prevent Justin's loss of affection toward her. Of course, calling him Malcolm in the heat of passion had been the absolute wrong thing to do, but aside from that, she could have been more trusting of him and more open with her feelings instead of holding back. She had no doubts that he had been completely honest with her from the very beginning. He had held back nothing. She, on the other hand, had been too afraid to give in to her feelings, despite the strength of them for him. She knew he would never hurt her, that was something she felt in her heart. She knew he cared for her children and would take care of them and look after them as if they were his own. She knew he loved her like he'd said so many times. Why had she been so reluctant to let go of Malcolm? She knew their love would never be equaled, but she also knew that it would never be forgotten.

Rachel sat through the game and cheered Malcolm's team on along with the other onlookers in her immediate area, though her heart really was not in it. She was functioning almost mechanically; when the people around her cheered, she cheered.

During the halftime break, Rachel stayed in her seat and spoke to no one. She watched Justin covertly the entire time. *How could I have been so stupid,* she asked herself, *to let such a good man get away.* She knew how hard it was to find a good man just from listening to some of the stories Janice and other women she worked with relayed to her about their experiences. Justin was a rare find. Not only had he shown how much he cared for her, but he had taken her children into his care as well. She knew a lot of men didn't want to be bothered with a woman's kids, especially if they were the ages of Malcolm and Jennifer—but when Justin would visit, he never excluded them from his time. As a matter of fact, he more often gave them his time than he did Rachel. They would all sit around the den watching television together or laughing and joking around as though they were one big happy family. One of the things she loved about him was the way he interacted with her children. As she sat there watching him, Rachel realized just how important he had become to her. She missed him desperately.

Justin was trying his damnedest to concentrate on the game. Knowing that Rachel was in the stands made it almost impossible. He wished Malcolm hadn't told him she was there. The only way he had managed to do what he had to do every day was knowing that he wouldn't see her. During the first game after their breakup, he had been on pins and needles until almost the end of the second half. He hadn't known whether she would show or not. He had breathed a sigh of relief when she didn't. He was trying to forget what she had done to him: not calling him by her husband's name, but the way she had come into his life and took control of his heart and mind without the slightest effort. She had become a part of everything he did. Her absence at the games had made his broken life somewhat bearable, but now she was here. He wanted nothing more than to run up into the bleachers, pull her into his arms, and kiss her sweet mouth. *When the game is over,* he decided, *I'll get out as quickly as I can so I don't have to talk to her.*

At the end of the game, Malcolm and Jenny waited for Rachel

at the base of the bleachers until she descended. Rachel hugged Malcolm. "You played great, baby!"

"Thanks, Mom. How you doin'?" he asked. The concern he felt showed on his face.

"I'm fine, baby."

Jenny added, "You sure?"

"Yes, I'm fine," Rachel said, looking from one to the other, trying to convince herself as well as her children.

As they stood amid the crowd leaving the gym, Malcolm noticed Justin approaching a few feet away. "Hey, Coach," he called out, making sure that Justin did not have the opportunity to pretend he didn't see them.

Reluctantly Justin turned toward them. "Hey, Malcolm, Jenny."

"Hi, Coach Phillips," Jenny responded as her eyes darted back and forth between her mother and Justin.

"Hello, Rachel."

She could have won an Oscar. Her performance was that good. Though her heart was shattered, she smiled brightly as she said, "Hello, Justin. Great game!"

"Thanks," he answered solemnly.

Anyone that didn't know her would have never guessed that her heart was aching for his touch or simply his smile, but Justin knew her. Despite her outward show of happiness, he could clearly see the sadness he saw in her eyes on the night they met. It was torture for him to be so close to her and not be able to touch her, so he said, "See you kids tomorrow," to Malcolm and Jenny and to Rachel, "take care."

Though she felt as if she would cry, Rachel held herself together and asked the kids, "Are you guys going to stop for pizza with your friends?"

Jennifer looked at Malcolm quickly before she answered. "No, Mom. I'm going home." She didn't think her mother should be alone.

"Me, too," Malcolm quickly added.

"Well, okay. Mal, you go change. We'll wait for you in the car," Rachel said.

"Naw, I'll go home like this," he said and put his arms

around his mother's and sister's shoulders and led them out of the gym.

Malcolm ordered Chinese food for them, but when it arrived at the house, Rachel had no appetite. Though he and Jennifer tried to get her to eat something, she opted instead to go to bed.

Rachel went up to her bedroom, and as she prepared herself for bed, she tried not to think about Justin but he would not leave her mind. She sat on her bed and cried. After ten minutes or so, there was a knock on her bedroom door. She quickly tried to brush the tears from her face as she didn't want her children to know how upset seeing him tonight had made her.

"Who is it?" she asked as she wiped her nose and eyes with a tissue from the box on her nightstand.

"It's me, Mommy," Jenny called through the door.

"Come in."

Rachel would not face Jennifer immediately.

"Mommy, can I go to the movies with Marvin tomorrow night?" she asked.

"Sure, baby, I don't care," Rachel answered quickly, trying to keep her voice from trembling but to no avail.

"Are you okay, Mommy?"

"Yes, I'm fine," she stated, but immediately the tears started anew. She could not hold her feelings in.

Jennifer rushed to her side and wrapped her in a tight embrace. "Mommy, please don't cry. Please?"

"I miss him, Jenny. It's all my fault. I did something really stupid, and I hurt him."

"What happened?" Jennifer asked.

Rachel's head was lowered as she tried to catch her breath once more. She shook her head slowly before she said, "I'm not going to tell you what happened, but I don't want you to think that this is his fault. It's not. He didn't do anything wrong. It's all my fault."

"Mommy, it'll be okay," Jennifer said, trying to reassure her. She prayed that it would be. She missed having Justin around, too.

* * *

The next day, Rachel went to work as usual, and when she came home, still feeling depressed, she once again retreated to the privacy of her bedroom. Jennifer and Malcolm both had plans to go out that evening, so she was looking forward to a quiet night alone with her thoughts.

When Marvin picked Jennifer up, Rachel came down to greet him and to see them off.

"Eleven o'clock, Jenny."

"Okay, Mom." She kissed Rachel's cheek and asked, "You okay?"

Rachel smiled gratefully at her. She nodded in the affirmative.

When Malcolm was getting ready to leave, he asked, "Mommy, are you planning to go out tonight?" knowing that she wasn't.

"No."

"Can I borrow your car?"

"No," Rachel answered without hesitation.

"How come? I'm only going to pick up Juanita and go to a movie or something."

Malcolm had a driver's license, and Rachel knew that he was a good driver. In truth, she trusted him with her car. He had always proven to be responsible when behind the wheel, and she had let him use the car many times before.

She sighed after a moment and said, "Malcolm, if I let you use my car, I better not find a single ... No, if any of your friends smoke cigarettes, I don't want them in my car. I do not want to get in my car tomorrow morning and be smelling anybody's cigarettes."

"Okay," he said.

"And I better not find a single candy wrapper, potato chip crumb, or any other garbage in my car. Do you understand me?"

"Yes."

She looked at him a moment longer without comment before she said, "Go ahead."

His face split in a wide smile and he grabbed her and hugged her and kissed her cheek. "Thanks, Mom."

"Be home by eleven."

He had started toward the kitchen to get her keys from the counter drawer but stopped in his tracks at her words. "But my curfew's midnight," he protested.

"Well, you can either take public transportation and be home by midnight, or you can take my car and be home by eleven. The choice is yours," Rachel said nonchalantly.

He frowned slightly but said, "I'll be home by eleven."

As he was going out of the door, Rachel called to him, "Be careful, Malcolm."

Once both the kids were gone, Rachel decided to turn in, though it was still very early. She took off her clothes and got in bed. She wasn't the least bit sleepy, but she had no desire to do anything. She thought about everything that had happened with her and Justin, and though she was extremely sad, she did not shed a tear.

Chapter 18

"Malcolm. Malcolm, honey, I'm going shopping. I'll be back in a little while," Rachel said as she shook her son awake Saturday morning.

He turned over and groaned. "Okay."

When she stepped into the hallway, Jennifer was heading for the bathroom.

"Good morning, Jen."

"Hi, Mommy. Where you going?" Jennifer asked sleepily.

"Grocery shopping."

"Ooh, can I go with you?"

"If you hurry up and get dressed. I'm ready to go."

"Okay. I'll be ready in fifteen minutes," Jennifer said, suddenly wide awake.

Rachel went back downstairs and decided to toast a couple of slices of bread while she waited for her daughter to get dressed.

"You want some toast?" Rachel asked when Jennifer entered the kitchen fifteen minutes later, fully dressed.

"No, thanks. I'll eat later."

"Well, let's go."

Rachel was dressed in a pair of jeans and a sweatshirt. She

grabbed her waist-bag and strapped it around her waist. As they stepped into the garage, Jennifer asked, "Mommy, can I drive to the store?"

"Sure, I don't care."

She had been giving Jennifer driving lessons for the last few months, and though initially Jennifer had been a slow learner, the last few times Rachel had let her behind the wheel, she had much improved.

"Are you and Mal planning to do anything tomorrow?" Rachel asked.

Jennifer looked over at her mother briefly before she answered, "No." She was disappointed that they would not be able to surprise her by preparing a big meal for her while she was out.

"Well, since it's Mother's Day, would you mind hanging out with me tomorrow?"

"Of course not, Mommy. We'll do whatever you want to do."

"I hope Malcolm won't mind," she said softly.

"He won't mind. I don't think he had anything planned."

Jennifer and Malcolm had saved their allowance for the last three months and chipped in and bought Rachel a gold chain and pendant that read *NO. 1 MOM*.

"I hope you'll come with me to the Mother's Day service at church tomorrow."

"Sure, Mom."

Though as little children, Rachel and Malcolm had taken their children to church every Sunday, when they became teenagers, or more appropriately after Malcolm Sr.'s death, they lost their desire to go to Sunday School, and Rachel hadn't forced them. Every now and then, Jennifer would attend services with her of her own accord, but Malcolm Jr. seldom did. She hoped he would come with them tomorrow.

As they moved up and down the aisles in the supermarket, Rachel asked Jennifer, "How was your date last night?"

"It was okay. I think Marvin's going to tell me he doesn't want to go steady anymore."

Rachel looked over at Jennifer in surprise. "What makes you think that?"

"Because last night when we were in the movie theater, we ran into this girl named Sandy that goes to our school—and she pulled him aside to talk to her, and they were standing there, laughing and everything, like they were keeping a secret or something. When I asked him what they were talking about, he wouldn't tell me. I've seen him talking to her a lot at school, too."

"Does it bother you that he might not want to go steady anymore? I mean, it hasn't really been that long since you've been dating."

"I know, but I don't even care. You know how you can really like a guy a lot when you don't know him—then when you get to know him, you realize that you don't like him as much anymore?" Jennifer asked.

Rachel smiled and said, "Is that how it is?"

"Yeah," Jennifer answered, returning her smile.

They had reached the end of the aisle, and were laughing together about the mood swings of teenagers, when Rachel's shopping cart crashed into another entering the aisle.

"Oh, my goodness. I'm sor—" The words never quite made it out of her mouth when she noticed that the person on the other end of the shopping cart she had just crashed into was Justin.

"Excuse me. I'm—" Justin was saying when he, too, realized he was standing cart to cart with Rachel. "Hello, Rachel. Hi, Jenny."

"Hi, Coach Phillips," Jennifer said with a meek smile.

"Hi, Justin. I'm sorry. I wasn't looking where I was going."

"That's okay. I guess I wasn't, either."

They stared into each other's eyes for only a few seconds, though it seemed like hours had passed. Justin finally broke the uncomfortable silence. "How have you been, Rachel?"

"Okay, I guess. How have you been?"

"Okay."

"How's your mother?" Rachel asked, trying to sound cheerful.

118   *Cheryl Faye*

"She's fine, thanks."

"Good. Tell her I said happy Mother's Day."

"I will. Happy Mother's Day to you, too," Justin said softly.

His eyes traveled only briefly to meet Jennifer's. He felt guilty for letting her and Malcolm down.

"Thanks."

They stood again in silence for a few seconds before Rachel said, "Well, I'll see you later."

"Yeah."

She maneuvered her cart around his and started past him.

"Bye," Jennifer said to him softly.

"Bye, Jenny."

By the time Rachel reached the next aisle, she was fighting tears. She tried very hard to keep her emotions in check. "Jennifer, don't let me forget, we have to get some syrup," she said in a shaky voice.

"Mommy, are you okay?"

She smiled at Jennifer, though her smile was more like a grimace of pain. "I'm fine, honey. I'm okay."

Later that afternoon, Rachel sat in the den by herself, staring out of the window in quiet contemplation of what she had done and what she had to do in order to be happy once again. Seeing Justin that morning made her realize exactly how empty her life was without him. She saw, too, just how much she had truly hurt him.

"Mom, I finished cleaning out the garage," Malcolm said as he suddenly entered the room.

She turned to him slowly and said, "Thank you," then turned back to the window.

Malcolm was tired of seeing his mother moping around and saddened by what had happened with her and Coach Phillips. Thus he was unable to control his tongue.

"You shouldn't worry about that creep, Mom. If he really cared about you, he would have called you. He wasn't good enough for you, anyway," he said angrily.

"Stop it! You stop that right now, Malcolm," Rachel said,

turning back to him. "You don't know what happened between us, and you have no reason to be angry with Justin. If you want to direct your anger at someone, direct it at me. It's my fault that we broke up. It wasn't because of anything that he did. It was because of something I did. I hurt him! He's perfectly justified in not calling me."

"But—"

"No buts, Malcolm. Justin is the same man he was when he was coming here before. He's a good man, and he always will be. He did nothing wrong."

Rachel could see that he was confused. She wished she could tell him more, but she would never tell them what had happened to cause Justin's alienation. She felt she had to tell him something, though.

"Malcolm, go get your sister. I want to talk to both of you."

Malcolm and Jennifer returned to the den moments later.

"What's wrong, Mom?" Jennifer asked as they entered the den.

"Nothing, baby. Come here and sit down. Both of you." When they were seated beside her, Rachel turned to face them. "Listen, kids, I want you to understand something. Your father was the best thing that ever happened to me. What we had was so special. The best years of my life . . . Most of my life, he was a part of me, and I know I'll never meet another man like him for as long as I live.

"It's been very difficult for me to let go of the love that we had between us. It always made me feel safe and secure. He was my friend, my very best friend. He gave me the most precious gift of all, too." She smiled. "He gave me you. Every time I look at you two, I see him.

"I know you both think that I should forget about Justin since he hasn't called in two weeks, but you don't understand what happened with us. I won't tell you the specifics because that's not something you need to know. But you do need to know that he's a good man, and he was a good friend to all of us. He cared about you as well as me. I destroyed his trust and I hurt him, and I'm sorry for that.

"I know you're tired of seeing me walking around here with

a long face. I'm tired of it, too. I'll never forget your father. He will always live in my heart, but I realize that I've been cheating you and myself by holding on to him so fiercely. He was my first love, and that's always special, but there comes a time in everyone's life when you have to grow. I've been fighting that, and I've been losing. I lost a good friend." She paused and lowered her head for a moment. The children waited in silence. She looked up at them and continued, "I love you both so very much. I don't know what I'd do without you."

Rachel rose from the couch suddenly and turned to them. "I'm going out for a while. I need a little time . . . I'm going to see your father."

"Do you want us to come?" Jennifer asked as she, too, rose from the sofa.

"No, I'd rather be alone with him, if you don't mind."

Malcolm was silent through all of this. Rachel looked down at him for a moment before she placed a hand gently on his shoulder. "Honey, you okay?" she asked.

He looked up at her with the saddest eyes. "Are you?"

She smiled tenderly at him. "Yes."

He stood before her, and she put her arms around him. "Come here, Jenny."

Rachel held both of her children close for a couple of minutes.

"I love you, Mom," Malcolm said softly.

"Me, too, Mommy," Jennifer concurred.

"I love you, too," Rachel said with a smile as she kissed both of them on their cheeks. "I'll be back in a little while, okay? I don't want you worrying about me. I'm fine. Honestly."

It was a beautiful day. The temperature was a comfortable seventy-five degrees, and as Rachel drove her car through the cemetery gates, the old adage, "April showers, bring May flowers," immediately came to mind.

Once she was parked, she found Malcolm's grave easily, though she had not been to visit it since last year on Father's Day. His plot was situated near a large elm tree.

His gravestone was engraved with the words LOVING FATHER.

DEVOTED HUSBAND. She stood there for a few minutes, remembering how he had so personified those four words. He had always doted on their children, though he was a fair-minded disciplinarian. Malcolm and Jennifer adored him, and he returned their adoration twice over. He showered them with love every day. Whenever he had to discipline either of them, he never held on to his anger or disappointment. An hour later, he would be hugging them and telling them how much he loved them.

He had always shown her, too, how much he loved her. Every single day of their life together, he told her that he loved her. And he was a pure romantic. He always found time to romance her; to make her feel as though she was the most beautiful woman in the world. He was unselfish, generous, caring.

Rachel's eyes began to water as she knelt in front of his gravestone.

"Hi, Malcolm. I'm sorry I haven't been here in so long, but it's really hard for me to come here. I only want to remember you the way you were.

"I know you're probably up in heaven watching over us, so I'm sure you know what's been going on down here. The kids are doing well. Malcolm's playing ball for his school. He's the team's star player. You should see him. You'd be so proud of him. Every time I look at him, I see you. He looks so much like you. He'll be graduating from high school next month. He's going to start college in the fall. He was accepted at five different schools, but he chose Rutgers because that's where you went.

"Jenny's doing great, too. She's grown up so much, baby, and she's such a beautiful young lady. You probably wouldn't recognize her, she's grown so much. She's an excellent student. She's been bringing home straight A's for the last year. She's still taking dance class, and she's on the cheerleading squad at school, too, so she's right there cheering her brother on. They're both such a big help to me, too. I don't know what I'd do without them. Thank you for giving them to me."

Tears were flowing freely down her face by this time.

"I miss you so much, Malcolm," she cried. "I miss you. It's been so hard for me to let you die. I wasn't ready to let you go. I'm so angry with you for dying on me and leaving me here! I've been so afraid to live without you. You were always there for me." Her body shook with the emotions she was finally releasing after all these months. When she was calmer, she went on.

"I've met a man, Malcolm. His name is Justin Phillips. He's a teacher at the kids' school. He's also Mal's basketball coach. He's a good man. You would like him. The kids both like him. We were dating for a while until I messed it up." She looked off into the horizon as she tried to collect her thoughts. She continued, "I've been so afraid of letting you go that I lost him."

She covered her face with her hands as her emotions spilled forth. "I love him, Malcolm, and I miss him. I don't want to live without him, and I know that the only way I can be with him is if I let you go," she cried. "I'll always love you, honey, but I have to let you go. I can't be happy if I don't. I hope you understand. You were my best friend, and you know how much I've always loved you, but I have to go on. I want to be with Justin. I want him to be in my life. I want to live."

Minutes passed before Rachel spoke again. She calmed herself by acknowledging that Malcolm's first concern had always been that she be happy.

"You know I'll never forget you or what we had, and no one will ever take your place," she said softly. She rocked slowly on her haunches, taking comfort in the wonderful memories she had of her dear beloved husband. She bowed her head under the weight of melancholy that filled her heart, and her tear-filled eyes focused on her hands as they rested in her lap. She had been unconsciously playing with her wedding band. "I came to say goodbye, Malcolm." She slowly slid the ring off of her finger. "I'll see you again one day. We'll be together again."

Rachel rose slowly to her feet. She placed her right hand on his gravestone. "I love you, Malcolm. I always will." She bent over and pressed her lips to the stone. When she straightened herself, she removed her hand, took a step back, and wiped her eyes one final time.

"Bye, baby."

Chapter 19

It was four thirty by the time Justin returned to his apartment. He had been at the health club with his old friends, playing basketball and shooting the breeze in between.

When he returned home after seeing Rachel and Jennifer in the supermarket that morning, he knew that if he didn't do something to work off the anxiety he was feeling, he would bust.

How ironic, he thought, that he would actually bump into her, of all people, at the supermarket. Ever since he saw her on Thursday at the game, he had tried to do nothing but forget her. He had thought . . . He had hoped that she would have come to him before now, to tell him that she was ready to get on with her life—that she was ready to share her life with him. As much as he wanted to, and had considered going to her over the last two weeks and asking to start over, he knew that unless she came to him, their relationship would be a lie. He could not force her hand. She had to take that step on her own. He was disappointed when he realized that it would probably never happen. It had already been two weeks.

He missed having her in his life. He missed her smile, her laughter, the way she would blush when he expressed his feelings for her. He missed her children, too. He and Malcolm had begun to develop a closeness that he thought was very special. Justin figured since his father's death, Malcolm had probably kept a lot of his feelings inside as he felt a duty to step into his father's shoes and be protector to his mother and sister. He noticed that Malcolm had begun to open up to him—that he felt he could confide in him when he needed a break from being the "man of the house."

He missed Jennifer, too. He had begun to look on her as a daughter. He always felt that she was his biggest supporter in regard to his relationship with Rachel. She had always made him feel that she wanted him there with her mother.

He was genuinely saddened by the realization that he and Rachel would probably never be. He had been so sure that they could have a wonderful life together.

Justin opted not to shower at the health club, instead he waited until he got home. When he stepped out of the shower, after drying himself off, he went straight to his kitchen and removed a beer from the refrigerator. He popped the top off the bottle and placed it to his lips and took a long swallow as he stepped back into the living room. As he passed through, he grabbed the remote control from the end table next to the sofa and pressed the power button. The television sprang to life. The NBA finals were in progress. He stopped momentarily and watched as Michael Jordan made one of his picture-perfect drives to the basket, scoring and being fouled in the process. Justin shook his head and smiled as he continued to his bedroom to get dressed.

He was sitting on the edge of the sofa, praying silently as Shaquille O'Neal stood at the foul line, preparing to make the second of two foul shots. He had already missed the first one. His intercom sounded at the same moment Shaq released the ball. It bounced off the rim and was captured by Dennis Rodman of the Bulls.

"Aw, Shaq," Justin moaned as he rose from the sofa and went to answer the buzzer. He gave no thought to who it might be. He wasn't expecting anyone.

"Who is it?" he asked when he pressed the TALK button.

He then pressed the LISTEN button and was surprised when he heard, "Rachel."

His heart did a somersault at hearing that single word. He pressed the button, releasing the door in the lobby.

He stood near the door as a frown creased his brow and his heartbeat quickened. He tried not to get too excited, for he had no idea what she wanted. He didn't want to assume that she was there to tell him what he longed to hear. After a few minutes, though, he realized that he was happy she was there, period.

When his doorbell rang, Justin opened the door immediately.

She looked sad, that was the first thing he noticed. Sadder than when he'd seen her earlier anyway. His heart sank, as he automatically thought the worst.

"Hello, Justin," she said apprehensively. She stood outside his door, making no attempts to enter.

"Hi," was all he could manage.

"I was wondering if I could talk to you for a moment," she said as she looked up into his eyes.

"Sure. Come in," he said quickly as he stepped back and opened the door wider so she could enter.

When she was inside, he offered her a seat, but she declined it. "I just came by because I wanted to tell you how sorry I am for hurting you. I never meant to hurt you, Justin, and I know it's no excuse for what I did, but I've never known anyone else besides my husband, and he was a part of my life for so long that I was just too afraid to let him go."

A tear slid down her face, and she closed her eyes in an attempt to control them. She took a deep breath before she continued. "I don't blame you for being angry with me. . . ." She began to cry.

Justin moved closer and put an arm around her shoulder. "Come in and sit down, Rachel," he said as he guided her to the sofa.

She lowered her head and cried, unable to go on for the next few seconds. Justin sat beside her and waited patiently until she could. After a while, she wiped her eyes with the balled-up tissue she held in her hand and looked into his eyes. Tears continued to stream down her face. "I miss you," she cried. "I love you, Justin."

His own eyes began to well with tears at her confession. He reached over to the coffee table in front of the sofa and picked up the remote control, clicking the television set off. He then reached for her.

She wrapped her arms around him and held him tightly. A tear slid down his face as he returned her embrace just as strongly.

"I'm so sorry, Justin. I was so afraid to live without him, but I'm not afraid anymore. I don't want to lose you. I need you. I love you so much," she wailed.

"Shh, shh, Rachel. It's okay, baby. It's okay," he said with a caress. "I love you, too."

Tears of joy fell from his eyes unbidden. This was what he wanted, what he had prayed for so many times. They sat there for the next few minutes holding each other, taking comfort in the knowledge that their love was not lost, that it was only beginning.

When Rachel had calmed down, she took Justin's face in her hands and kissed his lips softly as she stared into his eyes with love.

"I love you so much, and I can't believe that I was so foolish to almost let you get away."

Justin could not speak, he was choked up with emotion. He had never been so happy before in his life.

"I want you in my life, Justin. I want to be a part of your life. Mine is so empty without you. Please forgive me for what I did."

"Rachel, there's nothing to forgive. I know how much you loved him, and I know how hard it was for you to let him go. I know you'll always love him. I don't want to take that from you. I'll never try to take his place. I only want to give you . . . to make the rest of your life as full and as happy as the time you had with him."

He held her close once more. "I've missed you, Rachel. My life is empty without you, too, baby." He took her by her shoulders and once again looked into her eyes. "You understand why I haven't called you, don't you? I don't want you to think that I stopped loving you. I never did. I never will."

"I know. I understand," she told him. She caressed his face and thanked God for sending him to her.

"I went to see him today. To say goodbye," she said softly.

"Rachel."

"He would've liked you," she said as she smiled at him.

"I'm sure I would've liked him, too. And if he's looking down on us right now, I hope he knows that I'll love you and Malcolm and Jenny for the rest of my life," Justin said sincerely.

"I'm so glad I have you. I'm so glad I have you, Justin," she repeated emotionally.

Their lips met in a passionate kiss as each of them was finally sure that they had arrived at that point in life where they knew they would always be thankful for the many blessings bestowed on them. They had each matured enough to know that everything happens for a reason, and everything has its time.

"Will you make love to me?" Rachel asked with her lips close to his ear.

He took her face gently in his hands, kissing her tenderly, and answered, "For the rest of my life."

Later in the evening, they lay together quietly, basking in the afterglow of the love they shared only moments before. Rachel rested her head on his chest and was comforted by the beating of his heart. Justin was overjoyed at having her in his arms this way.

"Rachel?"

"Yes," she sighed happily.

"What'd you have planned for tomorrow?"

Justin remembered that Malcolm and Jennifer had wanted him to keep Rachel out of the house so they could prepare a special dinner for her in honor of Mother's Day.

"After church, I was just going to hang out with the kids," she answered.

"A month ago I bought tickets for you and my mother for the gospel concert tomorrow at The Theater at Madison Square Garden. Kirk Franklin & the Family are going to be there along with Yolanda Adams and a couple others. I figured after the concert, we could go back and get the kids, then I'd take us all out to eat. Do you think they'd mind?" he asked, knowing they wouldn't.

"I don't know. I'm the one that asked them to hang out with me. They might be upset if I brushed them off like that," she said.

"Well, when we get back to your house, we'll ask them. If they want to be with you, that's all right," Justin said, playing the innocent.

They lay together again in silence for the next ten minutes or so.

"Honey, can I ask you something?" Justin said, breaking their silence.

"Sure."

"I know, Malcolm and Jenny . . . Well, they're damn near grown. I mean, Malcolm's going off to college in September, and Jenny will be, too, next year. I know you're probably looking forward to them being out of the house and you having some time to yourself. But . . . I was wondering . . . Do you think you'd ever want to have another baby?"

Rachel lifted her head from his chest so she could look into his eyes when she asked, "Do you want me to have a baby for you, Justin?"

He gazed into her eyes. "Yes," he said softly. "Yes, I do, but I want you to be my wife, first."

She smiled at him. "I'd love to be your wife, Justin, and I'd love to have a baby with you, too," she said sincerely.

"You wouldn't mind starting all over again?" he asked.

"But we are starting all over," she murmured.

Justin's face broke into a smile, then a chuckle escaped his lips. "Yes, you're right. We are starting over."

* * *

When Rachel returned home that evening, it was almost eight o'clock. She heard the television blaring, so she headed straight for the den. Justin was behind her.

"Hey, kids, I'm home," she said with a bright smile.

They turned from the television to greet her, but were both silenced immediately when they noticed Justin.

"Hey, y'all," he said with a tentative smile.

Neither of them spoke right away, but Jennifer's face broke into a smile that would have lit Times Square. "Hi, Coach," she said, trying to contain herself.

Rachel was pleased that she was so happy to see him. Justin was, too.

"How you doin', Jenny?" he asked with genuine affection.

She rose from the floor where she had been sitting and started toward them. "Fine," she answered. "How 'bout you?"

"Fine," he answered.

Jennifer looked at her mother and her eyes began to water, she was so happy. Then she looked up at Justin. Before she could stop herself, she grabbed him and hugged him as tears fell from her eyes. "I'm so glad you're back. I missed you," she cried.

Justin was so moved by her show of affection that he was speechless for a moment. He held her in his arms before he placed a gentle kiss on her forehead. "I missed you, too, Jenny."

Jennifer released him, then hugged Rachel.

Throughout this tender moment, Malcolm sat where he was. Inside, he was glad to see Justin with his mother. He knew that was what she wanted, but he wondered if he was there to stay or if this was just a one-time visit.

"Hey, Malcolm," Justin said as he moved closer to him.

"What's up?" Malcolm answered solemnly.

"How you been?"

"All right."

Justin sat beside him on the sofa. He could see that Malcolm was doubtful about him, and he could understand his feelings.

"I'm sorry I haven't been coming around. Your mother and I had some things we needed to work out."

"Yeah, so did y'all work them out?" Malcolm asked, full of skepticism.

"Yes, we did."

"So how long are you here for, this time?"

"I'm here to stay."

Malcolm looked at him for the first time since their conversation began.

"I hope we can be friends again, Malcolm. I've missed you," Justin admitted. He offered Malcolm his hand, hoping they, too, could start over.

Malcolm looked at Justin's outstretched hand for a long moment, then looked into his eyes. He rose from the sofa and looked down at Justin for only a moment before he took his hand. "I missed you, too," Malcolm whispered.

Rachel's face broke into a smile.

Justin rose to face Malcolm. He held on to his hand as they stared into each other's eyes. Malcolm's face broke into a smile, and he reached out with his other hand to embrace him. "I'm glad you're back."

Chapter 20

Sunday morning Rachel arose when she heard knocking on her bedroom door.

"Come in," she grumbled. She looked over at the clock on her nightstand. It was seven twenty.

Her bedroom door opened and in walked Malcolm and Jennifer. Malcolm was carrying a tray with her breakfast on it, and Jennifer was carrying a vase with a bouquet of roses beautifully arranged inside.

"Happy Mother's Day," they chorused.

She smiled as she sat up in bed. "Thank you."

"We made you breakfast," Malcolm said as he placed the tray over her lap on the bed.

He kissed her cheek and said, "I love you."

Jennifer did the same after she placed the vase on her dresser. "Me, too, Mommy."

"Oh, I love you both, too. This is so nice," she said, fighting back tears.

They made her French toast and bacon. A fruit cup with fresh strawberries and chunks of honeydew melon, her favorites, rested beside her plate. A tall glass of orange juice completed the menu.

"We have something for you, Mommy," Jennifer said as she reached into the pocket of her bathrobe and handed her a small gift-wrapped box.

"Oh, what is this?"

"Just a little something. We wanted to get you something else, but we didn't have a whole lot to work with," Malcolm said.

"I'm sure I'll love it, whatever it is," Rachel assured them. She began to remove the paper as quickly as she could, tossing it aside, anxious to see what was in the box.

When she removed the lid and the square of cotton on top, she sighed with joy as she lifted the chain and pendant out of the box.

"This is beautiful," she said with a smile, though tears were streaming down her face. "Thank you so much. I love it."

"We love you, Mom. You're the best mother in the whole world," Malcolm said as his eyes, too, filled with tears.

"Come here," Rachel said as she held out her arms to them. She hugged them both in turn and kissed their lips. "You're the best kids in the whole world, too. I'm so proud of you both. Thank you."

"You're welcome, Mommy. Enjoy your breakfast," Jennifer said. "I'm going to run you a nice warm bubble bath, so when you're finished eating you can just step right in."

"Thank you, baby."

"Let me know what you want to wear to church. I'll get it ready for you," Jennifer added.

"Coach said he'd be here at nine to get us, right?" Malcolm asked.

"Yes."

"Okay. We'll be ready when he gets here."

After services that morning, they all stayed at church and had lunch before Justin took Malcolm and Jennifer back to Rachel's house. So that Rachel could hear, he told them they would be back by six o'clock to pick them up, then he would take them all to dinner.

Rachel did not know that Janice was coming by that afternoon. She had not gone to church services that morning at Calgary Baptist Church, but had attended the services at Mrs. Phillips's church instead.

When Justin had Malcolm and Jennifer out of Rachel's earshot, he told them that he would call them when they were ready to leave the concert on their way home.

That morning, before he came to pick them up for church, a huge bouquet made up of roses, carnations, violets, and lilies was delivered to Rachel from Justin. The note simply read: *I love you. Happy Mother's Day.*

Malcolm answered the door when Justin arrived.

"Hey, dude," Justin said cheerfully as he stepped into the house.

"Hi, Coach. How you doin'?"

"I'm great. How are you?"

"Good."

"Good morning, Justin," Rachel said softly as she stepped out of the den.

Justin's face broke into a wide grin. "Good morning, Rachel. Happy Mother's Day."

"Thank you."

He stepped over to her and gently embraced her as he kissed her lips.

As she stood in his embrace, she smiled up at him. "Thank you for the beautiful bouquet."

"I have something else for you." He released her and reached into the pocket of his jacket and removed a small black velvet box. He handed her the box as he kissed her cheek. "When our child is born, we'll add his or her birthstone."

Rachel opened the box and sucked in her breath at the beautiful ring inside. It was a gold band that held two stones, a garnet and a ruby, the birthstones of Malcolm and Jennifer, respectively.

"It's beautiful, Justin. Thank you," she said as tears of joy filled her eyes.

He had purchased the ring early on the day they broke up.

He was overjoyed they were back together, and he could give it to her now.

The concert that afternoon was spectacular. Mrs. Phillips and Rachel were both overjoyed by Justin's thoughtfulness. There was so much love going around in that concert hall that afternoon, that one would have to be dead to not be moved simply from being there.

Justin was happier than he had ever been. His mother was doing better, healthwise, than she had in a long time, and she was thrilled that he and Rachel were back together. Rachel simply glowed with a happiness that he had never seen before, and it made her even more beautiful than she already was. His heart was so full of love for her that it felt close to bursting.

When the show was over, Rachel and Mrs. Phillips both wanted to use the ladies' room, which gave Justin the perfect opportunity to call Malcolm and Jennifer to let them know that they were on their way home.

When they arrived forty-five minutes later, Justin helped Rachel and his mother out of the car.

Before they started up the walk to the door, Rachel hugged him as she said, "Justin, thank you so much for taking us to that concert. It was so wonderful."

He kissed her softly on her mouth and murmured, "You're welcome, sweetheart. I'm glad you enjoyed it."

"Oh, honey, what was not to enjoy?" Mrs. Phillips added. "God was in that house this afternoon. Praise the Lord!"

When Rachel unlocked the door to the house, her nostrils were immediately assailed by the smell of fried chicken. "We're home! What are y'all cooking in here?" she asked as she turned toward the kitchen.

Out of the corner of her eye, she noticed that the dining room table was set with her good dishes, and she immediately wondered what was going on.

As she was about to enter the kitchen, Janice exited with a dish filled with candied yams.

"Hi, honey. Happy Mother's Day," she said cheerfully and kissed her on her cheek before continuing to the dining room. "Hi, Justin. Hello, Mrs. Phillips, I'm Janice."

"Hi, Janice. What are you doing?" Rachel asked.

"Hi, Mommy," Jennifer said as she emerged behind Janice with a dish full of fried chicken. "We cooked dinner for you."

"What? But Justin was going to take us out," she said, turning back to him.

He stood against the wall with one hand in his pocket and a smirk on his face.

Mrs. Phillips was smiling brightly as she was in on the charade, too.

"You knew about this?" she asked him.

He nodded his head.

"It smells wonderful," Mrs. Phillips said.

"Hey, Mom," Malcolm said as he emerged from the kitchen with a dish full of greens.

"What did you cook?" Rachel wanted to know as she moved into the dining room, astounded that they had pulled this over on her.

"We made fried chicken and barbecue chicken, candied yams, turnip and collard greens, mixed, red beans and rice—and Mrs. Phillips gave us the recipe for her dinner rolls that I've heard so much about," Janice said. "And by the way, Mrs. Phillips, they are great!"

"Oh, gosh," Rachel said with a sigh. "I can't believe this."

Justin moved up behind her and put an arm around her waist and kissed her on her neck. "Believe it, baby. This was in the works for weeks. I almost screwed up everything."

She turned to him and looked up into his eyes. "No, I almost screwed up everything."

She kissed him tenderly before she turned back to her family. They all stood around the table, smiling at her.

"This is great. You guys are just too much."

"This is your day, Rachel. And you, too, Mrs. Phillips. Happy Mother's Day," Janice said.

Janice, Malcolm, and Jennifer continued to lay the food out while Rachel, Mrs. Phillips, and Justin washed up for dinner.

When they had all returned to the dining room, Rachel stood back and admired the beautifully decorated table before she took her seat next to Justin.

"This is so beautiful," she sighed.

"I'll say grace," Malcolm then said.

"No, baby, let me," Rachel asked.

They all took hands around the table and bowed their heads.

"Thank you, Lord, for all your many blessings. Thank you for this wonderful day that you have allowed us to wake up to. Thank you for this meal that you have made possible for us to share, to strengthen our bodies in tribute to you. Thank you for my loving family; for my dear sweet Malcolm, whom you have called home to be with you; for our beautiful children, Malcolm and Jennifer; for my sister-in-law, Janice, who is always there for me; for my new friend, Mrs. Phillips, and for this wonderful man that you have sent into my life, Justin." He squeezed her hand gently. "I know through you, all of our blessings come forth, and I know as long as we live by your word, our blessings will continue. Thank you for watching over us in our times of sorrow, for being with us when we were afraid to go on, and for opening my eyes and giving me a second chance to love and be loved again. Through Jesus Christ, Our Lord . . ."

In unison, they all said, "Amen."

Dear Readers,

I would like to thank everyone that wrote to me about my debut novel, *At First Sight*. I appreciated every letter. I hope you've enjoyed this story of Rachel and Justin. I would love to hear your thoughts. Please feel free to write to me at:

Cheryl Faye Smith
Bowling Green Station
P. O. Box 1445
New York, NY 10274–1445

Please enclose a self-addressed, stamped envelope if you would like for me to write you back.

Sincerely,

Cheryl Faye

Cheryl Faye

MY MOTHER'S CHILD

Monique Gilmore

1

"Kasey, I told you to leave Baseem alone!" Geraldine Copeland warned through pursed lips. Her control and will to stay composed completely deflated when she pushed back her daughter's long, thick braids to survey her swollen and discolored cheek.

"I can't believe you want to marry that street thug. If your father was still living—had he still been able to grace this world with his presence—he would not have any of this."

Kasey cringed. The thought of her mother still pining away, for a father she never had a chance to meet, irritated her beyond words.

"Dad's been dead and gone for countless years now, Mom. Let him rest, would you?"

Geraldine Copeland towered over her lanky daughter. That flippant remark was not even necessary, she thought. Gingerly she tilted Kasey's chin upward and to the left in order to examine the bruise closer. Kasey's mahogany complexion glowed against the dim ceiling light. Twelve years as a registered nurse at Newark, New Jersey's, Beth Israel Hospital emergency unit had bestowed many valuable life lessons on

Geraldine. And one of those learned experiences warned her that her only child was driving down the wrong avenue.

Kasey withdrew, being careful not to seem too unappreciative of Geraldine's sometimes overwhelming attention. She glared up into her mother's cinnamon-complected face, which was not only full but worrisome. Age lines that were never visible before had begun to wrinkle around the corner of Geraldine's wide eyes. A crease dented her forehead suddenly. Kasey sighed heavily, glancing down at the tattered, colorful shag carpet. *A life—a makeover. That's exactly what her mother needed,* Kasey thought quietly.

"I'm fine, Mother. Really," Kasey mumbled as she backed away from the dank dining area into the tiny kitchen. Her lips still unwilling to engage in much movement—the pain excruciating, no thanks to a flying apple that pummeled the side of her face. "I told you. They're upset because Baseem chose to marry me over them. That's all. It's not that big of a deal."

"Not that big of a deal?" Geraldine squeaked. "Lord have mercy, Jesus," she exclaimed, shaking her head. "What kind of sam-blasted statement is that, Kasey? Twenty-six years old and already life has dealt you some tough blows. This is no way for a young woman to live."

Geraldine eyed Kasey more sternly. "Having strange women sabotaging your car is bad enough, but this?" She reached out for her daughter's bruised cheek again. Kasey moved away. "This is dangerous. It's assault. It's a sign, sweetheart." She sighed. "Must I outlive another child? Bury you, too?"

When Kasey refused to answer her mother—even acknowledge the rhetorical question—Geraldine sucked her teeth, rolled her eyes toward the faded ceiling, and spoke again.

"I love you, Kasey. That's the honest to God truth, and it's because of my love for you that I got to tell you this, baby." Geraldine inhaled a deep bit of air, then let it trickle outward. She walked toward Kasey, who stared blankly out the kitchen window at the gutted house behind them. Geraldine laid a caring hand on Kasey's shoulder. "You've got to make a decision."

Geraldine paused. "I'll never accept Baseem as my son-in-law. He's no good for you. It's got to be me or him.

"Mother's Day is a few weeks from today, and nothing would mean more to me than celebrating it with my only living child." Geraldine coated her next sentence with all the sweetness she could muster, considering the situation. "But I can't go through this no more, Kasey. I won't. Because if his blatant indiscretions with these half crazed, supposed ex-girlfriends aren't bothering you none, it's certainly bugging the heck out of me."

"There are no indiscretions, Mom," Kasey barked. "Just a bunch of envious women." She began pacing the floor. "They all want what I have." She stopped and stood in front of Geraldine. "Baseem and I will be fine. I will be fine. He loves me."

Denial, Geraldine thought. That's what Kasey was suffering from. A bad, terminal case of denial when it came to this Baseem boy. Really. Not to see and accept that Baseem was obviously messing around with half of the women in Newark, New Jersey? Come on, she wanted to scream at Kasey. It would take more than a rage of envy to cause an adult to purposely throw an apple out the window of a speeding car at another adult. If anything warranted such a behavior, it would be broken promises or commitments forsaken.

Tears rolled down Geraldine's face as she bent forward and kissed Kasey on the cheek. "Make a decision, Kase," she whispered before leaving the room.

What else could she do? Geraldine thought. Certainly she wouldn't leave her only living child stranded on the streets. But really, there was no other seemingly way to shake some sense into her. The prayers had been sent up on many, many late nights. It felt like God was preoccupied with other folks with more important problems. Lord, if she could just fight the devil all by herself to protect her child, she gladly would.

It was the likes of Baseem who were the real culprits responsible for her son's death. Sure, Baseem's story was typical. A neighborhood kid with the intelligence of a neurosurgeon, Baseem Rashad, formerly known in the hood as Dwight Clarke, had given up his life to the streets of Newark, New Jersey, as many bright brothers had. Having a mother hindered with cancer, and three younger siblings to support, one might agree that Baseem's way of survival was valid. But hell, everybody had a similar story to whine about south of Clinton Avenue.

It was street thugs like Baseem, who conveyed the messages to young brothers that the head-turner cars and the fancy cell phones and the state-of-the-art pagers were cool—necessary to own. It was the Baseem types who lead naive brothers to believe that it was better to be on the streets and master survival skills than in a classroom gaining education. It was the Baseem types who drove around town with that god-awful rap music blaring, glamorizing the violence, which ended Kenny's life.

Geraldine sighed heavily. It had been three years, and still it hurt too much to think back to that day. Kenny had just phoned from his car phone. He had promised to meet her and Kasey at Corky's restaurant after church around 2:30 P.M. Their plans were simple enough—like that of most small families on any holiday. Kasey and Kenny had agreed to take her to dinner for Mother's Day. Especially since Kenny was too busy to cook a home meal—and Kasey, well, just hadn't got the knack of how to cook.

Much of Kasey's inability to throw together a meal, the family supposed, had a lot to do with the fact that she spent all her time in their ailing uncle Chitty's barbershop, raking in the cash. Brothers lined up early on just about any day—but more particularly Saturday mornings—to have the honor of Kasey's clippers humming through their hair. Her ability to master barbering came at an early age. This was partly due to the countless after-school hours of watching Uncle Chitty work his magic in the barbershop while Geraldine worked the 12 to 8 P.M. shift at the hospital.

Kenny, on the other hand, preferred to spend his spare time in the kitchen, with his aunt Pearl, Chitty's wife. His lifelong dream was to become a chef, owner, and operator of a posh gourmet restaurant in New York City one day. But then that dream was suddenly yanked away on an unusually warm spring day—Mother's Day, three years ago.

She and Kasey had waited until 3:15 P.M. before finally placing their menu order at Corky's. The restaurant, which hosted many famed Newark born and raised stars, was cramped with folks returning from church, ready to treat their mothers and grandmothers with a day off from their aprons. The aroma of fried chicken, grits, gravy, biscuits, and ham floated through the air, further agonizing her and Kasey's famished bellies. The way she figured, Kenny had become sidetracked, as he often did, and had forgotten about his commitment to meet them for dinner.

Three hours later, and after a trip to the famed Carvel's ice cream parlor in Bloomfield, New Jersey, Kenny still had not phoned or returned home. And it was unlike Kenny not to show up for a Mother's Day dinner. Waiting and worried, she had paced the floor—Kasey had straightened the house.

When the tiny faux grandfather clock finally bonged for the eighth time, there was a still moment, before another chime rang through the air. But unlike that of the clock, this ringing was more precise. Geraldine had walked over to the front door and peered through the tiny peephole.

"Oh, sweet Jesus," she had murmured nervously on seeing brims of blue hats, bouncing off the early evening moonlight.

Geraldine's inner spirit had already told her the news before she opened the door.

"Mrs. Copeland?" the lanky officer had questioned. Kasey had gathered in the tiny foyer with her mother, anticipating the worst.

The officer removed his hat with the shiny precinct number displayed on the front and continued, "I'm afraid we have some bad news."

She and Kasey had screamed. Nothing else needed to be said. It had always been the three of them: her, Kasey, and Kenny. But as they stood before the two men in blue, it became painfully obvious that it would be only the two of them from then onward.

It was a high-speed chase. The drivers were fleeing from the police, the officers had told them. *Your son was an innocent*

*bystander—standing on the corner when the stolen car jumped
the curb and ran him over.*

Kasey stood in the archway of Geraldine's bedroom door.
She could tell by the glassy film that sheathed her mother's
quarter-sized eyes that she had slipped off into a reminiscent
trance about Kenny. Her mother appeared much stronger, sitting
fully postured, rocking back and forth with her broad shoulders
and big bones. Kasey knew Geraldine meant business. But so
did she.

Staring down again at the trampled carpet, Kasey sheepishly
mumbled, "I'm going to Uncle Chitty and Aunt Pearl's for a
while."

Geraldine continued to rock back and forth, her gaze shifting
toward the colored family portraits of Kasey, Kenny, and herself. Twins. *They were seventeen when we took that picture.*
Her eyes scanned over to the yellowing, eight-by-twelve, black-
and-white photo hanging next to the colored trio. Geraldine
sighed heavily. *Oh, James—my sweet, sweet, James. I sure
wish you were still with me—help me get it through Kasey's
thick skull that Baseem doesn't mean her any good.*

A tear folded over her eye. It had been twenty-five years,
and still she mourned her fiancé—Kasey's daddy. She had tried
to date—find someone to fill her lonely nights and empty heart,
but no one could ever quite fill James Bullock's shoes. Ever.

She still reminisced of the night James had proposed to her.
They had gone to Coney Island to spend the day. The day was
sizzling and sticky. The Italian Ice had melted down her arm,
leaving a streak of green and red food coloring after just a few
slurps. James was playing with his cotton candy, twirling the
pink stuff round and round as he nibbled at it from the side.

"Let's get on the Cyclone," he had said, with foamy pink
stuff stuck to the side of his mouth.

Geraldine had wiped the side of his mouth with her soggy
napkin. "The Cyclone? You must be crazy, James. There's no
way I'm getting on that thing. Not with you or anybody else."

"Would you get on with your husband?" he had asked her.

"Yeah. I suppose."

"Then marry me, Geraldine Copeland."

She had laughed aloud, placing her clean hand on her narrow left hip. "Just because you want me to ride the Cyclone with you?"

"No," he had replied deeply. "Because I love you." Then he pulled out the toy ring he had found in his Cracker Jack box earlier that day and slid it onto her finger. "This until I can get the real thing next month. Don't lose it."

And she hadn't lost it—had kept that Cracker Jack gag prize even after he replaced the silver plastic ring and its gaudy diamond with a 14 quarter-carat diamond ring. She wished she still had the ring now to show it to Kasey. Perhaps if she saw it, was able to hold it and listen to the story once again, she'd understand what love was truly about with a special man. A man that Baseem was not.

Kasey cleared her throat deliberately. "Mom? I said I'm leaving. I'm going to Uncle Chitty's for a while."

The rocking ceased. Geraldine's face stiffened. Her eyes locked with Kasey's eyes. She folded her plentiful arms and tucked them beneath her bosom, thoroughly observing her daughter's lean physique. *Need some more meat on them bones. The child is just like her daddy was—tall and skinny. Lord, what is she going to do at Pearl and Chitty's house? Pearl don't even cook dinner anymore.*

Geraldine pursed her lips. "You're going to Chitty's so you can be available for that boy." She shook her head disapprovingly. "I don't understand this, Kasey. This is your home. Don't you have enough good sense to recognize Baseem is nothing short of a streetwise con man?"

"Mom, you need a life. You need to get out and date once in a while so that you won't be consumed with my dating life. I don't need or want you to be the same way with me that Grandpa was with you. All right?" It had tripped out her mouth unexpectedly. She didn't mean for it to come out, really. Or sound so brutal, so disrespectful. But good gracious, this was getting to be too much—her mother orchestrating her dating life like some fledgling maestro.

She couldn't really blame her mother's action. They say the child begets the ways of their parents sometimes. And true to form, her mother had inherited some of Grandpa Jason's— better known in the Englewood community as Colonel Jason Copeland—ways. Even after he divorced Grandma Clare and moved to Englewood, he continuously tugged the cords to Geraldine's life until he died. There was no way Kasey would allow her mother to do that to her. No way.

Geraldine turned away. There was no need for Kasey to say that. She did have a man at one time. A man named James Bullock. Didn't Kasey know? Hadn't she told her time and time again that no one could ever replace her James? Even Sylvester Peterson—her platonic male companion of many years that her father forced her to attend the military dance with all them years ago, and James's best friend—hadn't been able to meet the criteria before he permanently fizzled out of her life five years ago when he died of cancer.

A pang of guilt streaked through Kasey. "Mom . . ." She paused. "I didn't . . ."

Geraldine threw up her hand. "Don't. If that boy is so important to your life, if the way he seems to speak to you and treat you with regards to all these so-called ex-women friends don't seem to matter to you, just go on and get your things and leave."

Geraldine stood up and walked over to her bedroom door. Gripping the rustic doorknob, she peered into her daughter's face once more. "I'll be praying that the Lord will remove the soot from your eyes, Kasey Copeland," she promised before hurling the door shut.

Kasey sped her worn-out Hyundai down South Orange Avenue, clearly preoccupied by her mother's intended power play comment. *She'll pray for me?* Kasey thought. *Humph, I'll pray for her. After all these years of not having anyone special in her life since my daddy's death, I'll be praying that God sends her a new man. Her own man.*

There was no sign of "Red," Uncle Chitty's 1981 Cadillac

Seville, so Kasey parked the car in the narrow driveway. Friday night. They must be in Atlantic City, rolling the dice, Kasey assessed as she cautiously made her way up the rickety wooden steps. The weatherbeaten, two-family house was in need of something new, something lively.

Kasey slid her key in the double-door lock. As soon as she saved enough money from barbering, she'd get a real car, treat her mother to a cruise to the Caribbean Islands, purchase some new carpet for the house, and pay for a paint job for this peeling, pavilion, she vowed, stepping inside the house. Yup, she would do all this just as soon as she saved up enough money. Or as soon as Baseem paid her the money he promised her for assisting him with his business affairs.

The two-family house on Richeliu Terrace in a renamed section of Newark called Vailsburg was the worst-looking house in the neighborhood. At sixty-seven years old, her great-uncle Chitty was unable to get around like he used to on account of his rheumatism. The house was disturbingly dark. The musty smell assaulted Kasey's nostrils as she sniffed and recognized the odor as that of a pickle jar left open for too long. She flipped on the lights in the hallway to help guide her toward the spare bedroom in the back, where she dropped her bags on top of the twin bed. The hunt for the cordless phone began. She had to call Baseem and let him know of her whereabouts so he wouldn't worry.

"Yeah?" Baseem snapped, when he answered the phone.

"It's me. Just wanted to let you know I'm at my uncle's house in Vailsburg," Kasey told him.

There was a lengthy pause before the sounds of chewing and swallowing resumed.

"What you eating?" she said, breaking the silence between them.

"Crabs," Baseem answered abruptly. "So"—He continued smacking loudly—"You supposed to be my administrative assistant," he slurred. "What we going to do about them checks I got coming to your mom's house?"

Kasey's mouth dropped open. She had forgotten all about

the fact that Baseem was using her address for some of his business dealings. "You can have them sent here, I guess."

"You there permanently with old snaggletooth Chitty, or is this another one of you and your mom's temporary separations?"

Kasey paused to toss the question around for a moment. This was the second time this year she had left her mother's home to stay with Uncle Chitty. The first time had to do with Baseem, too. Suddenly she felt irritated. Yeah, so Uncle Chitty needed to make an appointment with the dentist. But how dare Baseem call her only uncle "snaggletooth."

"I'm not sure," she snapped.

"Well, you need to be sure. I've been waiting four months for three checks totaling over eighty thousand dollars to arrive at your mama's house on South Seventeenth Street. What's your mother going to do when you're not there to intercept the mail? You know that's seventy-five hundred dollars down the drain for you if I don't get them checks."

Kasey sighed. "I still don't see why the record companies can't send your checks to your house. Or why you don't get a PO box," Kasey told him.

"Because I had them sent to your house instead. All right?"

"All right, Baseem. Don't trip," Kasey responded, equally as threatening. "I'll swing by and check the mail tomorrow after I'm done at the shop, okay?"

"Well, I hope your mama got some kind of life planned during the day tomorrow. You know how busy you are on Saturdays. I suggest you take a lunch or something and get by there 'bout the time the postman is supposed to show up. You think you can do that for me, Kase?" he coyly cooed.

"Yeah, sure," Kasey aloofly replied. "I'll call you after I've checked the mail."

"Good enough. Hey, how's your cheek, baby?"

Kasey hesitated. She turned to peer into the film-coated hall mirror. Still discolored, she thought. "It's fine. A little swollen is all."

"What color was that car again?"

"Green, Baseem. It was green." She sighed. Hadn't they been over this a half dozen times?

"Drenna," Baseem mumbled. "I'll get her little butt squared away tonight. I got a good mind to send Kareema over her house to whup her behind."

"If I don't end up doing it first. No sense in getting your baby sister involved." Kasey let out a noisy sigh. "Really, Baseem. First all four of my tires are flattened, then my windshield wipers get snapped off, then two dozen or more eggs smeared all over the hood, and now this." She sighed even louder. "It's on my damn nerves."

"Chill, baby. I'll take care of it. *'Aight?*"

"Yeah, yeah. Anyway . . ." She paused. "I'm beat down. I'll buzz you tomorrow."

"You better," he told her before hanging up the phone in her ear.

Baseem bit into a crab leg, sucking on the salty juice, pondering. He had to get control of his ex-girlfriends before somebody got seriously jammed-up.

2

Saturday

"Not too high, Kasey," the robust brother sitting in her barber chair instructed. "Just a little on the side and a little higher on the top."

"Like normal, Roderick," Kasey reminded him as she glided the Wahl clippers down toward his ear. After engaging Roderick's continuous conversation, Kasey used the duster brush to clear away any lingering hairs from the back of his neck and set him free.

Only twenty minutes between the last customer, Roderick, and fifteen dollars. Stuffing the dollar bills into the tan waist apron tied around her blue jeans, she glanced up at the clock: 12:08 P.M. The postman was due to arrive at her mother's house anytime. She thought about phoning Geraldine under some false pretense but quickly erased that idea. Besides, she wasn't up for more lecturing, and that's exactly what would greet her on the other end of the phone had she dialed the digits.

More than likely, Baseem would either page her or stop by the shop if he didn't hear from her in the next couple of hours. She'd be sure to get by the house before two thirty. Even though such a trip across town from Central Avenue to South Seventeenth Street would surely toss a few bucks into the hands of the other two barbers who rented their space from her. She'd make up the lost money once Baseem paid her for helping him with the record business stuff he so evasively avoided discussing.

"Next up," Kasey called out, flinging the black and gray speckled, polyester-blended cape a few times.

"How you doing today?" she asked the tall, skinny man before she snapped the cape around his neck.

"Fine, thank you," he muttered, slowly taking a look at her left hand. "Nice ring. That must have cost him some pretty dollars."

Kasey looked down at the pear-shaped two-carat diamond and smiled. "Yes," she said. "I suppose it did." But then, did it really? Baseem was so secretive about his business. So aloof about the people he dealt with that it wouldn't be unlike Baseem to have picked it up hot from some booster.

"What you having today, uh . . ." she trailed off, trying to recall his name.

"Jay," the late fortyish man replied with a smile and piercing black eyes. "Whatever you think would be good."

Kasey spun him around in the blue chair with the chrome armrest until he faced the mirror. She gazed at the hardened face reflected before her. Other than his piercing black eyes that seemed to tuck away a great deal of pain, Jay appeared to be a nice, sane brother.

"This is only your third time in my chair. I don't have a feel for your hair and face yet. Give me some hints?" She smiled.

Jay paused purposely, staring back at Kasey through the oval mirror. "What happened to your face?"

Kasey wanted to look away but didn't. "Flying object," she replied.

"Flying object, you say? Like what?"

"An apple."

"An apple," Jay enunciated slowly. "An accident or purposely?"

"Accident."

"Really?" Jay said smartly. "I didn't think apples could be that cruel unless some pompous, egotistical maniac was the one hurling it."

"Nobody said anything about hurling anything, Jay," Kasey said tersely.

"Um-hmm."

Kasey's cheeks grew warm. Small wet circles began to surface beneath the arms of her powder blue T-shirt. Working too hard, she determined silently, picking up the shears. "Perhaps a nice, clean, sedate cut might satisfy you. Tone down the height a little," she said, ignoring his last remark.

Kasey began with the shears, trimming down the thick salt-and-pepper strands to perfection. She snapped on the clippers just as Baseem walked through the door.

"Kasey," Baseem greeted in a thunderous tone from his six-three, two-hundred-twenty-pound physique, his smooth, chocolate bald head playing host to the black futuristic sunglasses sitting on top. "Can I speak with you for a minute?" His statement was more of an order than a question.

Kasey slung a handful of braids across her right shoulder. "In a second, babe. Let me finish with this customer first."

Baseem walked toward her and said, "I just need a second." Then he looked down at Jay, who was staring at him through the mirror. "You don't mind, do you, brother?" Baseem asked Jay.

"Well . . ." Jay grinned. "Actually I do. I have an important engagement in a few minutes," he said, looking down at his watch. "She said it'll be just a few more minutes. Do you mind?" Jay asked.

Kasey cut a glare at her customer, remaining silently amazed. Seemed like the earth stopped moving for just that instant. Oh, Lord, she thought, glancing at Baseem. Hopefully he wouldn't turn this into a big deal. What was a few more minutes? Baseem could wait. The noise in the shop had practically ceased. The ten or so customers cramped in Chitty's seven-hundred-square-foot shop sat in awe of Jay's response to Baseem.

Baseem pulled his glasses from atop his head and handed

them to Rex, his partner, otherwise referred to as his bodyguard. Baseem smiled a lazy grin, exposing his two capped gold teeth, as he placed his hand on the back of Jay's chair. He leaned down toward him.

"Excuse me, Mr. um . . ." Baseem hesitated, waiting for this stranger, who obviously was unfamiliar with his reputation, to introduce himself.

Jay locked eyes with Baseem. Calmly and in a whispered tone, he replied, "Jay."

"Well, now, Jay," Baseem was saying. "Let me just explain it this way. I have some real important business to discuss with the lady here. Like I was saying to you earlier, it should only be about three or four minutes. That shouldn't be a real problem for you, should it?"

Jay pressed his long feet down on the ground, using them to spin the barber chair around. He stood up, unfastened the cape from around his neck, and handed it to Kasey. Obviously Baseem was threatening him.

"Jay," Kasey said, "if you just give me a second, I'll finish you up and have you out of here in no time. You can't leave looking like that. I still have to trim and fade the back. Give me five minutes tops. Or I can have Tony finish you off. You just can't leave with your head all tore up like that. It's bad for Chitty's reputation." She chuckled nervously, looking up at him. Gosh, he was skinny as a rail, she thought, waiting for his reply.

Jay smiled. "No offense, but I'd rather that you cut my hair." He reached down and grabbed his torn leather duffel bag. "Don't worry about it, Kasey. Apparently you and the owner, Chitty, here have some things to discuss. I'll come back on Monday. You may finish me up then. My head is not as bad as it was when I walked in." He handed Kasey a ten dollar bill.

Kasey put her hands up, forming a "keep it" gesture. "I'm closed on Mondays. And just so you'll know, I'm the owner of this shop. Chitty is my uncle." It bothered her that Jay presumed Baseem was the owner.

"I see," Jay said with a slight bow of the head before tucking the money back in his pocket. "I'll see you on Tuesday," he told her before turning toward Baseem. "She is here on Tuesdays, right?" he asked Baseem.

"That's what the lady said," Baseem snapped. "If she ain't, Tony or Larry will be here. You can go to one of them," he said, nodding his head toward the other two barbers. "That's if you're really here to get your hair cut."

Jay ignored Baseem. He stole a peek at Kasey's ring finger again. "Very well," Jay said, tossing his duffel bag across his shoulder. "You have a nice evening, Ms. Kasey. And you all be safe," he cautioned Baseem and Rex before leaving the shop.

Baseem walked over to the glass door and watched Jay walk down the block for a few seconds before turning to face Kasey again. Something strange about that brother he didn't like—couldn't get a handle on.

"Let's go to the back," Baseem told Kasey, leading the way past the other two barbers and the stunned customers.

"Who was that character?" Baseem asked, once the back door was closed.

"Just another customer." Kasey shrugged.

"I don't want him in your chair no more. Give him to Tony or Larry. But you leave him alone."

Kasey slung her braids over her shoulder and threw a furrowed brow at Baseem. If he was so bad, he should have said all this stuff in front of Jay. Why didn't he tell Jay flat out that he didn't want him sitting in her chair anymore?

Baseem knew he struck a nerve with Kasey when she refused to acknowledge his demand. "Okay, Kase," he sighed deeply. "My bag. This here is your operation. Handle your business. I just got a bad vibe 'bout that dude is all. He's up to something, babe. I know it. Ain't like I got something to be real worried about," he said. "Just be careful what you say to folks in your chair, all right?"

"Careful what I say? All I can say is that we're scheduled to get married in the fall." She grinned. "And that you're managing some rap groups I ain't never heard no music by."

"Funny," Baseem said. "Real funny. Did you go by your mom's yet?"

"Not yet. I was planning to slip out of here just as soon as I finished Jay and Benny. Now that Jay is gone. I can trim Benny real quick and then stop by Mom's."

"Forget Benny for now. We need to take a quick ride to your mother's house and check the mail."

"I can't just leave my customers for forty minutes and expect to keep them," she said tartly.

"You can't afford not to. Come on, Kasey," Baseem said, guiding her by the arm toward the exit door.

"I don't see why you're so down in spirit, Geraldine," Amy, Geraldine's best friend, told her before bringing the silver Mazda RX-7 to a halt at the top of the hill. "Kasey is grown. If the bed she chooses has Baseem in it, then she'll just have to lie in it." Amy adjusted the side mirrors a second time before reaching the S-curves on South Orange Avenue. "I hate these darn curves. That's why I always end up shopping at Menlo Park Mall instead of Livingston. Too many darn curves," she said, whipping the car around the bend.

"We could have gone to Menlo Park," Geraldine mumbled as she crouched her body farther back into the leather seat. "Can you slow down a little, Amy? That concrete divider is looking a bit close."

"There you go, Gerry. Always ready to clam up. Relax. Do you know what that means?" Amy crunched on the pieces of peppermint she had in her mouth. "Look at all these cars," Amy sighed. "Shouldn't people be home cleaning their houses on a Saturday afternoon instead of traipsing off to the mall?"

Geraldine laughed. The nerve of Amy making such a statement when she hadn't even made her bed this morning. She glanced over at her co-worker and best friend, a single, childless forty-three-year-old woman sporting a new honey blond color for the spring season. "Amy, I still can't get used to that blond color on you. It's so, so . . ." Geraldine took a moment to search for the right word.

"European," Amy cut in. "Yeah, yeah, I know. But see, that's the difference between you and me. I don't care what other people say about a cocoa-brown sister, like me, dyeing my hair blond." Amy laughed wickedly. "That's your only problem, Gerry. You should try not caring for a change."

"What? And dye my hair bright yellow to show folks I don't care? I'll take a pass, thank you very much," Geraldine said dismissively.

"Who knows. Stepping off the deep end every now and then might do you some good. It ain't like Colonel Jason is still with us to make you question your decision, right?"

Geraldine refused the temptation to respond, to lash out and blaspheme a man who was no longer alive to defend his guilt or innocence. The thought of having allowed her father to control her life still angered her. She turned to face the window, resting her head against the cool glass. Mature and lush green trees, lining the colossal homes with the half-acre manicured lawns, occupied her view.

"Sorry, Gerry," Amy said, guiding the sports car around more curves. "I didn't mean anything disrespectful. Really."

"It's fine, Amy. I'm learning to overcome most of the things my father did."

"Like being the man solely responsible for breaking you and James up?" Amy pushed some.

"Yeah. Especially that. I mean all this time I thought James had just been one of the unfortunate college-bound students tangled up by the draft. I would have never thought my father was responsible for having James's name pulled. Sending James over there like that, knowing we were engaged to be married. And then the kids . . ." she trailed off. "That was wrong, Amy."

Amy reached over and patted Geraldine on the hand. "It was, Gerry, but your dad had no idea that you were pregnant. All he could see was that James wasn't good enough for his little girl. That you were too young to be married to a man with no supposed career path."

Geraldine withdrew her hand suddenly. "I don't really want to go through all this, Amy. You've known me and my father for over fifteen years. You knew how controlling he was. How difficult it was for me to breathe without worrying about him correcting me on that.

"And to think, it took all these years, and for my father to be on his deathbed, to finally admit that he sent James to Vietnam on purpose. Dead or not, Amy, it still hurts me to know my father could be so damn hateful," Geraldine spouted.

Amy drove the rest of the way in silence. Just before reaching the signs for the mall, she looked over toward Geraldine and smiled. "I know what you need, Gerry. You need to pack some things and fly to D.C. with me for Mother's Day weekend. My cousin Daniel, who owns a computer business in Texas, will be visiting my grandmother in D.C. for Mother's Day. I already told him about you." Amy snickered.

"You what?" Geraldine gasped. "You did not! Why? How do I let you continue to embarrass me like this? Honestly, Amy, you should own one of them matchmaking businesses."

"So I take that as a yes?" Amy asked, pulling into the mall parking lot.

"Fly to D.C. for Mother's Day with you? I have to work the Saturday before."

"What shift?"

"I believe the one to nine P.M. shift."

"We'll catch a later flight then."

"Oh, I don't know about this, Amy."

"What is there not to know? You said you and Kasey aren't on good terms. And you agreed to start getting a life for yourself, right? What better way to begin your new life than to fly with me down to the nation's capital and meet my cousin Daniel? He's sure eager to meet you," Amy told her while squeezing into a tight parking space.

Geraldine smiled bashfully. She did promise her best friend that she would make an attempt to stay out of Kasey's business and attend to some of her own. Perhaps D.C. and Daniel weren't such a bad combination. She stepped out of the car, closing the door behind her. She hunched her shoulders upward, then slowly nodded her head in the affirmative.

"Good. I'll call my travel agent on Monday and set it up,"

Amy said, meeting Geraldine at the front of the car. "Besides . . ." Amy hesitated as she jogged across the crosswalk, leaving Geraldine to wait for the oncoming car. "I already gave Daniel your phone number."

3

Tuesday

Kasey reached down and picked up the daily newspaper left in front of the shop before opening the door. She flipped on the overhead fluorescent tube lights and locked the door behind her. In an hour or so, she would draw open the blinds and welcome the much needed natural light. Right now would be way too soon. It was Tuesday, which meant the shop wouldn't swing its doors wide open until 10 A.M. And the Omega watch Baseem had given her for Valentine's Day read 8:40 A.M.

Had she returned on Saturday afternoon, after leaving the shop with Baseem, she wouldn't be standing in the shop so early. But she had business to take care of before the other two barbers arrived. She unlocked her workspace and tossed her Doone & Burke bag and leather satchel in the cabinet before turning on the stereo. Flutist Phillip Bent whistled through the floor-model speakers while Kasey bee-bopped through the squared shop, watering her plants.

Twenty minutes into tidying the waiting area, Kasey heard the knocking sound on the front glass door. Instinctively she glanced down at her watch. 9:05. Surely the person on the

opposite side of the door could read: HOURS — TUESDAY — 10:00
A.M. She peeked around the corner, noticing the back of a tall
masculine figure.

Recognizing the person, who seemed to have no regard for
her posted business hours, Kasey turned down the volume to
the stereo, grabbed the keys off the counter, and unlocked the
door.

"The sign says ten o'clock, Jay," Kasey said tartly. She
stood with her body wedged between the door and the frame.

"I realize that, Kasey. But I was hoping to be the first one
in and the first one out." Jay smiled broadly. "If this is a bad
time, I can come back in, let's see . . ." He paused to look at
his watch. "Fifty minutes if you promise to hold my space for
me."

Kasey studied his lanky body for a few seconds. Didn't this
man know that barbers were not in high demand on Tuesdays?
And didn't someone tell him that Cache pants and Docksiders
were passé? She stepped aside to let him in. Earth, Wind &
Fire's "Love's Holiday" played in the background.

"Seems like you're just getting settled in here good yourself," Jay said, standing next to Kasey's chair.

Kasey nodded in agreement and motioned with a wave for
Jay to have a seat in her chair. She snapped the cape in the air
a few times before clipping it behind his neck. Might as well
open the blinds, she thought, walking over to the large front
windows that faced Central Avenue and Baxter Terrace Apartments.

"There, much better," she mumbled under her breath at the
sudden burst of natural light. Turning to walk back to her
station, she noticed Jay staring at the pictures of Bernard King
taped to the top corner of her station mirror.

"Who's the big fan?" Jay asked, lowering his head to the
directional movement of her hand.

"My brother was. He died three years ago," she told him.

Jay's head sprang up. He caught a glimpse of Kasey's face
reflecting in the mirror. "How?"

Kasey refused to maintain Jay's stare—diverting her attention instead to the black-and-white photo of the talented basket-

ball star who seemed forgotten by the very fans that cheered him on. Much like how Kenny had seemed to be forgotten in the neighborhood. It hurt too bad to dredge up all that stuff.

"He was run over by some kids in a stolen car," she finally blurted out, surprising herself as she said it.

"Jesus Christ," Jay murmured, lowering his head as if he might go into mourning. The morning breeze rustled the blinds. "So many of our young brothers are leaving this world." He let out a deep breath.

Kasey opted to change the subject. The last thing she wanted to do was get all emotional. "Your hair grew back over the weekend, I see." She ran her hand through the top of his head. "What you using? Miracle Grow?"

Jay laughed. "No. But I need to be using something that will get rid of all this gray."

"Naw, Jay . . ." Kasey paused to examine his hair some more. "Don't go covering up all that wisdom." She picked up the shears.

"Wisdom? More like worrying."

Kasey eased the shears across the top of his head. *Clip. Clip. Clip. Clip.* "Worrying? What you have to be worried about?"

"Things. My life."

"Well, maybe you shouldn't worry so much. Let things just take their natural course."

Jay raised his eyebrows in agreement, careful not to move his head while Kasey used the clippers to further fade the top of his hair. "So, is your bullying boyfriend at work this morning?"

Kasey cut off the clippers. Why would he be asking about Baseem's whereabouts? The phone rang unexpectedly, startling her.

"Chitty's," Kasey said after placing the receiver to her ear.

"Kasey? Kasey, it's Baseem—can you hear me?"

"Barely. Where are you?"

"I'm at the studio. Anything come in the mail yet?"

"No," she huffed. "Not since you asked me the same question yesterday morning."

"You going by your mom's later today, right?"

"Yes, Baseem. Quit worrying," she said with a slight attitude. "How's the weather in Atlanta?"

"Hey, I hope nobody's in the shop with you giving out all my business and whereabouts."

Kasey looked over at Jay, who was staring her right dab in the mouth. "No. Just us."

"Good," Baseem said. "I should be home Friday or Saturday night. This group needs a little more work than I thought. I'll call you later tonight or tomorrow. Be sure to check the mail while I'm gone, Kasey."

"You be sure you're back by Saturday afternoon. Don't forget we have that appointment with the caterers and then the real-estate broker for the condo."

"Yeah, okay. Let me give you a number to reach me in case the money comes in. Ready?"

Kasey took down the number and stuffed it in her back pocket. She picked up the clippers and continued to line Jay's head.

"I assume Baseem is your boyfriend?" Jay asked.

"Fiancé," Kasey coolly replied.

"Is that his real name?"

"Do you want me to trim your mustache for you?"

"Sure. Is it a religious thing or something?"

"What?" Kasey asked.

"Your boyfriend using the name, Baseem. Is it a religious thing?"

"Fiancé. No . . ." Kasey sighed. She was really beginning to lose her patience with Jay. "Tell me something, Jay," she said, lifting his head up so he could peer into the mirror. "Are you married? Got any kids?"

Jay tilted his head sideways and honed in on his clean haircut. Nice attempt to change the subject, he thought, while turning his head to the left, then to the right, to examine the sides. "I don't think I've met anyone who doesn't have kids. You?" he said, strategically steering her away from his personal life.

Kasey laughed. "There are some people in the world who don't have kids. Like me, for instance."

"Really? Doesn't your mother want grandchildren?"

"I'm sure she would be ecstatic to have another extension of herself to boss around," Kasey said.

Jay smiled. "Does she want you to have kids with Baseem?"

Kasey's face soured. She unsnapped the cape and removed it from around Jay's neck, then let out a tiring breath. "What's with all the questions, Jay? You got some other reason for being here besides getting your hair cut?"

"Is that what your boyfriend told you?" Jay pushed a little.

"Fiancé. Maybe, maybe not. But I find it strange that you should be so interested in our business." She grabbed the broom and swept the strands of hair to the end corner of her station. "For all I know, you could be some crazed fool. Or . . ."

"An undercover DEA or FBI agent," Jay said, completing her sentence before rising from the chair.

"Exactly," Kasey said, eyeing him suspiciously.

"You've got something you should be worried about?" Jay asked, pulling out his wallet and handing Kasey fifteen dollars—twelve dollars for the cut and a three dollar tip.

Jay watched her tuck the money into her front jeans pockets. They were so tight, he wondered how she was able to squeeze anything else in them besides her body. He gave a quarter-moon grin, picked up the newspaper he hadn't had the opportunity to read, and headed for the front door.

"Well, are you?" Kasey called out to the back of him.

"Am I what, Ms. Kasey?"

"An FBI or DEA agent?" she anxiously asked.

Slowly he turned to face her, leaving one hand on the handle of the door. God, she was a beautiful child. Too bad she's all mixed up about picking the right man, he summarized silently. Studying her pose thoroughly, he answered, "Perhaps, Ms. Copeland. Perhaps." With that, he was out the door and a good part way down the block.

Kasey fell back against her workspace, stunned. *Ms. Copeland? Who? How did he know my last name?* Her heart flipped into overdrive, pounding louder with each breath as she reached into her back pocket and pulled out the pink piece of paper she had jotted Baseem's phone number on. Trembling, she picked up the telephone. *Ms. Copeland? Lord, Baseem, I sure hope you're not involved in no mess.*

Geraldine coasted the old, rust-riddled burgundy Oldsmobile Cutlass up Bergen Street before making a left onto Lyons Avenue. Wearied from pulling a twelve-hour shift, the only thing she could muster up enough energy to do was take a hot shower. There was no way she'd be able to engage in a phone conversation with a complete stranger—even if he was Amy's cousin. She looked at the cracked clock on her dash, which read 7:20 P.M. Daniel had rescheduled and promised to phone her at eight fifteen tonight.

Lord have mercy, Geraldine sighed. Why in heaven's name did she agree to speak with him again? Should have just told him that she'd be working till eleven every night for the next year, she thought, stopping for the red light. This way, she wouldn't have to talk to him ever. Maybe she could convince Daniel that she was asleep, like she had last night. Perhaps even pretend like she had worked an extra shift and was too tired to hold a conversation. He'd never know the difference. Unless, of course, that bigmouth Amy told him otherwise. Or worse yet, gave him her work phone number.

This light is way too long, she thought, glancing over at the corner liquor store, which was cramped with folks waiting in line to play the Pick-it. Once the light turned green, Geraldine eased through the cross street, carefully awaiting any last-minute runners of the amber light. Her eight-year-old car had finally decided to accelerate just as a teenaged boy approached her with a towel in one hand and a Windex bottle in the other.

Well, at least he's willing to work for an honest living, she thought. Gliding up South Orange Avenue, she recognized the familiar four-by-four coasting alongside of her. Some rapper's lyrics blared from the deep hunter-green vehicle. She'd know that ugly truck anywhere. Baseem or one of his siblings—she was pretty sure of it, despite the dark-tinted windows. She wanted to give him a disapproving scowl, but he or whoever it was behind the wheel, peeled off suddenly, wickedly rounding a narrow street corner.

"Street thug," she murmured aloud. Lord, she sure hoped Kasey would get Baseem out of her system before the wedding. Geraldine felt the nagging urge to react like her own father might have in a situation like this. The first thing the Colonel would have done was flat-out refuse to attend the wedding—and if that failed, he would threaten to disown her.

Geraldine parked the beat-up but faithfully reliable Oldsmobile in front of the house, taking a second to acknowledge her neighbor across the street with a hand wave. Grabbing the bundle of mail out of the black iron mailbox, she slowly began her ascent up the rickety steps. She heard the telephone's faint ringing as she stuck her key into the deadbolt.

Thinking that in her attempt to outsmart Daniel with her ploy to be asleep last night, she might not have gotten the correct time when he was scheduled to return the call, she became surprisingly anxious. "Come on," she fussed, jiggling the crooked key in the hole. Once she slung open the door, she seized up the cordless telephone on the fourth ring.

"Hello," she breathlessly answered. She tossed her purse and the mail on the dinette table.

"Mom?" Kasey questioned.

Geraldine's eyes rolled to the back of her head. Perhaps she was a little more excited than she wanted to admit about Daniel's arriving phone call. She walked back to the front door and slammed it shut, turning the top lock till she heard the click.

"Yes," Geraldine said, taking a moment to catch her breath.

"Is everything okay? You sound out of breath."

"The phone was ringing when I walked in. That's all," she said, taking a seat on the dinette chair.

"Gosh," Kasey sighed. "Sounded like you were having an asthma attack or something. Hey, Mom, anything come in the mail for me?"

"Why? You expecting more of that bridal junk mail?" Geraldine rummaged through the bundle of mail while she talked.

Kasey kept quiet, trying to curtail the butterflies buzzing

around in the pit of her stomach. God, she sure hoped Baseem's checks didn't arrive today. She'd have to make more of an effort to get by and intercept the mail during the day. She could hear her mother shuffling through the mail.

"Nothing but your Visa bill, phone bill, some magazines, and some other junk mail," Geraldine told her, tossing the bundle onto the table again.

"How's Uncle Chitty and Pearl doing?" Geraldine kicked off the white shoes with the scuffed wedge heels. She ran her feet back and forth across the carpet several times, a ritual she'd acquired during the last fifteen years.

"They're fine. Uncle Chitty won five hundred dollars in Atlantic City this past weekend. Said he was going to use the money to get the house painted." Kasey laughed.

"Shh, he's been getting that house painted about ten times now. Tell him it's time to use something else." Geraldine snickered. It was easy for her and Kasey to laugh—slip back into their comfort zone. But then there was Baseem and all his women and Kasey's blindness to it all. Geraldine's face tightened.

"So when you planning to pick up the rest of your things?" Kasey sighed loudly. "This weekend, I guess."

"Then I'll guess I'll see you on Saturday. If I'm here," Geraldine said.

"Fine," Kasey told her. "Talk to you then."

"Oh, before I forget . . ." Geraldine paused as she flipped through the latest issue of *Jet* magazine. "I'm going to D.C. with Amy for Mother's Day."

"D.C.? Why?" Kasey was shocked.

"Never you mind. Like you said to me before, it's high time I get some business of my own. Just thought I'd let you know."

The big hand on the grandfather clock was approaching the ten. *Just a few more minutes before Daniel's phone call, better use the bathroom real quick and grab something to drink.* "Look, Kasey I've gotta go. I'll see you Saturday. Be careful, honey."

* * *

Kasey hung up the telephone, befuddled. She leaned back on the rose-colored crushed velvet sofa, thinking. *For the past twenty-something years, we always spent that special day together. Now out of the blue she wants to push me to the side to spend Mother's Day with Amy? Fine then.*

After evaluating her reaction to her mother's news, Kasey realized that the truth of the matter was that her feelings were hurt. How could she choose to go to D.C. on Mother's Day? On the day that Kenny died? On the day that mothers and daughters are supposed to bond together? Probably just another one of her strong-arm maneuvers to pressure me into dumping Baseem, Kasey thought.

"Humph," she exclaimed aloud, picking up an old issue of *Ebony* magazine. She flipped through the magazine mindlessly. Yeah, well, Grandpa Jason might have been able to manipulate and taint your life, Mom, but I won't let you do it to me.

Geraldine hustled through the house, trying to prepare herself for the much anticipated phone call. She had just a few more minutes before Daniel's call. That's if he was a prompt man, she thought, washing her hands for the thirtieth time today. She reached for the plastic salad bowl and took it out of the refrigerator. She had to admit that she hadn't felt this stirred by a man's attention since that first time James Bullock had asked for her phone number during her junior year in high school, some twenty-plus years ago.

She crunched on a piece of cucumber. Sylvester had been serving as her convenient household handyman, best friend, and the kids' godfather for nearly two decades. He had wanted more, she knew. But no way could she ever forsake James in that way. Sylvester and James were best friends. A flood of treasured emotions engulfed her. The memory of being maneuvered by fear from her father's hand, more so than her proclaimed undying love for James, and then the death of her only

172   *Monique Gilmore*

son were all contributing reasons for the despondent way she often felt about herself.

The phone rang a second time. Geraldine sucked in a deep breath and let it flow out slowly. She stretched across her double bed, which was scattered with lots of stuffed animals, and picked up the telephone.

"Hello," she said in a perky tone.

"Good evening, Geraldine. It's Daniel. Did I wake you again?"

"Oh, no," she softly replied. "I was getting comfortable is all."

"Another stressful day at work?"

"Just the usual stuff: sick children, irresponsible staff members, and irate patients full of choice expletives." She laughed nervously.

"I always told Amy that it takes a special person to hold a career as a nurse, especially in the emergency room. Amy tells me you've been patching wounds and reviving hearts for as long as she. Are you as tired as Amy claims to be?"

Geraldine dug her left elbow into the green down comforter for support before resting her head in her hand. Tired? She thought of toying with the meaning of the word before replying. Heck, yes. She was sick and tired. Tired of sometimes dealing with ignorant family members of patients and tired of all the unimaginable bloody injuries. She let out a small sigh and replied, "Yes, I suppose you could say I'm suffering from burn-out."

"More reason for you to get away," Daniel told her. His voice took on a softer tone, engendering warmth and sincerity. "Enjoy a weekend away from the ambulance sirens and your familiar city streets."

Geraldine blushed. "You're sure right about escaping the flashing red lights and the constant double glass sliding doors. But then it would be just my chance the plane crashes, and I end up one of the passengers being rushed through familiar city streets with a piercing siren wailing above me."

"Now don't go jinxing yourself, Geraldine. We wouldn't

want anything like that to happen to you, so think positive,"
he teased.

"Oh, I do think positive as long as my body stays beneath
the clouds and not in or above them. I'm scared to death of
flying. I've been on two airplanes my whole life and got sick
both times."

"That's too bad about the illness part. But it's a short flight,
so hopefully you'll be okay."

"Short or not," Geraldine said shakily, "I'm still going to
be up in the air on a plane."

"Well, just remember, statistics support that flying is still
far more safe than driving. I mean, think about it ..." He
paused. "You're an emergency room nurse. How many people
have you treated from plane accidents?"

Geraldine pondered his question for a few moments. In all
her years of bustling around Beth Israel Hospital's emergency
room, she could honestly say that she had never treated anyone
from a plane accident.

"This is true," she reluctantly yielded. Regardless of all that
mumbo-jumbo statistical stuff, she still didn't like flying. Call
it paranoia or simple foolishness, flying was for the birds. "Still,
some people have a fear of water or heights—my phobia has
to do with large man-made machines soaring through the air."

"Humph, we're going to have to do something about that,"
Daniel flirted. "All I know is that I'm looking forward to
making your acquaintance in person. Amy speaks so highly of
you all the time. Actually I'm surprised we haven't met already.
But that will all change, come eleven days or so."

Geraldine sat in the middle of her bed, thinking, as she
wrapped her hair around the pink sponge rollers. She hadn't
felt this invigorated in a long while. Daniel's words seemed so
genuine—so caring. She'd imagined he'd be tall and built but
not rock solid like a high school boy.

"Eleven days or so," she repeated aloud with a girlish tickle
in her tummy. Time sure takes off the older you get, she thought,
clipping the last roller in place before tying a teal silk scarf

around her head. She wondered if she ate nothing but boiled eggs and toast for breakfast, salads and two quarts of water for lunch, baked chicken and fish with fresh vegetables for dinner, and walked around the hospital every day during lunch for the next ten days, would she lose ten or twelve pounds?

She looked over at the picture of her and James hanging on the dingy wallpaper. Would Daniel care about her oversized hips and behind? Would he be turned off by her bounteous breasts? Would he hold it against her that she no longer had a twenty-six inch waist or tight thighs like the days of her youth?

Geraldine closed her eyes, attempting to imagine what James would have thought about her body if he were here with her now. She sucked her teeth unconsciously. Makes no difference now anyway what James would have thought because he's no longer here. However Daniel was another story. A story that would hopefully and miraculously end with a resuscitated dying woman.

4

Friday

Geraldine Copeland propped an ashy elbow atop the speckled linoleum counter. Things were fairly quiet this evening, even had enough time to listen to a little music. She stood at the nurses' station, bobbing her head to some old fuzzy tune crackling from the boom-box. Aretha Franklin's "Look Into Your Heart."

Geraldine sang aloud, swinging her hips from side to side. It was Friday, and she had managed to finagle a weekend off and become like the rest of America and sleep in tomorrow. That's if Kasey didn't come to the house to retrieve some of her things too early. She felt weird on the inside for some strange reason. Well, actually she knew the reason, and his name started with *D*.

Geraldine could hear Amy's loud, ever moving mouth flapping in the near distance. Why her best friend always had to be the center of attention she had yet to figure. Although she had to admit she appreciated Amy's forwardness, which definitely complemented and challenged her own introverted ways. Geraldine grinned, turning to face Amy, who was now standing some two feet away and fussing with one of the emergency room doctors.

These new self-appointed gods in charge around here are about to cause me to blaspheme and be sent straight to hell— the unemployment line,'' Amy said, shaking her head. She had on a pale pink top with the matching pants and the white nurses' shoes. "I don't know why I can't just find me a millionaire in Atlantic City and become his housewife,'' she said, attempting to constrain a yawn. "Even somebody's mistress would be better than this.''

Geraldine laughed. "Amy, you can be real funny sometimes. You know good and well you don't mean that. We'll be in the break room,'' she told the desk clerk.

Geraldine pulled her arm and led her away. "Let's take five and get something to drink.''

"This patient is on her way out anyway,'' Amy said, tossing the file she had tucked under her arm onto the desk.

"Amy,'' Geraldine gasped. "That's cruel.'' She opened the door to the nurses' break room. A room with just two small round tables, a worn and wobbly sofa with wooden legs, and a couple of tweed-backed chairs.

"Whatever.'' Amy shrugged. "What's up with you swinging them hips earlier? You excited about something,'' Amy sang playfully.

"No,'' Geraldine responded quickly. "I was enjoying the song is all.'' She walked over to the coffeepot and poured herself a half cup.

"Um-hmm,'' Amy said with a speculative brow. "You were probably enjoying a fantasy of finally having your body by a strong man's hand after six hundred years of celibacy.'' Amy threw her head back and let out a wild laugh.

Geraldine rolled her eyes hard, scolding Amy with a tight-lipped stare. "You're a pervert, Amy Cherell Carter. I'm going to pray for your salvation,'' she joked.

Amy snickered some more, then dropped down on the sofa. "I hear Daniel is real excited to meet you. He's making all sorts of preparations for the weekend.'' Amy eyed Geraldine wearily. All joking aside, she really did hope and even pray that

Geraldine and her cousin Daniel would make a love connection. Especially since Geraldine hadn't been with a man in years.

Geraldine sat down across from Amy in a tweed chair. Her face had drooped downward, her eyes fixating on some inanimate object. She let out a deep sigh. Daniel was the person partly responsible for the bubbling feeling. But then there was the other feeling—a feeling of loss and emptiness—a feeling of guilt.

It had been so many years since she had lost the love of her life. Even though she and James had never officially made it to the altar, they had sworn before God—had made their vows to him one night on their knees—had pleaded love, life, and happiness till death do them part more than twenty years ago.

She heard Amy repeat her name a second time, this time louder, before she pulled her mind away. Geraldine looked up, coming face to face with Amy's.

"Yes," Geraldine replied.

"What mental trip did you just come back from?"

She hated that her best friend knew her so well. It was a pain in the neck sometimes. Geraldine shrugged her shoulders, then took a sip of coffee.

"*Elchk*. How disgusting," Geraldine said, spitting the remainder part of her sip into the cup.

"How ladylike," Amy said, turning up her nose. "You going to tell me why the long, agonizing face—or am I going to have to manipulate it out of you?"

Geraldine hesitated. Mainly because she wasn't sure if she wanted to deal with Amy's so-called pep talk, if she confessed to her that she was scared about meeting Daniel.

"I'm not sure about meeting Daniel or going to D.C. next weekend," Geraldine spouted out.

"What? You have got to be kidding me, Gerry. After all the feigning I did to get next Saturday off for you so that we can leave Friday night right after our shift? You have to go. That's all there is to it."

Geraldine frowned. "What lie did you concoct for scheduling in order that I would have next Saturday off?" She could feel her cheeks growing warm. Leave it to Ms. Busybody to work things to her liking. "Well?" Geraldine said after a few minutes of silence.

"Never mind all that. What matters is that we get to Newark Airport by ten fifty P.M. next Friday," Amy reminded her. "What's with you, Geraldine? Are you happy being alone and bored and tucked away from the world?" she said, flailing her arms about. "This is bull manure. Plain and simple. No, better yet, I bet this has to do with a dead man of more than twenty years. Get a clue, Geraldine Copeland. James Bullock is dead, been dead, still dead, going to still be dead when you're dead." Amy's voice was strident and strong, rising a few falsettos with each word. "You going to have to do better if you plan on standing me up, that's all I've got to say."

"Amy," Geraldine sighed, then continued, "I'm only trying to share with you how I feel. It feels weird, is all I'm trying to say. I never said it had anything to do with James, okay?" Although truth be told, it had a lot to do with James and being away from Kasey on Mother's Day. "I mean, Daniel seems like a nice man. And yes, I do have visions of strong hugs and soft kisses. But . . ." She hesitated. "I'm just not sure. I need to be sure, need a sign from God that I can move forward. That's all. You know how I am, Amy. You of all people should understand me." Her voice was weak and feeble.

Amy shook her head, then walked toward the door. The large metal door with the silver French handle flew open. On the opposite side of the door stood a human being, no doubt, hidden by a cascading bouquet of colorful flowers.

Geraldine stood up and walked toward Amy. Amy glanced at Geraldine and shrugged her shoulders. "Beautiful flowers," Amy said loudly, as if her speaking loud would compensate for the fact that she couldn't see the delivery person's face. "I think you have the wrong room. This is the nurses' break room. Check with the front desk."

"I did," the girlish voice responded. "They told me ya'll was in here."

"Who was in here?" Geraldine asked.

"A Miss Geraldine Copeland," the girl replied, walking farther into the room and placing the basket on the table. "I need you to sign here for me." The girl reached out and handed Geraldine a piece of paper and a worn pencil with several teeth marks indented in it.

"Lord have mercy," Geraldine said with amazement. "Who on earth? They're so beautiful." Her face was vibrant and smiling. She handed the girl the signed document and quickly snatched the tiny card from the plastic prongs. She tore open the envelope, which read: *Looking forward to spending Mother's Day with a beautiful woman. Always, Daniel.*

Amy peered over Geraldine's shoulder, having read the message simultaneously. She backed away grinning as she watched her best friend blush over a long-awaited romantic gesture. "They're absolutely beautiful, Gerry. Believe me, sweetheart, you deserve it." Amy grinned, walking toward the door again. She turned back to face a stunned Geraldine, gawking at her suspiciously. "Now you got your damn sign. So what ya gonna do?"

"Boy, you're crazy." Kasey laughed. She stuffed the dollar bills into the back pocket of her Cache pants, before waving her next customer, Crutch, to her chair. "Spike Lee's best movie was *She's Gotta Have It*. Hands down."

"Aw, Kasey," the dark-complected, pint-sized young man was saying as he walked over to the barber chair. "Come on, baby girl. *School Daze* was the phat-bomb, and you know this." Crutch tugged his oversized jeans up with both hands before sitting down in the antique barber chair.

"That's why they make belts to help keep britches up on narrow behinds like yours," Kasey teased, fastening the cape around his neck. "You just think *School Daze* is all that because it reminds you of your pledging experience in college."

"That and also because he made a good half-pint himself," Mike, one of Kasey's other customers, joked. "A tiny man with a severe short-man's complex. Pitiful," he said, shaking his head.

"That's 'aw-ight, least I ain't trying to do no jungle fever.

Always looking for some milks or high-yallers,'' Crutch said truculently. ''With your wannabe self.''

A moment of tense silence swept through the room before the bustle of the urban city streets, and the gruff sounds of the Wu-Tang Clan, recaptured the essence of the tight barber shop. Kasey swept the clippers through the top part of Crutch's head until his bronze scalp peered through. The clump of thick hair toppled to the lumpy linoleum floor.

''What you getting into tonight, Kasey?'' Crutch asked.

''Sleep,'' she told him, buzzing the clippers from the top of his head to the back once again. She had to be careful not to cut it too close. Crutch wasn't that fond of the bald look.

''Sleep? You mean you and Baseem ain't going over to the city to see Janet J. swing that fine body across the stage at the Palladium tonight?''

''Nope. I'm dog tired, and Baseem is in Atlanta till tomorrow,'' she replied. And thank God, too, she thought, brushing another ball of thick hair onto the floor. She wasn't up to dealing with Baseem of late—spending hours in his Range, roving the city and stopping everywhere to complete errands. She didn't feel like massaging his bulging muscles or listening to his frustrations.

She was enjoying the free time away from Baseem. His absence afforded her the opportunity to really assess how she was feeling about him, about the entire marriage thing. Knowing that her mother was going to spend Mother's Day in D.C. was something else that didn't sit well with the rhythm of her heart. After all these many years, years of spending every holiday together, she couldn't accept her mother's decision to spend *their* mother-daughter day with other people who weren't family.

A complete stranger by the name of Jay and his derogatory comments about Baseem had also bothered her. Perhaps Baseem wasn't the man she was supposed to marry and spend the rest of her days with. Maybe it wasn't normal for one's fiancé to have ex-girlfriends who were always bothering her.

Hearing loud, roaring sounds of laughter pummeling through the glass door, Kasey lifted the clippers away from Crutch's head and glanced up. Baseem. Now what's he doing here? she thought, quickly flickering her rehearsed smile.

"Hey, hey," Baseem yelled out to everyone in the shop as he walked over toward Kasey. "Ya'll miss me?" He grinned diabolically. His brawny body was donned in a soft-as-a-baby's-bottom, black leather jacket, a pair of loose-fitting black jeans, and a pair of black Timberland boots.

Snickers and grumbling "hell, naws" rang out in response to his presumptive question. Baseem stepped behind Kasey, lowered his head, and planted a wet kiss on the back of her neck.

"Hey, pooh," he crooned. "Got you a little sumtin—sumtin," he whispered lower. "Meet me in the back in a few, 'kay?"

" 'Kay," Kasey said, pretending to be more enthralled with Crutch's lumpy head than necessary.

Minutes later she had collected yet another fifteen dollars, making her total somewhere around two hundred twenty dollars so far for the day, with only two heads left to cut. She used her pointer finger to impart a "just a minute" gesture to Mike, who was now engrossed in the Knicks vs. Houston game lighting up the nineteen-inch color TV. Kasey hurriedly walked to the back of the shop to greet Baseem.

"Hey, baby," Baseem whined before wrapping his big arms around her slender back and planting a mouthy kiss on her lips. His lips were so big and full that they immediately claimed and devoured Kasey's.

Kasey had wanted, even tried, to force herself to be sparked by the kiss, like she had been so many times in the past. But Baseem's forceful kiss hadn't ignited her. Baseem detected the distance immediately. He pulled away from their embrace, eyeing Kasey suspiciously.

"What's wrong with you?" He frowned.

"Nothing," she told him. "I'm tired. Feels like I might be coming down with something," she lied.

Baseem licked his lips several times as he studied his lady love. He took a seat on the round bar stool. "You're lying, Kase. I can see it. What is it?"

Kasey exasperated heavily. Reluctantly she said, "It's my mom. She's going to spend next weekend in D.C."

Baseem, grinning, scratched the top of his bald head. "Well, there is a God. You mean to tell me Ms. High and Mighty is actually going to venture outside the 201 area code?" He laughed some more. "Good for her. Maybe she'll be lucky and get a man while she's down there."

Kasey cut a hard glare at him. "That ain't funny, Baseem. I'm a little hurt to know she's not spending Mother's Day with me." She lowered her eyes to the floor.

Baseem grabbed her by the hand and drew her nearer to him. "I've got some news that will make you feel better." He sucked her cheek. "First, here's a little sumtin—sumtin I picked up for you in Atlanta." He pulled out a red velvet box from his jacket pocket and handed it to her. "My gift to you for always being by my side, baby."

Kasey blushed with batted eyes. She flipped open the box. Her eyes bulged wider, and her lips fell open at the sparkling gems meeting her glare. Carefully she lifted the tennis bracelet and ogled it more thoroughly. "It's absolutely beautiful!" She stared into Baseem's droopy eyes. "Thank you, sweetie," she told him, placing a kiss on his lips. "Here." She handed him the bracelet. "Help me put it on."

Now that's more like it, Baseem thought, regarding the fire he felt in that kiss. "This ain't all." He smiled, clipping the safety lock to the bracelet in place. "Spoke to my peoples about the checks. They were mailed yesterday from California. We should have us some real paper by Tuesday—Wednesday at the latest. So be on the lookout for the mailman. You hear me?"

Kasey nodded obediently, her attention mostly absorbed by the diamond bracelet than by Baseem's demand. The intercom on the phone buzzed from the front.

"Yes," Kasey yelled out.

"Phone call for you, Kase," Tony the other barber told her.

"Thank you," she said, lifting the phone off its cradle. "This is Kasey." She leaned against the cool wall, with the phone

balanced between her chin and right shoulder, while she used
her left hand to toy with her newly acquired piece of jewelry.

There was a brief pause before the person on the other end
spoke. "Can you talk?" the male voice asked.

"Yeah. Why, who's this?"

"It's me, Jay. I was thinking about you, wondering how you
were doing. Is everything okay?"

Kasey froze. She stopped playing with her bracelet. Her
facial expression turned serious at the sound of Jay's name.
Calling to see if I'm okay?

"I'm fine, thank you," she told him politely. "What can I
do for you?" She knew she sounded too official, too stiff, but
how else was she supposed to sound? Especially with Baseem
around.

"Can't talk, huh? Must mean that thick-necked bully boyfriend of yours is near," Jay taunted. "Anyway, I didn't want
anything in particular. You were on my mind, that's all."

Kasey said nothing. She could feel a tension knot threatening
to set right between her eyes. Baseem stood up and began his
approach toward her. She'd have to hurry and get Jay off the
line. "All is well," she said through clutched teeth. How is it
this strange man felt completely at ease dogging her man to
her face? Something eerie about this Jay character she was
beginning not to like—to trust. Baseem was standing so close
to her now he would almost be able to hear her heartbeat.

"I take it he's really on top of you now. Before I let you
go, how's next Thursday for you?" Jay asked her.

"I beg your pardon?" Kasey spouted unintentionally.

"Who is it?" Baseem demanded of Kasey.

Kasey hushed him off with a slight wave of the hand as she
buried her ear farther into the receiver, pretending that there
was a bad connection and she couldn't hear. She didn't want
to chance Baseem discovering that it was Jay on the other line.
He had warned her to stay away from him.

"Oops, I hear Gigantor beckoning," Jay teased some more.
"Put me down on your books for Friday evening. I'm looking
forward to seeing you. Bye for now."

Just as the line disconnected, Baseem had snatched the phone out of Kasey's hand.

"Baseem!" she yelled. "What do you think—"

"Hello! Hello!" Baseem screamed into the telephone. Hearing a dead phone line on the opposite end, he slammed the phone back into the cradle.

"Who was that, Kase?"

Kasey shrugged. "I don't know. I was playing along, hoping I could recognize the person's voice at some point," she lied. "But I couldn't quite get the voice. The connection was awful."

Baseem furrowed his bushy brows. His thick body more erect, he towered over her. "If it's someone I need to get straight, you just let me know. You hear me?"

Kasey gaped into his bloodshot eyes. Yeah, I hear you loud and clear, she thought. Did she and Baseem have what it took for the makings of an everlasting marriage? Would he continue to be so overwhelmingly demanding and pushy? She sighed. God, she sure hoped not.

5

Wednesday

Geraldine stood over the egg yolk–colored stove, draped in a pink, full-length, terry-cloth robe, stirring a pot of grits. Half the morning had slipped by already. It was eleven thirty, leaving her with just three and a half hours to bathe, style her hair, stop by the bank to cash her check, and go by the cleaners to pick up her clothes before her three to eleven work shift. She had to beg Lucy, her hairdresser of ten years, to squeeze her in tomorrow night for a perm touch-up and manicure. It was Mother's Day weekend, and with her own personal excitement overwhelming her, she had almost forgotten how swamped the hair salons and retail stores would be.

Earlier in the week, she had tried to come up with every excuse in the book not to go with Amy to D.C. this weekend. She had, unsuccessfully, attempted to convince Daniel, after thanking him time and time again for the lovely floral arrangement, that not spending Mother's Day with Kasey would damn near kill her. Daniel had listened attentively but still had not been swayed. He had simply told her to bring Kasey with her if she couldn't handle being without her mother on that day.

Geraldine had laughed easily at the comment, which was to
serve both as comic relief and an effective persuasive tactic.

Her skepticism was further inspired this past Sunday after
church, when Amy let it slip out that Daniel was going through
a divorce. Geraldine was sure that she had the out she needed
to cancel on the trip. But that Monday night, Daniel had phoned
and run off a list of activities he had scheduled for them once
she arrived in D.C. On Saturday morning, he planned to take
Geraldine on a tour of the White House, Capitol, and Pentagon
before driving to Baltimore Harbor for lunch and back to D.C.
for dinner and to the theater house to see August Wilson's
Seven Guitars.

On Sunday he had tickets to see Kirk Franklin & the Family
gospel ensemble after they attended church and stopped off for
a late brunch in Georgetown. Geraldine had wanted to contain
the bubbling feeling churning in the pit of her stomach all
week. But the more she thought about escaping away from the
hustle of Newark's city streets to the presence of a debonair
gentleman to serve as her personal tour guide, the feathery
feeling magnified to the tenth power.

Kasey was very distant with her on Monday evening when
she had come to the house to pick up more of her things. "I
still can't believe you're not going to be here for Mother's
Day. We always spend that day together," Kasey had bitterly
said.

Their visit had been cut short when Kasey quickly responded
to the loud, beckoning horn outside the window. Baseem. Ignorant thug, Geraldine had thought, staring at her daughter as she
threw pieces of clothing into a small duffel bag and raced toward
the front door. "Have a good trip," Kasey had dismissively told
her, slamming the front door shut on her way out.

Geraldine let out a deep breath as she dropped a heaping of
grits and a few pieces of bacon onto her plate. She chewed in
silence, listening only to the steady drip of the kitchen faucet
plunking into the plastic washtub. The spigot needed repairing
as did the one in the bathroom. So many things needed fixing in
this house—her mother's house, which served as her permanent

place of residence after her father traipsed off to live with his new wife.

Geraldine slid the empty plate into the half full dishtub, leaving the pot she had cooked the grits and the fryer pan she had used for the bacon to soak till she returned from work. She ran a tub with hot water and sprinkled in some of the bath salts that Amy gave her for Mother's Day last year.

God, how she wished she was living in one of them new apartments or town houses that offered a heat lamp and a fan blower in the bathroom; central air and heat; new, plush wall to wall carpet; a modern kitchen with a dishwasher, garbage disposal, frost free refrigerator, self-cleaning oven, microwave; a little sun deck on the patio; and a fireplace in the living room with vaulted ceilings. But the money landlords wanted for new apartments these days was out of the question. Especially since she still had this house—her mother's house.

If she won the lottery, she would move to Arizona where the weather was warm year round, and the homes and apartments were new and clean—where the city streets died down at a decent hour and where the only plants she'd opt to have would be cactuses. If she could win the Pick-six, she'd gladly leave her two-weeks' notice on her manager's desk, gather up her most precious personal belongings, and catch the next train smoking out of Newark, New Jersey.

She'd find a homeless person and give them the key to this old raggedy house and her rusty Oldsmobile. She'd leave all her clothes, dishes, bedding, furniture and start over—fresh— new. Plucking a pair of panties and a bra from her dresser drawer, she paused to look up at the pictures hanging on her bedroom wall.

She'd leave every darn thing right here in this pitiful house and drab state, including Kasey. Yes, she'd hightail it out of here with only the clothes on her back, the money in her wallet, and the pictures, her memories of her babies, Kenny and Kasey, and the only man she ever loved, James Bullock. If she won the lottery.

* * *

Kasey slung back her head, sending her individual braids swaying back and forth, as she gulped the last bit of her Pepsi. Baseem was late again. She pushed up her long denim sleeve and glanced at her watch: 4:45 P.M. She'd have to be back at the barbershop in thirty minutes. And with traffic being the way it was for this time of the day, it was hardly likely that she'd make the twenty-mile drive from Glenwood to Newark in time.

Baseem had promised to meet her here, at the newly erected condominiums, between four and four fifteen, to put down a deposit on the place that would serve as their new home after the wedding. Mr. Baldwin, the realtor for the builder, had offered her the Pepsi while she waited for Baseem. He assured her that he would wait with her as long as he could. Or at least until five thirty, when he'd have to leave to pick up his son from baseball practice. Kasey pulled her pager out of her pocketbook and checked it again. Nothing. "Sheesh," she exhaled.

She'd give him another fifteen minutes before making the tedious drive back to the neighborhood. Standing in the lobby of the plush, ten-story condos, Kasey waited. She wondered how she had come to agree to marry Baseem in the first place. No one had really approved of her relationship with Baseem.

Baseem? What kind of name is that? Her mother had laughed aloud when Kasey had admitted to seeing Baseem. He says he doesn't need an American slave name given by a white man, she had remembered telling her mother. Now as she stood staring out the window toward the cozy residential street with the large, nicely painted houses, she wondered if Baseem was really the man God intended her to marry.

Trickles of rain tapped against the glass, blurring the post-card-perfect view of the lush green bushes and neatly edged lawns. She let out a deep breath. *Dangit! Now it was raining.* Baseem knew how much she hated driving in the rain. He should have been here by now. This is ridiculous, she thought, glancing down at the diamond-studded watch again. The rain fell heavier, creating a harmonious beat as it pelted against the side of the building. *Splat, splat, splat. Splat-splat-splat.* She turned toward the elevator doors. Better reschedule again, she decided, pressing the UP button.

Once inside the elevator, she leaned against the dark rich wood with its thin slats of mirrors and dim lighting. She peered at her reflection bouncing off the mirrored double doors. If her mother could take a chance and risk traveling to D.C. to meet a man that she had had only five or six phone conversations with, why couldn't she risk meeting someone more to her liking—more suitable—less conspicuous—more considerate—who didn't want to talk down to her every time he was stressed?

Baseem had swept her off her feet at Virginia Beach, during her annual Fourth of July trip she'd made with her girlfriends from Connecticut, three years ago. Baseem had walked up to her while she was basking in the sun on the beach and invited her and her entourage to a party at the beach house he was renting with some other guys from Newark. After discussing it with her girlfriends later on that day, they had all agreed to go and check it out. Turned out it was the best time she had ever experienced during her young adult life.

The house had been overstuffed with about a hundred brothers and sisters eating, talking, laughing, playing cards, and dancing. Baseem had a flock of women chasing him the entire night but had selected her as the lucky winner. So she had thought then. He had made a fuss over her the entire night, catering to her every need or whim. They had walked the beach arm in arm talking, laughing, and snuggling. He had made a small bonfire, and they had watched the sunrise.

From that point forward, their relationship forged forward. Baseem courted her for the first six months, lavishing expensive gifts on her and taking her to the best restaurants in New Jersey and New York. Even Kenny was happy for all the attention she was receiving. Colonel Jason and Geraldine, on the other hand, didn't like the boy from the get-up. Said something about him being a refined street pimp with no real friends or bold enemies.

But Kasey didn't see what her mother saw. All she knew

was that Baseem worked part-time as a limousine driver for some big-time Newark politician, while trying to start his own business. And that once he quit his job and followed his dream to own a music company, he gave away turkeys in the neighborhood around Thanksgiving and presents during Christmas for all the less fortunate kids in the neighborhood. He had even given Kenny money to tide him over before he got hired by the express-mail company.

She tried to explain to her mother that Baseem wasn't a street thug—perhaps street knowledgeable but not a thug. That he was an up-and-coming record producer and a businessman with a heart of gold. Baseem had been there for her in a way that no man had ever been—not her godfather, Sylvester, and certainly not her deceased father.

Kasey stepped off the elevator and was once again greeted by the spicy potpourri. She began the long walk toward the end of the hall, her gait somewhat stifled by the thick carpet. Carpet she wished she could put in her mother's house. Mr. Baldwin's office door was ajar when she reached his office. She knocked lightly before proceeding into the office on command of his invitation.

"He must have gotten tied up in a meeting or something," Kasey began explaining as soon as her eyes met his. She shrugged and said, "I don't know what else would have kept him."

Mr. Baldwin, a tall, bony white man with a protruding nose, small eyes, and a head full of curly brunette locks, grimaced. He began gathering his things off his desk—tossing papers into his black leather attaché case that seemed fairly packed as it was.

"Don't worry about it," he said with a limp wave. "I'm sure that's the case. You all can call me when you're both ready to come out together. We have a few units left but none like the penthouse you're interested in. You know, Kasey, you can go ahead and write me a good-faith check for five hundred dollars to hold that unit. I won't deposit the check until you sign all the paperwork."

Kasey bunched several of her braids and twisted them

together as she considered Mr. Baldwin's suggestion. If she wrote a check for five hundred dollars, Baseem would definitely have the money to cover it. But what if he didn't like the unit? The area? The price? Mr. Baldwin? Then what? No, she thought. She'd better wait for Baseem.

She smiled and said, "Thank you, Mr. Baldwin, but I think I'll wait for my fiancé."

"Suit yourself," he told her, locking his file cabinet and the other office door. "I just thought it would be sort of a good-faith act. That's all."

Kasey entered the elevator, standing in the same spot she had on the ride up. Baseem's disregard for their appointment had ticked her off. This newly developing habit of his was beginning to irk the mess out of her. How dare he not even as much as page her.

She slammed her car door shut, cranked the ignition, and flipped on the windshield wipers. *A good-faith act, humph,* she thought, pulling off into the street. With the strange way Baseem had been acting lately, it was going to take more than some good ole faith to keep her from telling him to take a trip to the curbside. She braked for the stop sign, noticing the familiar vanity plates of the Jeep approaching in the opposite direction.

Kasey could see Baseem's smile through the streaked windshield. He flashed his lights off and on and honked his horn twice. She looked at her watch: 5:05 P.M. I'll be damned, she thought, easing through the intersection where Baseem was facing and waiting at the opposite stop sign. He waved toward her. She glanced at her watch a second time, returned the wave halfhearted and sped off. Now this was an act of good faith, she smirked, merging onto the main road leading back to the Parkway.

6

Friday

Geraldine raced around the house, tossing her toiletries in the new carry-on bag she had purchased from Stern's last night before going to Lucy's to get her hair done. She stood with her hands on her hips, taking an account of the items sprawled out on her dresser: toothbrush, toothpaste, deodorant, powder, soap, Estée Lauder perfume, makeup, cotton balls, lotion, and Pond's cold cream. Okay, she thought, putting the items into the bag.

The matching garment bag lay open on her bed with just two outfits hanging inside. She chose the peach silk knee-length dress with the ruffled sleeves for church on Sunday and her basic black dress with the flared bottom as her outing attire. After her shift was over tonight, she would change from the nurses' uniform into a pair of jeans and a scoop-necked knit top.

Now if she could just figure out what to wear during the day tomorrow while Daniel toured her around the nation's Capitol, everything would be set. The red numbers on her alarm clock read 1:00 P.M. Hurriedly she swept the hangers back and forth in her closet, looking for just the right outfit. Bingo! She'd wear the gold-colored cotton pedal pusher pantsuit with the hand-painted and beaded top.

Geraldine snatched the bag of caramel rice cakes off the kitchen table and stuffed them into the overnight bag. Just in case she got a craving for a snack late at night, she thought, locking the door behind her. She had tried to walk the block during her lunch break all this week, but to no avail. The only thing she was successful at achieving was no fatty snacks or late night meals for the past two weeks. Though she hadn't lost the ten to twelve pounds like she had envisioned, she was just elated to have shed four pounds.

After loading the bags into the trunk of her car, Geraldine looked up and saw her neighbor sitting on the porch. She waved to her and said, "Keep an eye on my place for me, Brownie, okay?"

Brownie, who was an old gray-haired woman with no business of her own to mind, nodded her head staunchly. Geraldine took in a deep breath and stuck the key in the ignition. She hesitated. It would be just her luck that her car would stall out today. Anxiously she turned the key toward the ON position. The car's boisterous engine roared. Thank God, she praised, wiping her sweaty palms on her nurses' smock.

She was already feeling out of sorts today and didn't need any outside forces making this trip to D.C. more challenging than it already was. For one thing, having to fly on an airplane, for however short a period of time, was a major task in itself. Not to mention, being able to leave her shift at nine tonight in order to make the eleven o'clock flight. Seemingly enough, things were falling right into place. The way things should when something good is for you, Geraldine determined, pulling into the street.

"Well, well, well. Look at you, Ms. Sassafras," Amy was saying to Geraldine when she stepped through the emergency room's automatic doors. "I see we went and got us a new style." Amy grinned seductively, checking out Geraldine's new look. "That color looks good on you, Gerry. What is it?"

"Gingerbread," Geraldine told her, placing her pocketbook

in the cabinet behind the desk. Her hair had been dyed the color of gingerbread, and her new style was labeled the "boy-cut." "Lucy suggested I get something to spin heads." She laughed. "You don't think it's a little young?"

"Young?" Amy asked with a raised brow. "Ain't no such thing, Gerry. I think it further accentuates your beautiful features. Especially those round eyes of yours." She looked her over more thoroughly. "Umm, even got your nails done. I'm going to have to watch Daniel around you," Amy teased, smiling. "I'll see you later. I've got to call social services about that little girl with the severe facial bruises. Mother claims she doesn't know how it happened." Amy turned and walked away.

"Gerry," one of the doctors called out as he walked past her and Amy. "Like your new style. Whose heart are you trying to capture?"

Geraldine blushed. My, my, my. It had been such a long time since she received so much positive attention. Wonder how Kasey will like it? She flipped through one of the charts sitting on the counter. Admittedly she was still a little unsure about her decision to fly to D.C., leaving Kasey here to spend Mother's Day alone. She probably would call her before she left to say goodbye—to tell her that she loved her.

It was the Friday night before Mother's Day, and the barbershop was swollen with brothers waiting in line to get buzzed, clipped, shaved, and trimmed for the monumental weekend. Kasey had completed fifteen heads already and had six or seven more to finish before she could call it a night.

She wasn't feeling very sociable or vibrant for several reasons: *1.* It was that time of the year that she longed for her brother, Kenny. *2.* She and Baseem had been fighting since Wednesday, when she drove away from the condos in spite of seeing him approach. *3.* With her and Baseem barely speaking, except for him calling to find out if the checks were in, it was likely she'd be spending Mother's Day alone.

The new bells she had hung on the front door handle, to serve as a signal to her and the other barbers when someone came in and out of the shop, rang for what seemed like the hundredth time today. She glanced up and noticed it was Jay with that battered satchel in his hand, squeezing in behind a group of brothers standing along the wall. He was donned in a black denim shirt with matching black jeans and a pair of cowboy boots. Finally gone shopping, Kasey thought, as she acknowledged Jay with a head nod.

"Hey, Kase," Mike, the closest barber to her station, yelled. "You seen the remote?"

Kasey shook her head no, as if opening her mouth to reply would require too much effort.

Obnoxiously loud voices coupled with thunderous laughter boomed in the background. Someone yelled out, "Where's the remote?" while another voice replied in agreement, "yeah. The Knicks are playing the Magic."

"To hell with the Knicks," someone had said.

"No, to hell with those sorry Nets." Someone laughed.

Kasey tried her best to stay focused. But all the noise and male bravado was beginning to rake her nerves.

"This my cut, hit the volume," someone else yelled out at hearing D'Angelo's "When We Get By."

Kasey sighed heavily. They would have to pipe it down a notch or two before she lost her mind and told everybody to get ta steppin'. The bell jingle-jangled again. Apprehensively she looked up. This time she saw an agitated Baseem and his bodyguard, barreling through the door with a menacing scowl on his face. Something had obviously pissed him off royally. She could tell by his pursed lips, the pound of his gait, the squeeze of his eyes. He blew past several brothers who were seated and standing—blew by several greetings, straight over to Kasey's station.

"Let's go to the back," Baseem ordered, clutching Kasey by her left elbow, while she held a pair of shears in her right hand. The noise that had cramped the shop, just a few seconds earlier, had simmered down to a near silence, all except for the referee's whistle on television in the background.

Kasey wiggled her elbow free, frowning as her heart rate accelerated. "I'm in the middle of cutting a client's hair," she snarled barely above a whisper. She had no intention of increasing the scene if he didn't, she thought. "Furthermore, I'm running a business here, in case you've forgotten," she added. "I can't just drop everything every time you come in here, Baseem." She was feeling stressed. *How many times is he going to storm in here and demand my immediate attention,* she questioned silently. *This has got to stop.*

"You will drop everything when it comes to my damn money!" he huffed, his voice getting louder with each word. "Now let's go!" He reached for her arm again, this time more forcefully.

Once again Kasey snatched her arm free. "I ain't in the mood for a scene, Baseem," she said, glaring at him. "Give me a minute, and I'll be right with you." She turned her body sideways to reach for the clippers so she could finish up her customer.

"I don't have a damn minute, woman. I need to talk to you right now. You got some explaining to do if you don't want me all over you right here. Now let's go, Kasey!"

"Explaining to do about what?" Kasey snapped with a slight roll of her head, causing her braids to shake.

The shop was completely silent, besides the milk commercial that was drilling through the TV speakers. All eyes were on Kasey and Baseem, including Jay, who had maneuvered his way closer to Kasey's chair.

Baseem lurched closer into Kasey's personal space, so much that she could see his chest rising beneath his jacket. "Who the hell told you to cash them checks?" he fumed with a strained voice. He didn't want everyone in the barbershop knowing all his business.

"What?" Kasey said, placing her free hand on her narrow hips. "I haven't cashed none of your damn checks."

"Well, somebody did. You the only person that could have done it! Now don't make me ask you again, Kasey. Who do you think you messing with, girl?" His voice was harsh sounding.

"Baseem," Kasey said with a raised voice, "I don't know what you're talking about. Like I said," she spewed angrily,

"I haven't seen or cashed no checks. Maybe you better retrace your steps and go threaten somebody else." She eyed him. She'd be damned if he was going to continue to come in here, bullying her around and being disrespectful. He must be losing his mind—trying to manhandle her like some street thug.

Jay had inched his way up, near Baseem's bodyguard, who was eyeing Jay with his hands jammed inside his pockets.

"Come here," Baseem yelled, snatching Kasey by the arm and pulling her toward him. She tried unsuccessfully to fight back, but Baseem had too strong of a grip on her.

Scrape the shin of his leg with my shoe, then stomp on his inner foot, Kasey frantically thought, recalling some of the survival techniques she had learned while attending a women's defense class. She tried to use the heel of her shoe to pounce on his foot, but he had on those darn Timberland boots again. Her eyes pleaded through the familiar faces as Baseem began pulling her toward the back. Lord, please—wouldn't somebody step in and stop this idiot?

God answered Kasey's prayer right then and there, because Jay plowed through the rest of the brothers toward Kasey.

Things were moving in slow motion to Jay as he sprang forward, and with an open palm, popped Baseem in the face. Instantly blood gushed out from Baseem's nose. He screamed a piercing yelp, releasing his hold on Kasey as he used both hands to hold his broken nose. With the same smoothness he had exemplified a few seconds ago, Jay lifted his right leg up high and used the bottom of his cowboy boot to slap Baseem across the side of his face, causing him to fall forward onto one knee. He waved for Kasey, who was trying to catch her breath, to move away.

"Back away," Jay whispered to Kasey. His eyes were squinted with fury, his nostrils flared with anger. Kasey obediently did as she was told, cowering toward the corner of the barbershop near the rest of the brothers in shock. "Somebody call the police," Jay yelled out.

"Now young brother," Jay said in a soft tone, "it's not acceptable for a big, overgrown man like you to muscle a beautiful sister around. That's just unbecoming behavior."

Baseem's bodyguard had drawn his gun. "Let him go," he warned Jay.

"Or what?" Jay smiled. "You're going to shoot me? Please, I've been shot more times than you've probably been laid. No, you drop your gun, or I'll be forced to twist his fat neck off."

Baseem's struggle proved fruitless. Jay had a firm death grip around his neck and Adam's apple. "Better yet," he told the bodyguard. "Why don't you just hand your gun to that brother right there." He nodded to one of the customers, sitting next to the bodyguard.

A few seconds more elapsed before a curling sound emerged from Baseem's throat. "Go ahead man," he whined. "Do what he says. He's cutting off my breath," Baseem said, slightly above a whisper.

The bodyguard did what he was told, grudgingly handing the gun over to Tony, one of the other barbers.

"Now get down on your hands and knees and face the door. And don't move till I tell you to. Me and Mr. Baseem here are going to have us a quick, brief overview of how things are going to go down from this point onward." Jay took his left foot and slammed it against the back of Baseem's right leg. Baseem immediately fell face forward onto the linoleum. Jay kneeled into his back.

The sirens were wailing close by. Kasey gasped with fear. Though she was happy that Jay was the one to step up and save her from God only knows what, she certainly didn't want Jay to kill Baseem.

Jay cleared his voice and spoke calmly, loud enough for everyone to hear. "Now I'm going to tell you this only once. If I ever see you putting your hands on Kasey again, I will pluck out your eyes, then snap off your neck! You hear me!"

Jay was raging, had had a flashback of some sort. His eyes protruded outward, and he started shaking. "Don't you ever put your hands on my daughter again! Ever! Ever! Ever!" He planted his foot in the back of Baseem's neck and stood up, giving Baseem one final mash before the police rushed in.

"Police! What's going on here?" one of the officers asked as he surveyed the area.

"This lowlife tried to accost my daughter, while the rest of these pussycats stood by and watched," Jay told the officer.

The officer knelt down beside Baseem. "Well, looky here. If it ain't Baseem, the big man in town," the officer said. He noticed the pool of blood lying beneath Baseem's face. "Did you do this?" the officer asked Jay.

"Yes," Jay proudly answered. "And I'd do it again if I had to."

The officer nodded. He ordered Baseem up on his knees before he cuffed him and the bodyguard and hauled them out of the shop. Tony handed the other officer the bodyguard's gun.

Kasey stood in the corner with quivering lips and a river of tears pouring down her cheeks. She trembled lightly at first but began shaking uncontrollably when Jay pulled her into his chest. He held her tight, absorbing her wet sobs, which were loud and uninhibited. She stood there for minutes on end, being consoled in the arms of the strange man, who had just claimed to be her father. *My daughter, my daughter,* she replayed over and over in her head, trying to make the words stick and hold. It can't be true, she thought. How could it? My father?

7

Kasey sat in the back room, cautiously sipping on a cup of hot tea that Jay had asked one of the customers to go down to the corner store to get. 8:44 P.M. The last few clients were finally straggling out of the shop. Mike and Tony had been kind enough to take Kasey's last two customers. That's the least they could have done, considering neither one was brave enough to stand up to Baseem and intercede on her behalf.

She took the crumpled-up pieces of tissue and wiped her runny nose, taking an exaggerated deep breath as she dabbed. What was she supposed to do now? After all these years of not having a daddy to help her blow out her candles on her birthday cake; to give the third degree to the boys she brought home to date; to step in and tell her mother to quit nagging her.

The tears came slowly at first. *A father—her father? Oh, Lord.* The tears were steady now—spilling down her cheeks like an overflowed bathtub. How would Jay fit in? She dabbed at her tears with a tissue. What would her mother do when she found out that after all these many years of holding on, believing, praying, standing on a half a leg of faith, the love of her life was still alive? Jay went to hug her. She let him but not for long. Hesitantly she pulled away.

Jay took a seat on the stool opposite of Kasey. *God, she looks just like Geraldine did before I left—crying and all.* Ever since he learned that he had a daughter, he imagined a time like this. When he would be able to support her in some form or another, even if she was grown and had a life of her own. *Kasey sure is a beautiful child.* His chest protruded outward. He was proud.

This was his daughter, with the same slender build and lanky legs, sitting before him. Surely Baseem or anyone else would never do her any harm. Ever. He had already lost a child he had never had the fortune to meet. He'd be damned if he'd lose another child.

Kasey cleared her throat. She wanted to speak naturally, like she had done the last few times she and Jay—*dad*—had spoken. But her sentences were tight and careful.

"I should call my mother, Jay," she peevishly said, standing. "She'd . . . she'd want to know." Kasey went over to the telephone to place the call, thinking the entire time what she would say to her mother, who she hadn't really been on good terms with for the last few months.

Jay touched her arm. "You don't have to do this right now, Kasey. There's a lot we need to discuss. Many things I need to tell you and your mother. First thing I need to tell you is that my real name is James Bullock. Jay is a name I latched on to much later."

Kasey's face was weary. Dark circles from smeared mascara gave her a ragged appearance. Her nose was red from crying; her lips pale with little to no hint that they had been colored a deep mahogany only hours ago. Silently she lifted the receiver and dialed the hospital. Of course she had to do this right now, because if not, her mother would be on a plane headed for D.C. sometime tonight. Or was it tomorrow? If she had only paid attention this one time to her mother's rambling words, she might have recalled when it was that she was scheduled to depart.

"Beth Israel Hospital," the operator answered on the fourth ring.

"Emergency room nurses' station, please," Kasey replied. Her voice was heavy and scratchy, like a cigarette smoker of many years. She listened to the *hold, please,* classical music as she waited to be connected. *Was Mom even working today?* Three more rings later, she was connected to the nurses' station.

"ER desk," a tired, apathetic voice answered.

"Geraldine Copeland, please." A few seconds later, she was back to listening to the continuation of the same song. She looked down at her watch—that darn watch Baseem had given her. *Who told you to cash them checks?* She heard Baseem's words taunting her. Her mind tossed and turned while she waited for her mother to come to the phone.

"Gerry is gone for the weekend," a more enthusiastic voice told her.

"Gone for the weekend?" Kasey said, shocked. "When?"

"She just left here a few minutes ago. Who's this?"

"It's Kasey. Her daughter."

There was a brief pause before the lady responded, "I'll take a message for her if you'd like. Is everything okay?"

No, Kasey wanted to scream, taking a chance to look over at Jay, who was still eyeing her protectively. She needed to speak to her mother, tell her that the man she had been holding a lit torch for the past twenty-some years was sure enough alive and standing in the back of Uncle Chitty's barbershop.

Disappointed, she said, "Sure. I'll try her at home. Thanks."

Kasey hung up the telephone and turned to face James. How was she to tell him that her mother was probably on her way to spend Mother's Day in D.C. with another man? She lifted the receiver again and dialed her mother at home. No answer. She hung the phone back up.

"Kasey," James softly called out. "Please," he said, pointing to the chair. "Have a seat. There is so much I need to say—get off my chest. I can't wait anymore. Please."

She walked back over to her chair and sat down, grabbing her lukewarm cup of tea for security—to give her hands something to toy with. Hearing footsteps approaching the back of the shop, she looked up alarmed. Some traces of fear from the earlier episode still blanketed her eyes.

It turned out to be Tony, coming to the back to bid her and James a good night.

"I'm out of here, Kase. I'll lock up the front," he said, looking down at the floor. "You okay?"

"Sure." Kasey nodded. And with that, Tony had disappeared. She heard the final jingling of the bells and realized that, alas, she was alone with Jay—James—her father. She ran a fidgety finger through her braids. Now what? She hadn't been nervous around James before this.

"I've got some leftover Chinese food. I can warm it in the microwave if you're hungry."

"No thanks, Kasey. Unless of course you're hungry," James quickly added.

Kasey shrugged her shoulders. No, her stomach wasn't in the mood for any food. What she wanted was her mother to be sitting beside her, experiencing the joy, the uncertainty and pain of James resurfacing after all these years. *Good gracious, Mom, where the heck are you anyway?*

"I know me coming here like this must be a shock to you, Kasey. But believe me, it was as equally shocking for me to find out that after all these many years . . ." He paused to reflect for a moment.

"If you are my father, where have you been?" Kasey burst out suddenly. It was the only rational or concerning question she cared about more than a long explanation or a host of pitiful excuses.

James stared at Kasey for a moment, taking in her pencil-thin eyebrows, which were both arched high, giving her eyes a wider look. He let out such a deep breath that his stomach contracted against the waist of his pants.

"In Cambodia," he softly murmured, looking down at the ground. "I didn't know . . . I never knew . . ."

"Never knew what?" Kasey asked. "That you left behind a woman you claimed to love and never looked back? That you had two children, who needed to have their father in their life?" Kasey's eyes filled with speckles of water again. "If you could have at least come to see us once in a while, perhaps Kenny would still be with us.'' The tears spilled over again.

James continued to stare at the uneven linoleum floor, counting the squares in his immediate radius. Twenty-two. That's how many of the gray, white, and black speckled squares he counted between and around he and Kasey.

''I would have been here had I known,'' he finally replied. ''I didn't know, Kasey. Honest to God.''

''How could you not know? You know now, don't you?'' she spewed.

''I'd really rather explain it to you and your mother at the same time. I . . .'' He paused to look away at the tiny table with the clear salt and pepper shakers. Need to wash them tops in some vinegar—get them sparkling again, he thought. He pulled his self back to the space occupied between him and Kasey.

''It's too painful to go through it twice,'' he said. ''I just didn't know. You have to believe me, Kasey.'' He shook his head back and forth a few times. ''I didn't know, I didn't know,'' he continued to say as the tears streamed down his face.

Carefully Kasey examined the man sitting across from her. Her mom was absolutely right. She did favor her father. They had the same complexion, similar slender build, identical eyes.

The compassionate side of her wanted to reach over and grab her father and console him as he had done her just a while ago. But the angry side of her—the side of her that wanted to shake him for not making such a miraculous effort sooner in their lives—wouldn't let her.

''Gerry and I were engaged to be married many, many years ago. I was supposed to attend the community college here in Newark to get my associate's degree in business. But then, out of nowhere I get this letter delivered to me telling me I've been drafted to go to Vietnam. Ended up over in the bush . . .'' He trailed off again, staring off to some safe corner of the room, shaking his head back and forth. ''I still can't believe him . . .'' he whispered under his breath.

"Who?" Kasey curiously replied. She also wanted to know the rest of the story, no matter if he had to tell it over and over again and again. She deserved to hear the reason why, after all these years, some stranger who had been hanging around the shop for the past three weeks suddenly was staking a claim at fatherhood. They couldn't go any farther until she heard the story.

"I need to know, Jay—I mean, James. I deserve to, don't you think?" Kasey said curtly.

James nodded his head up and down, then proceeded. "Some of this stuff may affect the way you think about some folks. Are you prepared to deal with that all by yourself?"

"Yes," she answered hurriedly. She'd been handling a whole lot more all by herself the past twenty-six years. She eyed him extensively. "Go on."

"He hated me from the very start. Told me I'd never amount to anything. That's what he told me the very first time I met him. Can you believe that?" James said tightly, reflecting on the bitter words. "Said he knew my kind from way back, and we was nothing but transplanted cotton-picking 'Bamas with big bodies and small brains." He paused again, letting out another deep, frustrating breath. Kasey listened eagerly, patiently waiting.

"Colonel said he be damned if he'd ever let me marry his Geraldine. *Over his dead body* were the exact words he used. Said *just because you sweet-talked my daughter into losing her virginity don't give you the right to make the rest of her life miserable.* Humph," James sighed.

"Forgive me, Kasey. I know he died of stomach cancer, and I'm truly sorry to hear that. Despite his regulating ways, he had a heart. Deep down I know that he thought he was only looking out for Geraldine's best interests."

Kasey's mouth dropped. Had she not used some restraint to keep James from truly suspecting how truly shocked she was, her mouth would have really hit the floor. "My grandfather?" she mumbled.

"I knew I should have waited till Gerry was around," James

sighed, looking down at the worn lino. "She'd understand. She'd tell you." He shook his head up and down. "Kasey, I don't want to skew your view about your grandfather. Please, let me finish when Gerry can hear it, too. Please."

"I want to know for myself. Why do I have to wait? I'm not a little girl anymore. Besides, I deserve to know!" Kasey shrieked loudly. Her hands began trembling again. She placed the Styrofoam cup down on the table. *She hadn't been this perturbed about anything since Kenny's funeral arrangements.* "Please, James."

James hung his head low for a few seconds, contemplating. Could he tell this story a second time to the woman he had abandoned twenty-some years ago? Could he tell it to his daughter now, without the support of her mother? He guessed he would have to, he decided.

"One second," he told Kasey as he stood up and walked toward the front of the shop to retrieve his bag.

Seconds later, James returned with his bag, taking his seat again. He unbuckled the tattered leather piece, shuffling through some papers before pulling out one letter addressed to him at his Cambodian address and another dingy letter addressed to him while he was stationed in Vietnam. He stared at the saffron-tinted letter much longer. His eyebrows lowered into a menacing scowl as he reached over and handed Kasey the second letter.

Kasey held the letter between her thumb and her pointer finger, reading the print. There wasn't a return address, and the postmark had read: NEWARK, NEW JERSEY, P.M. 25 FEB, 1970. Kasey's heart skipped frantically until she took a few deep breaths to calm the beat, get her natural rhythm going again. She opened the envelope and pulled out a folded letter. A picture spilled out of it, floating downward. She caught it before it touched the floor.

The back of the picture faced her. It had little ridges around the edges and pieces of worn tape at the top of it. There was something typed on the back of it. *December 17th, 1969—Mr.*

and Mrs. Peterson. She flipped over the picture and stared at the couple. She gasped lowly as she pulled the picture closer to her face. *My God,* she heard her mind plea. The Mr. and Mrs. Peterson in this photo was a picture of Sylvester and her mother.

8

"Is it safe to travel in this kind of weather?" Geraldine yelled out to Amy as they jogged from the parking terminal toward the airport entrance. Should have packed an umbrella, Geraldine thought, reaching inside the terminal. She lowered her pocketbook, which she had used to shield her hair, and shook the water from it.

Amy slipped out of her lightweight jacket and flung it out a few times. Droplets of water sprinkled to the floor. "It's not raining that hard, Gerry. Planes have taken off in much worse weather than this. Believe me," she said, rubbing her hands against the denim material covering her thighs. She lifted her bag again and slung it across her shoulder. "Let's get down to the gate. We don't want to miss our flight." She walked over to the TV monitors hanging from above and scanned the departure monitor until she located their flight number and the departing gate.

"Ready?" Amy turned and asked Geraldine.

"I suppose," Geraldine said, following Amy toward the escalators. *No, not really* is what she should have said to Amy, but the cat had obviously gotten ahold of her tongue. She had tried to reach Kasey earlier in the afternoon at the barbershop, but the line stayed busy for twenty minutes, and she had had to get back to work.

They reached the security checkpoint. Geraldine mimicked Amy's actions, loading her overnight bag on the conveyor belt, then walking through the metal detector doorway. The beeping sound alarmed Geraldine, and she jumped back. She stared at the security officers standing to her left.

"What?" she mumbled softly. "What did I do?"

"Go through and try it again," one of the security guards told Geraldine.

Geraldine backed through the door frame, then walked through it again. The alarm sounded once more. The woman motioned for Geraldine to come toward her. She scanned over Geraldine's body with a hand-held metal detector, then waved her through. "It's your belt buckle."

Amy stood off to the side, holding the bags. When Geraldine finally came over, she smiled at her friend and said, "Getting attention already, are we?" They both laughed. Amy loudly— Geraldine nervously.

"Gosh, I guess with all the bombings, airport security has really tightened these days," Geraldine said. "I haven't been to an airport in . . ." She paused to recollect. "God, a very long time."

"I've been trying to tell you, Gerry, you need to get out more, become more rounded. Praising God and living a serene life is beautiful and all, but there's a big world out there, and you need to go get some of it."

The customer service agent took their tickets, logged them in on the computer, and confirmed their seat assignments. "The flight is delayed due to the weather conditions," the agent said. "We anticipate a departure time of eleven thirty-five P.M. We apologize for the wait, but we're dealing with mother nature."

"Eleven thirty-five?" Geraldine repeated when they had walked away from the ticket counter. "That's forty minutes from now. Why so long?"

Amy shrugged her shoulders and tossed her bag down into one of the gray plastic chairs. "It's like that sometimes. Don't worry. We'll get to D.C. tonight." She opened her pocketbook and pulled out a five dollar bill from her wallet. "I'm going to get a cup of coffee. You want anything?"

"I'll have a cup. Black, no sugar, please," Geraldine told her. She looked over and caught Amy staring at her. "What now?"

Amy grinned sideways, then replied, "After almost twenty years of friendship, I know how you take your coffee."

Geraldine laughed as she watched Amy saunter away. *Of course she knows how I take my coffee. What was I thinking? We've been friends longer than most people been married. She knows me better than any other person besides Kasey. She would also know that I need to call and speak to my baby before we take off. Yeah, she knows that, I'm sure. I'll try her again just as soon as Amy gets back.*

Amy handed Geraldine the large cup of coffee wrapped with two napkins to ward off the heat of the cup. "They had some Tastycakes coffee cakes, but I figured it's a little late for us to be eating junk food. Besides, better save our appetites for the good stuff tomorrow." She winked.

Geraldine smiled tightly, then sipped her coffee carefully. Coffee cake did sound so good right about now. She had practically starved herself the last two weeks—denying herself such pleasures as chocolates, candy, cakes, and all other sugar-infested treats. Certainly a little bit of cake wouldn't harm her none. "I'm going to get me that piece of coffee cake," Geraldine said, standing. "You sure you don't want any?"

Amy shook her head. "You just trying to make me gain more unnecessary weight, aren't you?" She reached out to give Geraldine the two dollars and the rest of the change from the coffee.

"Just watch my stuff for me. I'm going to call Kasey, too, while I'm up."

Geraldine placed the bag with the coffee cake on the ledge and dropped a quarter into the pay phone. She sipped on her coffee while she waited for someone to pick up the phone at Chitty's house. Three rings, four rings, five—no answer. Oh, that's right, Geraldine remembered—Chitty and Pearl were on their way to the Poconos for the Mother's Day weekend. Kasey, on the other hand, must be out with that man, she thought, looking down at her watch. 11:28 P.M. She hung up the phone and walked back over to her seat. Amy had her head buried in the latest issue of *Heart & Soul* magazine.

Amy never lifted up her head, but she sensed Geraldine standing before her. "What she say?"

"Nothing. She wasn't home." She reached down and handed Amy her coffee cake.

"Page her," Amy said, lifting her eyes from the page. She ripped open the wrapping of the coffee cake with such strength that pieces of crumbs toppled to the carpet.

Geraldine sighed. "I don't remember her pager number. It's all right. I'm sure she's fine."

"You bet she is," Amy mumbled with a full mouth. "The girl is twenty-six years old. She should be able to deal with her mother getting on with her life."

Yeah? Geraldine wondered. But could she deal with Kasey getting on with her life with Baseem? She felt a nagging urge to cancel her trip and go home to spend Mother's Day with Kasey. Lord, how would she be able to stand Amy up at the last minute? If she canceled the flight, she'd certainly pay Amy for the ticket and any other incurred expenses.

Geraldine chewed the piece of cake slowly, savoring each bite of the cinnamon and sugar coated crumb topping. My, my, my. How was she ever going to lose twenty pounds if she couldn't keep her trap shut long enough to change her diet? Looking up at the clock, she bit into another piece of cake and began chewing faster when she heard the customer service agent's voice over the speaker.

"Flight 177 from Florida has just landed and will be taxiing to the gate shortly. We will empty the plane and clean it as soon as possible so that we may begin boarding passengers for flight 56 bound for Washington, D.C. Thank you for your patience. We will be boarding shortly."

"See," Amy said, leaning over toward Geraldine. "That wasn't too bad. Just a little under an hour's delay. That's pretty good, considering the weather." She placed her hand on Geraldine's hand. "It's going to be just fine, Gerry. Really."

Geraldine smiled faintly, trying to believe her best friend's words. *It's going to be just fine, Gerry.* She closed her eyes for a moment and thought about her daughter. Hopefully Kasey wouldn't hold it against her for not spending Mother's Day together. She opened her eyes, then sighed. And another thing, it was about time she got over James Bullock. There was no reason on this earth why she couldn't find her a nice gent to cozy up with and have a real relationship with. God hadn't given her any concrete signs—evidence that he didn't approve of this trip. None whatsoever.

Kasey rattled her key in the lock a few more times before the latch finally caught. She stumbled into the darkness, gauging her steps until she reached the burgundy lamp with the ivory plastic-covered lampshade and flipped it on.

"Like I said, James, Mom never spoke of being married to anyone. From all the stories I've heard, you two were supposed to get married. I don't understand that picture."

James stood stiffly under the archway of the front door, like a man who had seen a ghost. A chill shivered his body. It had been almost twenty-eight years since he had stood in this very spot, with a bouquet of white and pink carnations, trying to reassure Geraldine's mother, Mrs. Clare Copeland, that he'd take good care of her baby girl.

"I don't understand it, either, but you saw it for yourself. You even said that Sylvester was around ever since you could remember. Sounds suspect to me," he whispered.

Kasey gently pulled him by the arm into the living room before locking the door behind him. "You don't have to whisper, James. Doesn't appear that Mom is here anyway." Although she knew this long beforehand, when they pulled up to the house and the four-door sedan was nowhere to be found. Glancing up at the grandfather clock, which read 12:05 A.M., she quietly hoped that her mother was out on the town with Aunt Amy and not down in the D.C. area.

"You want something to eat? Drink?" Kasey asked. Not waiting for a reply, she began walking toward the kitchen.

James's eyes perused the living room and the dining room area as he followed Kasey to the back of this house, which he knew all too well. Long gone was the old tattered Queen Anne sofa, where he and Gerry had spent many late evenings watching TV and swapping kisses. In the royal sofa's place was an off-white one adorned with several pillows. The old black-and-white that sat wide on the gold wire TV stand was gone. And someone had covered the creaks of the hardwood floors with this multicolored carpet. Damn Sylvester! He sucked in a deep breath and widened his stride until he was standing under the circular fluorescent light cover in the kitchen.

James watched Kasey scurry around the kitchen, swinging cabinets and drawers open and closed, clanging pots and bowls, and rinsing glasses and dropping ice cubes. He began chuckling, under his breath at first, then more loudly as he watched his daughter bouncing from one area of the kitchen to the next.

Kasey began laughing, too—a tension breaker, she supposed. "Mom always told me I need to think things out before I take on a task. Keep me from running around like a chicken with its head cut off." She laughed some more. "Guess she was right, huh?" She was stirring a pot of New England clam chowder.

"Uh-hmm." James smiled.

"Hope you like chowder," she said, sprinkling some pepper into the pot and stirring some more.

"I sure do. Haven't had any since I got to New Jersey," he told her.

Kasey tossed the tin can into the trash. She sat down at the table, facing James. "Straight from Cambodia?"

"No," James said with arched brows. "California. I spent the last six months in the Bay Area, trying to get a worthwhile trade."

A look of confusion sheathed Kasey's face. But he said he was in Cambodia all this time, she thought silently.

James sensed Kasey's thoughts and quickly interrupted. "I was in Cambodia until seven months ago. I stayed at a friend's home in San Francisco, while I enrolled in a computer program. I even saw a shrink a couple of times to get my head screwed on right." He raised his head a good bit and stared at the top of the window ahead of him. "I had planned to major in business computers at county college before your grandfather—" He stopped suddenly.

A few minutes ticked by. Kasey rose to stir the pot of soup again. She knew her grandfather was considered by many to be overbearing sometimes. But hearing a complete stranger, claiming to be her father, making the same accusations made it even harder for her to swallow. She poured the soup into the bowls, placed a tablespoon in each one, and carried them to the table.

"Thank you, Kasey."

"You're welcome," she told him, placing the two glasses and the large bottle of diet Pepsi on the table. "What about my grandfather, James? What were you going to say?"

"Nothing, nothing," he hurriedly replied. "When are you expecting your mother?"

Kasey chased away the steam rolling from the spoon with a soft blow before taking her first bite. She swallowed and said, "I don't know. I thought she'd be here by now. But maybe she left for D.C. already."

"D.C.?" James let the spoon rest against the rim of the bowl. He lowered his head and closed his eyes. Hell, if he and Gerry didn't have the worst timing.

"Yeah, she and my aunt Amy, mom's best friend, are going to spend Mother's Day in D.C. I thought they were leaving tomorrow night. But I guess Mom found someone to work her shift tomorrow and they flew out tonight. She'll be back on Sunday night."

Sunday night? James echoed over in his head. That was too late. He needed to speak to Gerry tonight, right now! Too many years had gone by for him not to get some answers—too hard to push all that pain and recollection back down. No matter what that second letter he refused to show Kasey swore, he had to hear from Gerry's own lips why in God's name did she run off and marry Sylvester and not tell him she was pregnant?

* * *

Geraldine flipped through the complimentary airline magazine a second time. This time she took special notice of a page advertising some exquisite wooden furniture. One day, she vowed inwardly, she would have a living room just like this. She slammed the magazine shut, reached above her head, and punched the button until the little reading light clicked off. 12:40 A.M. and they were still sitting on the ground, even thirty minutes after the flight attendant promised that they would taxi to the runway just as soon as they had clearance.

"Jesus," Geraldine mumbled under her breath. The flight had been delayed nearly two hours, and she was beginning to feel all the hard week's work kidnapping her body. All this fuss to get to D.C. She could have very well been asleep in the comforts of her own bed by now instead of being squashed in this air-stifling piece of machinery like pennies in a wrapper.

"Relax, Gerry," Amy whispered over her left shoulder to Geraldine. "We'll be airborne in no time. I told you it's like this sometimes." She nudged her playfully with her elbow. "Take a few more deep breaths. You'll be fine. Remember to think, you're doing this for you." Amy buried her head back into her magazine, giving no further thought to Geraldine's apprehension.

Geraldine let out a stint of deep breaths. *I'm doing the right thing, I'm doing the right thing, I'm doing the right thing,* she affirmed over and over until she felt less antsy. She heard the faint sound of the overhead speakers breaking through. Oh, Lord. Now she had to use the bathroom. The wild pounding in her heart resumed. *I'm doing the right thing, I'm doing the right thing, I'm doing the right thing. Right, Lord?*

"Ladies and gentlemen. Thank you for your patience and understanding. We should be ready for takeoff just as soon as we get a favorable report about some technical problems we're experiencing. Not to worry, our mechanics are checking the engine."

Several loud disgruntled voices ribbed through the cabin.

"This is ridiculous," cried one lady.

"Yeah!" yelled another man. "What the heck is going on?"

Geraldine unlatched her seat belt and stood up abruptly, bumping her head against the overhead cabinet.

Amy's eyes widened with alarm—her mouth dropped open. "Where are you going, Gerry?"

Geraldine didn't respond. She reached for her pocketbook, tucked it under her arm, and stepped into the aisle. She couldn't wait any longer. She had to go right now.

9

Kasey dunked the rosemary tea bag in the steaming mug of water several times. Spring's breeze swept through the partially open window, bringing with it the dank scent of the city streets.

"I can't understand why you won't just tell me the story," Kasey said, flinging her braids back over her shoulders. "Do you really think it's fair for you to pop back into my life and not give me a full explanation?"

She eyed James wearily. "Wouldn't you want one if it were you sitting on this side of the table?" She didn't want to sound so brash, didn't want to lose her composure and start boiling uncontrollably from all the mounting events that had affected her life: the death of her twin brother, the deteriorating health of Uncle Chitty, the dilapidation of this house, the silent death of her mother's life, and her recent episode with Baseem.

James dumped another teaspoon of sugar in the clay cup, bringing the total heaping sum to three. "Got back to the States and got hooked on this stuff again," he grinned as he stirred the liquid vigorously.

Leaning against the back of her chair, Kasey surveyed James under the yellowish light. His oval face tapered down to a pointed chin, another feature she shared with her father. "How long you say you been in the States again?"

My God, she was just as determined as he had remembered Gerry's mother being. Definitely a trait acquired from her grandmother. "Seven months. Came just as soon as—" He stopped, took a sip of tea, and continued, "Man! Now that'll get me going way into the night." He laughed uneasily, an attempt to avoid the inevitable subject that had been lurking about him and Kasey for the past few hours. "Got any lemon? I think I got a little beside myself with the sugar."

Kasey ignored his request. Not a hospitable thing to do, she knew. After all, her mother had taught her better, but she had more pressing things on her mind. Things that James was apparently reluctant to share with her.

"Perhaps you should come back when my mother is here. This way maybe I can get some completed answers out of you."

"And out of your mother," he curtly replied before taking a few more gulps of his tea. "Sorry to have barged into your life the way I did. I should go." He placed the sodden tea bag and spoon into the empty cup. His welcome here was obviously overextended, though it would have never been years ago. James rose from his seat.

The piercing ring of the telephone caused Kasey to jump. No one ever called the house this time of the night, she thought standing. *Hopefully, it was Mom calling, she wished as she reached for the white phone hanging on the wall. Maybe she heard what happened, maybe she was too embarrassed to come home yet. Maybe she knew she'd have to explain to me why, after all this time, she felt it necessary to hide the fact that she and Mr. Sylvester were married.* Kasey lifted the receiver on the third ring.

"Hello?" she answered with grave uncertainty.

"Kase? This Kareema. Do you know Baseem has been arrested?" She was breathing heavy and speaking fast.

Kasey clamped her eyelids shut. *Did you know your brother tried to whip my behind in my own shop tonight?* she wanted to scream out. "Yeah," she finally said.

"Rumor is he may get ten to twenty in the pen. I can't get with that."

"What?" she was shocked. *Ten to twenty?* "For what happened tonight? It was wrong but not ten to twenty years' worth."

"What you talkin, 'bout Kase? You don't think check fraud and embezzlement is serious biz?" Kareema began laughing uncontrollably. "Baby girl, you sure are as naive as Baseem said."

Check fraud? Kasey gasped. Kareema kept laughing.

James detected the transformation in his daughter's face. He moved closer to her, trying to promote eye contact. If he could just grab hold of her eyes, he'd know if she was in some kind of fix. When she finally glimpsed up into his eyes, he smiled, feeling a sense of tranquility engulf him.

"Is everything okay?" James whispered to her.

She nodded yes with an equally brilliant smile and waved for him to sit down. She followed the same hand gesture with a single index finger, signaling one more minute.

"Kareema," Kasey said strongly. There. That should do it. It didn't take much to push her into alignment, just a firm tone, a commanding voice. She was so weak that way, unlike her elder brother, Baseem. "What do you mean they got him for check fraud? Explain."

"Girl, you know I can't go into details over the waves. I was on my way to post bail when I got the call that the judge won't be available until Monday." Kareema sniffed. "Mom won't be able to handle this with her chemo and all. It might push her over the edge. Damn, I hope they don't do anything that would keep Baseem from paying for her doctor bills." She let out another deep breath. "I'll call you as soon as I know more. He wants to see you ASAP. Don't know how you could manage that, but you better pay him a visit soon, baby girl. Anyway, I's be out. Peace."

"Baseem?" James inquired with an arched eyebrow.

"No, his sister, Kareema. Baseem was arrested for check fraud." She sat down at the table again. Could that have been why he wanted these so-called record company checks sent to her house?

"You're kidding, right?" James asked.

"No," Kasey said solemnly. "I wish I was."

James eyed her more closely. The wrinkle pinched in the middle of her forehead revealed a little more. "You didn't have nothing to do with it, did you, Kasey?" His voice was soft and syrupy.

"No!" Kasey snapped, springing up from the chair suddenly. She paced the kitchen floor in four quick steps before rotating on the balls of her heels. "I thought he was getting checks for his rap groups from the record company . . . he said he wanted them to come here cause he trusted me more than the mailman in his neighborhood . . . said he didn't want to open a PO box cause it wouldn't look good for business."

She was pacing the floor. She hurried over to the table. A look of fear consumed her wide eyes.

"Do you know if the checks were payable to you?" James asked.

Kasey shook her head. "No, I think they were in his name. Or his company name. I don't know," she whined.

James stood up. "And you're sure, sweetheart, that you didn't cash them. Right?"

"No!" she shrieked. "I didn't cash them. I didn't see them. I don't know nothing about check fraud. They can't arrest me, too, can they, James? I swear I didn't know. I can't go to jail! Mom is out of town." She began sobbing out of control.

James drew her into his chest for the second time today. Consoling her the best way he could, the way he had done Gerry the night he told her he had been drafted to go to Vietnam.

"There, there, sweetheart," he said, rubbing her frail back. Glory be, he thought. If he had been here sooner, had been a part of her life all them lost years, if Geraldine would have just answered his letters and told him that she was pregnant, Kasey's life would have turned out very differently. That, he would have seen to.

* * *

Geraldine handed the cab driver ten dollars before stepping out of the blue vinyl interior into a monsoon downpour. The whole flying ordeal had ruined her nerves. She walked through the bustle of people cramping through the sliding glass doors. It hadn't been twenty minutes, and she had to use the bathroom again.

She rinsed her hands with warm soapy water and left the ladies' room in a huff. Shouldn't have ever agreed to going to D.C. in the first place. She pushed the elevator button. Crazy. Plain and simple, she determined, stepping into the empty elevator. Obviously God hadn't wanted her to complete that trip. She pulled her car keys from out of her pocketbook and unlocked the car door.

Amy's harsh words, which were nothing more than a best friend's attempt to save a ruined moment, replayed in her head. *Are you just going to punk out like this, Gerry, and leave Daniel hanging?* Geraldine cranked over the ignition.

Nobody was going to convince her to stay aboard a cursed flight, no matter who the person was. She didn't want to fly to begin with. She had told Amy that time and time again. Why else hadn't she ever made the trips to Bahamas or Jamaica with Amy before? Geraldine pulled out of the parking garage. Didn't make no sense for a flight to be that dang-blasted delayed or boggled down with problems. It was an indisputable sign that she should spend Mother's Day weekend with Kasey. If Kasey wasn't with that con man Baseem.

Still no excuse for Baseem to be involved in whatever mess he was in, she thought. *He was old enough to know better— make something of his life. If James was here, had been around to raise Kasey, he'd never approve of Baseem. Never. Just like Daddy never approved of James. Or anyone except Sylvester, Daddy's best friend's nephew.*

Squinting her eyes into half slivers, Geraldine flipped the windshield wipers on high. The harsh sloshing sound of rain pouncing underneath her car warned her that if she didn't slow down, she'd soon be hydroplaning. Wet pavement was hazardous, especially mixed with sloppy city drivers. If she had purchased a car phone for emergency use, like Amy had often suggested, she would try Kasey again. Then again maybe not, she thought, glancing down at the clock. 1:10 A.M.

Got to clear up these windows, she thought, turning on the DEFROST button. God, she couldn't wait to slide under the soft downy-scented sheets of her bed and drop off into a deep, dauntless sleep. Just a few more blocks, she thought, turning onto her street. Later in the morning, she would phone Kasey at the shop and tell her she had changed her mind. That she hadn't gone to D.C. after all, and that she would be most obliged, honored, and blessed to spend another Mother's Day with her.

"I can't believe Gerry still has this old picture," James said as he moved his head closer to the wall to inspect the black-and-white photo. Al Green's "Let's Stay Together" played from the living room, where Kasey had tossed on a few greatest-hits CD's. So far he had been thrown back into a familiar time warp with sounds of Marvin Gaye, Al Green, Temptations, Smoky Robinson, and Aretha Franklin shuffling through the five-carousel CD changer—only one of the few items that seemed new in the house.

"God, it seemed like just yesterday when we took this picture," he said, turning to look at Kasey, who was smiling and bopping to the music. "We had gone to Wildwood for the day. Had signed up for the church bus trip." He paused momentarily.

"Your mother," he began again, as he faced the picture once more. The word *mother* had come forth sweetly from his lips. "She was something else." He chortled. "I met her at a birthday party in North Newark. I walked into the room, scanned the beautiful daisies standing against the wall, and *pow!* Just like that, I caught eyes with Gerry. Wooo, that woman could dance her fanny off." He ran his fingers across the glass casing that had preserved the picture so well.

"Yes," Kasey said, standing directly beside him, eyeing the

picture as well. "She told me how you smooth-talked her into dancing with you during the Temptations' "Just My Imagination." And that you smelled of Jade cologne and your hair was saturated with Afro-sheen." She laughed lightly.

"Let me see," she said, rubbing the right side of her temple with two fingers before closing her eyes. "You had on a pair of blue bell-bottom pants and a bright colored shirt with a spiral neck and some two-inch-thick platform shoes. You whispered in her ear that you thought she was the prettiest lady in the entire room, and that any man would be honored to have her on his arm. You told her that if she was any softer, you'd give up butter and just have her brush her arm across your pancakes."

James busted into a hearty chuckle. He laughed that way for a few minutes, reminiscing and admiring the fact that Gerry's memory had been so well tuned in. "Gosh, I can't believe she told you all that." He looked up at the picture again.

"She told me lots of stories, James. More than me and Kenny had wanted to hear. Trust me."

"Then I suppose she told you that it was this time," he said, pointing to the picture, "in Wildwood, New Jersey, that we fell in love." He laughed. "There was this old white man, peddling his camera around the boardwalk. He asked to take our picture."

"Yes, that would be Mr. Zimmerman from South Orange. He charged you all four dollars and fifty cents for the picture."

James spun around slowly to face Kasey. Geraldine had remembered their every moment spent and had filled his daughter's mind with such memories. A bothersome feeling groped at him. Why would Gerry go through such lengths when she was married to Sylvester? What did Sylvester think about her pining for him and filling the kids—his kids—with images and stories about him? Had he not gotten the word that Sylvester had died when he got the other news, he would have gone straight to him first. Threatened to twist his neck off for stealing his Gerry from him like he had. He was supposed to be his best friend.

James's face turned even more frigid. "When I come back

from the bathroom, Kasey, I want you to tell me about Sylvester. I want to hear all about your stepdaddy.''

Kasey stood still, not fully understanding what James wanted to hear. She watched him as he easily found his way toward the bathroom. What about Mr. Sylvester? He was a kind man, a reliable man—her godfather. He had been there for every birthday that she and Kenny shared since she could remember. He had put her bike together, taught her how to ride it, roller skate, and hit a softball.

Mr. Sylvester, the only man in her life to define just exactly what a man should be, had given Kenny a flip over his knee whenever he got out of hand and sassed her mother. He had attended Kenny's track meets and football games whenever he could. He had never brought another woman by the house, had never seemed to care about another woman as much as her mother, as far as she knew. What exactly was she supposed to say about a man, that come to think of it, had been the only father-figure she'd ever really known.

Geraldine shut off the engine, grabbed her bag, and stepped out of the car. The street was crowded with parked cars, crunched behind each other like Saltine crackers bunched in their packaging. Someone must be having a party, she determined, making her way up the front stairs to the dimly lit porch. She hadn't remembered leaving the porch light on when she left. She reached inside the mailbox, which was empty. Kasey's been here, she thought, instinctively turning around to survey the string of parked cars and recognizing the Hyundai.

A steep flight of steps met her gaze after she locked the second, inner, hall door behind her. She had counted these stairs so many times, she knew the number like the back of her hand after all these many years, but couldn't recall offhand how many she had to trample right this minute. Lord, have mercy. As soon as she hit the lottery, she was going to buy a home with no steps.

Partway up the steps, she heard the muffled voices. Who in the world would be at her home visiting Kasey at this hour of the morning? Her disposition quickly turned icy at the idea that the other voice penetrating the thinly insulated wall was her future son-in-law. She was out of breath by the time she reached the top landing. She must do something about the extra pounds she was buoying about unnecessarily. She placed her key in the lock and wiggled it back and forth for some time. Darn door lock, she'd have to find someone to fix this blasted thing before her key broke off in the lock once and for all.

Kasey's eyes bulged with anxiety when she heard the familiar sounds of the key turning into the lock. "It's Mom," she shrieked with excitement. "Quick," she whispered to James. "Hide over there." She pointed to the back of the bedroom door. "Oh, God . . . I'm so nervous. Oh, man, she's going to be sooo thrilled. No, maybe she'll faint." Kasey was giggling with nervousness. She raced out the bedroom, where she and James had been viewing the photos on the wall, toward the front door, and opened it.

"Mom!" she shrieked with excitement. "I was so worried. I thought you had already left for D.C." She freed the bag from her mother's grip and flung it to the floor, pulling her mother inside. She hurled the door shut and gave her a tight hug before breaking free. "Wow! Mom, you look great! Look at your hair. It's beautiful. When did you get it done like that?"

Kasey was asking too many questions. Something definitely was not right, Geraldine thought, as she stood in the living room examining her daughter's uncommon behavior. Yup, she was surely up to something, Geraldine resolved.

"Well, it's good to see you too, Kase." Geraldine smiled. "But we got to get that door fixed. My key nearly broke off in the lock."

Whatever it was Kasey was up to, Geraldine had to admit that she enjoyed her vibrant attitude. Geraldine couldn't remember the last time Kasey was so smitten with her.

James stood behind the partially cracked bedroom door, peering through the open slit at the back of Geraldine. His heart rate had accelerated toward stroke level. He exhaled several choppy breaths in an attempt to retard his pounding heart. No such luck.

All the emotions of years lost had flooded every inch of his body, from the beads of sweat forming at the tip of his forehead, down to the throbbing of his heart, through the butterflies in his stomach, past the pounding throb in his groin, to the cramps he felt in the arch of his right foot. *Geraldine, Geraldine.* After all these many years, what was he going to say? What was he going to do? He rubbed his hands together in excitement. *Lord, please help me. It's been so long—it's been so much.*

"Come, come," Kasey said, tugging Geraldine by the arm and leading her to the sofa. "Here, sit down, Mom." Kasey nearly pushed her down onto the sofa. "You thirsty? No, never mind," Kasey said. She couldn't chance leaving her mother alone while she went to the kitchen, because she just might end up in her bedroom and bump into James.

"Kasey, what the heck is the matter with you, girl? Have you lost your mind? Why are you acting so strange? And who was that you were talking to just a while back? I heard some voices when I came up the stairs." Seeing Kasey's eyes jump to the size of a walnut, Geraldine knew she stumbled onto something. "Well?" she said.

Kasey began pacing the floor. This was all so exciting, all so fairty-tale like. All too much. A camera. She needed a camera or a camcorder or something to capture the moment that was about to change her mother's life *for-everrrr*. She parted her lips together and blew out some air. Geraldine went to stand up. Kasey stood in front of her, motioning her to sit back down. Geraldine obliged, reluctantly.

"What the sam-hill is going on, Kasey? Who you hiding in here? I know I heard voices coming up the steps. You got that boy in here, don't you?" Geraldine was attempting to lift herself off the sofa, whose sunken pillows from years of butts being pressed down in them had nearly swallowed her. "Girl, it's late and I'm tired," Geraldine said, extending out her right hand. "Now please help me up, honey."

"Mom, wait!" Kasey told her with flailing hands. "You're right. I am hiding something." She smiled widely. "I . . .

I . . ." she stammered. "It's your gift." There—she blurted it out.

"What are you talking about, Kasey? Gift for what?"

"Your Mother's Day gift," Kasey told her. "It's sort of unusual, a real surprise—something you weren't expecting. Not in the least, teeny-weeny bit." She grinned diabolically. Lord, she sure hoped the first-aid kit her mother always had stuffed in the hallway closet had some smelling salts. Because after seeing James's face, Kasey was sure her mother would pass out.

Geraldine scooted up to the edge of the sofa, another failed attempt to free her behind from the grip of sunken pillows. Though she really could appreciate Kasey's thoughtfulness in wanting to give her a Mother's Day gift right now, she'd really prefer to get some sleep. However, she'd fight to stay awake just a little longer to appease Kasey's theatrics.

"Okay." Geraldine smiled faintly. "If you say so." She leaned back into the hollowness of the twelve-year-old sofa, feeling the wooden structure beneath the cushion grazing her back. Her mind slipped off to thoughts of Arizona.

"I'll be right back," Kasey said, slipping between the bedroom door and closing it behind her.

Lord, if this child don't hurry up with it, Geraldine thought. *If she only knew that the only thing I cared about right now, after that whole dilemma with the airplane, was sleep, she wouldn't be dragging her feet on whatever this thing is she has to give to me tonight.* She clasped her hands together, then let her mind wander freely, visualizing her plan. Eleven thousand dollars was enough money to leave this rat race and move to Arizona. She could sell this matchbox piece of house for twenty-five or thirty thousand dollars, purchase that Honda she always wanted, quit nursing altogether, and open up a little coffeehouse with homemade sweet potato pies, apple pies, peach cobblers, and pound cakes right in the center of Phoenix, Arizona.

Heck with the money in her 401K fund—she could sure enough open a business and use the money from the sale of this house for a down payment on a house in the Cactus State.

Why shouldn't she move? Everything had played out for her in Newark, New Jersey, anyway. Driving across country and seeing some of the other states would be well worth it. She'd pick a date sometime next year and do it! Her father was no longer a hindering force to reckon with, Kasey would be married to that boy, and she would still be alone. The word *April* popped into her mind. With her eyes still shut, Geraldine let out a half-moon grin. It was settled then. She'd make plans to head to Arizona next April.

"Come on," Kasey whispered to James. "Here's your chance to see the woman of your dreams and ask her all the unanswered questions you have regarding her, me, Kenny, and Mr. Sylvester."

At the mention of Sylvester's name, James's face hardened. His heartbeat had tamed down from the mambo rhythm it had sung earlier. Yes, he did need to get some answers.

"I'm ready," he said, eyeballing Kasey anxiously. "I suppose it's time I find out why the woman who claimed an undying love for me, before I left for 'Nam, would marry my best friend."

Kasey stood in the doorway, peering out at her mother, who appeared to be sleeping with her head laid back against the sofa. She eased out of the bedroom with James towering behind her. She could hear light snoring sounds coming from her mother's mouth. How could she go to sleep at a time like this? Kasey thought, tapping her on the shoulder. Geraldine cracked her eyes open lazily, trying to keep them open enough to acknowledge what Kasey was saying.

"Mom," Kasey said. "Your Mother's Day gift . . . wake up." She tapped the nodding Geraldine once more. "Mom."

"Oh, Kase, what is it? I'm so tired," she said groggily, turning away from her. "Can you just give it to me tomorrow?"

"It is tomorrow," Kasey told her.

"Well, later on today," Geraldine said annoyingly.

Kasey looked over her shoulder to James, who shrugged his shoulder. She nodded her head toward her mom. "Say something to her, do something," she whispered to James.

"Gerry," James bellowed in a deep voice. "Fall out," he

said, using the military term that Geraldine's father had used with her whenever he wanted to wake her up.

Geraldine's eyes snatched open. Was she dreaming? She hadn't heard that term in some years. And that voice—it sounded so familiar. Slowly, uncertainly, she turned her head to face the voice. When she saw the tall figure standing before her—the tall gentleman with the salt-and-pepper hair and copper complexion, she sprang up straighter.

"Gerry," James called out again. "It's me," he said softly. God, even after all these years, she still looked as innocent as then, he thought. She had filled out, of course, becoming much more woman since he last laid eyes on her. Having the babies put some good, healthy weight on those once slender, border-line-bony shoulders and fragile hips. Once she stood up, though, he'd be able to tell just how much womanhood she had gathered since their last meeting in this very room, twenty-seven years ago.

Geraldine leaned forward on the sofa, inspecting the handsome gent standing before her. "Me?" she said cautiously. No, she told herself quietly. I'm having a bizarre dream. Shouldn't have eaten that coffee cake so late. Late night sweets always give me weird dreams, she determined, using Kasey's arm to pull her off the sofa, until she was standing on her own.

"Yes, it's me, Gerry. James Bullock."

Geraldine's eyes jutted out with disbelief. *James?* Her mind turned over and over. James Bullock. She stood slowly, gawking blankly at the man standing in front of her. She scanned his physique: tall, slender, minimal percent body fat, bright smile, big round eyes, long eyelashes. A spell of dizziness swarmed over her. Her knees trembled, threatening to give way. James Bullock after all these years?

No way! No damn way! This is some sort of sick joke. Oh, Lord, she thought, surveying him some more. Wide hands, long nose, full lips—yes, yes, she heard herself agreeing. No, wait, wait, she exhaled deeply. It can't be. Her knees gave way as she took in the last feature—that well-known freckle above the corner of his right eye.

10

Kasey waved the smelling salts beneath Geraldine's nose a few more times, until she began to stir. James was seated beside Geraldine, stroking her dry hand. When Geraldine pushed Kasey's hand away from her nose, Kasey leaned back against the sofa, next to her mom.

Geraldine shook her head a few times as if gathering her thoughts. She caught a glimpse of Kasey, whose face was filled with alarm. "I'm okay, Kase," she said, patting Kasey with her left hand. It wasn't till then that she realized that her right hand was being caressed by someone besides Kasey. She turned to her right, coming dead smack, face-to-face with James Bullock. "I'll be damned," she whispered weakly. "After all these years—you finally decide to turn up.

"Not that I ever believed you were dead, see," Geraldine said, pulling her hand away from James's caressing strokes. "The way I figured it, you had been captured—probably even tortured, and held as one of them political prisoners. But when all the POW's were released from 'Nam . . ." She paused to push back the lump in her throat. The tears were filling up in her eyes. "I stopped speculating. Just held on to the fact that no one ever turned in your dog tags or officially claimed you dead.''

She cried just then, letting out all her mixed emotions about James Bullock being seated next to her after all these many lost years: the loss of Kenny, the loss of her parents, the loss of her life.

Geraldine was bawling hard and heaving. ''How come you didn't call? Didn't write me? Why?'' she said, raising her voice with each question, till it was practically at yelling level. ''I wrote and I wrote, but you never responded! You said you loved me, and I never heard from you again.'' Her face had turned hard and agitated. ''How come you didn't call? Write? What are you doing here anyway? We don't need you now!'' she said bitingly. The tears poured forth steadily.

Kasey placed her arm around her mother's shoulder, rubbing it softly. Her mother had a point—had several points. Maybe now James would confess and tell the whole story. Isn't that what he said he'd do once Mom was here to listen, too?

James blew out an exaggerated breath. He wanted to lash out, too, but knew that somewhere deep down, in the middle of all this mess, lay a culprit by the name of Colonel Jason. ''Gerry, I did write you several times, but I got only one response—one letter,'' he spouted, reaching into his shirt pocket and pulling out the envelope with the picture of her and Sylvester in it. ''This one,'' he said, handing her the envelope.

Reluctantly she took it from him and examined the outside of it. She noticed the Newark, New Jersey, postmark, the date, and her return address in the left-hand corner. This didn't even look like her handwriting, she thought, opening the envelope and pulling out the picture of her and Sylvester. It was the night they had attended her father's military ball. She attempted to hand it back to him. Okay, so maybe Sylvester had sent him a copy of the picture and used her return address. That still didn't have anything to do with the fact that he hadn't been in contact with her for more than twenty years.

James pushed the picture back into her hand. ''Flip it over,'' he told her.

Kasey leaned over her mother's left shoulder to view the photo again that James had showed her earlier.

Geraldine eyed him wearily. She turned the photo over and read the words: *Mr. and Mrs. Sylvester Peterson*. She read it a second time, a third time, then turned the picture over and stared at the powder blue spaghetti-strap dress she had worn and the navy blue, pinstriped suit Sylvester had on. She turned the picture over and read the words a fourth time.

A stupefied look veiled her face. After a few seconds, she looked him in the eye and asked, "Where did you get this picture from?"

"Where does it say I got it from?" he said gruffly.

Geraldine stared at the return address again: *575 South 17th Street, Newark, New Jersey. This address,* she determined. She put the picture down on the table. "I didn't send you that picture, James. I don't care what that envelope says. Sylvester and I were never married. Is that some kind of joke?"

"I would have liked to think that it was back then," James said, reaching over and picking up the picture. "But seeing you looking so elegant and festive with Sylvester while I was in 'Nam, with those words typed on the back, let me know that it wasn't my imagination playing a trick."

"It was that damn military ball thing that my father made me and Sylvester go to. He was the one who made us stand and smile for the photographer. If you thought we were married . . ." She hesitated. "I'm sorry," she continued. "It was only an outing that my father forced me to go to. Barring that picture, James, how come you didn't write me? How come you didn't return my letters? Call me?"

"I couldn't call. I was in the jungle, remember? So I wrote you, Gerry," James said softly. "I wrote and I wrote and I wrote until you sent me that picture of you and Sylvester. That crushed my heart in half—did you know that? Of course you didn't, because you were so busy with Sylvester."

"I wasn't busy with Sylvester!" she spouted. "I was busy thinking about you, crying over letters that were never answered, phone calls that never came. Home leave that never materialized.'' The tears began dousing her cheeks again. ''I never got your letters, James. Never!''

''Mom,'' Kasey whispered, stroking her shoulder some more. ''It's okay. Maybe you all should talk about it later. It's already very late.''

''No!'' Geraldine snapped at Kasey. ''I'm sorry, honey.'' She quickly apologized, patting Kasey's thigh. ''I want to know where he's been all these years, and how come now all of a sudden he can waltz back into our lives.''

James stood up and walked over to the other side of the room, where he pulled the La-Z-Boy chair in front of the coffee table, facing Kasey and Geraldine directly. Well, if she wants to know where he's been all these years, fine.

''I spent the past twenty-three years in Cambodia as a retired kick-boxer competitor. I lived with Mia, a lady friend of mine. I helped raise her three children until she passed away a year and a half ago. She was special to me, but I never married her. Mainly because I couldn't get my mind off you.

''When I got that picture from you—when you didn't send me any other letters but that one after a year—I wanted to die. I would have just run across enemy lines and let them kill me. But a good friend of mine, who's deceased now, encouraged me to stay strong—stay focused enough so I could get home and see you for myself.

''But the more and more I stared at that picture of the two of you, smiling and all happy-like, and the more I read the words 'Mr. and Mrs. Sylvester Peterson,' I became less and less interested in ever seeing you or any other American person again. I had just one more year to fulfill my two-year tour and come back to attend college,'' James huffed. ''I decided what else did I have to come home to America for? My parents were dead a long time ago. So I defected and decided to stay in Cambodia, where I met Mia.

''I traveled the entire Asian continent: Burma, Hong Kong, Thailand, Taiwan, and Kampuchea. I learned how to kick-box to release my frustration. And after years of practice and successful bouts, my instructor encouraged me to tour the kick-boxing circuit. So that's what I did. I blew you and Sylvester and America off and became a semiprofessional kick-boxer and a Cambodian citizen.'' He stopped to catch his breath and to absorb Kasey and Geraldine's facial expressions. They were enthralled all right, he thought, continuing.

''I lived my life that way for years. Thinking about you off and on, wondering why Sylvester would go behind my back and steal you, wondering why you'd let him. Why God had let my parents die, wondering why your father hated me so much.'' He lowered his head into the palms of his hands, where he wept. All he ever wanted to do was have a family of his own—be around to raise some children, unlike his parents.

Kasey and Geraldine looked at each other. Geraldine lowered her eyes, letting a few teardrops drip onto her lap. Kasey leaned her head closer to her mother's until they both touched. Silence dropped over the room, giving hidden pain an opportunity to come to light.

Geraldine sniffled softly, then wiped her eyes with the back of her hand and spoke first. ''Why did you find us now? How did you know we existed?''

James swiped his cheeks with the palm of his hands, before looking up at Geraldine and Kasey. He let out a frustrating breath, reached into his shirt pocket again, and pulled out another letter. He reached over the coffee table, with the plastic bowl hosting the colorful plastic fruit, and handed the letter to Geraldine. He glanced over at Kasey and shook his head up and down. ''That is why I didn't want to say something before, Kasey.''

Kasey leaned over and read with Geraldine as she reviewed the postmark on the outside of this envelope: *Englewood, New Jersey, 1995.* There was no return address, but she didn't have to speculate who might have sent it. Trembling, she tugged the letter loose from the envelope, wondering the entire time what its contents were.

James: I write this letter from my deathbed, not for absolution but in a desperate last attempt to try and correct some of my many ruthless wrongs. I've been following your career off and on for many years. You're one hell of a kick-boxer that I hope I'll never have to contend with.

Let me cut to the nitty-gritty. You need to know that you have a person here in the States who needs your help and guidance. You are the father of two wonderful children—Kasey and Kenny, twins that Geraldine had twenty-six years ago. She was pregnant when you left for 'Nam (another thing I neglected to allow you to know). Unfortunately Kenny died a tragic death two years ago, but Kasey is alive for now, as long as she doesn't marry that thug of a boyfriend of hers, Baseem.

Kasey is a barber at Chitty's Barbershop on Central Avenue in Newark. I'm sure you know the place. Geraldine didn't make it to medical school like I wanted. But she got close enough to wear a smock as a registered nurse at one of the local hospitals in Newark. Sylvester, who pitched in where he could, has gone on to be with the Lord. I am soon to be on my way out of this world, although I know my journey will not be toward heaven.

I apologize for some of the pain I may have caused you. Namely, being the one responsible for your enlistment into uniform. I shared this with Geraldine. I did not tell her that you were still alive. If you want her to know this, I'm sure you'll find your way. Sorry to hear about the loss of your love.

Front and Forward, soldier— your march has just begun. Colonel Jason Copeland (Do not let me down, or I'll see you in hell, and I know you wouldn't want to meet me there, too.)

Geraldine shut her eyes. *Well, at least he tried to make amends. God rest my dad's soul.* Before this moment, she wasn't sure if she had completely forgiven her father—but now she had. It was time once and for all to let it go. "Guess he forgot to mention that Sylvester and I were never married."

"He probably forgot he sent the picture."

"Probably," Geraldine huffed. "I just wish I could really understand the reason he'd do such a thing to you—me—us."

James shrugged his shoulder. "There's a lot of reasons. For one, I was not from an educated family. Secondly, I was a foster child who he saw as an idiotic jock. And thirdly, I was too dark-skinned for the light-skinned, wavy-haired Colonel. Don't you remember?" He laughed weakly.

Geraldine cracked a partial grin, recalling the time her father had called her mother, screaming and yelling about seeing her out with some baboon-looking man with a long nose. "But still, James," Geraldine said somberly, "it's been a hard battle all my life with my dad. But it's time to leave it behind me." She let more tears flow. James came over and sat next to her, pulling her head into his chest. Kasey looked on, savoring the moment.

Feeling the need to leave her parents alone, Kasey stood up. "I'll get us something to drink." She winked at James before leaving the room.

A few minutes passed away before Geraldine spoke again. "Now what? What does this mean?" she mumbled.

"I don't know, Gerry," James said, stroking her cheeks. "Figure out if you have anything left for me."

She smiled, looking up at him—her mascara smeared beneath her eyes. "I've never stopped loving you, James. That much you can believe."

"But we've got to do something about Kasey. She's got this God-awful boyfriend. I just know if you met him, you wouldn't approve of him. Lord, James, I don't want to sound like my father. But we've got to do something to make her see that this guy is all wrong for her."

James nodded in agreement. "Baseem, I believe his name to be. We've met," he said with a raised brow. "I don't think we'll have to worry about him anymore. He's been taken care of."

Geraldine looked up in amazement. "How?"

"Oh, just a father-daughter-don't-mess-with-her-again thing.

Don't worry 'bout him no more, Gerry. Just concentrate on you and what you want for a change."

"I know what I want," she said.

"Really? What's that?"

"I want me a quaint coffeehouse of my own. And I want it in Arizona, along with a little stucco ranch-style house."

"Arizona, huh? I think that's feasibly possible. You've got a plan?"

"I'm working on it," she said, allowing James to cuddle her hands.

"Is there going to be any room in your life for a handyman?"

Geraldine smiled. "Depends on who it is."

James laughed. "Do I take that as a yes?"

"We can talk about it." Lord, it was like he had never departed. Her heart was bursting with happiness.

Kasey stepped back into the living room with two steaming cups of tea. Now this was the picture she had dreamed about all of her life. Her mother tickled silly and happy with a man she loves. And a man, a dad, loving her mother back.

"Lord, girl, you about the most tea-drinking person I know in America," James teased.

"She gets it honest from her mother," Geraldine said, taking the cup from her.

The telephone rang out, stopping everyone in their tracks. Kasey lifted the cordless phone from the cradle.

"Hello," she said.

"Operator with a collect call from Baseem," the operator told her.

Kasey hesitated, taking a moment to look at her parents. Wow, she could finally think that word—even say it aloud and it be for real. Geraldine and James watched suspiciously. James motioned the word *Baseem* with his lips. Kasey nodded in the affirmative. James took his pointer finger and slid it across his neck from corner to corner, symbolizing a cut throat. Kasey smiled.

"Kasey, this your man, girl," she heard Baseem say in the background.

"Ma'am, will you accept the call?" the operator asked.

Kasey sighed heavily and spewed, "No." She looked over at James. "Tell him I've got me a true man now. I've got my dad."

Kasey clicked off the power on the telephone and placed it back into the cradle. She looked at her mom, who was clinging on to James. "I'm going to my bed," she said, walking over to them. "See you tomorrow, Dad." She kissed James on his cheek, then reached over toward her mother. "Happy Mother's Day, Mom. I love you."

Epilogue

Thirteen months later

Geraldine moved the red, triangle-shaped lever to sixty-eight degrees on the thermostat. It was only six twenty in the morning, and already the temperature had soared to a sweltering seventy degrees. Going to be another scorcher, she thought, pulling the last of the peach cobbler and sweet potato pies from the sizzling oven racks. Thank God, she didn't have to whip up the chocolate or carrot cakes today. She offered those specialties only on Saturdays and Sundays, and today was Wednesday.

She wiped the sweat from her brow with the back of her lightly floured hand, leaving a speckle of white flour on her forehead. The first set of customers, Mr. and Mrs. Clarke, a retired couple from Brooklyn, New York, would be waiting outside the tinted glass door at precisely 6:50 A.M. With a newspaper under Mr. Clarke's arm, and the latest fiction novel by some African-American author clasped in Mrs. Clarke's hand, the strongly resembled couple would bid good morning before beelining over to their favorite seats. Seats that faced west and overlooked the staunch cactus plants and the arid mountains.

Geraldine placed the pie pans and the peach cobbler tray on the cooling racks, before pouring herself a twelve-ounce glass of spring water. Her pale peach, short-sleeved cotton shirt began to show wet spots of perspiration. She tossed a piece of lemon in the water, and chugged a quarter of the glass away before coming up for air. Hearing keys jiggling in the background, then the creaking sounds of the back door opening, she walked to the door with her cup in hand.

"Need some help?" she asked, using her body to hold the door open.

"I got it, Gerry. Thanks," James said, stumbling over the top step. He caught his balance in enough time not to send five keyboard-sized boxes tumbling to the ground. "It's supposed to get to 104 degrees today," he huffed, placing the boxes on the counter, then wiping his face with a nearby paper napkin. His biceps, raised through a white, sleeveless tank top, weren't as hard as the days of his youth, still threatened their strength.

Geraldine handed him her remaining glass of ice water. "Here," she said, watching him swallow the water at record speed, while she wiped the residue of condensation on her light blue cotton skirt, already stained with vanilla flavoring. "Slow down, honey, before you end up with stomach cramps." She could see James's stomach, which now resembled a tiny pouch due to a year of good eating, beginning to push over the black leather belt which secured his wrinkled blue jeans.

"Whew! I needed that," he said, placing the empty glass on the tiled countertop.

"Are these the rest of the keyboards?" Geraldine asked, lifting the top to one of the cardboard boxes, her face glowing with excitement.

"Sure is. Now we have everything we need to get the computers up and running on the Internet." He lifted the boxes and headed through the kitchen to the front, humming an old Archie Bell and the Dells tune.

Geraldine had nearly clipped his heels more than once, following so closely behind him. He stopped at the right corner of the tiny café and lowered the boxes down onto the elongated computer table. When he turned around to face Geraldine, his mouth was wide open and welcoming.

"This is it, my darling. Arizona's first and only coffeehouse with Internet-cruising capabilities." He smiled smartly. "Who would have ever thought Sip & Chat would be up and running so soon? You did it, woman," he said proudly.

"We did it, James. I would have never been able to do this without you. Thank you, honey." She walked over to him and placed her arms around his narrow back.

"No, thank *you.*" He kissed her forehead. "Sip & Chat," he repeated again. "A place where people can sit down over a glass of something refreshing and catch up with one another and the rest of the world. Brilliant, darling."

"Our story is the inspiration behind the name, James. Always remember that."

"I will," he said, pulling her head closer to his chest until he felt the warmth of her temple against the warmth of his own skin. He rubbed her back gently, further mixing the mounting beads of sweat dipping down her back and onto her cotton shirt. They stood this way for some time, letting the sun rays angling from the east further heat their bodies.

"Thank you, Geraldine, for letting me back into your heart."

She pulled back from the embrace just enough to stare up into his shiny face. "You were never out of my heart, James. Never." She smiled easily.

"I'm not ever leaving you this time. Unless of course . . ." He paused to look up at the ceiling. "God sends for me this time."

"I pray it won't be no time soon. We still have a lot of lost time to make up." She kissed his left arm, just below his shoulder and above his biceps. The taste of salt glazed her taste buds. Such a hardworking man, she thought, kissing him again in that same spot.

James lifted her chin with his hand as he lowered his head until he met that spot—that area that only the two of them shared. He lowered his lips atop of hers, tasting the flavors of sweet potato batter as his tongue danced with hers. Their intertwining was rudely disrupted by the ringing of the telephone.

"Already?" she teased, using her thumb to wipe away the copper lipstick color from James's lip. She tried to break away to catch the phone. James held her tightly.

"It's not quite seven o'clock yet, Mrs. Bullock. Don't be such a workaholic. Isn't that what you tell me?" he teased.

She looked rather anxiously at the continuous chiming of the telephone. "But it could be Kasey calling. Her plane could be delayed—she could be stranded in Chicago. Or she could have missed the plane altogether. I really should get that." She attempted to pull away again. He restrained her once more.

"Believe me," he said, drawing her into his chest again. "Kasey's got everything under control. I know that she and that new fellow of hers . . ." He searched to remember the name. The phone stopped ringing.

"Dennis Hazel," Geraldine offered quickly.

"Yeah, well, whatever the boy's name is. I'm sure they'll get here with no problems. Now . . ." He stopped speaking momentarily to capture her gaze with his for a few seconds. Once again he lowered his head and whispered, "Can we not worry about planes and airports and complete what you started, Mrs. Bullock?"

"What I started?" she crooned softly. "You mean what you started twenty-nine years ago."

His tongue engulfed hers like a lit gasoline trail searching for the explosion point. His long fingers slid across her back and around her side before cupping her right breast. He held her that way for some time, fondling and caressing, until he felt her nipples jut through the lace bra she wore.

Geraldine kissed him deeper, pressing her full body—less the ten pounds she had lost over the past year—into the hardness of his body. She had been amazed that she could have such feelings again after years of inadequate, simple pleasantries. The way James got her blood pumping, and her heart racing, alarmed her at times. Good Lord, she thought, tossing her head back as he kissed her neck passionately. If they didn't watch it, they'd end up in the back storage room, making love right on top of the floor freezer.

James used both hands to squeeze her buttocks before grabbing her by the hand and leading her back toward the storage room. The bug had bitten them once again. Geraldine stole a peek at the clock as she was being led through the kitchen. 6:40 A.M.

The shop was officially scheduled to open in twenty minutes, but Mr. and Mrs. Clarke would be waiting at six fifty. Lord, what would her customers think if she wasn't open by seven? 'Cause after all, she knew her husband and knew that if they got things heated up in the storage room, they might not be out until sometime after seven. Maybe.

James pulled her into the hazily lit room, but not before catching the questioning glare in her sparkling eyes. "What's the matter, sweetheart?" he asked, kissing the back of her hands softly. He slipped her index finger into his mouth and sucked it gingerly, while unfastening her blouse.

She unfastened his pants. "Nothing." She shrugged. *Nothing at all, Mr. Bullock. Everything is just right after all these many years.* She gasped a deep sigh as his soft, sweet warmth kissed her neck. *Tap, tap, tap.* It was the front door. She closed her eyes and concentrated on the rhythm that she and James were about to create. Frankly this was the only beat that Geraldine Bullock cared about. *Let it flow, let it flow, let it flow.*

NEVER SAY NEVER
Angela Winters

One

As she honked her car horn frantically, Nicole Cox felt sheer fright sweep through her as her brow broke a sweat. Alex was all she lived for and all she had left. She couldn't lose everything, she couldn't.

She cursed to herself aloud as she saw the light turn red and slammed on her brakes. She heard the loud screeching sound as her car came to an abrupt stop.

This was taking too long. Her baby needed her now. Checking her watch, her anxiety grew. The call had come almost ten minutes ago—the call every mother feared.

"Evanston Gallery." Nicole had answered the phone the same way she had every day for the past year and a half she'd worked at the suburban Chicago art store.

"May I speak to Mrs. Nicole Cox?"

Nicole knew then. She had a sense that connected her to her son. Her heart leaped as she took a deep breath.

"This is Ms. Cox," she answered with caution, trying to quell the sudden desire to panic. "What can I do for you?"

"Ms. Cox, this is Mira Van Deer, with the Evanston Day Learning Center. I—"

"What's happened to Alex?" Nicole jumped from her desk at the reception center. A few gazes set on her.

"Ms. Cox, please calm down," the voice said. "Alex will be all right. There was a little accident."

"What? Where?" Nicole reached into her desk for her purse and car keys.

"He's at Evanston Hospital. The ambulance just—"

Nicole slammed down the phone. The art gallery—with its eclectic style, boundless colors, and abstract statues—was full of people, unusual for the middle of a weekday. Nicole's eyes searched among them until they found who she wanted.

"Dee!" She ran to her boss, who had also been her best friend for the past decade. "Dee, I have to go."

"What is it, honey?" Delaney Smith, who always answered to the name Dee, responded with a concerned frown to Nicole's panic.

"It's Alex." Nicole searched for the words, fear knotting in her stomach. "He's been hurt. I have to go to the hospital."

"Oh, no." Delaney looked around the gallery. "Let me close up, and I'll drive you."

"I can't wait," Nicole said, shaking her head. "You'll have to get all these people out, and I can't wait for that."

"You're right," Delaney called after Nicole, who had already headed for the large glass doors. "Go ahead, but call me as soon as you can."

Nicole's life flashed before her eyes. Norman and Alex Cox were once all that mattered to her. She had already lost her adoring husband, Norman, to the water two years ago. Now Alex was all she had left, and she loved her baby with all her heart and soul.

As Nicole parked her car and ran toward the emergency room doors, she held back her tears. She didn't want Alex to see her cry. She had to be strong, whatever the case. She could cry later, after she was sure he was all right. He had to be all right.

"Can I help you?" The young woman behind the front desk, cluttered with papers and clipboards, looked up from her chart and opened the sliding glass protective window.

"Alex Cox," Nicole said after catching her breath. "A little boy. I'm his mother. Where is he?"

The young woman glanced at one of the various charts in front of her for a moment before motioning down the hall. "Room 4," she said. "Right down the—"

"Thanks." Nicole headed down the white hallway, seeing nothing and no one around her, trying to block painful memories of the past. She thought only of Alex and how much she loved him.

As she opened the door marked FOUR, she called to her baby even before seeing him.

"Mommy!" The whimpering cry came from behind a large nurse, who stepped aside when she saw Nicole.

"Baby!" Nicole ran to Alex, who sat up straight on a gurney that seemed to engulf his little body. She wanted to hug him, but saw his right arm was in a sling. Instead she gently grabbed his chocolate-colored face and kissed both of his tear-stained cheeks. "Are you all right?"

"I'm fine now, Mommy." Alex was all smiles after the kiss. His large black eyes were open wide, his ivory white teeth shining. "Now that you're here."

"What happened?" After kissing Alex again, Nicole turned to the attending nurse. The worst was over, she thought, now that she had seen him alive and in one piece.

"False alarm, I would say." The red-haired nurse removed her gloves before giving Alex an affectionate pat on the knee. "The young lady from the school said he fell off the slide onto his arm and was in a lot of pain."

"It hurt awful, Mommy." Alex squirmed a bit, wiping away a drying tear. "I thought it was gonna fall off."

"Silly." Nicole smiled lovingly as she pinched his nose. She felt her heart beginning to return to a normal pace.

"I was so afraid for you," he said with a little frown.

"Why me?" Nicole asked, surprised.

"You get so worried all the time. Even if I cough, you go bonkers."

"I do not," Nicole said with a playful pout. Although she hated to admit it, it was probably true.

She was always accused by family and friends of being overprotective, but couldn't help it. Alex was her life, but he was also all she had left of Norman. He was her baby, a bond that surpassed any other. She couldn't bear to have anything happen to him.

"We checked him over," the nurse continued. "Dr. Arscott is our ER pediatrician. It's not even a sprain."

"The doctor said it's just a very big ow-ee," Alex said as the nurse checked his sling.

"That's good news." Nicole winked at Alex and warmed inside at his smiling response. It was certainly good news. She then turned to the nurse. "Is the sling necessary?"

"Probably for a couple of days," she answered. "Just to get little Alex here to leave it alone."

"Can I speak to Dr. Arscott?" Nicole wiped Alex's tear-stained cheeks with a tissue, ignoring his little frown at her fuss.

"We have a car accident that just came in." The nurse looked in Alex's direction with concern. "Dr. Arscott is very busy."

"I see." Nicole understood from her look, the nurse was telling her that a child had been involved in the accident, only making her more grateful that Alex was all right. "Dr. Adam Childs is our pediatrician. Has he been notified?"

"Yes, the doctor is on his way down." The nurse headed for the door. "I'll leave you two alone for a few minutes, but we'll need the room soon."

"Mommy," Alex said, turning to Nicole with a saddened expression. "I'm sorry."

"Why would you apologize, baby?" Nicole gently pecked his forehead with a kiss, rubbing his soft cheek. "It wasn't your fault. It was an accident."

"Yeah." He shrugged, still with a pout. "But you always get so upset when I play on the swing and stuff and I fall."

"Those things may look like harmless fun, but they can also be dangerous, honey." Nicole held his face up to look into his eyes, loving the trust for her she saw in them. "You have to be careful to hold on to something the whole time."

"I know."

She loved him so much it couldn't be described in words. It was as if he had always been a part of her life, a part of her heart, even before she knew he existed. Despite her biased position, Nicole was sure he was the cutest five-year-old to walk the face of the earth. He looked nothing like her except for the milk-chocolate-brown skin. The similarities both inside and outside ended there.

Alex Cox was his father's son in every sense of the word. He had Norman's large black eyes and thick, wild eyebrows. His nose was tiny, and Nicole loved to kiss it like she had with her husband. Alex frowned constantly like his father had, whether he was happy, sad, confused, or tired. What Nicole loved the most was how Alex would rub his thumb and index fingers together when he was deep in thought. Norman had done the same thing. Being only three years old when his father died, it was uncertain whether or not Alex had observed the behavior, but Nicole believed it was genetic instinct. Neither of them knew when they did it, but she noticed it every time, and it warmed her heart.

"Ms. Cox."

Nicole turned to see a young woman poke her head into the room. "Yes?"

"I'm Mira Van Deer." The young blonde walked cautiously into the room, holding out a hand to Nicole. "I called you earlier."

"Hello, Mira." Nicole recognized the first name. "I'm sorry I hung up on you earlier."

"I understand," she said with a nod. "You were worried."

"He's all right now, though." Nicole smiled as the young girl looked affectionately at Alex, who returned the smile with emphasis. "I appreciate your bringing him."

"He was in a lot of pain." Mira gave Alex's skinny leg a squeeze. "The nurse said he's okay, though."

"Thanks again," Nicole said appreciatively.

"No problem. I have to get back to the school now." Mira turned to Alex. "I'll see you soon, Alex."

"See ya!" Alex waved his free hand at the young lady as she turned to leave.

Evanston Day Learning Center was one of the best summer programs in all of the Chicago area. Nicole had chosen the school because she liked the multicultural ethnic makeup of the class as well as the educational activities the program mixed with the fun trips. Mostly she liked that there was one adult for every three kids. She wanted to be sure an eye was kept on Alex, making sure he was always safe.

"Is this where they put my favorite patient?"

Dr. Adam Childs poked his head into the small emergency room before entering. He looked around with a searching gaze, purposefully ignoring Alex's presence.

"I'm here!" Alex laughed as he raised his hand. He was used to this scenario but always amused.

"I can't see anyone." Dr. Childs turned to leave. "I guess I got the wrong room."

"No!" Alex called after him between giggles. "I'm right here, Dr. Childs!"

"Oh, my goodness." The doctor turned with amazement as he "saw" Alex. "You're so tiny, I almost missed you."

Dr. Adam Childs was a pleasant man. Over the years, Nicole had come to respect and care for him a great deal because of the tender care he had shown her as well as Alex during their visits. He wasn't a doctor exclusive to the hospital or the clinic. He was always accessible. Always had been. He had been Nicole's pediatrician as a child, and she was proud to hand her son over to him. Dr. Childs always knew the right thing to say, presenting himself as a contrast to the sometimes impersonal feeling modern-day healthcare institutions evoked. He was frank and honest at times but always hopeful and positive.

He had a doctor's look, his tawny brown complexion was smooth and soft. He had a wavy white mustache. Alex called him the "Black Colonel" after the man on the fried chicken buckets and guessed him to be a hundred years old. Nicole wasn't sure how old Dr. Childs was anymore, but she knew he was getting up there in age. Despite that, he was as sharp as a tack.

"So you fell and went boom?" Dr. Childs asked as he studied Alex's arm.

"Yes, I did." Alex was always the helpful patient. "I fell off the slide at the park. It was awful."

"You exaggerate." The doctor spoke with playful doubt.

"No, I don't," Alex protested, shaking his head vigorously. "Then it was awful. Now it isn't so bad. Just sore."

Neither the doctor nor Nicole were surprised that a five-year-old knew what the word "exaggerate" meant. Alex was quite intelligent. He listened closely to adults and picked up new things quickly. The day-care center suggested he go directly to first grade in September instead of kindergarten, but Nicole decided against it. She knew there were skills other than the intellectual that needed their time to develop.

Alex's intelligence was from his father, another thing Nicole would always be grateful to Norman for. A straight A student throughout school, Nicole knew she was no dummy, but she couldn't compare to Norman.

He knew everything. A thoroughly educated man, Norman absorbed knowledge in college, from his work, and from traveling the globe in his early days. He was never resigned to leaving new technology to the younger generation. He was usually the first to understand a new scholarly concept or catch on to a revised social diagnosis. He was never too proud to ask questions and soaked up all the answers. If ever he came across something he didn't know, he'd learn it quickly. It was never in an effort to be smarter than others, simply a result of his thirst for knowledge, which Nicole loved. She remembered, with a soft heart, the light in his eyes when he shared something new with her.

Norman had been so proud to see his son talk and walk earlier than most boys his age. He did his best to contain his excitement because it usually distracted Alex from whatever he was saying and caused him to get excited as well. Nicole enjoyed watching that special relationship between a man and his son, loving them both so much. Remembering it, she felt tears coming, so she wiped the thought from her mind and concentrated on Alex. He was all right, and at that moment, nothing else mattered.

"You're going to be fine," Dr. Childs said after examining the boy. "I'm going to look at the X rays again, but it looks harmless."

"What about the sling?" Nicole asked.

"I'm going to have him keep it on just to keep Alex from bothering it." Dr. Childs took a seat on the bed beside Alex. "I want you to follow up in a few days so Dr. Jordan can check on the bruises."

"Dr. Jordan?" Nicole knew the doctor had assistants but didn't recall the name Jordan.

"Dr. Jordan is my replacement, Nicole. I've decided to retire."

"Retire?" Alex asked.

"It means I'm old, and I need to go fishing." The doctor answered Alex's confusion with a kind smile. "After two wives and five kids of my own, I feel a lot older than I look."

"You've earned it, Doctor," Nicole said with a somber smile. "Alex and I will miss you. How soon will it be?"

Dr. Childs winked appreciatively and said, "I've been telling my patients all week. I have a few more serious cases I need to see through, but I'm handing over most of them immediately."

"You recommend Dr. Jordan?" Nicole asked.

"Yes." Dr. Childs gave a self-assured nod. "Of course the choice is yours, but I highly recommend him. He's a fantastic doctor with a flawless reputation. I've watched him interact with kids. He's a natural."

"He can't be even half as good as you," Nicole joked. "You're the best."

"Yeah!" Alex added his two cents with enthusiasm.

"Even half as good as Dr. Childs would rank me in the top ten."

Nicole turned quickly toward the deep voice that was

responding to her comment. Her attention immediately perked up when she saw him and made a quick and involuntary appraisal of his features. Tall, dark, and handsome was the first cliché that came to mind—only in this case, it was no cliché. It matched this young man perfectly. With smooth brown skin, an enchanting smile, his towering figure demanded attention. He was a very good-looking man, and Nicole reacted strongly to him, feeling herself momentarily entranced by his appearance. She quickly broke from this trance, somewhat surprised at her reaction.

"Nicole." Dr. Childs stood up from the bed. "Meet Dr. Damon Jordan. Doctor, this is Ms. Nicole Cox and her son, Alex, my favorite patient."

"It's very nice to meet you, Ms. Cox."

The young doctor held out a strong, saddle-brown-colored hand with a warm friendly smile that showed perfectly shaped, white teeth.

"Hello." Nicole stepped forward to accept his hand, smiling in return. She was distracted by his hazel eyes and impressed with his strong, firm handshake. Feeling something inside that made her a little uncomfortable with his effective grip, she removed her hand immediately and backed up until she was again beside Alex.

"Is this little Alex?" Damon placed the X rays on the bed and extended a hand to the young boy.

"That's me!" Alex gave a proud, grown-up smile as he shook the doctor's hand.

"Well, Dr. Childs told me a lot about you," Damon said with an exaggerated wink and nod. "You are definitely his favorite."

"He was my mommy's doctor, too," Alex said. "When she was young, but that was a long, long time ago."

"Hey!" Nicole tapped her son on the leg with a humorous frown. "Not that long ago."

"Couldn't have been." Damon turned his attention to Nicole, his eyes lying softly on her gentle face. "Either Alex has his timing off, or you look incredible for someone who was a kid a long, long time ago."

"Thank you." Nicole, feeling a blush come to her smooth cheeks, turned away from the doctor's gaze. She tried to focus her attention on Alex again, but couldn't help feeling as if the young doctor were standing a little too close to her.

Damon shared his attention between Nicole and Alex as he discussed the X rays. Nicole saw the immediate connection between him and Alex that Dr. Childs spoke of earlier. Dr. Jordan appeared to be as friendly as he was attractive, and Alex took to him immediately. He was very thorough in his explanations of Alex's condition to her and Dr. Childs, relieving Nicole of any worry.

"So"—Dr. Childs clapped his two hands together, rubbing them quickly—"We need to get out of this room, but can we first confirm a follow-up in three days?"

"Why don't I leave," Damon said as he gathered some papers and the X rays. "I don't want to make Ms. Cox uncomfortable with any decision she has to make. You know the choice is yours. You aren't forced to take me on as Alex's pediatrician."

"I like him!" Alex interjected, now struggling to get off the gurney.

"Put in a good word for me!" Damon winked at Alex before turning to Nicole. "It was very nice meeting you, Ms. Cox."

"Likewise," Nicole said as she accepted his strong grip again. She felt a smile form on her face that was a little wider than she'd intended it to be. Although his attraction was not intimidating, she was still disturbed by her awareness of it.

"He's the guy, Nicole," Dr. Childs said after Damon closed the door behind himself. "You saw how he was with Alex."

"Yes, he was great." Nicole gently lifted her son off the bed and onto the floor. She held on tight to keep him from running around. He was a ball of energy that tired her even as young and fit as she was. "He's pretty young."

"He's thirty, and he's been in private practice for a year. He graduated top in his undergraduate and medical school classes. His current patients love him. I can give you phone numbers of professionals and patients who are willing to give references."

"I would appreciate it," Nicole said, impressed with what she was hearing. Dr. Childs was not usually free with compliments. "You know I trust your word completely, but I should make some calls."

"You won't be disappointed." The doctor gave her a sly wink. "He's single, too."

"Dr. Childs!" Nicole gave him a playful pat on the arm as the three exited the private room.

"Just a note. Not a suggestion." He leaned in closer to Nicole to whisper, "I know you always say you're not interested, but you never know."

"I know, all right," Nicole said with a confident but kind smile. "And I'm not interested."

"We'll see." He shrugged his shoulders and turned to Alex, who was trying to fidget his way out of Nicole's grip. "You take it easy, Little Bit, okay?"

"Okay," Alex agreed, looking up at his doctor. "If it would make you feel better, Doc."

Nicole laughed at her son's sense of humor. He was a silly one, she thought, as she picked him up and carried him out of the hospital. He oftentimes surprised her with his sarcastic jokes and observations of adult behavior, which he found extremely peculiar. He was just like his father in that sense. Sometimes it hurt Nicole to see so much of Norman Cox in his son. It reminded her of a love so deep that had been stolen from her. A love she would never have again.

Two

"Don't you touch that phone again," Delaney Smith said with a warning tone and darting eyes as she saw Nicole reach for the telephone.

"I need to check in," Nicole responded in a childlike tone, almost asking permission. She hadn't seen Delaney standing behind her at the reception desk. "Just to see if he's all right."

"You just called the school a half hour ago." Delaney paused to greet a couple of gallery patrons who entered the store. "Then a half hour before that and forty-five minutes before that."

"I know. I know," Nicole sighed, her eyes still on the phone. "If they don't keep their eyes on him, he'll run off and start playing again. You know how wild he is."

"I heard you on the phone all morning." Delaney placed a protective hand over the reception desk phone and looked sternly into Nicole's eyes. "You made it very clear to the school that Alex was to refrain from physical activity for the next three days. Let it go."

"One day you'll become a mother," Nicole scolded, "and the words 'let it go' will cease to exist in your vocabulary."

"Since I never will be a mother," Delaney said matter-of-factly, "I don't have to worry about it."

Nicole had known Delaney Smith for ten years and had come to love the petite, long-haired sister with a lot of attitude. They were college roommates their freshman year at Spelman College. Having lived a sheltered suburban life, it was Delaney who opened Nicole up to life full of parties and fun. Delaney had always been the risk taker, changing her major every semester, ready to give up everything to seek out fame and fortune. Nicole, on the other hand, was the shy art student whose dream was to be a wife, a mother, and an artist.

Delaney had been there for Nicole at the best and worst times of her life, and their bond went from that of two young girls who were friends to two women who felt like sisters from these experiences. Only two months after their college graduation, Nicole lost the only parent she had left, her father, Alex, to lung cancer. Delaney moved from her native Columbus, Ohio, to Evanston, Illinois, to be a comfort and companion for Nicole. She consoled her, let her know she wasn't alone and had family in her heart, where it counted. Delaney pushed her out into the world, getting her feet wet in the single life the city of Chicago had to offer.

Delaney had been the maid of honor for Nicole at her wedding. Despite her love for Norman, Nicole was only twenty-three years old at the time and more nervous than she had ever been. Delaney was a calming friend, finding humor in everything. Delaney was at Nicole's suburban home when she had taken the pregnancy test that came out positive. She was Alex's godmother and occasional baby-sitter and had earned the right, paying special attention to Alex during the difficult time after Norman's death.

Meanwhile, Delaney had made quite a life for herself. She met an investment manager, Ron Smith, and married, with Nicole the matron of honor. Together, Delaney and her husband purchased an old art gallery where many African-American artists sold their work, including Nicole. With a new, brassy decor and Delaney's superb marketing skills, it became one of the most popular galleries on the North Shore.

Nicole credited Delaney with giving her the strength to continue after Norman's accidental death. It was a heart-wrenching time for her, and Delaney cried along with her. She continued to remind Nicole of the happiness of the four years she had shared with Norman, three as husband and wife, and mother and father to Alex. Nicole hadn't thought she could make it, but she did. She did out of love for Alex and with support from Delaney. She would love her best friend forever for that.

"You keep saying that." Nicole frowned back at Delaney's mahogany-colored face. "But you mark my words. One day you and Ron are going to want a baby." She looked with loving eyes at the picture of Alex on her desk. "You're going to hold that little life you made with the man you love in your hands, and at that second, you'll know what it means to love something beyond reason."

"Not going to happen." Delaney shook her head as she smoothed an invisible wrinkle in her rayon ruby-red dress. "Sometimes I can't even deal with my cat. I certainly couldn't handle a little fireball like you have."

"It's not easy." Nicole smiled to herself, quickly recalling the many times Alex had brought her to her last nerve. There had been many. "But it's all worth it. I can say firsthand that the rewards are ten times the sacrifices."

"I'm happy with Ron." Delaney slapped at Nicole's hand as it reached for the phone again. "He's my kid, and I have my hands full."

"So do I."

"Do you really?" Delaney asked, a concerned rise in her thinly styled eyebrows.

"Don't start with me." Nicole knew what was coming next.

"You can't spend the rest of your life being just a mother, Nicole," Delaney insisted.

"Yes, I can." Nicole's retort and curt nod held plenty of sarcasm in response to the word "just." "It happens to be the hardest job out there."

"You know what I mean." Delaney gave an impatient sigh. "You're an artist. You should have your work displayed at a gallery, not answering the phone at one."

"Is my job here in jeopardy?" Nicole asked, knowing her

career was not exactly where she wanted it to be, but it was no longer a priority.

"No, the job is here as long as you want it. It's just that you haven't painted since Norman's death. It's been two years. Can't you at least try?"

"I'm not inspired," Nicole shot back somberly. "Norman inspired me. Before him, my art was nothing but teenage doodles."

"Your art sold even in college, sister." Delaney snapped her fingers in the air. "You made more then than you do now as a receptionist."

"Can we get off the subject?" Nicole asked, knowing inside she didn't have a strong argument, except for the fact that she hadn't had the desire to pick up a brush since Norman's death. The idea only brought back painful memories of joyous times she could never recapture.

"Fine." Delaney leaned over the desk, staring directly into Nicole's oval-shaped light brown eyes. "Another subject then. How about dating again?"

"Let's go back to painting," Nicole said, thoroughly annoyed. "Please."

"No, you don't want to talk about that." Delaney smiled, amused at her own maneuver.

"Listen, Dee." Nicole gave her friend a stern stare, determined not to rehash the dating issue. "I don't want to talk about painting. I don't want to talk about dating."

"I know you loved Norman with all your heart," Delaney continued, ignoring Nicole's protest. "But it has been two years. It's time to move on. You are a beautiful, vibrant, and young black woman. Look at yourself."

"I don't need to," Nicole said stubbornly. "I know what I look like."

She was very well aware that she was an attractive woman. An awkward and thin girl, she had blossomed into an alluring, shapely woman. Her eyes were large and welcoming, her lips full and curving. Average height, she had cinnamon-brown hair that flowed lightly just past her shoulders, which she usually wore up to reduce the hassle, but down when she wanted to feel a little free. Her chocolate-brown-colored skin was smooth and soft. Norman never ceased telling her how much he loved touching her skin. His love had made her feel like the sexiest woman in the world, awakening her to a passion that went beyond the physical and turned on her soul.

She never thought of herself as exceptionally beautiful, as others had told her she was. She kept in shape from chasing after Alex, but she also ran and lifted weights when she got a moment to herself, which as a single mother wasn't often. Her father had told her she looked exactly like her mother, Ana Mae, who had died from cancer as well, when Nicole was eight years old. Looking at the pictures of the beautiful woman, Nicole felt grateful if she was even half as pretty.

"There are plenty of brothers who would love to—" Delaney went on.

"There was only one brother for me," Nicole interrupted in a calmly confident tone. "Norman was everything. I had my time with him, and there will never be another."

"So at twenty-eight years old, your love life is over? Is that what you really believe?"

Nicole had no immediate response for Delaney's comment. It was difficult, which was why she did not like to discuss it. She had tried to ignore the fact that she would never love again, just accepting it as price to pay for her tragic misfortune and feeling grateful for the time she did have with Norman. It was all the more love left for little Alex.

"Not selling today?"

Both women lifted their heads to see William West. Billy, as they called him, a Northwestern University teacher's assistant and also a longtime friend of Nicole's. Nicole had met him six years ago at a community-sponsored art exhibit. It was the same night she'd met Norman. Billy had been interested in dating her, but Nicole had eyes only for Norman from that night on. So instead, the two became friends and pretty good ones. Billy had helped her through Norman's death as a shoulder to cry on and continued to help by being the obligatory platonic date on social functions—and most importantly, a father figure and male role model for Alex.

Nicole was very grateful for Billy's involvement with Alex had no strings attached for her. Now that he was five, Alex's interest in sports had grown, and Billy stood in for Nicole, who was unable to tell a touchdown from a free throw. She was also grateful for Billy's sudden appearance in the gallery, hopeful it would divert Delaney from the current topic of conversation.

"What do you mean by that?" Delaney asked, her hands coming defensively to her hips.

"Those somber looks on your faces." Billy winked a hello in Nicole's direction. "Doesn't look like you're having such a great day."

"Actually I've already sold several pieces today." Delaney's tone was playfully smart as it usually was with Billy.

Nicole smiled at her comeback. She got a kick out of watching the two, who very much enjoyed their constant sparring. It was how they wanted their relationship, with Delaney pretending to be insanely annoyed with him at all times and Billy completely ignoring her.

"As a matter of fact," Delaney continued, "those two ladies that just walked in look very interested in those Uganda family sculptures. Excuse me."

"So what is the reason?" Billy let Delaney walk by before approaching the desk. He snatched a piece of candy from a glass jar.

"She's getting on me about my painting and not dating again," Nicole said, her eyes darting toward the phone every now and then. She hoped they were watching Alex at the school.

"And you told her to mind her own business again, huh?" He mockingly rolled his eyes like a woman.

"Yes, I did," she answered with a flippant gaze.

"Good for you." Billy gave a fisted gesture of support. "So what about your painting and your dating?"

"Not you, too," Nicole moaned. "Nothing. Nothing. Those are my answers. I have my hands full with Alex."

"How is our little invalid anyway?"

"He's fine." Nicole pouted at Billy for his reference to her son, containing a smile. "He's not an invalid. It's just a sore arm."

"The way you talk about it, it would seem otherwise." Billy shrugged as he walked around the counter, took a chair from the wall, and sat down as he usually did on his many visits to the downtown gallery. "We were going to play catch at the beach today. I guess that's out."

"Maybe this weekend." Nicole swiveled around in her chair to face him in his new position. Her maternal antennae perked up at the word "beach." "If you promise to keep him away from the water. He has an appointment with his new doctor Thursday. We'll know then."

"New?"

"Yes. Dr. Childs is retiring. Dr. Jordan is taking over." Nicole unintentionally blushed at the mention of the young doctor's name, remembering how attractive he was.

"What do you know about this guy?" There was a suspicious line at the corners of his mouth as his eyes squinted and arms folded across his chest. "After all, we're entrusting our boy to him."

"Dr. Childs highly recommended him." Nicole smiled appreciatively at Billy's obvious concern for a boy he cared a lot for. Billy spent a great deal of time with Alex and regularly asked about things such as his health and progress in school. "I haven't checked his references, but I plan to this afternoon. Alex really liked him."

"Is he an old fogey like Dr. Childs?"

"Not at all. He's very young and attractive," Nicole said, acting nonchalant, although she was overly conscious of her compliment to the doctor.

"Very?" Billy's brows centered as he eyed his friend. "Was 'very' necessary? Does he look that good?"

"My mother sure thinks so."

Nicole took a deep breath as she swung around in the chair. Damon had a deep, smooth voice—she had noticed so yesterday and immediately recognized it today. As she stood to face him, she felt her entire face redden in embarrassment, and her eyes widened in surprise. Not only because he had overheard her refer to him as very attractive, although that would be enough, but also because her first thought at seeing him was that he looked terrific in a T-shirt and blue jeans.

"Dr. Jordan." She finally found her voice, although it was a little shaky. "What are you doing here?"

"Professional business," he answered with a smile that showed a left cheek dimple. "If you have a second."

"I'll just look around," Billy said as he stood. He gave the young doctor a quick look over before heading off.

"Is something wrong?" Nicole asked as she walked around the desk.

"Everything is fine." Damon shoved his large hands into his pants pockets and peered at her with a tender gaze. "You look great."

"Thank you," she said, her voice calmer and more controlled now in contrast to the way she felt.

Abruptly aware of her modest attire, Nicole straightened the sleeveless cotton dress. She had worn it so many times, thinking nothing. Now she noticed the V-neck cut seemed low, and the hem, more than a couple of inches above the knees, seemed to have shrunk since she wore it last. She was very conscious of his closeness to her and his eyes on her. His presence provoked an unreadable emotion that bothered her tremendously.

"I talked to Dr. Childs," Damon said, his eyes looking directly at her, letting a little of his shyness show as they blinked several times. "He said you agreed to see me Thursday."

"Yes. Yes, I did." Nicole could tell she was nervous inside, assuming it was a reaction to the unexpectedness of this visit. What else could it be? "For follow-up on his arm. I still haven't decided about a permanent basis."

"I understand," Damon said with a nervous smile. "You need to know someone very well before you trust them with your child's health."

"I really do trust Dr. Childs' opinion," Nicole said, not wanting Damon to get the idea she didn't believe he was a capable doctor. She wondered why he didn't call for this. Why would he come to the gallery? Why was she happy he did? "I still need to call the references he gave me."

"Of course." Damon stared at Nicole with a look of hesitation. "There is another way . . ."

"Yes?" Nicole asked as he seemed to hesitate. She realized
she had taken a step closer to him. Her first thought was to
step back, not wanting to seem as if she were flirting, but her
second thought said no—stay where you are.

"I hope you don't find this inappropriate in any way."
Damon ran a nervous hand over his short black curls. "If so,
I apologize and would never—"

"Wait a minute," Nicole said with a laugh as she held up
her hand. "You're apologizing for something you haven't ever
said yet? Why don't you try me? I'm a mother of a five-year
old boy. I couldn't do my job if I was easily offended."

Damon calmed a bit at Nicole's humor before speaking again.
"I was wondering if you would have dinner with me."

Nicole's light eyes winked in surprise. This was not at all
what she expected. The nervousness that had gone away briefly
with the humor returned full force. It wasn't that Nicole wasn't
used to being asked out. She was approached often for dates,
mostly by gallery patrons. It had been a simple routine in the
past. A man would ask her out, and she would politely refuse.
Some would bow out gracefully, but others would try again.
She would continue to refuse, and eventually they would all
go away. She made it clear her heart belonged to one man only.

Then why, she thought to herself, was she so pleasantly
surprised by Damon's invitation? Why was she hesitant to
refuse?

"Do you ask all your prospective patients' parents out to
dinner, Dr. Jordan?" Nicole noticed her silence had lasted long
enough and was beginning to make things awkward.

"Well, I thought it would be a good opportunity for you to
get to know me." Damon's eyes flirted with her as they blinked.
The dimple showed again.

The dimple sent a surge of energy through Nicole and forced
a smile to her face. It was as if something other than herself
was in control of her reactions.

"It would give you an idea of how I practice," he continued,
then seemed to realize the insinuation that could be interpreted

from his words. "I-I mean about my medical beliefs and style
. . . that kind of practice."

"Is this a professional dinner you're referring to?" Nicole
noticed his last blunder and was amused by his nervous attempt
to cover it up.

"If you want." There was a look of question on Damon's
face as he studied her, apparently trying to get an idea of what
she was thinking. "Mostly I'm asking because I like you and
would like to have dinner with you."

"You don't even know me," she said, not happy with the
sudden pleasure she felt at his expression of his feelings. "You
met me only yesterday."

"Yes, and in such a short time, I already know I would like
to get to know you better."

"I'm very flattered by the suggestion," Nicole said as she
pasted on a friendly smile. She wanted to appear certain, but
inside she felt confused at her hesitation and her feelings. "Only
I'm sorry I must refuse."

"I hope you didn't find my suggestion inappropriate in any
way." Damon's disappointment was evident, although he was
valiantly trying to hide it.

"Not at all," Nicole said reassuringly. Unlike the others,
she felt sad about disappointing him. Unlike the others, there
was a curious pull from within her in response to his suggestion,
making her reluctant to refuse him. He seemed like such a nice
guy, and the only thing dangerous about him was his appeal.

"Well," Damon said as he smiled shyly and began backing
up toward the door. His gentle eyes were appraising her in more
than a mild interest, fettered only a bit by his disappointment.

He continued to stare for a moment longer, as if he wanted
to say something other than what he finally did, which was,
"I guess I'll see you and Alex Thursday afternoon."

"Dr. Jordan," Nicole called after him, although she wasn't
sure why. She had surprised herself with the fragile tone of
her voice.

"Yes?" With eager eyes, Damon halted in the doorway.

She wondered what she would do now as his gaze made
her restless. She had called him but with nothing to say. She

swallowed tightly as the hopeful look on Damon's face told her she had to come up with something.

"I want you to understand that it's nothing personal," she said in just above a whisper as she saw Delaney approaching. "I'm just not dating right now. There just isn't any . . ."

"I understand." Damon smiled and nodded at her. "I'll see you Thursday."

Nicole felt herself sigh quietly as she watched him turn and walk out. He was very appealing from both angles. She fought the pleased smile that tried to form at the edges of her lips as Delaney stepped in front of her, her eyes demanding answers.

"Don't give me that look." Nicole headed back for her desk, suddenly in a better mood.

"What look?" Delaney followed closely behind.

"That 'who was that and when are you going out with him' look." Nicole's tone and demeanor mocked her friend's usual behavior.

"Well, who was he and when are you going out with him?"

"He's just Alex's new doctor." Nicole wasn't always warm to her friend's persistence.

"Why is he here? Is Alex okay?"

"He's fine." Nicole appreciated Delaney's affection for Alex. She had taken her role as godmother seriously and was like an aunt to him. "Dr. Jordan just came by to confirm an appointment."

"Yeah, right." Delaney smirked. "Isn't that what phones are for? What did he really want, and what's his full name?"

"His name is Damon Jordan, and—"

"He asked you out on a date, didn't he?" Billy joined the two women again, an unamused look on his face.

"How did you know?" Nicole asked, feeling more uncomfortable now that the "d" word was again the topic of conversation.

"He asked you out?" Delaney's curiosity peaked. "A *doctor* asked you out?"

"Hold on, Dee." Nicole freed her arm from Delaney's grip and turned to Billy. "How did you know he asked me out? Were you listening?"

"No." Billy frowned, apparently taking offense at her words. "I don't eavesdrop. I can just tell. All guys get that heart-on-their-sleeve look when they ask a woman out for the first time. He had that look."

"You said yes, right?" Delaney asked, crossing her fingers and waving them in the air. "Please tell me you said yes."

"Of course not." Nicole said, surprised she would even ask.

Delaney made a frustrated fist and shook it in Nicole's direction. "Don't you give me any of that talk about not being ready to get back into the dating world. I don't want to hear it."

"I'm not ready." Nicole's tone was defensive now. She wished people could understand.

"Don't you think that's a weird situation?" Billy asked with an uncertain stare.

"For who?" Delaney asked, her eyes shooting him an annoyed glance.

"I don't know." He shrugged. "Just . . . well it's your kid's doctor."

"I don't think it sounds weird," Nicole said.

"Then why did you say no?" Delaney asked.

"Because I'm not ready," Nicole answered with impatience. Her eyes moved downward, staring at the marble gray and white floor. Inside she felt torn, knowing she was still young. "I don't know if I ever will be."

"You have to let it go, honey." Delaney appeared about to give comforting words but instead turned to Billy. "Can we women have a few minutes alone?"

"Why?" Billy asked, although it was apparent what Delaney meant. "There's nothing going on here I don't know about. If she isn't ready to date, you shouldn't try to force her."

"What do you know?" Delaney's words were very sarcastic. "This is a woman-thing."

"No, Dee." Nicole smiled at Billy. "Billy understands. He's been there with me just like you, and he's right."

"How can it be right that you never fall in love again?"

"It's not right," Nicole said, feeling the anger, pain, and unfairness of it all rising within her. "None of this is right. I should still have my husband, and Alex should still have his father, but we don't. Maybe one day, things will change, and I'll consider seeing someone else—but now I feel no attraction for another man, and any dating on my part would still feel like cheating. In my heart, I'm still a married woman.''

"I don't believe that. I saw the way you looked at that doctor when he was leaving." Delaney's face showed compassion, but her eyes showed frustration. "But if you say you don't want to, then you don't want to.''

Delaney gave Nicole a comforting pat on the shoulder and went to help a customer that was calling for her. Nicole felt embarrassed because she knew Delaney was right. For the first time since her husband's death, she had been more than aware of an attraction to another man. She was beginning to feel the young doctor was more than just pleasant to look at, and that disturbed her.

"Thanks." Nicole winked in Billy's direction.

"No sweat, sister." Billy returned the wink.

"What did you come by for anyway?" Nicole gave Billy her undivided attention, hoping to clear her mind of thoughts of Damon Jordan.

"I was in the neighborhood. Summer classes start in a couple of weeks, but I'm pretty loose right now. Do you want to go for some lunch?''

Nicole looked at her watch and noticed it was almost noon. "Lunch is fine. Just let me check on Alex once more, and I'll be ready.''

Nicole picked up the phone and was set to dial but was frozen in place. To her sudden surprise, she was drawing a blank as to the numbers to dial. She concentrated hard, jogging her memory to find the seven numbers she had known by heart for the last two years now, but nothing came to mind. She laughed with astonishment at herself as she had to reach for her Rolodex to find the number to Alex's day-care center.

As she dialed the numbers, she shook her head at her own confusion. What could cause her momentary disorientation? She knew something else was on her mind—someone else— but she chose to ignore it. She chose to ignore the vision of Dr. Jordan's face in her head and hoped it would go away.

* * *

"Come on, Mommy!" Alex flapped his skinny arms impatiently at his sides as he stood in the middle of the ladies' room outside Dr. Jordan's office.

"Stop flapping your arms," Nicole ordered. "I'll be just a minute."

As she brushed her hair, Nicole took a look at herself in the full-length mirror. She had made a point to dress casually in a pair of long baggy jean shorts and a soft peach T-shirt. Her purpose was to distract attention from herself.

Nicole hadn't admitted to anyone, but Damon's visit to the gallery had been on her mind constantly these past few days. It was a brief visit, but her mind seemed determined to go over every second, every smile, and every gesture. It made her uncomfortable as she had never thought about a man that much since Norman. For one short moment, she had even wondered what would've happened if she had agreed to dinner with Damon. She quickly threw the thought from her mind, believing the summer sun must have gotten to her.

She had prepared herself for today's checkup. She was sure Damon would be nothing but professional but was still a little nervous. Trying not to focus on romantic possibilities, Nicole instead concentrated on Alex's quick recovery. That was, after all, the only important thing now. The first couple of days had been hard on both of them. Alex was frustrated with his limited movement, and she, being a mother, felt for him and was tempted to set him free more than a few times. But now he was out of the sling, and his arm was as loose as ever.

"Let's go," Alex urged. "Hurry, before another lady comes in and I have to cover my eyes again."

"Okay." Nicole grabbed her purse and raced him to the door. She always slowed down just before the end to let him win. She loved to see his champion dance at the end as he shook his hips from left to right. "I would let you wait outside, but you always run off, scaring me half to death."

"Do not," Alex responded with a guilty giggle.

Dr. Damon Jordan's practice was located in Lincolnwood,

another suburb of Chicago. Its decorative style fit his youthful
and fresh look with a modern design that was still accessible
to children, making them feel comfortable. There was a comical
sign on the door that said: ENTER AND ENJOY. EVERYTHING
HAS BEEN SCOTCHGUARDED. Nicole smiled at his sense of humor
as she waited with the other mothers and a couple of fathers
until the young receptionist called Alex in.

She felt a little embarrassed as she had expected to sense
some tension from Damon due to her turning down his dinner
invitation. Far from it, he was as cordial as ever with her,
focusing most of his attention on Alex, whom he gave the green
light to go back to his normal play routine. If there was any
tension at all, it was all her own as she found herself distracted
by his handsome profile more than a couple times and had to
tear her eyes away.

Damon seemed pleased to hear that Nicole had checked his
references and decided to keep him as Alex's physician. Besides
that, he appeared very nonchalant toward her during the short
visit.

Leaving the office, Nicole felt very silly. What made her
think she was so much that a gorgeous doctor would think
twice about her rejection. He probably had women lining up for
his attention and had probably forgotten all about the incident
himself. She had spent three days worried about nothing.

She should feel better, Nicole thought to herself as she drove
out of the parking lot. He wasn't thinking about her at all. She
should feel great. Then, she asked herself, why didn't she?

Three

As Nicole parked her car outside Jessica Cox's apartment building, she paused and smiled. The four-story redbrick unit placed oddly in a neighborhood of two-flat homes in the suburbs always brought back memories, all good. She and Norman had spent many nights there—talking, eating, doing nothing, and doing things that made her blush. If only Jessica knew, Nicole thought with a giggle to herself as she let her mind return to days of love.

It was a warm July night six years ago when Nicole Bradford walked into the Forest Community Center. A twenty-two-year-old budding artist, she was excited about meeting and making valuable contacts in the art community. This community-sponsored art exhibit was as good a place as any to start, she thought. Delaney had reluctantly accompanied her, only going in the hopes she would meet a guy. That seemed to Nicole to be Delaney's only objective since moving to Chicago a year ago.

Billy West's only objective seemed to be to flirt with every woman in the room. Or at least it had seemed that way to Nicole. She saw him as soon as she entered the room, here and there, always talking to a woman or women, laughing up a storm. He had a sporty, youthful appearance and seemed to be more than fond of himself. She found his behavior amusing and was receptive to his eventual introduction as a Northwestern University graphic arts student. Eager to meet new people and make friends, Nicole took to him immediately, warming to his friendly fun-loving personality and humor. He was candid and open, making her feel comfortable with him only minutes after he had arrived.

Delaney, on the other hand, seemed less than impressed and excused herself as soon as she spotted a prospect. Nicole didn't expect to see her for a while that night.

"What does she mean by prospect?" Billy asked, seemingly unaffected by Delaney's social rejection.

"It's a long story," Nicole said with a smirk and a wave of her hand. "Never mind her."

"Am I boring you?" he asked, cupping his chin with his hand and centering his brows. "You're looking a little bored."

"Not at all," she assured him, "I'm very interested in hearing the story about your uncle delivering a baby in the elevator of the Wrigley Building. That's what you said, right?"

"Yes." He smiled at her doubting grin. "It's a true story, mind you. It's also long, so let me quench my thirst first. Would you like a drink?"

"Certainly." Nicole was incredibly thirsty and grateful for the offer.

Waiting for his return, she turned her attention to a painting she had been intrigued by since walking in. It was simple in its description—a family with a father, mother, and child—but in appearance was anything but simple. She was visually attracted to its dark colors of deep rose, umber brown, and charcoal gray, and their contrast with each other. But it was the deep sadness in the eyes of the subjects that pulled her in, drowning out the noise of the conversing crowd. An artist herself, she knew that the expression of art in all its forms came from the heart and could see that this artist's heart was heavy.

"It's one of mine," said a deep, husky voice from behind.

A startled Nicole turned quickly to face her fellow observer. She was stricken with a sudden smile as she felt a lurch of excitement within at the sight of the older man. Devastatingly handsome, he looked to be in his midthirties, with large dark eyes and thick eyebrows. His skin was a ginger-brown hue and smooth, except for a few lines on his face that made him look experienced and distinguished. Clean cut around his face, his wavy, jet-black hair wasn't quite the beginnings of an afro but very thick. He was tall and a little on the thin side, but looked very appealing in a sport jacket and blue jeans. Despite the warm weather, he didn't seem to break a sweat, projecting an image of coolness and contentment.

Nicole immediately knew she liked what she saw. More than his physical appearance, which she felt would be enough, she was drawn to an aura of self-confidence and togetherness he seemed to have. He wasn't overwhelmed with it but stood tall and stared proud, as if he knew who he was and would not be questioned about it. Her curiosity, as well as her own vanity, were aroused by his inherently strong presentation.

As he took one step closer and smiled kindly, Nicole felt her heart dance with excitement, and the very air around her seemed to electrify. She knew at that moment her life would never be the same again.

"This is your work?" she asked, wondering if she had made the wrong assumption about the artist. He did not look like a hurt or heavy man.

"Not mine," he answered, looking down at her five-foot seven-inch stature. His gaze dropped from her eyes momentarily, quickly and respectfully observing her figure, then returned to her deep pools. "One of my students. What do you think?"

Nicole was embarrassed that she had to make a conscious decision to tear her eyes away from him reluctantly to view the painting again. "It's sad. It seems very sad."

"He lost his parents in a car accident when he was twelve." The older man smiled at Nicole's obvious preoccupation with him as she returned to staring at his face. "Sometimes he'll paint this same picture, but the parents have no face."

"Has he ever considered professional help?" Nicole asked honestly.

"This is his therapy," he answered, pointing to the painting.

Nicole turned to the picture, again feeling sad for the painter. She sympathized with the loss he had suffered. Although she barely remembered her mother, she missed both her parents.

"Here we go!" Billy West wormed his way between the two observers. "Two fruit punches."

"Thanks, Billy," Nicole said as she turned to her new friend, just in time to see his joyful expression change to a nervous one.

"Hello, Mr. Cox," he said, holding out his hand after wiping it on his pant leg.

"Hello." Mr. Cox shook the younger man's hand but was apparently not acquainted with him.

"My name is William West. I'm a senior in graphic arts. I took your class last semester."

Nicole cleared her throat, hoping to be included in the conversation. So far, she had the dashing stranger's last name and knew he was a college professor, but she wanted to know more. Much more.

"I'm sorry." Billy laughed nervously. "You two don't know each other?"

"I've been speaking with this lovely lady, but I can't say I've had the pleasure of knowing her name." The professor's eyes went soft as he turned to Nicole, his generous smile showing pearly white teeth.

"Nicole Bradford, this is Professor Norman Cox. He teaches American art history and art history of ancient Egypt and Africa at Northwestern. Professor, this is Nicole Bradford. Nicole is an artist."

"It's very nice to meet you, Ms. Bradford." Norman held out his hand to her.

Nicole could swear she felt a lightning bolt run through her arm even before their hands touched. He had called her lovely, and it sounded so different than when she had heard it in the past from other men. It sounded sweet and sincere, romantic and heartfelt.

"What types of art do you do, Ms. Bradford?" Norman asked as he still held her hand.

"I paint," Nicole answered, more than aware that he still held her hand in his. She wasn't about to pull free. She could see an instant attraction in his eyes, and she was positive he could see it in hers. More than physical, it was an energy that drowned out the rest of the world. "Mostly what I see but also what I feel."

"Anything on display here tonight?" Norman glanced around the large room.

"No," Nicole said, extremely aware their hands were still joined. "Not yet."

"That's the right attitude." Norman finally let go of her hand but still held her with his eyes. "You'll go far, Ms. Bradford. I can tell."

"Thank you." Nicole lowered her eyes and smiled flirtatiously. "And please call me Nicole."

"And please, Nicole," he said, "call me Norman."

This was magic, her heart told her at that moment. This man would bring her magic.

Billy had said something next, Nicole remembered, but she wasn't listening. No one else existed at the moment except for the professor. Nicole believed that lust at first sight was true but had always held her reservations about love. That was, until now. She could swear the whole room could hear her heartbeat.

For three hours, they got to know each other better. The thirty-four-year-old professor told her about his Chicago upbringing. He grew up poor in the city, his mother the only parent he ever knew. She had taught him strength through adversity and given him goals. Always wanting to be a teacher, he had come to love art from a college trip to Paris, seeing how even the most basic of statues were beautiful. Everyone in Paris is an artist, he told her.

Nicole told him of her Evanston upbringing and childhood. She felt no qualms about letting him know of the loss of her mother and the recent loss of her father. To tell that to anyone else she had met only an hour ago would seem out of place— but not Norman. When she told him, he said nothing. Not the usual "I'm sorry." He merely took her hand in his and held it. She felt the sympathetic squeeze and found it more comforting than any words she had ever heard.

He invited her to attend his summer class anytime and offered to give her names of artists and galleries he knew of in the area that were looking for new talent to showcase. She gave him her phone number, telling him to call her with any contacts he could think of, but it was a front. Nicole didn't care if he gave her one contact ever. She had been two feet off the ground from the moment she met him until she went to sleep that night. She wanted to know everything and anything about him, from the inside out. She had fallen and was sure he was at least smitten with her. She had pulled out all her charm on his behalf. He liked her, she was sure. She could feel it.

She had been right. It was barely past breakfast time the next morning when the phone rang, and it was Norman on the other end. He seemed nervous this time, and Nicole found some satisfaction in that. Her heart leaped when he asked her to lunch. She remembered saying yes before he even finished the question.

So went the beginning of what Nicole was sure would be the rest of her life. Never had she been so happy. Her ideas of being in love couldn't compare to the reality of truly experiencing it. It was immediate and mutual. Norman had some misgivings about the age difference, but Nicole assured him age meant nothing when true love was at play. She helped him stay young and vibrant, and he helped her mature and grow.

It almost frightened Nicole how her love and desire for Norman grew with every day that passed. He awakened her to passion and erotic pleasures that she had never imagined in her young years. He encouraged her independence and inspired her talent with his support. Her art flourished as her creativity seemed to grow with the love, breaking into avenues of warm and colorful artistry she hadn't done before. She began to sell at local galleries and make a name for herself. Life was magic. Love was magic.

They were married seven months later, both eager from the heart to be husband and wife. Forever was in the palm of their hands. Nicole's heart warmed beyond compare when she found out she had gotten pregnant on her wedding night. This baby would be the first in a big, happy family she was so excited to begin.

Norman hit the ceiling when he found out he was going to be a father, and that excitement only intensified when his son was born. Starting a family in his late thirties, he was anxious to begin fatherhood. He told the world, screaming his joy from the hospital window that night. Old fashioned as he was, he spread cigars around the entire maternity ward. Of course there was no smoking allowed, but he made everyone promise to light up when they reached the outdoors.

He made about twenty calls that night, stopping only when Nicole ordered him to take a rest. She was thoroughly amused by his happiness and touched deeply inside as she remembered how he had kissed her over and over again, saying the words "thank you" repeatedly before falling asleep at her side. Nicole stayed awake a little longer to say thank you to the little miracle she held in her arms and named him after her father. She didn't need to tell him she would love and protect him forever—she knew he could feel it when his tiny hand squeezed her pinkie finger with all its might.

For three years, they were the perfect family, growing together and learning to depend on each other. Nicole had to pinch herself sometimes to believe it was true, giving thanks in her prayers every night.

Then it was taken away. Like a thief in the night, it was ripped from her and Alex before she could blink. She was stunned, heartbroken, and torn apart to realize that what she had thought to be forever was now a few years of memories. Pictures in an album. All that was left was Alex—and Alex was everything.

Alex was hungry, Nicole remembered as she returned to the present. She hardly ever worked at the gallery on Saturdays, but when she did, Alex was left with Jessica Cox, his grandmother.

Norman and Nicole had moved Jessica from her Chicago apartment to Norman's condo in Evanston when the newlyweds purchased a new home. Jessica was happy to be out of the city, and everyone was happy she would be closer to the baby.

Jessica loved to baby-sit, and although she and Nicole were never as close as Nicole wanted to be, they both loved Alex with all their heart. So whenever Delaney begged for weekend help, Jessica kept Alex. To make up for losing a day with him, Nicole promised McDonald's for dinner. She wasn't too fond of fast-food, but every once in a while it made Alex's day.

"Come on in, Nicole." Jessica stepped aside as Nicole entered the apartment.

Physically, Jessica Cox reminded Nicole of Norman. The same color, both tall, he had inherited her mysterious eyes and thin figure. The inner similarities were there as well. Norman was selfish when it came to his wife and his son, not wanting to share their love and attention with anyone else. Jessica had been that way with Norman, her only child. It had been a great cause of friction between the two women when it was clear to Jessica that Nicole would be a part of Norman's life forever. Nicole wasn't proud of it, but the only two times she could remember the two of them being close was when Alex was born and when Norman died.

"How was today?" Nicole asked as she situated herself on the living room sofa.

"It was fine," Jessica said in her usually calm voice. "We had a short disagreement on whether or not he had to wear shoes when we went for our walk in the park, but I won in the end."

"That's a change." Nicole knew Alex had his grandmother wrapped around his little finger.

"He's so much like Norman." Jessica's eyes wandered out the window next to her seat and stared at the blue sky. "You should have seen him."

"What did he do?" Nicole never tired of hearing stories about how similar Alex was to his father.

"He actually tried to reason with me as if he was an adult." Jessica laughed as she remembered. "No tantrums or public displays, he promised. 'Grandma,' he said, 'we'll just have a discussion on the topic.' "

"Norman was like that," Nicole said. "He used to drive me crazy. I wanted to argue, but he wanted to reason."

"Since he was a child." Jessica shook her head with an emotional sigh. "He was always so smart."

"He would be so proud of his son," Nicole added. "So proud of how he's turning out."

"Thanks to you." Jessica returned her gaze to Nicole with a smile. "You've done such a fantastic job."

"Thanks." Nicole took pride in such praise from Norman's mother. After all, Jessica had raised Norman all by herself and had done a terrific job also. She hoped she could do the same with Alex. She was determined to. "It's all I want to be."

"A good mother?"

"Yes, for Alex." Nicole was committed to the task ahead of her. "He's been cheated, losing his father. He deserves someone who is committed to being both mother and father to him—as you were to Norman."

"I did put everything I had into that kid," Jessica said. "I feel lucky to say he made me the proudest mother ever. I know you'll be able to say the same about Alex."

"Speaking of Alex"—Nicole stood up as she glanced at her watch—"I better get him. It's getting to be dinner time. Is he napping?"

"Not at all. He's playing, and you're going to have a hard time getting him out of that pool. He's having such a—"

"Pool!" Nicole shouted, all of her senses coming alert. "He's in a pool?"

"Yes." Jessica jumped up from the chair, her face in total confusion at Nicole's sudden excited reaction. "What's wrong?"

"How could you let him near a pool?" Nicole, trying to control her panic, ran for the door. "Where is he?"

"Next door, like I told you." Jessica followed Nicole out of the apartment.

"Are you crazy?" Nicole asked. "He could drown. How could you?"

"Nicole, I put the floating gear on him myself. I've been out there watching him all afternoon. I just came in when I

saw your car drive up. There are four of us adults out there.
You know Alice Henry and Frank Kent. They've been my
neighbors for years. Since I moved here. They both promised
to keep a close eye on him while I got you.''

"Why didn't you tell me right away?" Nicole was fuming,
her anger obvious in her tone.

"We haven't even been inside five minutes, Nicole." Jessica
gave an exasperated sigh. "You know Alice and Frank are
reliable. They've raised six kids between the two of them."

"I don't care." Nicole jumped over the bushes that separated
the building and the house next door, desperate to reach her
baby. "I don't want him anywhere near water."

Nicole called out for Alex as soon as she reached the backyard. Her heart relaxed as she saw he was out of the pool,
playing with trucks on the back patio. When he saw her, he
jumped up and ran to her.

"Are you all right?" Nicole asked as she hugged him. She
hurried to remove the floating gear from his arms. At least they
were on, but it was still no comfort.

"Yes," Alex said as if it was a silly question. "I went to
the park, played Nintendo, and we swam in the pool."

"I told you not to ever go near a pool." Nicole grabbed his
arms and held him still as she looked sternly into his eyes.

"I know." Alex spoke with hesitation, aware his mother's
temper was warming. "But it was hot, and Grandma said it
was okay."

"It is *never* okay," Nicole corrected. "I don't want you
anywhere near water. Do you understand?"

"I like to swim!" In an angry move, Alex freed himself
from her grip, and with a pout headed for his grandmother,
who picked him up.

"You're being overprotective, Nicole." Jessica kindly
waved goodbye to the adults of the house as she spoke through
clenched teeth.

"I don't need your opinion," Nicole snapped as she followed
Jessica back to the apartment. "I decide alone how to raise my
son."

"You can't shelter him from life."

"That's not what I'm trying to do," Nicole sighed, wondering why it seemed she could never get through to anyone her concerns. "You of all people should understand."

Jessica did not respond. No words were spoken between the women as Nicole gathered her son's belongings and led him to the car. Nicole did not want to say any more in Alex's presence, so she only said a quick goodbye and left.

In the car, a still-fuming Alex said he wasn't in the mood for McDonald's, making Nicole feel terrible. She hated it when he was angry, especially because of something she had done. Despite that, she had to do it. She could take no chances with Alex. Everyone treated him like he was just another kid, but he wasn't. He was her son, and he was all she had.

Four

When she arrived home from work after picking up Alex, Nicole took a second to try and relax herself on the sofa before starting dinner. This Tuesday had not been like any Tuesday in the past. It was unique because the night before she had had a dream. A romantic dream. She'd had romantic dreams in the past two years, all involving herself and Norman. She had not dreamt of Norman last night.

As she'd sat on a bench overlooking the lakefront on a moonlit night, she heaved a satisfied sigh, feeling herself relax all over. Then, a strong hand affectionately touched her soft shoulder, and she felt the warmth of it reach through her skin. A feeling of contentment washed over her. She tilted her head to the side and brushed the back of that hand gently with her cheek.

"My love," the deep voice said to her.

It wasn't Norman's familiar husky voice, and when Nicole turned her head to face him, she saw Damon Jordan's face. Then she awoke, almost horrified as if she had been dreaming a nightmare.

Nicole had tossed and turned all night, unable to return to sleep. She was wracked with confusion and guilt. Why would she dream of Damon, and how could she dream of anyone other than Norman? She was utterly annoyed with her preoccupation with Damon Jordan, and this only served to increase her frustration.

Nicole admitted to herself that she was somewhat frightened. Even if it was only a dream, she had never thought it possible to let another man make her feel that way. She had to conquer these involuntary feelings she was having and needed to ignore the thrilling current that moved through her every time she remembered his touch on her shoulder.

The dream had stayed with her all day, keeping her silent as she pondered its significance. She ignored Delaney's pleas to know what was bothering her and tried to keep busy, but there was no avoiding it.

Back home, she tried to find excuses. It made sense she'd dreamt of a good-looking man she'd just met. It didn't mean she was attracted to that man in real life. It wasn't a true betrayal of Norman's memory, because she hadn't wanted to dream of Damon. She would never want to dream of anyone besides Norman and was resolved and determined to see that it never happen again.

"Mommy!" Alex ran into the living room with a confused expression. "Aren't you gonna get the door?"

"Why?" Nicole snapped out of her trance.

"The doorbell rang." He laughed at her absentmindedness. "Didn't you hear it?"

"I . . . I . . . Yes, I did." Nicole jumped from the sofa and headed for the door.

"Hello." Billy West stood like a choirboy on the front steps of the Cox household with his hands straight at his sides.

"Come in, Billy." Nicole stepped aside. "This is unexpected."

"Well," Billy said as he opened his arms for a jubilant Alex to jump into, "I was pretty bored, so I thought the three of us could go out to dinner. My treat."

"The three of us?" Nicole was used to Billy coming over to pick up Alex for dinner, but she was usually not included.

She liked the time for herself and knew it was important that Alex spend time alone with a responsible male role model.

"Yes, why not?" Billy carried Alex around the living room, pretending he was an airplane. "I think it would be nice for Alex for the three of us to go out together."

Nicole wasn't sure what to think of that comment but quickly let it go as the telephone rang.

"Hello?"

"Hey, girl. It's Dee. What are you doing tonight?"

"Well—"

"You're coming over here for dinner."

"Billy just came over and suggested we go out to dinner."

"Billy?" Delaney paused. "You know what he's up to, don't you?"

"Dinner. Like you are?"

"Nicole," Delaney said in her motherly tone. "We have discussed this. Billy is attracted to you. You know that he's just waiting in the wings."

"I really can't talk about this right now," Nicole whispered as she eyed Billy playing with Alex just steps away. They were making enough noise that she was sure he couldn't hear but did not want to risk it.

"I know his affections for Alex are genuine," Delaney said, "but lately. Well, lately you've noticed he stops by the gallery more often. Think about it, Nicole. Do you want to encourage him?"

"I'm not encouraging him," Nicole said defensively, recalling that Billy's visits to the gallery had picked up in frequency.

"The three of you going out to dinner sounds like a nice, cozy little family to me."

Nicole had to admit to herself that Delaney was right. Despite his active dating life, Billy had always shown a tendency to want more than friendship with Nicole, but she had made it clear to him that was out of the question, and he had told her he understood. She had never had any problem since then, but she also knew that actions spoke louder than words.

"I'll think about it," she said.

"Don't think," Delaney urged. "I made way too much pot

roast. You know Ron is out of town, and I need a little company. Let Alex go out with Billy. Please."

"All right." Nicole knew it was useless to fight Delaney when she was prepared to beg. Besides, she always enjoyed a girl's night with her best friend. Between Alex and Ron, it didn't happen too often. They always had fun together, even when they stayed indoors.

"Seven thirty. Plenty of time to change and get over here."

"Billy," Nicole called to him after hanging up the phone. "I'm so sorry. I forgot I told Dee I would come over for dinner. Ron is out of town on business, and I promised I would keep her company."

She hated to lie to a friend, but what else could she say? *Sorry, but I think you're suggesting romance, and I want to cut you off.* That wasn't necessary and would only serve to hurt him. He was far too important to Alex for Nicole to do that.

"That's fine," Billy said, trying to hide his disappointment. "Maybe another night."

"You and Alex can do something." Nicole tried to avoid answering Billy's last comment. "Alex doesn't want to hang out with two gals."

"Pizza! Pizza!" Alex jumped up and down on the sofa. Knowing that was against the rules, he quickly jumped off before Nicole could swat his rear end.

"Pizza, it is," Billy said. He glanced at his watch. "How long will you be?"

"Just a few hours. Is that all right?"

"Sure. Give me the keys and I'll bring him back then just stay and watch TV until you get back."

"You're a great friend, Billy." Nicole went to kiss his cheek, as she usually did, but stopped herself to pat him on the shoulder.

Nicole was a half hour early to Delaney's. The far north suburban house, Victorian in style and immense in size, was one Nicole had always loved visiting. It was lavish and well decorated, befitting a modern upper-income family, each room decorated in what Delaney referred to as a separate theme. Nicole and Norman had opted for a small-town-style home, more fitting their own personalities. Despite Norman's generous salary as a distinguished private university professor, he was never eager to display his wealth, and Nicole respected him for that.

On the other hand, wealth was appreciated by Mr. and Mrs. Smith. They had the big house, the Mercedes, and the BMW. It was no surprise to anyone when the couple decided to have a tennis court built in the backyard, even though neither played tennis.

What was a surprise to Nicole, when she rang the doorbell, was that it was answered by Dr. Damon Jordan.

"Dr. Jordan," she said, completely surprised. Her mouth and her eyes opened wide at the sight of him, wondering for a quick moment if she was back in that dream that had consumed her thoughts all day.

"Please call me Damon." He cracked a friendly smile, that dimple standing out.

"You're early, honey." Delaney strode from the hallway to the door, grabbing Nicole by the arm and pulling her into the house. "You're both early."

Knowing now what had happened, Nicole glared searingly at Delaney. A setup. Delaney had attempted them before, until Nicole finally threatened to never go anywhere with her again. She thought it was over, but apparently she was wrong.

"What have you done?" Nicole asked in a quietly controlled tone, not wanting Damon to know how angry she was with Delaney.

"Why don't you show Damon around the house," Delaney said with a flip of her head as she was already walking away from the two of them. "I need to set the table."

Nicole turned to Damon with an embarrassed grin. He looked fantastic as usual, his flawless face smiling warmly down at her. He knew he was attractive as he held his head up with an air of self-confidence, but he wasn't arrogant about it. He stood calm and collected in a white cotton button-down shirt and khaki shorts that showed off his muscled legs, his smile squarely set and intended for Nicole.

Overly aware of his inspection, Nicole suddenly remembered what she looked like. Not expecting anyone but Delaney, she had carelessly put her hair into a ponytail and threw on a wrinkled pink tank top and cut-off white denim shorts. She wished she had dressed better, but more so, she wished she didn't care.

"Delaney lied to me, didn't she?" Damon placed his hands on his straight hip and gave Nicole an amused stare.

"What did she tell you?" Nicole nervously tucked in her shirt, attempting to look somewhat presentable.

"She called my office today and said you had reconsidered and were interested in meeting me—in getting to know me— only you were nervous and she decided to call me."

Nicole found that suggestive enough. Now Delaney was acting as her pimp, practically handing her over.

"She does this sometimes," Nicole said apologetically. "You can see from the way I'm dressed that I wasn't expecting anyone."

"I think you look terrific." Damon surveyed her quickly.

"You do?" Nicole felt a tingle in the pit of her stomach as he looked her up and down. Her mind was urging, begging, her heart to stop beating so fast. She did not want to be attracted to this man, but what she wanted to feel and what she was actually feeling were quickly becoming two completely different things.

"Yes," he answered. "You look about eighteen years old but very attractive."

"That compliment will get you a tour of the house, Doctor."

"I really don't want to impose if it wasn't your intention to see me here."

"It wasn't, but you're here. There isn't any reason why the three of us can't have a friendly dinner." Nicole leaned in to whisper, the smell of his masculine cologne touching her nose and delighting her senses. "Your presence here will probably be the only thing that keeps me from strangling Dee for lying to both of us."

"I'll do my civic duty." Damon placed a firm hand on Nicole's shoulder. "My part in preventing a crime."

Nicole smiled despite the quiver she felt surge through her veins from the feel of his hand on her bare skin. The touch was warm, too warm for her liking, but she didn't remove it. She simply walked ahead of him, causing it to slip off. Yet she still felt it for a long time afterward.

She felt the tension, like a cool friction, between them as she became too aware any close contact with him made her temperature rise a degree. The warmth returned as he brushed her hip with his own accidentally when they returned to the kitchen after the brief tour. She couldn't even look him in the eye, afraid of saying something she'd regret, or worse, feeling something she'd regret.

She could feel him looking at her. It wasn't in an aggressive, intimidating way, but admiringly. Nicole was annoyed with herself for letting him cause such a distraction to her senses. That annoyance was accentuated by the fact that she actually liked it. A sense of alarm swept over her. She realized that she found pleasure in his admiration. She could tell he was still interested in her, and despite her resolve, she found it a little exciting. More than a little.

Nicole made a promise, in the form of an order, to herself to get an iron control of her feelings and stop this nonsense. It was up to her, after all, wasn't it? She had no intentions of romance and that was that. Wasn't it?

Her mind told her to stick to her guns, for this night would be over soon, and she would be safe at home with Alex. Her body, with a mind of its own, rebelled and took a seat next to Damon at the dinner table. Nicole felt the tension sweep through her as she realized this struggle would continue all night.

"So, Damon." Delaney spoke with inquisitive enthusiasm as she served the food. "Let's hear about you. We know you're a doctor with an impeccable record, but what about Damon Jordan the man?"

"Well . . ." Damon's dimple made a brief appearance as he shyly smiled. "Where do you want me to start?"

"Childhood is fine." Delaney poured the wine.

"Dee, please," Nicole said. "That's not necessary."

"I don't mind." Damon took a sip of water before speaking again. "I was born in Muncie, Indiana, the only son of Davis and Alanis Jordan. I have a younger sister who is in law school at Princeton."

"Impressive." Delaney winked in Nicole's direction.

"Stop." Nicole scowled at her. "Go on, Damon."

"My family moved to Northbrook, Illinois, when I was sixteen. I went to Howard University for my premed studies and—"

"That's all great," Delaney interrupted, with her usual impatience. "What about now? What do you like to do now?"

"My practice is only a year old, and it keeps me very busy, but I also volunteer at the Free Clinic on the West Side of the city every two weeks."

Great, Nicole thought, the struggle raging on inside her. He's not only gorgeous, sexy, and friendly, he's also generous and caring. Why couldn't he be a jerk and make it easy not to like him?

"You said you live in Lincolnwood now?" Delaney asked.

"Yes, I need to be close to my practice, but I've driven around Evanston and I like it very much." He turned to Nicole with a charming smile. "You have a great town."

"Thank you." Nicole gave a nervous laugh as she lowered her head to look at her plate. She felt her temperature take that creep up again. Just because of a smile?

She couldn't let him know the effect he had on her. She needed to depict an ease of nature despite the turmoil that was threatening inside. Quit looking at him, her mind told her. Choose your words carefully and avoid eye contact. You'll be home soon.

Nicole felt strengthened as she lifted her head again, only to connect her eyes with his, seeing the romantic tension they held. He's so cute, her body told her. He seems very nice and funny. There's no harm in a friendly dinner. It told her that her mind was working overtime, and she needed to shut it down. Just for a moment. You'll be fine.

Nicole didn't speak much for the rest of the evening, which

was normal when Delaney was around. She volunteered, to Damon, Nicole's life history. There was an awkward moment for Nicole when Norman was brought up in the discussion, but Damon put everyone at ease when he explained that Dr. Childs had informed him that Nicole was widowed.

Despite that, Nicole quickly changed the subject. She was very protective of her history with Norman. Not just anyone could hear about it.

"What made you choose pediatrics as your specialty?" she asked politely, taking a sip of water. Her throat felt incredibly dry.

"I love kids," Damon answered with a shrug. "I love their honesty and innocence. With the kind of world we live in today, being with children keeps me positive and gives me hope for the future."

"That's great," Delaney said, staring at Damon with dreamy eyes of her own.

"That," Damon added, "plus my father is a doctor, and he told me I would be one whether I wanted to or not."

"But you did want to be one?" Nicole asked, genuinely interested.

"Yes, fortunately I did. Mom and Dad wanted me to be a surgeon or something powerful like that, but I prefer pediatrics."

"I know how that can be," Nicole said with a nod. "My father didn't make a lot of money, and he was always concerned with my financial well-being. He wanted me to be a lawyer or a business executive, but I've always loved art, and I had to go with my heart."

"I enjoy art myself." Damon's eyes centered on Nicole as he spoke, not bothering to hide his attraction.

Nicole felt her pulse leap as she was captivated by his gaze. If he weren't so attractive . . . If his voice weren't so soothing and sexy . . . She wanted to look away but couldn't. Her body was pummeling her mind in the struggle so far tonight.

"Is that so?" Delaney's eyes lit up. "You like art?"

"Yes," Damon said after he took more than a moment before

turning away from Nicole to answer. "I like to collect family and antebellum era portraits."

"That is such a coincidence." Delaney looked in Nicole's direction, as obvious as ever. "There's a major art fair downtown Evanston this weekend. Nicole is going. You should go with her."

Nicole bit her lower lip to keep from yelling at Delaney. If she were closer, she would have stepped on her toes.

"I don't want to impose." Damon, obviously aware of Delaney's intentions, appeared nervous.

"You wouldn't be imposing." Delaney shook her head with a frown as if it was silly of him to even ask. "Alex is going to be with his grandmother that day, and Nicole asked me to come along. Remember? You said you didn't want to go alone cause you might need help carrying stuff."

"Well, I . . ." Nicole couldn't think fast enough to get out of what Delaney was trying to get her into. She wasn't trying as hard as she knew she could.

"You did," Delaney continued, then turned to Damon. "I told her I couldn't go because my husband, Ron, is coming home Friday."

"I'm sure Damon's very busy this weekend," Nicole interjected nervously, her voice abrupt and sounding uncertain.

"Actually my practice is open only two Saturdays a month," Damon said with an innocent grin. "I'm free this weekend."

Nicole's frustration grew, but she concealed it under a nonchalant smile.

"And look at those arms." Delaney reached across the table and pinched one of Damon's half-bare muscled arms. "These arms could carry quite a few paintings—don't you think, Nicole?"

Nicole nodded compliantly as she realized Delaney wasn't giving up. Why was she being so persistent with Damon?

"I'm sure Damon doesn't want to spend his valued weekends as an arm for hire." Nicole heard the rigid tone of her voice but hoped it wasn't as obvious to Damon.

"I don't mind," Damon said with childlike enthusiasm. "I'd love to go."

"That is, of course," Delaney said as her eyes widened in feigned innocence, "unless you don't want him along, Nicole."

The smile was getting harder to fake as Nicole felt she could surely reach across the table and strangle Delaney despite Damon's presence. She knew Nicole would never say she did not want Damon along right in front of his face. Nicole had to think of something else to get out of this.

"I think that would be nice," Nicole said in the calmest voice she could muster.

"Sounds very nice." Delaney leaned back in her chair with a look of fresh success all over her face. "Sounds perfect."

Nicole was patient as she participated in small talk for the rest of the evening, doing her best to fight the urge to flirt with the handsome doctor. She and Damon exchanged phone numbers as she agreed to call him to confirm a time they could meet. It wasn't until he left that she began her assault, but Delaney was unfazed as she stood by her actions.

"What do you mean you did what you had to do?" Nicole made a sufficient amount of noise as she placed the dirty plates in the sink.

"You know that saying 'a man's gotta do what a man's gotta do'?" Delaney kept a straight face as she poised herself for the onslaught. "Well, so does a best friend. If you're not going to care about your future, then I will."

"I care about my future," she spouted off in frustration. "I care about Alex's future."

"Alex isn't going to require his mommy's attention all the time." Delaney sighed, seeming annoyed at the thought of repeating a speech she had given hundreds of times before. "Pretty soon, he's going to only want to be with his friends. Then comes the girls. Then college—and guess what?"

Nicole gave no answer, wishing now that she had never started the conversation.

"He'll get married and have a family of his own." Delaney began rinsing the dishes, passing them back to Nicole to place in the dishwasher. "What will you do then?"

"I'll be happy for him and proud to pieces." Nicole smiled proudly as she flipped back with confidence.

"Oh, shut up," Delaney said with mild disgust. "It's just an art show."

"I'm canceling."

"You're what?" Delaney's head swung around, her mouth wide open. "You said you would go."

"You gave me no choice."

"You can't cancel," she pleaded.

"I'm going to call him tomorrow and apologize." Nicole shrugged. "I'll be apologizing for your behavior."

"I worked so hard on this one, Nicole. I invited a practical stranger to my house for you."

"Another bad move I'm sure Ron would be very happy to hear about," Nicole added with emphasis. "Hey, I tried to stop you quite a few times. You saw those looks I gave you."

"I couldn't help it. I saw the sparks."

"What sparks?" Nicole feared her attraction could be detected. She wondered if Damon had noticed and hoped he hadn't.

"I know chemistry when I see it. I saw it when he came to the gallery last week and here tonight. Don't try to lie to me."

"I won't lie," Nicole said, trying to hold her head above water in this conversation. "He's an attractive man. So is Denzel Washington. There are a lot of attractive men out there. It doesn't mean I want them."

"Don't try to block him in with the masses and the unattainable." Delaney placed a stubborn hand on her hip, flinging water across the kitchen. "He's right in front of your face, and he's after you, girl."

"Stop." Nicole placed the last dish in the washer, closed it, and turned it on. "I'm canceling. I don't want to encourage him."

"Not only will you *not* cancel," Delaney said in a self-assured tone, "but you'll be dreaming about him tonight in your sleep."

"With all the garlic you cooked those potatoes in, I'll be lucky to get any sleep tonight." Nicole grinned sarcastically, trying to hide her embarrassment at the mention of a dream. If only Delaney knew.

Nicole fell asleep that night with a familiar feeling she couldn't quite identify. She was confused and a little upset with herself for her behavior in Damon's presence, but there was more to it, and she couldn't tell what it was. She wasn't looking forward to another sleepless night.

Five

Nicole sat quietly on a rose-colored towel, feeling the hot, soothing sand beneath her legs. She watched Alex concentrate as he built his castle, where he would rule for one second before trouncing all over it and moving on to whatever caught his interest next. She was happy, so serene, as she watched her little love.

She felt a blissful radiance ignite throughout her body as a strong, dark hand touched her bare, firm thigh. His touch was hotter than the sun as it caressed her gently. Nicole turned her head, her eyes half closed in comfort. She could stay where she was forever.

She met Damon's seductive smile with one of her own. Slowly she let her long fingernails run down his chest, feeling the smooth black curls with the tips of her fingers. He closed his eyes. She smiled at the pleasure she gave him.

His hands went to her waist, resting above her bikini string. His fingers gripped her soft skin, and Nicole felt on fire. As he pulled her to him, her eyes closed as well.

The touch of his lips on hers turned her to putty as she wilted into his embrace.

"Nicole," he whispered as his lips parted from hers.

"Damon," she answered back as she opened her eyes.

Only it wasn't Damon anymore. Now it was Norman who held her tight.

Nicole almost fell off her bed, she jumped so high when she awoke. It took a few seconds for her to register where she was and what had happened.

She sat in silence for a while, cursing Delaney under her breath. Confusion and guilt found their way into her head, and she could not let go of them. It had happened again, and this time it was much worse. This time she had known it was Damon who was touching her, arousing her. She had expected to see him when she turned her head—and not Norman. The thought terrified her. She wondered what was happening to her.

Nicole was happy to have a busy day on Wednesday. With a youth art exhibit in the morning, and the usually active afternoons, she was distracted from her dream. More importantly, Delaney was far too preoccupied to hassle her about last night and try to discourage her from canceling. There could be no discouraging, Nicole knew that. Last night's dream had told her so. She would call and cancel the first chance she had.

Wednesday passed. Nicole found herself far too busy. Work was more hectic than usual, and Alex chose that evening to go bike riding with his mother. When they returned, it was well past dinner time, and Nicole didn't want to disturb Damon. She was sure he was tired after a long day at the clinic. She made a note to call him first thing Thursday.

Thursday came and went. Morning was no good—she had to rush Alex off to day care, couldn't call from work with Delaney always around, and was so tired after grocery shopping. Besides, she hadn't figured out exactly what she would say. As she tucked Alex in for the night and kissed him softly on his forehead, she promised herself she would call Friday.

"You're getting excited, aren't you?" Delaney asked as she handed Nicole her biweekly paycheck.

"About what?" Nicole said, pretending to be oblivious to whatever it was Delaney was referring to.

"Don't act coy with me, sister." Delaney was obviously not falling for it. "I can see you're getting excited. I'm excited for you."

"Well, don't be," Nicole said in a cutting manner. "It's not going to happen."

"Don't start all that canceling talk." Delaney waved a dismissing hand. "You are not going to cancel. You are just as excited as he is."

"I am going to cancel." Nicole busied herself at her desk, searching her mind for excuses. "I just haven't gotten around to it."

Delaney snatched the Rolodex from Nicole's desk. Finding the card for Damon's office, she pulled it from the bunch. Then grabbing the telephone, she handed them both to Nicole.

"So call," she said. Her tiny lips were pressed tightly together.

"I will." Nicole's tone faced the challenge brought before her. "I plan to, today."

"Do it now. You have my permission, as your boss, to take the time off and do it now. You know I don't mind you making personal calls." Delaney took Nicole's hand and placed the card marked ALEX'S DOCTOR in it. "I don't think you'll do it."

With a stubborn glare, Nicole snatched the phone and dialed Damon's office. She had spent the last few days thinking of what she could tell him. Little white lies were not her style, and she wouldn't feel comfortable seeing Damon after lying to him. She would just tell him she decided not to go and wouldn't go. No lying there. She could go to another fair. There were tons of them during the summer.

"Hello?"

"Dr. Jordan?" Nicole was surprised to hear his voice, expecting to first speak with his receptionist. It would at least give her a little more time.

"Yes, this is Dr. Jordan."

"Hello." Nicole turned her back to Delaney, whose expression was beginning to soften. She would show her. "This is Nicole Cox."

"Nicole." His deep voice suddenly sounded upbeat and pleased. "How are you?"

"I'm fine and yourself?"

"All right, except my secretary took the day off, and it's been crazy around here."

"Oh." Nicole felt stupid as that word slipped from her mouth. She was nervous and reluctant and starting to get angry with herself. She turned to Delaney, who could sense her hesitancy, and the crooked smile returned.

"How is little Alex?" Damon asked.

"Alex is fine. Bad as usual." She could hear the tap of Delaney's fake nails on the marble countertop of the desk. She would show her. "Dr. Jordan?"

"Please, Nicole," he said with a soft laugh. "Call me Damon."

"I'm sorry." Nicole heard herself giggle. She couldn't remember the last time something made her giggle like a school-girl. "Damon, about tomorrow . . ."

"I'm looking forward to it," Damon said. "I'm trying to find some nice pieces for my office. Something the children will like."

"Yes, well . . ." Nicole felt herself weakening. She couldn't even look in Delaney's direction.

"Is something wrong?" the voice on the other end asked.

This is your chance, Nicole told herself. He was a nice guy and she was more attracted to him than she was willing to admit, but this was wrong. She could stop it now, before any trouble came down the line. To agree to this date would be starting something she had no intention or ability to finish. To cancel might hurt his feelings for a moment, but to falsely encourage him would cause more problems in the future. Her dreams had warned her, but her gut feeling was in charge of her now.

"I know we suggested noon as a good time to meet at Delaney's house, but why don't we meet at eleven instead?" Surprised at her own reaction, Nicole heard Delaney let out a gasp of air. "All the best art goes first. If we miss it, the day would be wasted."

"Good idea," Damon said. "Outside the first level of the parking garage, right?"

"Yes. You can't miss the garage. It's the only one in the area."

"I'll see you tomorrow then."

"Yes, tomorrow."

It was only a fair, after all.

They said their goodbyes, and Nicole slowly hung the phone back on the receiver. She had been all ready to end this "date." Her mind meant to cancel, but her mouth suggested they start this date an hour earlier. She took a deep breath and turned to Delaney, whose face held the widest smile she had ever seen.

"You say one word," Nicole warned, "and I'm going to smack you."

Delaney pressed her lips together while her eyes danced.

"This doesn't mean anything," Nicole said defiantly. "I just didn't want to disappoint him. He was looking forward to it. And as you said, I need someone to help me carry my art if I choose to buy any."

Delaney simply gave a thumbs-up sign as she backed up before turning and walking away.

Nicole felt as if she had failed. Those excuses no more convinced her than they had Delaney. She wondered what she was getting herself into. Did it have to be something? Couldn't this be a harmless occasion among two friends?

Nicole knew Norman had been the only lover for her, and now Alex would be the only man in her life. So why was she nervous? Did she doubt herself? Did she doubt her strength and the commitment she had made to Norman to love him—and only him—for the rest of her life?

Never. It would never get to the point where love was at question. Nicole was sure of that. No, everything would be fine. A harmless afternoon was nothing to be concerned about. That's where it would begin and end. After that, she would never see him socially again.

* * *

"Mommy," Alex screamed as he threw off his seat belt and struggled with the door. "Open it up! Open it up!"

"Slow down, precious." Nicole flipped the lock controls on the car. "What's the rush?"

"We're going to the carnival!" He jumped from the car, his Chicago Cubs cap falling to the ground. Anticipation and thrill was on every inch of his face.

Nicole laughed as she watched him jump twice, before picking up the hat. She loved to see him so excited. She loved the way his eyes danced as his tiny arms waved in the air. This was the one-hundredth time he had reminded her of the carnival Jessica was taking him to.

"You act like you never go anywhere." Nicole held his hand tightly as they crossed the street to the apartment building.

"Grandma! Grandma!" Alex dragged Nicole as he ran to Jessica, who was waiting outside the building.

"You sure you're prepared for this?" Nicole asked, pointing to the boy, who had turned into a little brown jumping bean. "You can see he's already gotten started."

"I have my aspirin." Jessica lifted her purse. The smile on her face turned sideways as she looked Nicole up and down. "I thought you were going to the art fair."

"I am," Nicole said, letting Alex go now that they were safely away from traffic.

"You look so . . . Well, nice."

"As opposed to other times?" Nicole's eyes shifted nervously.

Had she overdressed? She was already embarrassed by all the time she had spent getting dressed. She wanted to ignore it but knew Damon was on her mind when picking out her clothes.

Her first inclination was to wear a T-shirt and shorts. The weather was warm, and she knew she would be walking for a long time. After trying on shirt after shirt, they all seemed too tight or too low cut. She didn't want Damon to think she was trying to show herself off. She was ready to pull her hair out after trying on her shorts. Too short, too tight. Had she gained weight in the past week? After finding the baggiest shirt and pair of shorts she owned, Nicole realized she no longer matched. Besides, she looked like a bum with the clothes hanging, practically falling off her.

As Alex's impatience threatened to tantrum, Nicole quickly decided on a light green short jumper with suspender straps over a plain white T-shirt. She hadn't thought she looked like anything in particular but now wondered if she looked too "cute."

"No," Jessica said. "You always look nice. It's only ... Well, you look very nice. Are you and Delaney going out to lunch afterward?"

"Not exactly." Nicole tensely scratched her chin. Sometimes she wished she were a better liar.

"Well?" Jessica's brows centered as Nicole's behavior turned curious.

"Delaney isn't coming with me." Nicole's eyes diverted everywhere except at Jessica.

"Going by yourself?"

"Actually, no. A friend is coming with me." Nicole had hoped that would be sufficient information, but could tell from the look on Jessica's face that they were going to stay right where they were until she knew everything.

Nicole explained her planned afternoon with Damon, who Jessica was already aware was Alex's new doctor. Despite her insisting there was nothing between them, Nicole saw a look of mild surprise on Jessica's face. That look stayed with her as she drove to the parking garage near the fair. It made her feel guilty and a little angry at the same time. Why was what she did any of Jessica's business? Why was she letting Jessica and this harmless, meaningless afternoon matter so much?

Nicole knew why as she laid eyes on Damon, standing outside the parking garage. She felt a lightning bolt run through her at the sight of him. He looked ruggedly sexy in a navy blue tank top and black shorts. His brown-skinned muscled arms and legs gave him an athletic physique Nicole found very sexy. Yes, she knew why she was worried. She was very attracted to Damon Jordan, and it distressed her. She hadn't been this physically conscious of a man since Norman. It was a feeling she was once certain she would never have again.

As she emerged from the dimly lit garage, she called to him. She saw his eyes widen and a smile come to his face as he turned to her. She knew he was pleased to see her, and she liked that. She liked that his smile was because of her.

"We can start at Church Street," she said as she pointed to the next block, "and take a left on Sherman Avenue or start right on Sherman. That's where the food stands are."

"What types of food?" Damon flipped on his sunglasses.

"Ribs, chicken-kabobs, and funnel cakes." She made a quick note that he looked good in sunglasses. Very good.

"Funnel cakes?" Damon licked his lips. "Lead the way."

"Follow me." Nicole smiled as she turned and headed toward Sherman Avenue. She told her nagging mind to shut up and have fun for a few hours.

As the lakefront breeze cooled them in the hot sun, Nicole and Damon walked together along the streets of downtown Evanston. She felt only a little uncomfortable when Damon would accidentally touch her or when he placed a hand on her arm to protect her from oncoming crowds of people. Each time it happened, everything else seemed to stop, and Nicole felt a tingling sensation run through her.

She enjoyed listening to him talk about his upper-middle-class upbringing. He got into trouble a lot, but his parents kept him on the straight and narrow. Nicole could tell he was still someone who liked to have a lot of fun. He had a lot of stories to tell about growing up, college, and being a doctor. Nicole could see that he really did love kids and believed strongly in helping others. She found him interesting in many ways: easygoing and refreshing.

As they searched for unique and original art, Nicole told Damon everything there was to know about Alex. Her son being her favorite topic, she continued for a long time until Damon stopped her.

"Alex sounds like a great kid," he said as they both took a seat near the Fountain Square. "But I'll have plenty of time to get to know him. I want to hear about his mother."

"There isn't much to say." Nicole shrugged and turned her attention to the water as it flew into the air. "I'm Alex's mother."

"That's not all you are." Damon slid in on the concrete bench to where he was less than a foot from Nicole. "There's more to you than your son. What about your painting?"

"Really, there isn't more to me than Alex." Nicole wasn't looking directly at Damon but could tell he was closer now. She could feel he was closer now. The tingling sensation was returning. "It's all I want to be. I barely have enough time for that."

"I don't believe that Alex is the only thing you care about." Damon removed his sunglasses and looked directly into Nicole's eyes as she turned to him. "You're an interesting, intelligent, and beautiful young woman. There's too much out there to ignore."

"If you're talking about dating, I—"

"No, I'm not," Damon said as he shook his head. "I'm talking about you. Just you. What about art? You had such insight into the pieces we saw today. Your perspective on the clown painting turned me 180 degrees. I thought it was just a textbook piece until you brought out the tenderness in the background. I can't wait to place it on my wall Monday morning."

"So what's your point?" Nicole asked, smiling appreciatively in response to his compliment.

"The other night when we were at dinner, Delaney said you used to paint and you sold your art. Why don't you anymore?"

"I'm too tired." Nicole was reluctant to tell him she hadn't been inspired enough to even pick up a brush since Norman's death. After all, she was exhausted. "Despite how much I love it, raising a rambunctious little boy all by myself takes all the creativity and energy I have. Nothing is left for the canvas."

"That's too bad." Damon lowered his head as he looked at the coin he had just taken from his pocket. "I'll bet your art was beautiful. I'll bet if you were here today, you would have had to close up already because you'd be sold out.''

''Aren't you a charmer?'' Nicole gave him a playful slap on the leg.

''It's not a line.'' Damon flipped the coin between his fingers. ''I mean it.''

Nicole took a moment to look into his eyes. He was telling her what he thought, she could see it. She saw honesty and confidence directed at her, and she wasn't sure how she felt about that, but her first inclination was to feel flattered.

''So if that isn't a line,'' she said, choosing to change the subject, ''I believe you, but what is?''

''What is what?''

''A line. Some of your lines.'' Nicole liked seeing him suddenly nervous. At least the spotlight was off of her now. ''I know you have plenty.''

''Says who?'' His tone was coy and evasive.

''Says me. You're obviously an attractive, eligible man. I'm sure you don't need many, but you have to have some. Don't you all?''

''You mean like, 'Hey, baby, what's your sign'?'' Damon asked with a mocking tone. ''Those kinds of lines?''

''I think you have a little more class than that.'' Nicole let out a quick laugh. ''At least I hope.''

''I don't use lines.'' Damon kept his eyes on his coin. ''Can we change the subject?''

''Sure.'' Nicole, letting her playful side have a little fun, decided to push a bit more. ''Where is marriage on your time-line?''

''Wha—'' Damon's head jerked up as his eyes widened in surprise. ''Can we go back to the last topic?''

''No, no.'' Nicole laughed as she pointed her finger and shook her head. ''You said to get off that topic. We're on another one now. Let's give.''

''Give what?'' Damon appeared to be stalling.

''Some info!'' Nicole said. ''Hasn't some woman singled you out yet for marital harmony? You're a good husband candidate. You're an attractive, successful, and mature man. You don't have any obvious chemical imbalances or compulsive behaviors, although I don't know you that well."

"Thanks for the compliment, I think." He gave her a stern frown. "The truth?"

"Nothing but," she answered.

"Marriage doesn't fit into my plans right now. When I was younger, I liked to play the field. A resident's life doesn't allow for a committed relationship. Now I'm married to my practice. It's only a year old, and I'm putting everything I am into it. It would be unfair to make any woman my wife right now."

"That's refreshing," Nicole said as she sighed.

"What's refreshing about that?" Damon asked. "My mother is pulling her hair out about grandchildren."

"It's just nice to hear someone have their priorities in order. You understand that to be married means that's what is most important in your life, and you have to give your all to it. If you aren't ready to do that, then you shouldn't get married. It's how I feel about Alex."

"How does it relate?" he asked, his brows gesturing confusion.

"Everyone is always telling me to get out into the world and party. They don't understand that being a mother is my priority. It's a choice that I've made willingly. Those partying days are over for me."

"I don't know, Nicole." Damon's eyes turned to the fallen water as it joined the pond from the stream in the air. "Everyone has to have balance in their life. They can't just stick to one thing. I do plan on getting married one day and still run my practice."

"Good for you," was her only response, his words making her feel a bit awkward. She wondered what exactly did he mean by that, if anything. She nervously glanced at her watch and said, "It's getting late. We've been here for hours. I need to get back to Alex."

"All right." Damon stood up from the concrete bench, stretching his arms wide. "Just a minute."

Nicole watched as he shut his eyes for a moment, then threw his coin into the pond. His eyes opened and stared directly at

Nicole as he smiled widely. Unable to turn away, Nicole stayed her eyes in his path. She was suspended there for a moment in time, afraid to ask what he had wished for. She was afraid he would tell her and was afraid she already knew.

There was a prolonged silence between them as they returned to the garage. It wasn't until Damon safely placed the painting Nicole had purchased into her trunk that they spoke again.

"Nicole." Damon slammed the car trunk closed. "I had a great time today."

"So did I." Awkwardness forced Nicole to lower her head. She felt silly and uneasy, like when she was in school on a first date with a boy. "I really appreciate you helping me carry—"

"Nicole." Damon shoved his hands into his pockets. His eyes moved nervously from Nicole to the ground as he spoke. "I know you were . . . we were forced into this by Delaney."

"I could have canceled," Nicole said. "Really, I don't mind. I had a great time."

"It would be nice if we left it at this," Damon said with a thoughtful expression. "If we said our goodbyes and saw each other only whenever Alex needed a checkup. Only I wouldn't be able to stand myself if I didn't ask again to have dinner with you."

"Damon, I—" Nicole protested.

"You've made it very clear," he interrupted, "that you aren't interested in dating right now."

"It has nothing to do with you, Damon." Nicole hoped he could understand. "It's me. In my life right now, there's just Alex. My husband and I were—"

"You have very good reasons," he said, nodding in agreement. "You're still in love with your late husband, and you want to concentrate on raising your son. On the other end, I need to concentrate on developing my practice. Neither of us is interested in a commitment."

"So what are you saying?" Nicole asked, confused as to his intentions.

"Why don't we just have fun?" Damon asked. "No commitment. No strings attached. I like you, and I think you like me. I'm not a mind reader, but something clicks between us.''

"I'm flattered, Damon," Nicole said, blushing at the knowledge that he'd sensed her attraction to him, "but I don't think it's a good idea.''

"I think it's a great idea." Damon spoke confidently. "Nothing serious. We could just spend time together like we did today. No harm, just fun.''

"Sounds like dating to me." Nicole hated to admit the suggestion appealed to her. She had enjoyed herself very much today but had made herself a promise that this would be it. She was never to see him socially again.

"More like a platonic friendship with options," Damon said. "All options would be yours.''

"Why mine?" she asked, not believing that she was actually curious about this arrangement.

"You're obviously a woman who likes to control her situations. I'll give you that control.''

"Emotions can't be controlled," Nicole said with a staid tone. "To underestimate them would be dangerous.''

"I don't want to push you." Damon raised his hands in the air, indicating that he was backing off. "I think it would be fun. Something new with no expectations or requirements. It's up to you. You have my number. Have a nice evening, Nicole.''

Nicole watched as Damon turned and headed out. She was sorry to see him go but also glad he had left. She wasn't so sure how much longer she could've held out. Despite the wants and beliefs she had built up within herself for two years, she had let a few hours on a sunny afternoon bring her doubts.

No matter what he said, Nicole knew if they went out it would be dating, and that was out of the question. How could she share her time and part of herself with any man other than Norman? It seemed so wrong. No one understood that despite her attraction to Damon, in her heart and soul, she still belonged to Norman. Besides, Alex needed his mother, and she was more than satisfied being that and only that.

Six

Nicole felt exhausted Sunday morning. Not only had she not gotten any sleep last night, but she had tossed and turned throughout, unable to get Damon and his proposal off her mind. She had wanted to acknowledge her attraction to him. It was there, she admitted, hoping in facing up to it, she could figure out a way to make it go away. That wasn't happening. Damon had been right when he said something clicked between them. He radiated an energy and vitality that drew her like a magnet to him, despite her desire for the opposite. It was a pull Nicole had been sure only Norman could have on her. She wanted to get past that and block it from her mind, her heart—but it wasn't working. At least it hadn't last night. She found herself weighing the pros and cons of Damon's suggestion, then chastising herself for even going that far.

She did not want or need this confusion and complication in her life. She had come to grips with the fact that she would never wake up in Norman's arms again and had found peace in holding on to Alex. She loved that boy more than life itself and got immense pleasure from caring for him. This life was not necessarily what she had imagined for herself, but it was comfortable and safe. Damon was taking that away as he invaded her dreams and now her daytime thoughts. To continue seeing him would completely tear down the level of comfort she had taken two years to build.

"Grandma is gonna call," Alex said as he reached across the kitchen table for a blueberry muffin.

"Why would she call?" Nicole asked, breaking from yet another daydream involving Damon. She wondered what Jessica had to say about her "date."

"Because you woke up late, and we didn't go to church." He broke the muffin in two, concentrating on one half. "She always calls when we miss church."

"Oh," Nicole sighed.

"She's also gonna ask you about your date." Alex spoke with a mouth full of food.

"Don't do that, Alex," Nicole scolded. "And what do you mean, my date?"

"With Dr. Jordan." Alex spoke after swallowing his food this time. "She was curious."

"What did she say?" Nicole wasn't surprised, because the look Jessica had given her yesterday warned of this.

"She just wondered how long you've been dating him." Alex kept his eyes on his plate as he spoke. "I said I didn't know, so she said she'll ask you."

"I'm not dating Dr. Jordan." Not at all hungry, Nicole picked at her food. "He's just a friend like Delaney or Billy."

"So he won't be my new daddy?"

Nicole's mouth flew open as her fork dropped out of her hand. Alex had never mentioned a new father before, and she was unprepared as to how to answer him.

"Where did you get that idea?" she finally asked with a stunned look.

"Sean Davis's mother just got married again. You know Sean? He's at the Day Learning Center."

"Yes, I do."

"Well, his mother had a husband like you had Daddy, and he died, too. He was sick."

"Well, I'm very happy Mrs. Davis has found love," Nicole said, "but I don't plan on getting married again."

"Why not?" Alex gave a confused frown.

"Your daddy was the only man I was meant to love."

"He was a great guy, wasn't he?" Alex smiled proudly.

"Yes, he was, Alex." She leaned over and kissed her son on the cheek. She wondered if he still remembered his father at all. "He was the greatest, and he loved you so much."

"But what about me now?"

Nicole's heart turned inside as she saw a look of sadness on his face. "You want a new daddy?"

"Yes, I do." Alex's expression was completely serious. "Sean likes his new daddy. They have fun. I want a new daddy, too."

"I'm glad you've told me that." Nicole wasn't sure what else to say.

She felt guilty, knowing that she had only thought of herself as far as a future with another man was concerned. Alex was what was most important, and Billy wouldn't be around forever. One day he would get married and have his own kids he had to put first.

"Will you marry Dr. Jordan?" Alex asked.

"No, Alex. Well . . ." Nicole was flushed as she saw Alex's smile form. "You find this amusing?"

"Amusing?" he asked, confused.

"It's another word for funny."

"Yes," he said while laughing. "I find this very amusing."

Nicole smiled as she always did in response to Alex's happiness. It was contagious. The smile was only temporary, though, as Nicole knew things would be much more difficult from now on. When it came down to it, Alex was first. Nicole didn't have to think twice about that. She had vowed the day he was born to give him all he could ever want and need and recommitted herself to that vow even more after Norman's death. Now he wanted something Nicole wasn't sure she could give him.

"He wants a daddy?" Billy repeated the words Nicole told him.

He had stopped by in the afternoon to say hello. She hadn't intended on telling him, but he insisted after seeing through her pasted smile.

"That's what he said." Nicole poured a glass of lemonade for Billy as they sat at the back porch table watching Alex play in the yard.

"What did you tell him?" Billy leaned backward, taking a long sip.

"I thanked him for being honest." Nicole shrugged. "I didn't know what else to say."

"You really don't plan on being single the rest of your life, do you?"

"I don't know. I just never . . ." Nicole moaned and laid her head on the table.

Billy lifted his chin and lowered his eyes as he surveyed her for a moment before asking, "Why don't you marry me?"

Nicole's hair flew back as her head jerked up. Her mouth wide open, she was certain she had misunderstood. "What?"

"Marry me." Billy's tone and expression showed no sign of humor.

"You're very funny." Nicole laughed, but her chuckles went away as Billy's serious expression continued. "You have got to be joking. Please tell me you're joking."

"I'm not." Billy casually set down his glass. "I'm actually very serious."

"I don't even want to hear this." Nicole pushed away from the table. "I've had enough surprises to last me an entire week."

"You've made it clear you aren't interested in dating," he continued, despite her protest, as he followed her into the kitchen. "You say you'll never love another man, but Alex wants a father."

"You would want to marry a woman that doesn't love you that way just to give Alex the idea that he has a family again?"

"I know you care about me, Nicole." Billy closed the sliding glass door behind him. "And I care about you. I think it's a foundation from which to build."

"Build what?" Nicole's frustration grew as she was coming to understand Billy's suggestion of a marriage of convenience.

"A marriage. A family. We could grow to love each other."

"What if we don't, Billy?" Nicole asked. "What if after a few years, we still only see each other as friends. That would be a pretty unhappy and lonely situation."

"I don't think that will happen. It wouldn't be normal for us to never have needs again. We'll want to . . . need to . . ."

"I'm not an animal, Billy." Nicole couldn't ignore the glimpse of Damon that flashed in front of her face at the thought of needs.

"No, but you are a woman. You're a woman entering the prime of her sexual—"

"Enough!" she yelled. "I really don't want to hear any more of this." Nicole knew what Billy said was probably the truth, but she wasn't prepared to deal with it. In her heart, her prime had come and gone with Norman.

"Don't think about you or me," Billy said. "Don't think about your doubts. Think about Alex. Isn't that what's important?"

"Alex isn't served well by this," Nicole said, surprised that a usually level-headed Billy would even suggest such a thing. "He is better off with one parent who loves him truly and wholly than two that are lying to him. Anyway, I would never put myself in that position."

"But, Nicole," Billy said with a frown, expressing some confusion. "You talk as if Alex is all that counts. What he wants is all that matters. Are you actually saying that your happiness means something?"

"Of course it does," she answered adamantly. "I don't plan now to get married again, but if I ever do it will be for love as much as for Alex."

"But you said you'll never love again." Billy shook his head in confusion. "What about Alex?"

"Nothing is set in stone," Nicole said. "And besides, what about me?"

Nicole immediately deciphered what had just taken place when she saw the look of satisfaction on Billy's face. He had tricked her!

"You don't mean any of this, do you?" She was fuming, doing her best to keep from grabbing a pot and throwing it at him. "This was all a ploy to force me to—"

"I didn't force you to say anything." Billy lifted his arms in the air as he leaned back, indicating his innocence. "I challenged you, that's all. Teachers do it all the time with their students. If you challenge them, it forces them to express how they truly feel."

"I'm not one of your students," she yelled, growing angrier every second.

"But you are my friend, and I love you." Billy's face softened. "So we never happen. That's fine with me, but it's not fine that nothing ever happens for you ever again. You deserve better than that."

Nicole felt a sudden need to cry her eyes out. She fell into the nearest chair and wept silently. She didn't push Billy away when he offered consolation. She needed consolation.

She needed answers, but she knew Billy wasn't the one to provide them.

The frustration and confusion was growing for Nicole: her attraction to Damon, the dreams, Damon's suggestion they date, and Alex's desire to have a father. Now Billy's insane ploy to get her to admit she had needs was too much. So when Delaney called later that Sunday, only requesting news about yesterday's trip to the art fair, she got a lot more. Nicole told her everything from beginning to end, unable to keep it all to herself anymore.

"This is fantastic," was Delaney's response after a silent pause.

"Did you hear what I just told you?" Nicole asked. "My life is a mess."

"It is not a mess. You simply have a life now. Conflict, desire, confusion, and challenges. You're living again."

"If this is having a life, I don't want one." Nicole pouted. "What can I do?"

"Alex wants a daddy," Delaney said. "Then you will give him one. Only you'll give him one the right way."

"I've done that, with Norman. I don't think I could ever give him that again."

"You don't have to give him that."

"Give him something else but just as good."

"It would never be that good," Nicole said with surety. In her heart, she truly believed that it could never be as good as it was with Norman.

"How do you know unless you try? It's happened for people before. You're not the only woman in your situation."

"We've had this conversation several times before." Nicole took a second peek into the living room to check on Alex. "It's always the same."

"Not this time, honey. You said you dreamt about him? You've never dreamt about a man before Damon. This time it's different. You know that."

"I think you're right." Nicole paused, taking a second to let her own words sink in. "I just don't know what to do."

"I think you do. You're just scared, honey. But that's good."

"How can that be good?" Nicole felt herself almost laughing. "What's out there for me?"

"For starters, a very attractive young doctor who seems to like you very much."

After saying their goodbyes, Nicole took a deep breath and stood alone, silent in the middle of the kitchen. In the background she could hear Alex's precious voice singing along with the soda pop commercial. His singing, as terribly off-key as it was, made her smile every time. She wanted him to always be happy.

Was she really considering this, she asked herself. Dating again? As the image of Damon in his tank top and shorts flashed through her mind, Nicole felt fear and excitement. Was it simply physical, what she felt for him? Her heart warmed at the very thought of Norman, but it was her entire body that warmed at the thought of Damon. More than both of those, it was her soul that warmed at the thought of Alex. He was worth everything and anything. He was definitely worth trying.

No promises, no strings, just fun. Nicole remembered Damon's words in the garage as, with a shaky hand, she picked up the telephone receiver.

Seven

"You're beautiful."

"Delaney, please." Nicole was trying her best to act unaffected, but as she stood in front of her bedroom mirror, she had to admit she was impressed.

She looked stunning in the silver-sequined spaghetti-strap evening gown. It hung loosely on top, showing off her firm, shapely shoulders and tempting with cleavage. The style fitted around her hips, not tightly, but enough to move with her when she walked. The dress draped loosely again above her small ankles, adding a modest slit up the left thigh.

She wore her hair up, its reddish tints shining in the lights. Loose tendrils hung carelessly around her face, on her neck. Her delicately curved facial bones were highlighted with blush, her full curving mouth was dashed with red. She looked softly elegant and smelled like lilies.

"Pretty good." Delaney lay back on the queen-sized bed. "I think we'll have a first date proposal."

"That's enough," Nicole said. "There will be no proposal or anything like that going on here."

Nicole had been in anticipation of this night all week. Although seeing each other had been Damon's suggestion, she was concerned about rejection when she called. After all, Damon was a very attractive man. A man she was sure did not have to wait around for anyone to accept his dinner invitation. Relieved that he was happy to hear from her, Damon took any further pressure off by suggesting a perfect time to get together. The following Friday there would be a downtown Chicago charity event to raise money for inner city clinics like the one at which Damon volunteered. He had already purchased two tickets but was planning on going alone. Nicole thought it was a nice idea, and they made plans for him to pick her up at seven.

As the clock read six forty-five, her anxiety had reached its peak. It had grown as every day went by, but Nicole enjoyed it. She enjoyed frantically searching for something to wear as Delaney had teased her. Nicole had dreamt of Damon only once during the week, but the kiss they shared, that time on a yacht off the South Pacific, was enough to keep her blushing for days.

Both women jumped as they heard the doorbell ring. Nicole froze in place as Delaney leaped from the bed and ran out of the room, knowing she would have to be fast if she wanted to beat Alex. He was almost as excited as Delaney that she was going out with a "boy."

"What is wrong with you, Nicole?" she asked herself as she looked in the mirror. She felt so silly. Her stomach was trembling as if she was a teenager going to the prom. It was only a date.

She took two deep breaths and headed down the hallway. She could hear Delaney telling Damon how nice he looked, but Alex was loudest of all. Nicole hoped he'd listen to her when she told him not to mention anything about getting a new daddy.

Everyone turned with a wide smile as Nicole entered the living room.

"Mommy, you look fantastic!" Alex was jumping up and down on the sofa with his shoes on again.

He was showing off for Damon. Nicole chose not to get

after him about it for now, but she would remember later. Right now, she thanked him kindly for his compliment.

"I second that," Damon said, his eyes turning soft as they slowly trailed her figure.

"Same to you." Nicole returned the compliment but not for the sake of good manners.

Damon looked very handsome in his tailored tuxedo. His tall, muscular physique was refined and polished, tempting at what was underneath. Nicole raised her eyebrow at the thought.

"Would you like to sit down?" Delaney picked the jumping bean off the sofa and wiped at the seat covers. "We could talk a bit."

"Thanks for the offer, Mother," Nicole said sarcastically. "But we should really get going."

"I just had one question," Damon said as he took his eyes off Nicole for the first time since she entered the room. "Where did you get that beautiful painting?"

A wide smile came to Nicole's face as everyone turned to the painting that hung on the wall above the fireplace. It was her favorite. The first time she had seen the Louisiana Bayou at sunset on a summer evening, her breath was taken away, and she knew she had to paint it. The sky was a mixture of purple and orange, looking as if a fire was raging off in the distance. The bare trees cast a dark shadow against the murky blue waters with fallen leaves strewn about. The dense, plush greenery held the mystery of the area that Nicole found intriguing and inspiring.

"Mommy did that," the jumping bean said loud enough to be heard down the block.

"You did this?" Damon stepped in front of the painting, his eyes moving from it to Nicole. "This is beautiful. It looks like the South."

"It's Louisiana." Nicole tried to stifle a laugh at the sight of Delaney covering Alex's mouth with her hand. He was apparently under the impression that all questions were directed at him, and he was ready to answer every one of them. "My mother's family is from there. They used to own a cabin on the Gulf. That was the view."

"Did you take a picture and paint it?" Damon asked.

"No," Delaney said. "She painted it from view. Just sitting on the back porch."

"Now you told me Saturday, you were a basic painter." Damon squinted his left eye as he stared Nicole down. " 'Nothing special' were your words."

"She's too modest for her own good." Delaney took hold of Damon's elbow. "Let me show you."

Before Nicole could protest, Delaney had led Damon on the short tour of the small, welcoming home with Alex jumping right behind. She chose to stay in the living room, unable to hide her proud smile as she overheard Damon's compliments. She had kept her best work for her home, to be shared with her family.

It was well after seven before Nicole was able to get Damon out of the house. Promising Delaney she would be home by ten, she was met with a frown and changed her own curfew to eleven.

As Damon drove his BMW downtown, conversation was easy. Nicole's nerves were forgotten as he told her about the importance of these charities. She was impressed with his serious commitment to providing health care to people who couldn't otherwise afford it.

When they arrived at the Westin Hotel, dinner was already being served. There, Nicole met a few of Damon's peers, other doctors who volunteered or were sympathetic to the cause and its challenges.

"For three months now, I've run out of supplies just over halfway through," Donna Lee said.

Donna was an obstetrician/gynecologist who volunteered at a clinic on the south side of the city, giving prenatal care to pregnant mothers. To appearances, she was a petite lady with caramel-colored skin and light brown hair that waved down her shoulders. On the outside, she looked delicate, but after watching her and hearing her speak for a while, Nicole realized she was a very tough and determined woman.

"I had to buy prenatal prescriptions for a couple of girls myself," Donna continued. "They were only teenagers and too afraid to tell parents they were pregnant. They had no money of their own but refused to ask their mothers.''

"What about the fathers of their babies?'' Nicole asked.

"One girl refused to tell me about him.'' Donna's saddened tone matched her frustrated expression. "I'm thinking he isn't a kid from school, and she feels ashamed. The other one said as soon as she told her boyfriend, he split town.''

"Disappeared?'' asked Damon.

"Not really,'' Donna said. "Considering his family knew where he was. Apparently his mother approved of his leaving town. When this frightened girl went to his home, looking for him, his mother treated her like dirt. Told her that her son deserved a better life and wasn't ready to be a daddy.''

"She probably can't get any legal help tracking him down without her parents finding out.'' Nicole's heart softened at the situation she realized many young women were in.

"It's hard enough dealing with these kids' problems.'' Donna shook her head. "I can't deal with funding problems, too.''

"Tell me about it,'' said Terry Lindon, assistant director of neurology at the City Hospital. "I've always encouraged my residents to volunteer at least once a month at these clinics. They tell me that they open as early as six A.M., but there are people already lined up outside. The waiting rooms are filled all day. They have to turn sick people away. Residency is hard enough. The doctors are exhausted. We need more clinics.''

"We definitely need more,'' Damon said, "but that's farther down the line. What we need now is funding for the ones that already exist.''

Nicole could see the conviction in Damon's eyes as he spoke. This was very important to him. She was developing respect for him, knowing that he could have been satisfied with his private practice. Successful now, he could have left the unpleasant work for someone else to do. She could tell this was something Damon would do forever, no matter how successful he got. She liked that.

"You should have been on that stage tonight,'' Nicole said as the two of them sat at the table alone.

The dinner and the speeches were over, and dancing had

started. Nicole was glad to be alone with Damon to let him know how much she admired him.

"What do you mean?" Damon turned his chair around to face Nicole.

"Listening to you here, at this table tonight." She paused, trying to find the right words to express her admiration. "You have as much conviction as those people that spoke."

"Thanks." He looked down, attempting to hide his shy smile. A more serious expression returned when he looked back up. "I am very serious about this. It has a lot to do with my upbringing."

"From what you've told me, I thought your upbringing was very good."

"It was," Damon said. "I was very happy. I had the best of everything, and it made me want to give a little of that back."

"What about yourself?" Nicole asked as she scooted her chair closer to his. "What do you like to do for yourself?"

"I like to dance." Damon stood up from his chair and held out his hand to Nicole.

"No way," she said, shaking her head. "I don't dance. I haven't danced in years."

"It's a slow song. You won't have to move much." Damon took hold of her arm gently and pulled her up from the chair. "Don't be a wimp."

"Since you put it that way." Nicole threw him a challenging stare, turned herself around, and began leading him to the dance floor. "I'll show you who's a wimp."

Nicole's senses leapt to life as he held her body to his. Her eyes closed as if by instinct as she felt his arms wrapped firmly around her waist. She felt a heady sensation as he held her to him with one hand, and with the other, grasped hers and laid it against his chest. She could feel his heart beating as she looked into his eyes, feeling a hint of desire reach within her.

"I like bike riding."

Nicole's eyes flew open as she realized she was drifting off into her own world as he was talking to her. His hold was comforting and so distracting at the same time. "Excuse me?"

"You asked me what I like to do for myself." Damon led her delicately along the dance floor. "I like to dance and go bike riding."

"Oh, yes. Of course." She could smell his cologne faintly and liked its masculine scent. "What else?"

"I don't know." He shrugged his shoulders as he looked down at her face. "I'm sure I would have more hobbies, but I don't have the time to explore them."

"I know what you mean." Nicole found his smile engaging. "Your practice keeps you occupied like Alex does for me. After I come home from work, I spend all evening with him. We talk and we play. Sometimes he'll play at a friend's, and I get a couple of hours to myself. Then we have dinner, and pretty soon he's off to bed. By that time, I'm too exhausted to do anything. I know I have to get up early the next morning, make breakfast, and help him get ready and off to day care before I go to work."

"Compared to you, my day sounds almost empty."

"Don't get me wrong," Nicole said. "I love every moment I get with him. He's the sweetest boy in the world and means everything to me. It's just that there is very rarely time for anything else."

"Little time for painting, either?" Damon asked.

"Yes, I suppose that, too." Nicole averted her eyes from his and lowered them to his chest.

"I really admired those paintings at your house. You must have sold well at the gallery."

"If Delaney told you that, you should know she exaggerates. She wants you to be impressed with me."

"I don't need Delaney for that."

Nicole stopped dancing and looked up. Her eyes met Damon's as he stopped along with her. There was a tenderness in his gaze that sparked wild excitement within her. As Damon passed her a lazy smile, Nicole knew she was in trouble.

They danced for an hour more until both were exhausted. On the way home, Damon turned the car radio up loud, and they sang songs together. Although very tired, Nicole was almost disappointed as they pulled into her driveway.

"I hope Delaney isn't angry with me," Damon said as he opened the car door and helped her out.

"Why would she be?" Nicole searched in her purse for her keys.

"You said you'd be back at eleven. It's a quarter to one."

"I had no idea." Nicole glanced at her watch. "I was enjoying myself so much."

"So was I, Nicole." Damon's tone turned serious as they stood on the dimly lit porch. "I hope we can do this again soon."

"I'd like that." The nervous schoolgirl with butterflies in her stomach had returned.

She smiled at the sight of him under the light. His tuxedo was worn after a night of dancing. He had taken off his jacket long ago.

"What's so funny?" Damon asked as he noticed her smirk, a smile treading his lips as well.

"Your cummerbund is sideways." Nicole covered her mouth with one hand as she laughed and pointed to the piece of clothing with the other. She enjoyed an opportunity to point out a flaw, despite the fact that it only made him more attractive. It gave him a fun look she found enchanting.

"Oh, no," he sighed, seeming embarrassed as he spotted his mistake. Quickly correcting it, he also tucked his shirt in tighter and adjusted his tie.

As he grimaced in good humor, Nicole enjoyed watching the animation in his face. She found it appealing that he could laugh at himself.

"It's okay," she said reassuringly, still laughing. "We had quite an evening. It's understandable to be a little worn."

"You're not." Damon's eyes roved Nicole's figure as he stepped closer. "You're just as devastating as when you stepped into the living room earlier tonight."

Nicole's lips parted slightly, but no words came out. He placed his compliments so well, catching her attention each time. His undeliberate charm was appealing.

Nicole stared into his eyes as she watched him step closer. She felt her breath inhale as his hand gently touched her neck.

Her eyes closed as his thumb softly tilted her chin upward. His touch was electric. A fire swept through her as she felt his full lips lower onto hers. They brushed softly but pressed harder as she let out a quiet moan.

As if by instinct, Nicole wrapped her arms around him and pulled him to her. She savored the taste of the kiss as its heat flowed from her lips to the rest of her body. It was sweet and smooth. She felt a tingle grow in the pit of her stomach as Damon's other hand wrapped around her small waist. She felt his fingers sear through her dress onto her bare skin, making her want more, and that frightened her.

Nicole pushed gently away, lowering her head. It took a moment for her to get her senses together. When she looked up at Damon, she could tell he'd been affected the same way.

"What about us being just friends hanging out?" Nicole's voice was choppy as she searched for words.

"Did I say that?" Damon smiled softly as he ran his hand over his head.

"Yes, you did," Nicole said. "And I agreed."

"You did, didn't you?" Damon pointed a finger at Nicole as he stepped back. "So this isn't just me?"

"No, it isn't." Nicole still felt the heat from the kiss on her lips. Even a cool summer night couldn't relieve that right away.

"What do we do?" Damon asked cautiously. "It doesn't seem like our initial plan is working out."

"We can take it slow," Nicole said. She understood and appreciated his attempt to give her control. "I need this to go very slow."

"Very slow it is." Damon stared at Nicole, his eyes showing satisfaction.

"I appreciate it." Nicole reached down for her keys again. "I really should get in. Dee's husband is waiting up for her."

"When can I see you again?" Damon's words were almost a whisper.

"Why don't you call me tomorrow," Nicole said, noticing he had stepped closer again. "We can do something next week or next weekend."

"Good night, Nicole." Damon took a step backward off the porch, never taking his eyes off her.

"Good night, Damon."

She gave him one last flirting glance before entering the house and locking the door behind her. She stood at the door, listening quietly, as she heard him start his car and drive off, hoping he would drive safely.

For herself, Nicole felt exhausted. She wasn't used to late nights, usually in bed by ten. Delaney awoke from her sleep on the sofa when Nicole turned on the lights, and still tired, called Ron to say she would stay the night. Nicole promised Delaney details in the morning.

The house seemed unusually silent to Nicole as she checked on Alex before going to bed. As she pulled up her own covers and snuggled comfortably into her pillows, a smile fixed itself permanently on her face. She had had a great time tonight. She hoped to have great dreams.

Then it hit her as sudden as a slap in the face. She had not thought once of Norman the entire evening. Nicole had expected feelings of guilt or remembrance to come to her on occasion while on a date with a man for the first time since her husband, but it hadn't happened. She had kissed a man for the first time since Norman, but no thoughts of him had come to her until now.

As she fell asleep in the bed she once shared with her husband, Nicole wasn't sure if that was a good thing or not.

Eight

The morning after the date, Nicole awoke with more energy than she expected. With the exception of sore feet from dancing the night away, she felt fantastic. She sent Delaney home with a brief review of the evening, promising to keep her informed, and started breakfast for Alex, who was anxious to know how his mommy's evening had gone as well.

Returning home from grocery shopping, the phone rang the second Nicole opened the door. An open-mouthed Alex stared stunned as his mother ran to the phone. Her eagerness surprised her as well.

It was Damon, as she had hoped. She was conscious of the current that ran through her at the sound of his masculine voice. Despite his pouting, Nicole sent Alex away for a little privacy. He always chose the times she was on the phone to demand her attention, but Nicole wanted to speak with Damon and enjoy the conversation.

They engaged in a little small talk, each repeating that they enjoyed themselves the night before. Nicole was aware of the happiness that filled her as she talked, enjoying the fullness of his masculine laugh in gracious response to her attempt at humor.

They made a date, including Alex this time at Damon's request. Nicole was hesitant at first, not sure if she should include Alex in Damon's personal life so soon, but the sound of his eager tone excited her, and caught up in his enthusiasm, she was convinced it was a harmless dinner. Damon was cooking for everyone at his condo on Tuesday evening.

Nicole hadn't looked forward to a dinner with such optimism in a very long time.

Damon Jordan's Lincolnwood condo was roughly the size of Nicole's entire house. With two bedrooms and baths, the kitchen and dining room were a normal size, but the living room was very large. Damon's taste was nice and simple. He obviously bought the finest of everything, but nothing was overstated or ostentatious.

As a result of Nicole's repeated warnings during the drive over, Alex tried his best to behave well. She could see the temptation was strong as he eyed Damon's belongings.

By the time Damon brought the dinner dishes to the table, everyone was ready to eat.

"What is it? What is it?" Alex's excitement was mixed with caution as he eyed the food.

"Alex," Nicole admonished him kindly. "Don't be rude."

"It's all right." Damon removed his chef's apron and laid it on the chair beside him. "Tonight we have skinless chicken breast broiled in olive oil and a bit of Dijon mustard and a variety of spices. We're also having shrimp salad and russet potatoes."

"What's for dessert?" Alex apparently enjoyed Damon's eagerness to please him and answer his every question.

"Strawberry shortcake."

"Yeah! Dessert first!" Upon hearing his favorite, Alex raised his tiny hands in the air.

"That's enough." Nicole lowered his hands, giving him a playfully stern wink.

Just then, the doorbell rang, surprising everyone. As Damon went to answer it, Nicole turned her attention to Alex. She placed a napkin under his chin as well as his lap. She knew it was futile because he always found a way to make a mess of himself. He looked adorable in his matching green and blue plaid shorts and T-shirt. She wanted to conserve it as best she could.

"What is De-Jon mustard?" Alex whispered as he looked upward at his mother.

"It's like the mustard you put on your hot dogs, except a little spicier." Nicole loved his inquisitiveness, always eager to know and learn. It bought her so much pleasure to be there when he heard a new word so she could be the one to teach it to him.

"Do I like spicier?"

"You like those buffalo wings Dee cooks for you, don't you?"

"Yeah." He licked his lips.

"Then you like spicier."

"Nicole." Damon called her name as he returned to the dining room. "I would like you and Alex to meet someone."

Nicole stood from her chair to face the attractive elderly woman that entered beside Damon. She was a beautifully austere-looking woman with oval-shaped eyes, a straight nose, and pursed lips. She was tall and willowy thin, every piece of clothing and accessories placed in the proper place. Nicole could determine this was due to years of etiquette, appearances, and very expensive care.

"Nicole Cox," Damon said politely. "This is my mother, Alanis Jordan. Mother, this is my friend, Nicole."

"It's very nice to meet you, Mrs. Jordan." Nicole held out her hand to the other woman, who gave a lukewarm handshake.

"Hello, Nicole." Alanis spoke in a quick tone as she hastily withdrew her hand. She gave Nicole a once-over look. "Damon has told me a lot about you."

"And this little man," Damon said, stepping next to Alex, "is Alex Cox, Nicole's son."

"Hello, Dr. Jordan's mommy." Alex waved from his seat, his eyes staying close to the food.

"Hello, Alex." Alanis's smile was a full one this time. "I hate to interrupt everyone. I should have called."

"We don't mind at all," Nicole said. "I'm sure we have enough food."

"No, I can't stay." Alanis took hold of Damon's arm. "I just need to borrow my son in private to discuss some *family* papers."

"I'll only be a minute, Nicole." Damon winked at her and Alex before leaving with his mother.

"I don't like her," Alex whispered as Nicole regained her seat next to him.

"Alex, don't say that."

"She's not nice," he continued. "She doesn't smile right."

"That's enough, Alex. We won't say another word about it."

Nicole corrected Alex for the sake of manners, but inside she had to agree with him. Alanis Jordan didn't appear to be the warmest of people. Her handshake and smile seemed forced, and Nicole was uncomfortable with the way she had looked at her when she said the word "family."

"Maybe she's just having a bad day," Nicole whispered with a nod.

"Maybe," he whispered back.

After seeing his mother out, Damon returned to the table. Alex provided the entertainment for the evening, talking non-stop. With the exception of a few flirtatious glances directed at Nicole, Damon gave the young boy his undivided attention, and Alex loved it. Nicole loved watching it.

After dessert, Damon pulled out a cartoon movie he had rented especially for Alex, making him feel very special. After setting everything up in the living room, Nicole helped Damon bring coffee for two onto his balcony. At her seat, she kept an eye on Alex from behind.

"Where did you learn to cook like that?" Nicole asked.

"I could lie and say I'm a fantastic cook, but I won't. That's really the only meal I know how to make. That and spaghetti."

"Well, you do it very well." Nicole checked on Alex for a

second. "Alex and I will have to return the favor and cook dinner for you."

"You're a great mother, Nicole," Damon said. After noticing, from her expression, that his words seemed out of place, he explained himself. "I say so because no matter what you're doing, you always keep an eye out for him."

"That's only to keep him from breaking your things." Nicole took pride in his compliment. She would never be one of those parents that let their kids run wild in other people's homes.

"I guess my place is not very child-friendly." Damon set down his cup, leaning back in his chair. "I'll have to make some changes now that a kid will be around a lot."

Nicole took a second to let the meaning of his words sink in. He expected Alex to be around a lot?

"I'm sorry." Damon looked concerned at her expression. "Suggestions such as those aren't what you'd consider taking it slow."

"Don't worry." Nicole found the words actually pleased her somewhat. She was glad he understood that having anything to do with her meant having something to do with Alex. "I'm not shy. I'll let you know if you're moving too fast."

"I'm sure you will." Damon's eyes lowered in a seductive fashion as he smiled lazily.

He knew he was gorgeous, Nicole thought. He knew when to smile that way and make her heartbeat speed up. His eyes were like magnets, making her unable to tear her own away from them. He knew she was attracted to him. The fervor with which she returned his kiss last night alone told him that.

Damon Jordan was smooth, but Nicole trusted her instincts and her smarts. She wouldn't be seduced so easily despite her attraction to him. Even though that attraction was growing every moment she spent with him.

After drinking coffee, Nicole and Damon sat mostly in silence, watching the stars in the sky. It saddened her to remember the peaceful summer nights she and Norman spent on the back porch of their home. She would put Alex to sleep in his bed most of the time, but sometimes he would fall asleep in Norman's lap. The three of them would stay out there for hours.

"Am I boring you?" Damon asked.

"No, not at all." Nicole hid her sadness with a smile.

"You didn't look too happy." Damon stood up. "Do you want to go inside?"

"If you do, but I'm fine."

"Actually I do." Damon slid open the balcony door. "I have something I want to show you."

Nicole's anticipation grew as she saw a spark of excitement in Damon's eyes. She followed him through the dining room, a curious Alex joining them. They went past his bedroom and into the second room, which Damon told them served as a weight room.

"A little present from me to you." Damon stepped aside, allowing Nicole and Alex inside.

When Nicole entered the room, she halted suddenly—shocked—and a soft gasp escaped her. Her mouth dropped open at the sight. Among the free weights was her present.

Along with several unwrapped, blank canvases of very fine quality in various sizes was a set of paints in every imaginable color under the sun. They were in gold, silver, and plastic containers of all shapes. Next to those were brushes neatly grouped together. Some were tiny, some regular, and a couple were very large. Nicole couldn't contain her surprise at the sight.

"It's painting stuff, Mommy." Alex's expression showed he was expecting more, possibly something he could use.

"What is this?" The shock caused Nicole's words to wedge in her throat as she stood frozen in the middle of the room.

"You got me thinking the other night," Damon said, his eyes jumping with uncertain excitement. "About hobbies and such. I really loved your paintings. I thought it was such a waste you weren't painting."

"So you bought me this stuff?" Nicole made her way to the gifts as Damon handed her the clean, recently unwrapped palette. She recognized it was the leading brand, the best and most expensive. He had gotten all of this for her? She was truly amazed. She was truly touched.

"My movie is on. 'Scuse me." Alex passed between them on his way out, his attention span reaching its end.

"Damon," Nicole stuttered, an unexpected warmth running through her as she met his eyes with her own. "I-I don't know what to say. I—"

"There is a catch." Damon lifted his index finger.

"A catch?" Nicole found his excitement amusing. She had no idea he was this interested in her painting, and it thoroughly flattered her.

"You have to promise me you'll find time to paint. I don't care when or how much, only that you do."

There was an earnest slant to his look that touched Nicole. He was a kind person, caring about her personal happiness. She didn't have the heart to tell him she hadn't picked up a brush since Norman's death.

"You're way too kind." Nicole placed the palette down. "But this is so expensive. I can't let you do this . . . spend all this money."

"I want to let you in on a secret." He gave her a playful wink and leaned closer to whisper. "I'm a doctor. I make a penny or two."

"I know you do." Nicole smiled, now by instinct at his closeness. "It's just—"

"It's just nothing." Damon put a finger to her lips to hush her.

They both fell silent as Nicole felt the heat on her lips. It was brief as he slowly removed the finger. Their eyes caught and held, Nicole knowing he had felt the same heat. There was a certain satisfaction she got from knowing he was attracted to her but also a danger in his knowing she was just as attracted to him.

"Just promise me." Damon stepped even closer this time.

Nicole kept her eyes attached to his as she felt the tips of his fingers touch hers. The tingle shot from her hand, up her arms, and through the rest of her body. Their fingers locked, and Damon swung her arms around his waist.

Their eyes still joined, Nicole felt her knees go weak as she watched his face lower to hers. She had wanted this since last

Friday night, the touch of his lips on hers and the fire it ignited from within her.

That fire returned immediately, and Nicole closed her eyes and savored it. His lips were soft, but the kiss was hard. She wanted it that way. He wanted it, too, she could tell. As she sensed the passion that was growing inside of her, she still found pleasure in sensing his. She sensed it grow as his lips pressured hers, wanting them to open. She obliged, desire driving her now. The taste of his tongue was like a blaze, and it sent a charge through her, landing in the pit of her stomach. Nicole heard him moan, and it only served to increase her craving. She wrapped her arms tighter, letting her tongue explore some as well.

She wanted this. She missed this. She had felt this yearning, since . . .

Norman.

Jolted by the image of her husband, she tore herself away from Damon. She stepped back a couple of steps and stared at him. This wasn't Norman, was what her mind told her. This man was not her husband.

"What did I do wrong?" Damon, his eyes still clouded with passion, gave Nicole a baffled stare.

"Nothing." Nicole stepped back again, wanting the passion within her to go away, but it wouldn't. "It wasn't you. It was me."

"I didn't plan that." Damon's brows centered, showing concern. "I touched you and—"

"I know, Damon." Nicole shook her head. "I promise it's not you."

"Then what is it?" He cautiously stepped closer. "You pulled away so fast."

"It's Alex," she lied. "I thought I heard him coming."

Damon frowned as if wondering whether or not to believe her. Nicole didn't want to lie to him, but how could she tell him the truth? She couldn't stand to offend him that way.

"I'm sorry," Damon said. "I should have thought about him."

"It's all right. You don't have any kids. It takes a while to get used to adjusting your behavior in their presence."

"I hope you'll give me that chance."

A thoughtful smile curved Nicole's lips. He was always so kind, even in rejection. "I hope I can."

"You promise?" Damon, seeming refreshed, turned to the paints and brushes.

"Promise . . ."

"Promise to paint?"

Nicole saw the look of thrill in his eyes. He almost looked like a kid, and it made her feel good to know it was over her. She felt like maybe . . . possibly . . .

"I promise." Nicole said the words quickly before she could change her mind. Maybe, she thought. Possibly.

Later that night after Alex went to sleep, Nicole brought up her easel from under the dusty blanket in the basement. She set it up in the den, in the same place from where she had taken it down two years ago.

Silently Nicole placed her new paints, brushes, and canvases beside the easel. She took a second before stepping back. Looking at the objects, sitting there, waiting for her, Nicole felt suddenly very alone as the memories rushed back to her.

She would paint every day, sitting at the easel with an eye on baby Alex as he slept or played in his pen. She had always been careful to buy nontoxic paints but nevertheless kept him at the other end of the room. She sang as she painted, many times causing Alex to fall into a peaceful sleep. The sleep was temporary, though, as he always awoke to the sound of the front door.

Norman was always all smiles when he came home for lunch or at the end of his day. Nicole couldn't wait. She was grateful that as a professor his hours were short, giving him plenty of time for the family before she started dinner. Alex always got his attention first, but Norman always remembered to hug and kiss his wife.

For an hour or so, they would all stay in the den. Nicole

would paint while Norman played with Alex and told her how his classes had gone. It had been like a fairy tale, Nicole remembered, as tears of happiness and sadness fell down her face. She had lived a fairy tale.

In the silence of the night, Nicole cried herself to sleep with quiet tears. She had enjoyed herself that evening with Damon, remembering their kiss with a blush. The loneliness she had felt for the past two years welded together with the confusion she had felt the past few weeks. Only she missed her husband terribly. She missed his smile, his touch, his kiss. She missed his love. She missed her fairy tale.

Nine

Nicole was pleasantly surprised on Sunday afternoon when she opened her door and saw Damon standing outside with a bag of groceries.

"Delivery service?" Nicole asked, stepping aside to let him in.

"To your door." Damon set down the groceries and leaned over for a kiss.

The brief kiss wet Nicole's lips, making her smile as she enjoyed the flutter of pleasure that flowed through her.

Nicole's attraction to Damon had grown over the past couple of weeks. They talked on the phone like teenagers regularly. They had gone on six dates, some alone and others with Alex along. Nicole had gone to the first movie that wasn't a cartoon in two years this past Friday. She wasn't sure what the movie was about, because she and Damon sat in the very last row, kissing throughout.

"Am I forgetting something?" Nicole peeked inside the bag.

"You're cooking me dinner," Damon said. "Don't you remember?"

"Oh, yes." Nicole suddenly remembered her promise to cook dinner tonight in return for his doing so for her and Alex weeks ago. "Why are you bringing the groceries? Wouldn't that be my job?"

"I decided I wanted rustic lasagna." Damon began following Nicole to the kitchen, doing his best to avoid the many toys on the floor.

"Be careful," she warned. "This place is a war zone on the weekends."

"If I hurt myself," Damon said, his voice lined with humor, "I'm suing A.J."

"That's fine by me." Nicole broke into a smile at hearing Damon use the nickname he had created for Alex. "I should warn you—he has a savings of about five dollars."

"Hey"—he shrugged—"it'll be five dollars more than I have now."

"You're shameless." Nicole laughed at his sense of humor, while she emptied the contents of the bag onto the kitchen counter. "What is rustic lasagna?"

"That's what I thought you'd ask. Which is why I bought the groceries." Damon grabbed a stem of broccoli in one hand and a pack of carrots in the other. "Rustic lasagna is vegetarian style, made like the Italians do it in the homeland."

"Does it take long?"

"A half hour to prepare and about forty-five minutes to cook." Damon glanced at his watch. "It's only three o'clock. We have plenty of time. Where's A.J.?"

"He's out." Nicole enjoyed the look of excitement in Damon's eyes as he mentioned her son. "Remember I told you about Billy West? Billy took him to a petting zoo at some area park."

"So we're alone?" Damon raised a brow mischievously and stepped closer to Nicole.

"Don't you get any ideas." Nicole acknowledged her heightened temper in response to his suggestive movement and evaded his embrace. She escaped to the living room. "He'll be home any second."

"Okay." Damon faked a pout as he looked around. "What are you doing now?"

"I was about to start my weekly cleanup of this house." Nicole looked around the apartment, cluttered with Alex's toys.

"No, no, no." Damon shook his head, stepping to Nicole. "I have a better idea."

"I just warned you." Nicole slapped away his strong dark hand as it reached for her trim waist.

"Not that," Damon said. "I want to see your painting."

"My painting?" Nicole was caught off guard. "What painting?"

"You promised me you would paint." Damon headed for the den. "You said you set up everything in the den. What have you done?"

Nicole followed Damon to the room. She watched Damon's expression turn to confusion as he saw that nothing had been done.

"What's going on?" he asked, a perplexed stare on his face. "You haven't done anything."

"I get started," Nicole said, feeling a bit of apprehension creep inside of her. "I lay everything out. There's just never time."

Nicole admitted to herself that was partly true but not completely. The truth was, she had entered the room several times in the past couple of weeks, wanting to try. The farthest she had gotten was to put an actual brush in her hands. She just sat there, sometimes for minutes, once for an hour. The strength it took her to fight away the memories blocked her from any creative ideas whatsoever. It was useless and made Nicole feel weak.

"Well, you have time now." Damon waved at Nicole to join him at the easel. "And I'm not letting you leave this room without making a little mark."

"Look at me, Damon." Nicole pointed to her clothes, a basic red T-shirt and white cotton shorts. "I'll make a mess of myself."

"We'll make a mess of each other." Apparently sensing her hesitation, Damon came over to Nicole and gently led her to the easel. "I don't want to hear any protest. You have to do this."

"I need to get started cooking." Nicole stopped in her sentence as Damon gave her a serious stare. He meant business, she knew.

Nicole reached for the palette and undid the cover that preserved the paint she had placed in the small containers.

"What are you doing?" she asked as Damon sat in the chair. "Are you painting or am I?"

"You are." Damon opened his arms to her, sweet sensitivity in his eyes. "Come on."

He knew, Nicole thought to herself. Despite her cover-ups, Damon knew there was more to this than a lack of free time. He could read her well.

Without protest, Nicole situated the palette in the easel holder. She turned her back to Damon and allowed him to help her into his lap. She tensed inside, not remembering being this close to him before. She could feel his muscled chest against her back and his firm thighs beneath her own.

"Let's go." His breath against her neck made loose tendrils of her hair fly, then settle again.

Nicole reached for the brush, hoping her arms would not visibly tremble. She could smell his cologne, and his breath was sweet and warm. She felt her arousal grow as Damon covered her hand with his own as she dipped the brush into the red paint.

"Why red?" he asked in a whisper.

"I don't know." Nicole shrugged, feeling her temperature rise. "Because."

She gave little resistance as he led her hand to the waiting canvas. Expecting him to connect, she was surprised when he stopped an inch from contact. He was leaving that to her.

"Why?" she asked, knowing she didn't have to explain her question.

"You have to, Nicole. You know that."

Nicole brushed the smooth canvas lightly, shooting a fire-engine-truck red line down the middle. It seemed so bright standing against the pale white of the canvas. She lowered their hands and leaned back to take in the view. It was a single red line, but it meant so much more. It meant a beginning. It was an opening. Nicole was abruptly reminded how much she loved color and all the expressions it produced.

Nicole's breathing picked up pace as she felt Damon's other hand come around her waist and stop over her flat stomach. As her heart pounded an erratic rhythm, she swept the brush again, this one right beside the first.

"What are you making?" Damon's voice was low and passionate, his breathing deep.

Nicole did not answer, although she had heard him. The third stroke went down and around, underneath the other two, ending with a soft curl. The fourth was a circle almost off the left edge of the canvas. She placed the brush down and picked up a clean one. After dipping it in black, she made several more slow strokes. Here and there, they made no sense unless you were making them. They made perfect sense to her as she was quickly caught up in the sensual moment.

Carried away by her own response, she failed to notice that Damon had taken his hand off of hers until she felt it lay on her thigh, sending a jolt through her entire body. She needed something bright but darker than red. She reached for the blue.

His first kiss came softly to her neck. Nicole closed her eyes to savor it. His lips were so moist as they tickled her neck and her shoulder. His hand pulled at her stomach, bringing her closer, as he moved to the other side of her neck. The kisses were harder now. So was he. Nicole felt his manhood as he pulled her closer. He was as aroused as she was.

As he whispered her name, she reached for pink and blended it with the green. She paused momentarily, her eyes closing again as his hand slid up from her stomach to her supple breast. He would feel her hard nipples and know she wanted him.

She wanted to dash some purple on the bottom right corner, but as she reached for a fresh brush, she lost her control. Damon's other hand had left her thigh, and both hands were caressing her breasts through the shirt. The kisses along the back of her neck were like fire.

With her back still to him, Nicole untucked her shirt ends from her shorts. She took his hands in hers and led them to her breast, underneath her bra, which she quickly unsnapped. All she wanted was to feel his hands on her. Everywhere.

Damon moaned as he caressed her. Nicole turned her head, and with her hand, took hold of his face and brought his lips to hers. The kiss was hard and hungry, lips bruising and tongues searching, wanting. She didn't think she could ever get enough.

His strokes were rougher now. Nicole wondered if he could sense that was what she wanted. She brought her other hand to his face and held it tightly as she kissed him deeper. She was moaning nonstop now—she could hear herself.

His hands left her breast and grabbed her waist. He picked her up effortlessly and sat up from the chair. They continued to kiss as he carried her to the sofa. Their lips parted briefly as he laid her down. Nicole opened her eyes to look at him. His eyes were on fire, and that fire was for her. She smiled as he lowered his body onto hers and took her lips again.

Her hands grabbed at his shirt, pulling it from his pants. She trailed the muscles of his back with her nails before grasping at his bottom. She squeezed, causing a deep groan to emit from him.

Damon jumped to the ceiling at the sound of the front door loudly opening and shutting. His eyes widened like a deer caught in headlights. Despite the passion that had overwhelmed her seconds before, Nicole could not stifle a laugh at the sight.

"What is that?" Damon was on edge, his voice deep with quick breaths. "What's so funny?"

"Alex and Billy must be home." Nicole noticed her breath was quick and her words were choppy as well. She rushed to get herself together before Alex ran in on them.

Damon nodded as if he understood but still appeared confused. Nicole assumed the transition from passion to fear was not an easy one. She felt light-headed herself as she stood up from the sofa and tucked in her shirt.

"I feel like I'm in high school," Damon said as he did the same with his shirt. "I'm outside on the porch kissing the girl, and her father turns the light on. Those are some scary flashbacks."

"I'm sure you had a few of those nights," Nicole said in a sarcastic tone.

"I don't like to brag." He lifted an arm to shield himself from Nicole's blow.

Still trying to cool down, Nicole took a deep breath before entering the living room, where Alex and Billy were waiting. Before anyone could say hello, Alex was yelling about his day.

"Mommy, it was fantastic!" He jumped around the room. "I petted a sheep, and I helped a guy feed a goat. Then I rode a pony. A pony!"

"Oh, my goodness!" Nicole opened her mouth in feigned surprise as she reached down and kissed her baby's dirty forehead. "You just had too much fun, didn't you?"

"No such thing," Alex said, resuming his jumping. "No such thing, I tell ya."

Nicole turned to Billy, whose happy expression suddenly changed as he saw Damon enter from the hallway.

"Damon!" Alex opened up his arms as he had become accustomed to do so Damon could pick him up. He let his arms fly as Damon swooped him up and swung him around.

"Damon," Nicole called to him, "I want you to meet Billy West. Billy, this is Dr. Damon Jordan."

As she watched the cordial handshake, Nicole could feel the slight tension in the room. Billy knew she was dating and was happy for her. Despite that, Billy felt it his responsibility to survey any suitors. Nicole would allow him the judgment, to an extent.

On the other end, Damon had asked about Billy the first time he'd called over and Alex wasn't around. He seemed nonchalant when Nicole explained the nature of the relationship, but she could sense a little apprehension on his part. "What kind of a name is Billy for an adult?" he had asked with a smirk.

The tension ceased quickly as the two men began a conversation about their cars, which led to more discussions. Nicole wasn't surprised. They were both friendly men, easy to get along with. She sat in a nearby chair with a tender, happy smile and her son in her lap as they all talked through the night. Alex was elated to be involved in the adult conversation despite the fact that he had no idea of much of what they spoke about.

Dinner in downtown Chicago with Alanis Jordan was an experience Nicole would not soon forget. Due to the cold reception she received the first time they met, Nicole was surprised when Damon told her Alanis wanted to join them for dinner. His father was away at a conference, and Damon hated to leave her alone for a long period of time, so Nicole agreed.

Nicole and Damon had been dating for over a month and had grown steadily closer. Nicole laughed when she remembered considering the idea that they could date casually, with no strings attached. Nicole was sure to be cautious, knowing it had been a long time since she had these feelings. Damon had gone slow as she requested, making it easier for her to handle the affection and desire she was developing for him.

The feelings came back to her easier than she thought. She found him affectionate, understanding, and funny. He was generous and caring and more attractive each time she saw him. She enjoyed herself with him immensely and was happy he had come into her and Alex's life. She still wasn't sure if she could ever love a man like she loved Norman, but she cared very much for Damon and looked forward to seeing him as often as she could. She no longer had images of her late husband flashing before her eyes when in Damon's embrace. No longer had feelings of guilt when she dreamt about him.

Nicole found herself many times as breathless as a teenager whenever he touched her or kissed her. She enjoyed the simplicities of early dates like movies and dinner. She was learning so much about him over dinner and was coming to respect him even more. He talked about his practice and desire to help children. She talked about her paintings and her hopes for Alex in the future.

Damon had told her, due to bragging on his part, his mother was anxious to get to know her as well and considered the dinner a great opportunity. Nicole was terribly nervous after Damon warned her that his mother was rather harsh, but he swore she was kind at heart. Nicole dressed her best in a peach sundress and let Delaney put her hair up in a casually elegant style. She wanted to impress, but Alanis made it clear she was not easily befriended. Despite Damon's many attempts to keep conversations going, there were several silent moments creating tension between the two women.

Nicole begged for the evening to come to an end, but could not find the nerve to protest Damon's suggestion they stop at his place for coffee. When they arrived, only moments after sitting down, Nicole excused herself to the bathroom, but halfway there realized she had forgotten her purse. Returning to the living room to retrieve it, she paused outside the doorway as she heard her name mentioned.

"What do you mean by that?" Damon asked. "How serious am I about this Nicole?"

"It's a valid question," Alanis answered. "You're thirty years old now, Damon. You need to start thinking about marriage."

"Let's not have this conversation again, Mother. Not now at least."

"Yes, now," she insisted. "I saw the way you looked at her tonight. You're getting entirely too serious."

"Who are you to determine that for me?"

"I'm your mother, Damon. I just want you to understand that a lot is expected of you."

"By whom?"

"Chicago society. You need to make a name for yourself. A great way to do that would be to marry someone more . . ."

"More what?" Damon's tone mounted in anger. "A socialite? Someone from a good family?"

"Someone with a real job would do." Alanis rolled her eyes. "She's a receptionist, Damon."

"That's enough, Mother," Damon warned.

"Your practice is becoming such a success." Alanis spoke in a pleading tone. "You're ready to shoot off. Don't let them hold you back."

"Them?"

"A single mother with a child is not the best thing for your image right now."

Nicole couldn't listen to any more. She hurried to the bathroom and paced the floor. She was angry and hurt, but more angry. How dare this woman judge her? Who was she to say what was best for Damon or anyone? Then she wondered, would Damon listen? Nicole realized she really did care if he would.

Nicole knew she couldn't stay in the bathroom too much longer, so she splashed her face with some water and headed out. If Alanis Jordan had any more to say about her and her son, she could say it to her face.

Only Alanis was nowhere to be found when Nicole returned to the living room. Damon stood alone on his balcony, looking into the dark skies.

"Where's Alanis?" Nicole asked as she joined him. The July night was hot and humid.

"My mother left." Damon's voice was curt and short as he continued to stare into the stars.

"Because of me?" Nicole reached over and placed her soft hand on his bare arm.

"Why would you think that?" Damon turned to her with a look of surprise and concern.

"I know she doesn't like me." Nicole's eyes lowered, concentrating on his thin cotton slacks.

"Nicole." Damon wrapped his arms around her, pulling her closer. "I told you my mother was a bit standoffish."

"Damon, I heard the two of you before. I didn't mean to eavesdrop. I was returning for my purse, and I overheard your conversation."

"Damnit!" Damon turned away, his hands gripping the ledge tightly. After a second, he turned to Nicole. "I'm sorry, Nicole—I wish you hadn't heard."

"It's all right." Nicole rubbed his back comfortingly. She didn't want him to think she blamed him for his mother's opinion. "I like to know where I stand with people. Which brings us to you."

"What does that mean?"

"I don't know, Damon," Nicole sighed, frustrated by her own confusion. "Sometimes I'm so mixed up about how I feel and what I want from you."

"I'm not." Damon reached out for her hand and squeezed it tight. "I know I don't have the obstacles to love that you do, so I thought it would be best to keep my feelings secret, but I can't do that anymore."

"Damon." Nicole stepped back, wanting to release her hand from his grasp, but he only held on tighter. Fear swept through her. "I'm not ready to hear this."

"I think you are," Damon said. "I think you're stronger than you give yourself credit for being. Besides, I'm not expecting anything back. You've made it clear that you have unresolved feelings for your late husband. I only want you to know my feelings."

Nicole looked off into the night, preparing herself for what was to come. She heard his words, but could she believe him? Did he really expect nothing back? She had told him she cared for him, he knew that. Was he about to ask for more? She turned her head back, her eyes softly connecting with his. Despite her apprehension, part of her wanted to hear this. A part of her she was coming to know again.

"Go ahead," she whispered with a sweet smile.

"I'm falling in love with you, Nicole." Damon shyly smiled as he stepped closer. "I know it's soon, but I can't deny it. I was attracted to you the first moment I saw you. You're beautiful, and you have no idea how sexy you are."

She blushed, feeling none of the anxiety and tension she had expected. Instead she felt happiness and joy. His words were spoken from his mouth as well as his eyes, she could see.

"Most of all, I love your commitment to Alex. You're loving and self-sacrificing. Your loyalty is so appealing. Your sarcasm and quick wit turn me on like crazy."

"You keep this up," Nicole said, "and you'll never be able to get rid of me."

"I don't plan to." He looked at her, his eyes pressing. "I plan to hold on to you, Nicole. You can try to fight loving me, but I'll fight you back."

"Damon, you're so sweet." Nicole was truly touched by his words. "I wish I could—"

"Could what?" His eager eyes blinked.

"I care about you so much, Damon. It's taken me a while to accept that. It's something I never expected to feel for another man."

"Then that's enough," he said. "For now."

"I want to give you more." Nicole wrapped her arms around him, feeling the desire that crept into her every time she touched him.

"I know you will when you're ready." Damon brushed her forehead with a soft kiss. "I promised I would never push you."

"You've kept that promise." Her lips touched the bottom of his chin. "It's let me know I can trust you."

"You can, baby." He held her tightly. "You can always trust me."

"It's made me want you." Nicole rubbed his arms with her hands. She was surprising herself with her behavior but knew it was what she felt.

"Nicole?" Damon looked down at her, anticipation and desire in his eyes.

"Don't talk," she said, giving him a seductive glance.

With his arms on her waist, she undid a couple of buttons on his shirt and kissed his chest softly. The soft, curly hair brushed her lips. She could feel his chest heave faster as his breathing sped up.

She undid the rest of the shirt and slid it off his shoulders. She loved his body, so firm and fit. She leaned back to watch her hands slide up his chest.

"We better take this inside." Damon's voice was thick with hunger as he led Nicole inside the apartment.

Taking her hand, he led her slowly to the bedroom. Nicole knew what was going to happen. She had anticipated this night for some time. Their passionate encounters had increased in frequency, but Nicole had always put a stop to them. She was very attracted to him but had to deal with her feelings of disloyalty to Norman. Damon made that easy with his patience and understanding.

She was still scared, but willing, as Damon reached behind her and slowly unzipped her dress. She felt a hot ache forming in the pit of her stomach as the dress fell to the floor, revealing her lovely womanly body. Having a child had had no effect on her body: her stomach as flat and smooth as an eighteen-year-old's, her hips tightly rounded. He undid her bra, gently sliding it over her shoulders. His hands stopped a moment as his eyes desired her supple breast before he tossed the garment aside. Nicole watched him as he surveyed her entire body, aroused by the fire in his eyes. She could tell he was more than pleased with what he saw.

He teasingly trailed his finger along the top front of her satin peach panties, gently tugging at them before sliding them down. Nicole swallowed tightly as she fought back from grabbing him and throwing him to the bed. She had waited two years to make love again and was willing to wait a little longer. Only a little.

He picked her up slightly by the waist and laid her on the bed. She resisted nothing, feeling her passion grow like a well-lit fire as it replaced the fear. He straddled her on the bed as she unbuckled his belt with urgency. His eyes never left hers, filled with a desire that excelled her wanting. She knew he would give her everything she wanted tonight. Everything she had missed.

As she slid off the rest of his clothes, Nicole's gaze moved over his body. With kindled feelings of fire, she had never seen a man so fit this close to her before. His closeness was like a drug, and his body was inviting. Looking at him like this, bare and exposed, only hastened her existing impatience. As he reached over to the drawer beside the bed for protection, Nicole caressed his hips and thighs in a commanding gesture. Sensing her impatience, Damon did what he had to do quickly and returned his attention to her.

His lips quickly reclaimed hers, but not with the gentle, awakening passion they had before. This time they were persuasively demanding as Nicole could feel his desire building. She could feel the movement of his breathing and smell his sweetly intoxicating musk. She fiercely wanted him now.

Everywhere his hands went, lit on fire. Her flesh prickled at his every touch as he caressed her body from head to toe with his hands, his mouth, and his tongue. She felt divine ecstasy racing through her bloodstream, threatening to send her to oblivion. Searching for and reaching her pleasure points again and again, he sent currents of overwhelming desire through her, making her scream his name in agony before he finally took her.

Her soft curves molded to the contours of his masculine, virile body as she invited him. The pleasurable pain made her tremble. She could only think how she had missed this feeling. How she wanted this feeling. She moved with him with every tantalizing stroke, feeling each moment of pleasure would send her over the edge at any moment. When it finally did, exploding tremors sent shock waves through her body. She said his name in a savagely passionate scream. When he reached his realm of ultimate pleasure moments later, he called out her name with as much burning intensity.

As she lay next to him, breathing fast and heavy, Nicole didn't think it could be any better than that. That was until he took her again moments later. Then she knew—this was only the beginnings of the pleasure they would share.

Ten

"What was Norman like?"

Nicole turned her head from its snug spot in his arms to face Damon. "What?" She was puzzled he would bring Norman up now.

"I don't want to pretend like he doesn't exist," Damon said. "He's always going to be a part of your life. A part of your heart."

"You don't have to deal with that." Nicole rested her head on his chest again. She would never want Damon to worry about Norman. She would never compare him to her late husband. She cared too much for him to do that.

"I want to," he said. "I'm falling for you so fast, Nicole. I want to know everything and anything about you. Norman is a big part of that, especially because of Alex."

Nicole hesitated, uncertain if this was a good idea. Here she was, naked in bed with her lover. Could she talk about her dead husband, a man she had vowed she would belong to alone forever?

On the other hand, she wanted Damon to know about Norman. She wanted him to understand how much she had loved him. She needed him to understand why it was so hard for her to give her heart to another man, whether she wanted to or not.

"There aren't enough words to describe him." Nicole smiled with the familiar comfort she always felt at the thought of Norman. "He was handsome, smart, caring, and funny. He always knew how to find the perfect balance in everything. He treated me like an equal but still made me feel like a queen. He gave Alex everything, but he never spoiled him too much.

"He always made our family his number-one priority. He was a fantastic father. He loved Alex with all his heart. He listened to me when I talked to him. He understood my emotions and saw the meaning in my art."

"Sounds like you were very happy," Damon said. "Very few people get in a lifetime what you had with him for a short while."

"I know." Nicole nodded. "What's important is that I knew it then, too. I didn't just realize it when I lost it, left with only regrets."

"Delaney told me he drowned." Damon's voice was compassionately cautious. "Can you tell me what happened? I would understand if you didn't want to."

"He was swimming with friends at the lake." Nicole felt a flicker of pain flash within her as she remembered that fateful day. "It was his getaway with the guys. He did it once a month with some fellow professors. He cramped, or at least that's what the doctors said probably happened. He was a good swimmer but not great." Nicole paused, remembering the day before. "The last time we saw each other, we said I love you. I'll hold on to that forever."

Nicole stopped there, knowing if she said any more she would start crying. She had that good memory to hold on to. He could remember her last words to him as saying she loved him. A part of her always would.

"I forgot to tell you another reason why I'm so crazy about you." Damon kissed the top of her head.

"Why?"

"You're a strong woman, Nicole Cox. You're very strong."

Nicole wanted to believe him. In the past month and a half, she had reclaimed a strength she didn't believe she had. Was there more undiscovered or forgotten strength within her? Maybe, she thought. Was she strong enough to love again?

Lying there, falling asleep in his arms, Nicole believed for the first time that she could.

It was eight in the morning. Nicole still held the glow from lovemaking on her face as she stepped onto her back porch. Noon was rolling around, and Alex would soon be home from his overnight stay, but for now she could enjoy the moment alone. Maybe later, she thought, she would paint.

For now, all she could think of was Damon and the way he had made her feel last night. He'd made her feel so desirable, a feeling she had long since forgotten. She remembered the gentle way he caressed her entire body, sending her to delightful insanity.

She anticipated every day for more than one reason now. Before, it was Alex and only Alex. She still looked forward to every day with him, but now there was Damon. Now there was the time to breathe in the fresh air and think about the future. It was a future of possibilities in every nuance of life. A future of seeing Alex grow and thrive. A future of painting again, expressing so many of the emotions that were flooding back to her. A future period.

Nicole wasn't so much changing as she was returning to her old self. It was September, but inside her heart it felt like spring. She felt alive and vibrant, welcoming the challenges and emotions that came with every day. So much was new, and her optimism in the small things, like someone to go to the movies with, brought her as much joy as the big things, like watching Alex and Damon play together. Alex was still the most important thing in her life, but now Damon had staked his claim on her heart, taking over her daily thoughts and nightly dreams. Caring so much for herself and the two men in her life would have been enough for Nicole, but that wasn't all there was to it. Good news was coming from everywhere.

"Here's your check." Delaney reached over the reception desk of the gallery and handed the envelope to Nicole.

"I never get sick of this," Nicole said as she hastily opened the envelope.

Her mouth dropped as she saw the amount.

"This is five thousand dollars." Nicole hadn't expected this much.

"Yes it is, girlfriend." Delaney's smile was as proud as the artist herself. "With your oh-so-busy schedule, you didn't even realize you sold another piece yesterday afternoon."

"Which one?"

"The one with the orange and the other stuff. I don't know what it was. It all looks crazy to me."

"It's the sunset on the lakefront painting." Nicole remembered every single piece of art she'd made. Delaney always put on her business face when she handed Nicole a check, but Nicole could see the happiness in her eyes. "I just painted it a few weeks ago."

"Well, some guy came in yesterday and had to have it. He gave me his card and told me to call him when you put out some more pieces."

"I wish I had been here," Nicole said, "but it was Alex's first day of kindergarten. There's a bus that drops him off a block away, but I wanted to pick him up."

"How is he doing with school?" Delaney leaned over the counter, ready for conversation.

"He's all right. I'm the one who's a mess."

"He'll be fine." Delaney continued her blank stare at Nicole, a mysterious smile pursing her lips.

"What?" Nicole asked. "What's that look for?"

"I'm just so happy you're so happy." She shrugged with a joyful smile.

"I was happy before Damon came into my life." Nicole knew Delaney was referring to Damon without being told so. "I had Alex and my friends and myself."

"But now ..." Delaney winked mischievously. "Now you're a little happier."

"I think about him all the time, Dee." Nicole rested her

chin on her hands, supporting herself with her elbows on the desk. Her smile widened as she felt herself go soft inside. "I feel like a schoolgirl every time I see him. I love it. Whenever he touches me, I light up like an inferno and my feet leave the earth."

"The question is," Delaney said, "do you love him?"

"He's great with Alex." Caught up in her own emotions, Nicole ignored the question. "Last week they went to the movies together. Alex wasn't exactly an angel, but Damon said he kept him in line pretty well. Alex is really starting to respect him."

"But do you love him?" Delaney repeated her question.

"Alanis is really coming around, too," Nicole continued. "I told you she was against Damon and I at first. Alex really brought her around. Even the coldest person would warm up to his precious love face. We're getting along a little better now, too."

"If you don't answer my question, I'm going to strangle you."

Nicole paused, enjoying her tease. Delaney was too nosy for her own good, but she understood her frustration. They were best friends and had shared everything, but they hadn't spent a lot of time together since Nicole and Damon started seeing each other. It wasn't that Nicole didn't care, she felt it was very important that Damon meet Delaney and Ron. It was only that every moment she had with Damon, she wanted to be alone with him.

"I don't know." Nicole blushed, lowering her eyes slightly. "I know I'm falling in love with him."

"What's taking so long?" Delaney asked mysteriously.

"We've only been dating for four months," Nicole said.

"And you don't know yet?" Delaney raised up from the counter as two elderly ladies entered the store. "You're lying to yourself."

Nicole childishly stuck her tongue out at Delaney's back. She wasn't about to let anyone rush her. She wasn't sure if she loved him or not, but she was sure she was falling for him. She found it endearing how she was quickly rediscovering those feelings she had thought she'd lost forever. Damon made it easy. He brought out the passion in her, patiently and willingly allowing her to explore once dormant needs and fantasies.

Her feelings for Damon were different than for Norman in so many ways. They had similar qualities but were two different men. She wasn't the least bit interested in comparing them. Neither man deserved that. She was just grateful they were both so fantastic.

Nicole couldn't easily describe her feelings for Damon, but she wasn't in such a rush to do so. She was too busy enjoying her life. She enjoyed watching Alex grow and be happy. She enjoyed painting as she explored abstracts now, a new avenue for her. She enjoyed talking with Damon, spending time with him, making love to him.

Nicole rushed to the door when she heard Billy's car roll into the driveway. Someone was getting into trouble.

"What took so long?" Nicole started in on Billy and Alex as soon as they entered the house.

"It's a long story," Billy said, taking a long look at Nicole. "You look fantastic."

"You look beautiful, Mommy." Alex kissed his palm and blew the kiss to her.

"Don't try to sweet-talk." Nicole held back her smile at his gesture. It was terribly hard to. "You were supposed to be home from swim practice an hour ago. Damon will be here any minute."

"Big plans?" Billy asked.

"Damon is getting an award for his service to the community." Nicole beamed with pride. "It's from the American Medical Association."

"Damon says that's big-time!" Alex winked at Nicole and Billy.

"You look big-time," Billy said.

Nicole thanked him kindly, clinging to what little modesty she had this evening. She knew she looked spectacular. Her hair was slicked back into an elegantly-styled bun. Her eyes sparkled with lashes that swept up, seeming as long as forever. Her full mouth was a cinnamon-brown. Her slender neck was tastefully adorned with a diamond necklace that had once belonged to her mother. The form-fitting lavender slip dress slid around her narrow waist and fine hips and touched just above her knees, revealing silky smooth brown legs held up by shimmering, sleek black heels.

She wanted to look special for Damon. She was immensely proud of him and knew everyone would be watching him. Tonight was his night, and Nicole knew he deserved it. She was just as excited as if she was getting the award herself.

"Did you shower?" Nicole caught on to Alex's waving hand as he passed her by.

"Why shower?" he asked. "I was in water for two hours."

"I don't have time to argue with you, young man," she sighed impatiently. "I made your overnight bag. You won't have time to change or shower."

"I'm hungry!" Alex headed for the kitchen. "I want a yogurt."

"You're having dinner at Dee's. You'll spoil—" Nicole gave up, not wanting the frustration to wear her out.

"Sorry, Nicole." Billy shrugged. "The class was over, but he was having so much fun, he didn't want to get out. I watched him the whole time. He really loves the water."

"I know." Nicole glanced toward the kitchen. "It makes me nervous as heck, but I can't smother him. I can't keep him from the things he loves because of my fear."

"You're doing the right thing." Billy smiled, stuffing his hands into his pockets. "Sometimes falling in love can open your eyes to other things going on in your life."

"You should know that better than anyone."

Nicole was referring to Billy's current state of affairs. He had been dating a beautiful young teacher's assistant for almost two months. She was thrilled for him, hoping he would find the happiness she had.

"I guess I would." Billy, embarrassed by his blush, backed up toward the door.

"Now if only—" Nicole turned with a start as the phone

rang. She hoped it was Damon calling from the car. They had to leave now if they wanted to be downtown by six.

"Hello?"

"Hello, Nicole. It's Alanis."

"Hello, Alanis." Nicole sensed something wrong with Alanis's tone. Usually unemotional, she sounded affected. By what?

"I want you to calm down." Alanis spoke slowly. "Damon wanted me to tell you that first."

"What is it, Alanis?" Nicole asked in a small, frightened voice. She felt her knees go weak as she reached for the sofa to support herself.

"Damon was in an accident on his way to your place." Alanis spoke quickly now. "A car accident. Someone ran a red light and hit him."

"Oh, my God!" Nicole felt her heart race, panic setting in. "Please don't—"

"He's going to be all right," Alanis said. "A few cuts and bruises. A broken leg."

Nicole felt her tears coming, her head spinning. "Where is he?" she asked, her voice choking back threads of hysteria that threatened her.

"He's at Evanston Hospital. He's in—"

"I'll be there in ten minutes." Nicole threw the phone to the ground and turned in all directions. She began to shake as fearful images from the past returned to her, plunging her heart into the pit of her stomach. She needed to do something but couldn't think! She was in panic, her mind seeing a million images in seconds. Damon! Alex! Norman!

"What is it, Nicole?" Billy grabbed her by the arms, holding her still.

"Damon," she said in a tortured whimper. "Damon has been in an accident."

"Is he okay?" Billy led her to the sofa and sat her down.

"He broke his . . ." Nicole could barely speak through her tears, trying to listen to her own words to calm herself down. "Cuts. B-Bruises."

"You stay right here." Billy reached for the phone. "I'm going to call Delaney to come and watch Alex."

"I can't wait," Nicole yelled, jumping up from the sofa. Damon needed her. "I have to get over there now. The hos-hospital."

"You're in no condition to drive." Billy dialed the number. "I'll take you there."

"Please hurry," Nicole begged. She was beginning to feel empty inside. It was a familiar feeling. All too familiar.

Eleven

Still made up, Nicole's hair and makeup contrasted with the sweater and jeans she had changed into, inviting a few stares in the emergency room. She and Billy were quickly directed upstairs and given a room number. Billy waited in the hall as Nicole walked inside. Anxiety was knotting in her stomach, through her entire body.

Hearing the door open, Alanis Jordan turned around. As she stepped aside to let Nicole closer to Damon, her worried face formed a genuinely happy smile.

Nicole's heart leaped at the sight of him. He looked fine except for a couple of stitches above his left brow and a bruise on his left cheek. He was sitting up in the bed, his casted leg under the covers.

She loved him. At that moment, in all happiness and despair, she realized without a doubt, she loved him. With all of her heart and soul. Nicole began to cry silent tears as he opened his arms to her, motioning for her to come closer. Slowly she took the steps, her feet feeling like thousand-pound weights.

"Are you all right?" Nicole reached over for a hug. She held him softly, not wanting to hurt him. Even a soft touch

sent chills through her with new meaning now that she under
stood her love for him.

"Stop crying, baby." Damon held her away and wiped a
her tears. "I'm all right. I had my seat belt on, and my airba
cushioned me. A couple of bruises can't keep me down."

"I was so worried for you." Nicole rubbed his right chee
with the back of her hand. She would do anything to take awa
the fear she felt inside, but it was going nowhere. "I just don'
know—"

"Don't finish that sentence," Damon said.

He turned to his mother, who read the message his eyes sen
her, and watched her leave the room.

"Don't get upset, Nicole." Damon rubbed her arm compas
sionately. "I'm all right."

"Don't console me, Damon," Nicole said. "You're the on
that was in the accident."

"I think we know there's more to it than that."

Nicole closed her eyes, fighting back more tears. Her hea
kept screaming that she loved him again and again. Even now
he was thinking of her first.

"You look beautiful." Damon's voice was warm and hi
eyes tender as he gazed at her anguished face. "I would hav
been the man of envy tonight."

"Oh, Damon!" Nicole let out a sniffle. "The dinner! You
award!"

"Mother left a message with the banquet office at the hotel."
He continued to comfort her with his caress. "Everything i
taken care of."

Nicole kept her eyes on his chest, the pale blue hospit
gown's little white dots beginning to blend together. Her hea
was spinning so fast, she felt dizzy. She fought the memorie
but they were forcing their return.

"Where is Alex?" Damon's voice cracked.

"Dee has him." Nicole wiped at her tears with a tissu
from her purse. She wished she could pull herself together fo
Damon's sake. He didn't need to be worried about her.

"I wanted to call you first," he said. "Before I called Mothe but I was afraid how you would react. With Alex around, I decided to wait until I knew the damage.''

"He was in the kitchen. He could tell I was upset, but I tried my best to hide it from him. I think he'll be okay."

"You're always thinking of him."

"I really should go." Nicole took a step backward, feeling the room close in on her. She hated her selfishness but was powerless to resist it. Here he was in a hospital bed, and all she could think of were her own feelings, her own pain. "I have to get him."

"You said he was with Delaney?" Damon seemed confused at her reaction as his words separated a little. "He was going to be with her anyway. Please stay a little while longer."

"I can't." Nicole felt him take hold of her hand, but she quickly pulled it away. "He saw me upset. He'll be wondering."

"Nicole." There was a slight hint of desperation in Damon's eyes as he reached for her.

"Don't look at me like that." The tears had returned as she snapped at him in defense of her confusing behavior. "You know he comes first. You always knew that."

Not able to take his pained stare, Nicole quickly turned and fled the room. She heard him faintly call after her as she passed by puzzled stares from Alanis and Billy and took quick steps down the hallway. She had to get out of there. When she finally did, Nicole inhaled the outside air so deeply it made her cough. Catching her breath, she took a seat on the concrete bench with her back to the place she had just left.

She had always hated hospitals. The scattered noises and locked closets. She was surrounded by pain and confusion. They reminded her too much of that day a little over two years ago. The worst day of her life.

Jason Stone, a longtime friend of Norman's, had called her on the way to the hospital, explaining what happened. Nicole quickly dropped her baby at a neighbor's house, because there was no time to drive up to Delaney's. She never felt faint or lost control of her senses, but was focused, her only goal in life getting to that hospital. She was sure everything would be

okay. Nothing could happen to her love, her husband, her bes
friend and the father of her child.

It was an unfamiliar hospital, but Nicole remembered finding
the men on her own. She had no time to wait for directions
She could almost feel where Norman was and let that lead her
right to him.

Jason met her halfway down the hall, and when Nicole saw
the look in his eyes, she knew she was too late. The last thing
she saw was his arms reaching out to her as he apologized
repeatedly. Then she fainted.

When Nicole was able to see the love of her life again, he
was already dead. She had no chance to say goodbye, give him
a hug or a kiss. That day, Nicole felt a part of herself die a
well.

She had found that part of herself again with Damon. It
wasn't exactly the same, because her life with Norman wa
only for the two of them, but it was a part of her heart she had
left for dead beside that bed in the hospital two years ago. With
Damon, it had been revived and had come back to life.

She loved him. It hurt that she had to see him in a hospita
bed to realize that, but it was as clear as crystal to her now
She hadn't been so much fighting it as she was simply no
expecting it. It was a bittersweet revelation. Today she ha
come close to losing that part of herself again. It was mor
than she could take. The thought of losing Damon, or anyon
she loved, tore her heart to pieces.

She had been fortunate this time. Everyone had been, wit
only cuts and bruises and a broken leg. But what about th
next time? The thought of Damon being hurt worse or eve
dying made Nicole's stomach turn in pain. It hurt so much
Too much.

She couldn't do it. Nicole turned her head slightly, lookin
back at the hospital. She couldn't go back inside. She couldn
face him. Her fear was almost paralyzing.

"Nicole?" Billy appeared beside her, his hand gently pres
suring her shoulder. "Are you all right?"

"No, Billy." Nicole's voice was soft and shattered, her heart fractured. "I need you to take me home. I need to see my son."

Billy said nothing as he helped Nicole up from the bench and walked with her to the car. The ten-minute drive seemed to last forever as Nicole stared blankly out the window. She was grateful for the silence, not able or wanting to explain her behavior.

She realized now that Damon had been wrong. She loved him, but he had been wrong. She was not strong. At least she wasn't strong enough. Nicole had only enough strength to love one thing in her life with all her heart and nothing or no one else.

When she was inside the sanctuary of her home, Nicole ran to Alex. She grabbed him, lifting him from the living room floor and his puzzle pieces into her arms. As usual, he responded with a happy smile and the tightest hug his little arms could offer. She sank in his affection as it always gave her the strength she needed in good times and bad. Here, holding her baby in her arms, she never needed to question the risk, the worth of such everlasting love.

Nicole held him away, taking a moment to look at him. She loved him so much. He was more precious than life. She knew he was going to look just like Norman one day. Just like his father.

She assailed his face with tiny kisses everywhere, causing him to laugh.

"That tickles," he said, pushing her face away with his tiny hands. "Stop it!"

"I can't." Nicole smiled back. "I can't help it. Your face is so yummy."

"Mommy?" Alex's little face turned serious. "Is Damon okay?"

"Yes, he is." Nicole took his hands in hers, looking into his big, innocent eyes. "Someone hit his car with their car, but he's going to be okay. He just got a couple of bruises and broke his leg.''

''Michael Patrick broke his leg last year when we were on the jungle gym.''

''Just like that,'' Nicole said. ''And like Michael, Damon's leg is going to be as good as new real soon.''

''Good.'' He smiled for a moment but then became serious again. ''How 'bout you, Mommy? Are you going to be okay?''

''Yes, baby.'' Nicole kissed his soft forehead. ''Mommy's going to be fine.''

Nicole held back the tears, for Alex's sake, as she felt her heart break into a million pieces. It was the only choice she could make. One woman could take only so much, and this woman had had her fill.

Nicole made the decision at that moment. The only man she could risk her heart and soul for was the one in her arms at this very moment.

Damon called the next day, leaving a kind message on the answering machine saying he was home now and was looking forward to seeing both Nicole and Alex soon. Nicole had to do everything to keep from picking up the phone and calling him back to tell him they would be right over. Just the sound of his voice made her heart race. Despite that, she knew she had to stick to her decision.

She knew she would have to face him soon. He was such a kind and loving person and deserved to hear her explanation. Only Nicole wasn't sure what to say. She hated the idea of hurting him, knowing how much he cared for her. She wanted to break it to him in the nicest way she could, which would take a little time and forethought.

Unfortunately for her, Nicole wasn't allotted the time she needed as Monday rolled around and Damon showed up at the gallery.

With her back to the door, Nicole didn't see him at first. It was Ellen, the new receptionist she was training, that saw him.

As Ellen's eyes lit up and a flirtatious smile came to her face, Nicole turned around.

What little pieces that were left of her heart melted. Crutches in hand, Damon leaned against the wall. His Howard University sweat suit was ruined now that the bottom of one leg was cut off to make room for the cast. She wanted to run to him and hold him. She wanted to kiss him and playfully make fun of him as she did so often during their courtship.

She wanted to, but she didn't, because seeing him made her realize she would have to tell him the bad news and say goodbye.

"Hello, Damon." Nicole stepped to him, a gentle smile hiding her pain.

"Hi, sweetheart." Damon spoke with uncertainty and cautious eyes. "Do you have a minute?"

"Yes, I do." Nicole could see he was concerned, and it wrenched at her heart.

She quietly led him to the back room, scattered with sold pieces and new items, some belonging to her. The tension caused by their silence was starting to build as Nicole quickly gathered her thoughts, wanting to hurt him as little as possible.

"Who is the new young lady at your desk?" Damon placed his crutches to the floor as he sat in the chair opposite Nicole.

"New receptionist," Nicole said, simply loving the sight of him and the sound of his voice. "I'm a consultant now. It gives me more time to paint."

"Your art is selling like wildfire." Damon's smile made it only halfway. "You must be making a fortune."

"It's doing well," Nicole said with partial pride. Her art meant nothing to her at this moment. "I have you to thank for that."

"No, you don't." Despite his words, his eyes danced a bit, showing he was touched by her compliment.

"No, you got me started again, and now I can't stop. It's like I want to make up for two years right now."

"It was just the right time." Damon shrugged humbly.

"Damon." Nicole lowered her head, promising herself she would be strong. "I'm sorry for not returning your calls."

"That's okay." There was the caution again in his voice as if he knew the icy waters they were treading were thin. "I know Alex keeps you busy."

"We need to talk." She took a deep breath and looked back at him. "I'm sure that's why you came here."

"I know there's a problem." He nodded somberly. "Saturday frightened you. I understand. I think if we talk about it, we can work it out."

"Oh, Damon," Nicole sighed, loving him so much. "I'm so sorry. I hate to say this."

"Then don't." Damon's expression became very serious, more so than ever before. "Don't say it. Hear me out first."

"I can't," she said, shaking her head. "It would only make the inevitable harder. I just want you to understand that I—"

"I love you, Nicole." Damon's voice was strong but emotional. "I love you, and I think you love me. We both love Alex, so we should—"

"This *is* for Alex." Nicole couldn't stand to hear any more. Knowing he loved her only made her throat fill up with painful tears.

"How can this be for Alex?" Damon asked.

"He needs me to be his mother. I can't do that if all I'm worried about is losing you."

"It was an accident." Damon's voice was rough with anxiety. "Don't make it more than that, Nicole."

"I don't have to. I lost my husband to an accident." She unconsciously twisted her soft hands together. "You could never in a million years understand that pain."

"Don't do this, Nicole."

"I have to, Damon." Nicole turned away from his burning eyes that seemed to be seeing through her. "I want you to know how much I care for you. You came into my life at a time when I needed someone. You helped me see life was for me again. I got so much from you, and I'll always appreciate that."

"And now you throw me away?" Damon's expression and tone were dark now as his anger began to show. "You're punishing me for something I have no control over."

"None of us do." Her hands were clenched at her sides. "Damon, please understand. I can't do it. I can't see you anymore. When you said I was strong, you were wrong. I'm not strong enough to risk losing two men I love."

"If you could listen to yourself, Nicole," he pleaded. "If you could step outside of your life and listen to yourself for one moment, you would realize this is a mistake."

"That's just it, Damon." Nicole turned to him again, her eyes begging for him to understand. "I can't step outside of my life and the tragedies it's retained."

"You said you were trying to let go of the past." Damon tempered his tone, sounding more compassionate than angry now. "It takes time, baby. Don't give up now."

"I can't let go of the past when it stares at me every day with big black eyes." The knowledge of her loss twisted and turned inside of her. "You have no idea how painful it is to know that no matter how much I tell him, no matter how many home videos or pictures I show him, my son will not have any memory of his father."

"Tell me how painful it is!" Damon tried to stand as he gripped the edges of his chair, but quickly sat down as he was apparently reminded of his physical state. "I can take some of that pain for you. I can help you deal with it."

"No, Damon!" Nicole wished she could hate him for being so loving, so kind. It only made this harder. "I can't let you do that. You don't deserve to be saddled with that kind of responsibility."

"Saddled?" He laughed a cold, ironic laugh. "I love you. I want to share everything with you. How can you think I would feel saddled?"

"Because I do!" She held her hand to her heart, her tears streaming. "Don't you know, sometimes I'm angry at Norman for leaving me alone to raise his son and feel this grief. Then I hate myself for it."

"You're not alone, Nicole. I'm here." He held out his hand to her in a gesture of support. "You won't have to raise him alone."

"Damon." Nicole tried to ignore his affectionate words,

knowing she had to if she was going to follow through. "When I love, it's with my whole heart and soul. That kind of love sets me up for a hard fall. I took that fall once and have come to accept it, but I can't set myself up for it again."

"Answer me one thing." His eyes bore into hers, demanding her honesty. "How is ending this going to make your life better? How is being alone going to make your life better?"

"I won't be alone," she retorted. "I'll have Alex. This is for him anyway. I have to risk hurting you and myself for him."

"Nicole." Damon bit his lip, seemingly in an attempt to control his angry words. "I understand your fear. I'm sure if I were in your situation, I would be afraid as well."

He stood up from the chair, grabbing his crutches. "But don't insult me and say you're doing this for Alex. You're doing this for yourself and only yourself."

"That isn't true." She shook her head violently, feeling the sting of his words in her heart.

"How could this be for Alex?" he asked. "I know that kid is crazy about me."

"I know." Nicole stood up from her chair. "I'm not happy about this, but I'm doing what I think is best."

"This is too soon." Damon shook his head as if not believing her words. "You need more time. This just happened Saturday."

"Damon, please. I—"

"No." The defiance in his tone silenced her. "You take the week to think about it. When you calm down, I'm sure you'll see that this is not the answer."

"I'm not hysterical, Damon. I have thought this through."

"I'll call you Saturday," he said, ignoring her words. "We'll talk then."

"This is hard enough," she pleaded. "Let's not drag it out any further. My feelings will be the same."

"They won't." He turned to her, his eyes now glossy as if he was close to tears. "I know you're upset, but you'll understand by Saturday. You've made me so happy. Alex has brought so much to my life, and I know you care for me. This isn't over Nicole. It can't be.''

Damon gave a silent, motionless Nicole one lasted pained stare before using his crutch to push open the door.

Nicole fell into the chair, emotionally and physically exhausted. She wanted to go after him, her heart begged her to, but she resisted. She felt the damage to her heart now but had to believe the pain would go away one day. She could hold on to the good memories and never have to deal with the tragedy as she had to for Norman.

She had been telling him the truth when she said she was grateful. Damon had added to her life at a time when she needed it. She would always leave room in her heart for him because of that. Only that was all she could give. Nicole knew she would feel the same a week from now, but she still wanted to avoid talking to Damon again. She also knew she would hurt the same again a week from now.

She stood up, wiping her eyes and straightening herself out. She wasn't sure how to face a full day of work feeling so heartbroken and guilty. Delaney had picked the wrong day to take a day off. Nicole wanted to crawl into bed and cry herself to sleep, only she knew that wasn't possible. Life goes on despite heartbreak when you're a mother. That's what she was first and foremost. Nicole only hoped that would be enough. Before Damon came into her life, she thought it was plenty. Now she wasn't so sure.

Through everything, she remembered most that he had told her he loved her. Those words stayed with her all day.

12

The next week seemed to last years to Nicole. The days were long and the nights lonely. She couldn't stop thinking of all the possibilities that a relationship with Damon could bring for her as well as for Alex. They urged her to try, but each time she thought she could, the fear and remembrance of her past, and the pain it brought her, stopped her. She couldn't go through it again, but neither could she get Damon off her mind. She had little solace in the hope that this was the first week, and maybe it would get better after a while.

Grief was coming from all angles. Not only did she have to deal with Delaney's constant urging to reconcile with Damon, but Alex was also behaving badly all week.

Nicole could hardly discipline him because she knew it was her fault. He had asked her on Monday night when Damon would be coming by again. She knew Alex looked forward to the weekly dinners they shared.

Nicole never lied to her son, which might have been easier. She sat him down and told him she had made the decision not to date right now. She assured him he had nothing to do with her and Damon not seeing each other, and that Damon still cared for him very much. It wasn't enough for Alex. Upset and confused at the sudden change in his life, he yelled at his mother, pulled away from her, and ran to his room. For the rest of the week, he was very difficult. He would not pick up after himself, no matter how many times she asked, got into a fight at school, and snapped back at Nicole regularly.

Nicole wished she could explain to him but knew better. A five-year-old boy could not understand fear. He had his mommy right with him, knowing she would protect him and take care of him forever, and she would. Even if it meant being lonely.

Saturday finally rolled around, and Nicole felt a knot in her stomach after another sleepless night. Fixing breakfast for Alex, she almost jumped out of her skin when she heard the doorbell ring.

What was he doing here? So early at that. He was supposed to call. She wasn't at all prepared for this. The last thing she wanted was to confront Damon in an emotional situation with Alex around. Her stomach shaking with fear, Nicole walked to the door. She felt her entire body release its contraction as she opened the door and Jessica Cox faced her with a smile.

"Jessica," she exclaimed. "What a nice surprise. Please come in."

"I was in the neighborhood." Jessica entered the house unaware her presence was such a relief to Nicole. "I thought I'd stop by and see my little man."

"Your little man is in his bedroom on punishment." Nicole motioned toward his bedroom as the two women sat on the living room sofa.

"What did he do?" Jessica pouted like any grandmother who never believed their grandchild should be punished.

"Last night I told him it was bedtime, and he looked me dead in the eye and said, 'Then I guess you better go to bed.'"

"You sure he wasn't joking with you?" Jessica asked. "He's such a joker."

"You didn't see that look in his eyes," Nicole said. "He was being a downright smarty pants."

"Can I at least say hello?"

"Sure." Nicole called to Alex, telling him to come out for breakfast. "I was just putting his oatmeal in the microwave."

Nicole headed toward the kitchen, happy to have averted the dreaded confrontation for at least a while. It was nice to have company. Nicole had been searching for diversions all week to keep her mind off of Damon and her heartache. It was useless. As soon as silence or calm set in, the pain and regret came rushing back. She wondered how long this would last. She wasn't sure she could go through many more weeks like this one.

"All right, little man." Nicole stood in the doorway to the kitchen. "You've said hello to Grandma. Now get in here and eat your breakfast. Then you go right back to your room."

"Aw, man." Alex pouted his little lips and brooded past his mother into the kitchen.

"Watch it, kid," she warned. His looks and sneers were tempting her already quick temper.

"What is this about you breaking things off with Damon?" Jessica asked as soon as Nicole returned to the sofa.

"Did Alex tell you that?"

"Yes. I asked him why he seemed so upset. He told me you and Damon weren't boyfriend and girlfriend anymore."

"It's a long story. I'd rather not get into it right now." Nicole changed the subject quickly, wondering what more she could do to help Alex accept this decision. "How have you been, Jessica?"

"Why did you break up?" Jessica persisted. "You seemed so happy."

"I was," Nicole said, understanding there was no avoiding the topic. Just recently she had told Jessica how fantastic Damon was and how much she cared for him. "We were."

"Then what happened?" Jessica slid closer on the sofa.

Nicole saw genuine concern in Jessica's eyes, and it triggered her emotions. In the past month, Jessica had apologized for her initial reaction to Nicole's new life, telling her she was pleased that she had found happiness. Jessica had been such a comfort after Norman's death, Nicole remembered. She wanted to talk about it, even if it was out of self-pity.

"Jessica . . ." Nicole almost sighed her name. "I can't do it."

"Can't do what, honey?"

"Damon was in a car accident last week." Nicole spoke quietly, not wanting Alex to hear her. "He's all right, but the fear paralyzed me. It brought me right back to two years ago."

"Scared you to death, didn't it?" Jessica nodded sympathetically.

"And beyond." Nicole put her hand to her heart. "I'm just not strong enough. I had to end it."

"Nicole, you shouldn't do this."

"What do you mean? You should understand—of all people. You know what I went through."

"But you've come so far." Jessica leaned forward with earnest eyes.

"I went too far." Nicole shook her head with regret. "I fell in love, and I shouldn't have done that."

"How could you have prevented that?"

"I did it for two years. It wasn't difficult then. I'll just have to do it again."

"You won't be able to." Jessica shook her head. "You did it before because you were still grieving the loss of your husband. Through time and through Damon, you've gotten past it. You've moved on to the next level. You can't go back from that."

"What am I supposed to do?" Nicole opened her arms, begging for an answer to her dilemma.

"Listen, Nicole," Jessica sighed, smiling at Nicole's good intentions. "You not only changed yourself. You changed me. I saw you falling for another man, letting him into Alex's life, and I felt like you were betraying my son. Then you were so happy, and Alex was so happy—it helped me heal some, too. It helped me realize what Norman would have wanted me to feel. He would have wanted me to want your happiness."

"What does he want for me?" Nicole rested her head on the sofa, her eyes weak with love.

"You have to answer that for yourself. Your relationship with him was different than mine."

"I don't know the answer." Nicole noticed Jessica's skepticism at her words. "Really, I don't. I'm so confused and stressed right now."

"What was it Norman always wanted for you and Alex when he was alive?"

"Happiness," Nicole answered quickly, never doubting the answer to that question.

"Where can you get happiness?"

"I don't need a man to be happy, Jessica. I'm not that kind of woman."

"I know that, but Damon makes you happier when he's in your life than when he isn't."

"So does Alex. So does my painting, and my friends and . . ."

"And Damon."

Nicole sighed, unable to deny it was true. "But what if I lose him?"

"What if?" Jessica leaned back with an endearing smile. "Remember what Norman used to say about 'ifs'?"

"Yes." Nicole wiped her tears, a faint smile appearing on her face. "If 'if' were a fifth, we'd all be drunk."

"You lost Norman," Jessica said. "But weren't those four years of memories and Alex worth any risk?"

"Any risk in the world." Nicole turned her head to the kitchen door, feeling her heart leap at the thought of the gift Norman left her. "I wouldn't take anything back for Alex."

"Norman wants you to be happy. He wants all of us to be happy. What's going to make you and Alex happy?"

Nicole knew the answer already. She knew her challenges and her goals. She knew her heart.

"Jessica?" she asked, feeling a spark of hope return to her. "Can you do me a favor and watch Alex for a while?"

"I'll watch him all day." Jessica's smile went from ear to ear. "Don't you worry about him."

"Thanks."

Nicole leaned over and kissed Jessica on the cheek. It made her happy to believe that their relationship had just reached another level. No longer tied only by a man and his son, there was hope for them to become friends now.

After telling a nonchalant Alex she would be gone for a while, Nicole grabbed her purse near the stand at the door and left her house. Her confidence grew as she passed every mile that separated her from her destiny. She was astounded by how clear everything seemed now.

She was the luckiest woman in the world. Not only had she been blessed with Alex, but she had been blessed with the chance to love two men with all her heart and have them love her back. Many people go their entire life without love like that. She was getting a second chance at it and was determined to take it.

When he opened the door and saw her standing there, Damon's eyes flew open.

"Hello, Damon." Nicole's light eyes sparkled at the sight of him, feeling the connection immediately.

Just seeing him helped her realize she had missed him terribly, not that sure she needed any help. She hadn't gone an entire week without seeing him since they started dating. A week was too long.

"Nicole." Damon's surprise was evident. "I . . . I just called your house less than five minutes ago."

"Did you speak to Jessica?" Nicole let herself in.

"Yes. She said you had gone out. She wasn't sure when you'd be back." With his crutches, Damon followed her to his living room. "I thought you were—"

"Avoiding you?" She turned to face him, giving him the warmest smile she could create. "I wouldn't do that to you."

"I'm glad you came," he said with a serious look as he sat on the sofa.

"So am I." Nicole sat down so close to him, their knees touched. She could see he wasn't expecting her to be so friendly and hoped it was a pleasant surprise.

"Nicole," he started. "All I could think about this week was you. These last months have been some of the happiest in my entire life. The thought of not having you or Alex in my life made me crazy. It took all the strength and pride inside of me to keep from calling you and begging you to come back."

"Damon . . ." Nicole whispered his name as she leaned in closer. "Don't say another word."

With her lips, she gently kissed his forehead, then his eyelids, his cheeks, and finally his lips. She pressed hard, having yearned for this connection for a week now. She laughed as she pulled away, seeing the delighted confusion in Damon's eyes.

"I'm sorry," she whispered. "In one bad moment, I forgot how much you cared about me. I forgot how much you and Alex love each other. I forgot how you helped me realize I could love you and still love the memory of my life with Norman. I forgot how strong I was and how happy we were together. I thought only of myself and my fears. In that moment, I hurt the two people I love more than anything, and I hurt myself as well. For that I am so sorry."

"Don't apologize." Damon's eyes beamed with happiness as he grabbed Nicole and hugged her. "You're here now, and that's all that matters, but I'm going to lay down some ground rules."

"Anything." She held his head in her hands, her face only inches from his.

"We share everything, whether it's about you, me, work, life, or Alex. Your problems are just as much mine as anything else. Everything belongs to both of us, not just one of us."

"You have a deal." She kissed his lips again, savoring the charge of electricity it sent through her. She loved him terribly.

"Any ground rules?" he asked her as their lips parted.

"Only one. That we tell each other how much we love each other every day. I'll start. I love you, Damon." Nicole smiled lovingly as she saw how happy her words made him. "I love you very much."

"Girl"—he shook his head and pressed his lips together—"if I didn't have this broken leg, I'd pick you up and carry you to that bedroom right now."

"I think," Nicole said as she pushed at his chest, forcing him backward on the sofa, "we can make do right here. Right now."

Damon's eyes lit up with desire as Nicole tore open his plain blue T-shirt. She would buy him another. Right now, it was in her way. She had a whole week to make up for and hoped he was up to it.

As he reached up and pulled her down on top of him, the fear Nicole had felt was swept away. She was living for now, letting go of any possibilities. Right now, she was making new memories.

"I love you, Nicole," he whispered.

Epilogue

"Can I feed her, Mommy?" Alex asked as he leaned over the bed.

"Only I can feed her right now," Nicole answered with a tired voice. "But you'll be able to one day soon."

"Can I dress her?"

"Sure, sweety." She leaned over, ignoring the pain, and kissed him on the forehead. She loved his eagerness. "When we get home."

It hadn't been that way at the start. Alex had been extremely pleased when he got a new stepfather a year ago. Nicole remembered how helpful he was as she planned the quick wedding. Her love for Damon, and his for her, grew fast—culminating in his Thanksgiving dinner marriage proposal. When she saw the ring in his hands, Nicole hadn't hesitated with her answer. She wanted nothing more in this world than to be his wife. The wedding was set for Mother's Day in April of the next year. At first, Alanis was displeased with the arrangements, wanting a large society wedding that took forever to plan, but soon came around.

The wedding and the honeymoon were delightful for Nicole. If she didn't miss Alex so much, she would have never wanted to leave their private villa in Italy. Alex was waiting, with open arms, for their return home—and they settled quickly into family life.

Three months later came the unexpected news. Nicole and Damon were ecstatic to discover she was pregnant. It served only to increase their love for each other. Alex, on the other hand, was not at all pleased, not at first at least. The only child for six years now, he was very protective of his mother and new father's love. His uncertainty soon disappeared as Nicole and Damon involved him in every aspect of the pregnancy.

It was a busy nine months as the Jordan family purchased a new home and Damon's practice grew even larger. Alex started the first grade. Not wanting paint fumes near her unborn baby, Nicole turned to clay sculpting for the first time. Her pieces sold as fast as her paintings had.

"Can I . . ." Alex stopped talking as he turned toward the doorway.

In walked Damon in sterile hospital clothing. He was holding his daughter and newest patient. The happiness and pride that beamed from his face could be seen from miles away.

"She's come for another feeding." Damon winked in Alex's direction. "Did the nurse scrub you good, Alex?"

"Up and down," Alex said. "Mommy said I can stand close while she feeds her."

"Let me hold my precious little girl." Nicole's eager hands reached out as Damon came closer. She couldn't wait to get her hands on the little darling again.

"Here you go." Damon kissed his wife on the forehead as he gently handed over one-day-old Danielle Elizabeth Jordan. He sat beside them on the bed, motioning for Alex to come around and sit on his lap.

Nicole felt her heart melt every time she laid eyes on her newborn baby. She was the most beautiful girl in the world. She had wondered, during her pregnancy, if she was being unfair by having another child. Surely she couldn't love any child as much as she loved Alex. She was wrong. Nicole knew that the second she heard Danielle's first cry.

As Nicole looked around her bed, Damon gave her a loving wink. Alex's eyes were as wide as saucers. Danielle was hungry. Nicole had her fairy tale again.

ABOUT THE AUTHORS

Cheryl Faye's first novel for Arabesque was titled *AT FIRST SIGHT*. She has been writing as a hobby for over twenty years. For her, it is the best form of relaxation. Aside from romantic fiction, she also writes poetry and short stories. She is the mother of two sons and lives in Jersey City, New Jersey.

Born in New Jersey, Monique Gilmore now lives in The Bay Area, California, where she works in real estate. She attended Rutgers University where she earned her Bachelor of Science degree. Her fourth romance for Arabesque is titled *SOUL DEEP*.

Angela Winters' first Arabesque novel was *ONLY YOU*. She majored in Journalism at the University of Illinois at Urbana-Champaign, with double minors in Speech Communications and English. She is a research executive at a Chicago area firm. She lives in Evanston, Illinois with her ten-year-old cat, Jordan.

Look for these upcoming Arabesque titles:

June 1997
RHAPSODY by Felicia Mason
ALL THE RIGHT REASONS by Janice Sims
STEP BY STEP by Marilyn Tyner

July 1997
LEGACY by Shirley Hailstock
ECSTASY by Gwynne Forster
A TIME FOR US by Cheryl Faye
THE ART OF LOVE by Crystal Wilson-Harris

August 1997
SILKEN BETRAYAL by Francis Ray
WISHING ON A STAR by Raynetta Manees
SLOW BURN by Leslie Esdaile
SWEET LIES by Viveca Carlysle